THE HAUNTING OF WILLOW TREE COURT

By

Jennifer Adele

D1496533

2012 Synthesis 365 Trade Paperback Edition

Copyright © 2012 by Jennifer Adele

Photos © Jeff Kornberger and Jennifer Adele

For Jeff, with love — always.

Thanks to my brother, David, for believing in me as I took this journey.

Many thanks to my support team of friends for all their technical and creative insights, which helped to make this book a beautiful reality: Brad, Dani, and Jenn.

In memory of my strong, beautiful, and wacky dog Hildegarde. She always made me smile and was a bold protector. She was with me as I wrote this book and stayed by my side to the very end. Even after death, her spirit reclines with mine as I hold her in my heart with all my love.

"Is all that we see or seem but a dream within a dream?"

— Edgar Allan Poe

THE HAUNTING OF WILLOW TREE COURT

Chapter 1

There have been many stories told about the sentience of place, about the particular effectiveness of a given spot. Hyper-awareness in animals, plants, structures, and places, is in fact a very old and universal master story. Within it are scary stories of places that harm and reassuring stories of places that heal and hold the answers to dreams, where a single wish breathed on the fullest breath or lost in a single tear has the magic to come true. As a child, I loved stories that fell into either category. Fairy tales filled with magical and malevolent forests, ghost stories, ethereal scenes from out of time, and haunted houses were the foundation stones of my impressionable years and what the underpinnings of my creativity hung upon. *The Fall of the House of Usher* as envisioned by Poe was a personal favorite, and for someone like me, how could it not be?

I consistently felt that there was an eerie sort of romance about a place being so alive that it haunted the living with visions of death. It's the undeniable connection in the obsession of an ancient home with those who dared to live there in more modern times, as though what was set in motion centuries before might be less powerful with the passing years. Of course, it never was. That was a twisted play upon life for me, for it seemed that in a checked reality, it was the living that haunted a place more than the dead. But, in lands of nod and fanciful stories, that truth was fulfilled through the opposite expression.

The stories of healing places were sometimes even more intriguing than the haunted manors on the moors, although not so much on a dark and stormy night. The thought that all the tolls of life could be erased completely by stepping over a precipice was enough to take my breath away. Sunlight on bare skin peeking through a fine summer top and ancient healing rituals in sacred groves on the pages between my fingers may have been the closest to heaven that I've ever come. And, that was captured at a time in my life before it would have made any tangible difference. The entire concept gave hope to me in a way that nothing else could. It filled me with the courage to consider braving the extremes, for who knew whether or not the scars obtained in the bravery would one day be erased. All I'd be left with would be the memories of the wondrous without any of the consequences. But, the confines of society impinged over the years, numbing a portion of my psyche so that the extremes went largely unexplored.

My mother, of all people, gifted me with James Hilton's *Lost Horizon* for my eighth birthday as both a cultural learning tool and a means of safe and acceptable exploration. And, that particular book grew to be my most prized possession. Even now, as an adult barely beyond the age of thirty, it is the tale I want to hear told and re-told above all the rest, even if it is a hard journey to complete sometimes, even if there are instances or episodes where I shove it aside.

To be fair, I don't suppose I ever really stopped looking for Shangri-La, and it would be far too easy to blame my mother for exposure to these absurd and obscure possibilities. In all honesty though, I sought them out. I must be honest at this point and right from the very start, because the entire tale that I tell at this juncture depends on my transparent truthfulness, if I am ever to be even half-believed. Yes, this is my story, and it is important to me to be credible. But, it is even more important because it's #18's story, too. It is also the story of a whole court of people, a whole segment of homes, and a whole mass of trees that might seem insignificant in the greater scheme of things, yet they are indeed and in part fully significant. One tree especially deserves to have this tale told and should in all accounts and accounting be believed. I admit fully that my soul called to them and my stubborn mind refused to believe they didn't exist. I would have found my House of Usher and Shangri-La on the bookshelves eventually. I found what I was unwittingly looking for in life eventually, too.

If I had to say I had experience in hard reality, prior to my move to #18 Willow Tree Court, with either extreme of sentient place, I would have claimed the House of Usher.

Only, it wasn't a house; it was a car. Perhaps it was a blending of cars in a jigsaw of crushed and twisted metal that molded horrifically into one. My car had seen its fair share of fender benders, and as it turned out, the other two cars involved in the accident had a colorful history as well. Combined in that one pristine moment of malcontent, we all manufactured the torqued reality in the essence of those cars, the essence that robbed and maimed and harmed on so many levels that it is pointless to count. We had all met our fates in that malicious automobile accident, one rainy October morning.

It felt like most of me died that day; it was a severe lessening that took place in a very palpable although incomplete way. My daughter died in every conceivable way. And when she died, a part of me that couldn't recover died with her, yet my body in a warped state lived on as if to simultaneously mock and remind me of the fate of those who dared to live within a realm of sentience.

Places can harm or heal those that reside there. Places are harmed or healed by those that reside there, even in a single moment's time.

"Three years," Brian said as he woke one early and auspicious October morning. The days had melted together, and I couldn't be sure whether it was a workday or a weekend, and in case of the latter he had all day to persist. He didn't move a muscle and repeated, "It's been three years, Sally."

Workday.

He had to get right to it.

I remained very still in our bed, waiting him out while the warm brown comforter buffered like a bed of earth around me. I wanted to bury myself alive in it. I knew it had been three years just as surely he did, maybe even more so. I felt the years keenly, every minute, hour, and day. I felt each second drop off like a withered leaf from a dying tree. It didn't matter that I couldn't recall the exact day of the week, as I was a cruel and exacting gatekeeper of biological time.

"I know you're awake," he insisted.

Yes, I was fully awake, shaken by a dream of Sonya and her little stuffed dog toy from the night before, a dream so vivid that it had physically rocked me, torqueing the sheets like the twisted metal of the car she'd died in. It had made me quake with such force that I was catapulted into the conscious dawn.

A sigh escaped me. "Then you also know I don't want to talk. Besides, it's too early," I moaned.

He moved, rolling over in bed to face my body with the agility of a man in his prime. I kept my back to him, not wanting to see the ripple of firm muscle in a youthful physique still moistened with the dew of life. His rosy flesh and lanky build aggravated me. The way I saw it, I was also doing him a favor. He wouldn't have to gaze upon his spotted and speckled maiden-crone of a wife, the remnants of what the wreck had left him, for better or worse. And, it was a little much in the sober first light of day. It was certainly unmotivating right before work.

"It's not about what you want anymore," Brian said firmly, the authoritarian coming forth out of professional habit.

When was it ever?

I accented my thought with a loud snort.

I knew he would catch my drift in that non-verbal retort, and I was not one of his work subordinates to be spoken to so callously. For three years I had made his life difficult, and I wasn't going to stop now. After all, what else was there?

I shut my eyes tight, still trying to blot out the dream that relied on lingering bits of reality floating about my brain, imprinted images. The image of Sonya specifically, in the back seat of my car in her bright, purple plaid dress with baby-fine blonde hair in a whisper of ringlets remained.

She was barely a year old.

I hadn't yet learned to live with her, and now I would have to learn to live without her.

Sunlight filtered through the meager cracks of the bedroom blinds, dappling the sandstone-toned wall I stared at as if it were the most interesting thing in the world. Irregular as it may be, I did look forward to that sight every morning. It was the one piece of organic art that didn't judge me as less than, the one source of natural light I could enjoy without fearing it would enhance all of my ugliness, all of my scars.

Brian placed a warm and heavy hand on my shoulder, just within range of my peripheral vision so that I could pick up the image of his dark and hairy knuckles. "It's about what's best for you, what's best for us," he assured.

"What do you want, Brian?" I cut to the chase.

It couldn't be sex.

Of course, he could have been referring to sex as a segment of conversation. We hadn't had that awkward delight in a little less than three years. Brian himself probably hadn't had it in a week or so by my estimation. Although, to be fair, he brought up the subject less and less and my estimates were poor ones. My flannel nightgown should've been made from steel wool. Nightgowns hung in my half of our bedroom closet like a never-ending line of armor suits, each cast and recast since the last episode of intimacy I indulged in with my husband.

A couple of months after the accident I had made the attempt at intercourse. I was home, life was quasi-stable, and the routines of the newer and less stimulating schedules were settling in with the two of us. It was one of those evenings where you can sense the spirits of what once was coming alive in the living space, the memories of every regular activity in each room calling out not to be forgotten. The main room in our apartment, which doubled as both a living room and dining area, was full of erotic energies, mostly Brian's. He'd always been the initiator, the one in pursuit. I could tell that Brian was trying to be subtle yet encouraging; and for his sake as well as my own, I let him encourage. I remember thinking that things might actually go back to the way they were before if I could just find a way to lapse into the rhythms of the life I'd once had. It may not have been great, but it was better than what had been visited upon me in the aftermath, after having been nearly swallowed up alive in the maw of the Cars of Usher.

Find the rhythm and you find the key.

It was a concept I'd clung to in the earlier days of recovery, and something I'd heard in cognitive therapy before abandoning it. Sulking and sniveling acted as a better refuge.

Brian and I were on the sofa, and a bad sci-fi movie was just ending on television. He'd slid very close to me and placed his hand on my upper thigh, running his fingers gingerly up and down the inner seam of my jeans. I placed my hand over his and began to caress his skin from fingertip to wrist, feeling the hairs on the back of his hand stand up. I could sense his hesitant determination and the subtle vibration of anticipation that hovered around us, as though we were captured in a bubble that could quickly burst and destroy us both. It might all end or bring everything back to life. Then came the inevitable kissing that led to courteous stroking. His clothes came off rather quickly to reveal his firm and erect manhood, the one part of him that never really bothered me, ever. But when it came time for me to remove my clothes, it took tremendous effort. Brian began to help me after several minutes of futile struggling, and then the once passionate play session turned into a caretaker's chore. By the time I was partially nude, his erection had subsided, and I felt the flush of embarrassment spread from the root source of my inner core. I was sure I felt the embarrassment alone.

Brian's long awaited reply to my curt question snapped me out of the shameful memory. "Out of this."

He wants out. Of course he does. Divorce would be justified from either perspective.

"Ok," I complied. "But, at least make coffee first." Perhaps that sobering and caffeinated beverage would scrub away the visions of Fido with its acidity. Fido – Sonya's stuffed dog toy, the one that had been lying with her in the back seat, her life force pooling up in his spongy outer fluff and soft, foamy insides. That dog's black button eyes had never blinked during the trauma, and they never blinked in my dreams either. Why would they?

A pregnant pause filled the room with hope and disbelief. I heard Brian's breath catch, and it drew me back into the painful moment we were sharing.

"So, you'll do it?"

"Do what?" I knew how flat I could make my tone, and I knew just how much that would set him on edge. He was never sure where I existed on the emotional spectrum from moment to moment. Unpredictable. It was the worst punishment possible for a man who thrived in an environment of habit, logic, and expected outcomes. With me, he never knew if he was dancing near the den of a wounded lioness. Brian probably thought I was still oblivious to his recent sexual indiscretions, that's how good I was.

Now it was his turn to sigh. "You'll agree to move away from here."

I rolled over, a clumsy husk of a person, and faced him. Morning sunlight be damned. "You can't be serious. Why in the hell would I do something like that?" He'd hit a nerve, the same old, raw, and unhealed nerve.

"Sally," he breathed, almost like a prayer. I used to love it when he'd say my name that way, even though I had never really loved him in full. "Sally, please don't keep fighting this. There is no reason to stay in this apartment."

"And, there's no reason to leave," I countered, knowing he wouldn't dare speak her name to me. It was blasphemy of the highest degree.

Sonya.

When I prayed these days, as rare as it was, I prayed to her.

"I mean, it's not like we're going to need more room or anything," I narrowed my gaze and challenged him in my own pathetically weak and terminally defiant way. Somewhere along the spinning spiral I had become a master at manipulation. I had even gotten him to give up on taking away all of the art and furniture that still made up her room, the vacant and yet disturbingly active nursery suite.

Brian ran a hand through his thick dark hair, parts of which stood up straight and gave him the most ridiculous version of bedhead I'd ever seen. It was such a personal relief to see him that way, to see the façade of order cracked and creased. "You need room, Sally. You need to leave this trap of an apartment and everything behind with it. I think you need to leave the city behind, too," he insisted. "Correct me if I'm wrong, but we moved here because of your work at the time and the yoga studio expansion, but that's over. For three years you've been trapped here with doctors and therapy aids and snake oil salesmen. Nothing has gotten any better. You won't get better here." It was rehearsed like an actor's soliloquy from the many fights before.

"I won't get better no matter where you drag me off to," I leveled.

Brian's jaw twitched and I could see him deciding whether or not to continue our quickly escalating debate. The gears in his mind were spinning. I could almost hear them grinding with some sixth sense that people develop after spending years in close contact with each other. He actually looked wickedly handsome when he became stony and silent, when he clenched his jaw and set his mind to murder.

How he must hate me! If I were him, there would be no end to my hatred for me.

It was comical, really. Here I sat so close to him and so helpless, a maimed cripple from the accident that had taken so much away from him, although it had taken nothing in comparison to what it had stolen from me. I was the perfect victim, and he couldn't erase me from his life no matter how much he wanted to.

I didn't doubt that he was capable of murder. His habitual and fastidious front only served to further prove that he was detailed enough to commit the act quite well. He had a brain that would automatically weigh the pros and cons in an irreversible decision. But, this was the twenty-first century, and we lived in a modern city with modern cops and crime labs that would undoubtedly catch him in the end. Plus, it's rather old hat to suspect the husband. Too bad for Brian that we weren't in an ancient manor surrounded by foggy moors in a different time period.

"I'll go make coffee. Get yourself ready for the day. Reggie will be here at ten." Brian fell back into routine, giving up the tired old argument uncharacteristically soon. Perhaps it was simply logical and reasonable for a workday.

As he left me in the bed, I tried hard to remove myself from the tangle of sheets and blankets, the physical clutches of last night's dream. And, as I did so, I couldn't help but notice the quiet that settled in, the shift. Silence had been a rare and welcome guest in the earlier days of my marriage, the days when we'd both been parents of a small child. But, Silence now was a tormentor. He was one come too often in the days that had followed.

Monday, Wednesday, and Friday were the days that I spent a good portion of my mornings with Reggie. Even though the relationship was purely clinical, I had spent the past couple years with the same independent physical therapy aid and had come to think of him as a confidant. Whether he wanted to be one or not was beside the point. He was stuck with me for two hours each session and had to listen. Professional courtesy. He also had the forethought to send me a friendly text before each appointment to let me know when he was on his way, and that led me to a sense of connection barely beyond the constructs of our appointments. The texts would simply read, 'On my way,' or sometimes even simpler, 'omw.' But, I took them as evidence of thoughtfulness, and I needed the head start.

I prepared myself for his arrival as if it were an impending date for a lover's touch. And looking back on it, I could see how that had made a sick sort of sense, seeing as he was the only person I really let touch me. Reggie was the only person in my life during that time that I allowed myself to have any sort of physical intimacy with, in any way. His hands on my legs and arms as a guiding force during exercise repetitions, a stabilizing embrace around my shoulders as I strove to peddle for five minutes longer may have been in the name of medical science on his end. But, to me, it had more romantic inclinations and forbidden implications. For some reason I was able to insidiously achieve that intertwining with him where I was no longer able to do so with my own husband.

"How was your weekend?" Reggie's standard lead-in to our Monday work, as he unpacked his equipment from the duffle. Thera-bands, weighted balls of all different colors, ankle weights, wrist weights, gait belt, and a portable peddling stand were the usual assortment. He laid them all out along the floor in the order in which we'd use them. I watched his ease of movement and meticulous flow from my plush plum recliner. We used the living room area for our workouts, as it provided the greatest space and the most comfort for me.

"Not bad," I lied. "And yours?"

His weekends were always far more interesting than mine. Most people with a pulse had weekends far more interesting than mine, so I wasn't really a good gauge. However, as a fit man in his late thirties and unmarried, Reggie had both freedom and some degree of earned experience. He carried himself with a great deal of confidence, too, and that was more than likely due to his chosen career. Getting people to do what they didn't want to do all day long, five days a week, had to provide both confidence and persuasion as well-honed skills. And with Reggie, there was a quality that was also dark and alluring about that persuasiveness.

"Busy."

As always... and as I am not.

"How so?" I pressed.

It's such a delightful torture to hear about the activities of people who have real lives.

"Well, Friday night I went out for a while. Played some darts, had a few beers, and saw a fire spinning show indoors. The performers almost set themselves on fire and did manage to set the overhead sprinklers off, which was not part of the act," he detailed, and then stopped to eye me rather brazenly, awkwardly. I'd told myself he was probably seeing if his words held my interest, but there'd been something off about the way in which he'd sized me up. There was a spark, a flame that hadn't been there before. It surprised me that he did it at all, for Reggie should've known that he'd permanently held my interest.

I was smiling though, smiling to show friendliness and kindness in the face of whatever cold fire had taken hold of my confidant. I tried to shake off the sullenness that was also coming between us, the mood that was so bizarre under the circumstances. I imagined myself in the exact same scenario on a carefree Friday night. After all, I was a few years younger than Reggie, despite what fate had done to diminish me, to prematurely age me.

I can shake this off.

As a share, I used to be wild… or, at the very least, wilder. I'd had untamed moments amid all the repression. Boxed away in the storage area of the apartment building were clothes that I used to wear and that probably still fit, but I had no occasion to wear them. I hadn't worn most of the really good ones since before Sonya was born, and some of the deliciously scandalous ones since before my marriage to Brian. All dressed up and nowhere to go would've been an apt expression, but I couldn't bear to part with any of my party clothes or pretty clothes or what they represented to me. I had countless camis and dress tops, skirts of varying lengths, dress slacks, tight jeans, and the rare item made from spandex. I also had an assortment of lingerie purchased for me and by me over the years.

Uncomfortable shoes with unashamedly high heels were what I missed the most. Wearing shoes for the sake of a desired look and never having to think about balance or endurance. Wearing what was sexy, regardless of whether it was appropriate for my age. I knew I still had my favorite pair of red snakeskin stilettos buried in the designated basement storage area. They mocked me in the closet one too many times and had to be banished to a box, innocuous box #5. I longed for them still, like a lost lover, even though I only wore them a handful of times — never to an event as a married woman, though. Salacious!

"Saturday," Reggie continued, attempting to take up normalcy, even though it was fraying at the edges all around him and making itself known through its native tongue in his strained voice, "I chilled out with a girl I met the night before. Did a brunch thing and then hit some yard and estate sales with her. She's really into repurposing."

That's what I need... repurposing.

"And, Sunday?" I urged.

I can bring this back around and straight on through to a balanced place, to a typical place, to a safe place where I can dream as I strive.

Reggie stopped and looked at me, his set up complete. He seemed to be weighing a key decision in his mind, in those flickering, cold flames. The thoughts might have been near sinister based on a flash of facial expressions. He ultimately decided to go on, even though the essence of brooding was fanning up near the surface. "Well, on Sunday I helped a friend prepare her garden beds for the rest of the year. We turned them over and mulched." There was something in his delicate brown eyes that caught me off guard; it was a pondering that came without words to follow, without syllables to explain the intent. It was simply a question in the eyes that begged to be answered. "Are you ready to begin?" He practically whispered, hoarse from the strain of holding back.

This is most unusual... and erotically unbelievable.

I was drawn in not so much by his words, but by the odd and unexpressed behavior, by the weird energy that was sitting below the surface.

I leaned forward in my chair with a conspiratorial advance. "Are you?" I had pressed in nearer to him than I ever would've dared to do with someone else. Reggie had seen more than his fair share of scars over the years, what with all the patients rotating in and out of his caseload. My scars were a handicap, but nothing spectacular to someone like him. The scars on my face and body that I typically and religiously kept hidden from others through distance at the bare minimum, and often coupled with make-up, I felt no need to hide from Reggie.

Reggie sighed and roughed up his short yet straggled strawberry blonde hair, shattering the indulgent illusion I'd been building, and after which he began pacing in frustration. It was a poor outlet for all the pent up energy. He must have been picking up on some super-sonic stimuli that I couldn't hear. Something suddenly had him actively agitated, and like any other unnerved animal, I let him be. I let him pace for several uninterrupted minutes. I also thought better of my positioning and leaned back and away, sinking into the cushions of my chair.

Something was seriously off, and it had gone off with a short fuse and the flip of an invisible switch. If I didn't know any better, I would have said Reggie's body language telegraphed a barely contained hostility. "What? What is it?" I eventually inquired with a tremor to my voice.

Reggie placed his hands on his hips and cocked his head to one side. If it weren't for the signs of inner struggle, I would have said he looked more curious than cutthroat. Instead I realized that he was holding something big back from me, and in doing so, his anger was spilling over the sides of an energetic wall. Reggie had a secret, maybe many secrets. My confidant was angry and holding out on me.

Not that he would see it that way.

Silence. The irrefutable argument and tedious tormentor was seated heavily in the room, and I felt the crack of an invisible whip for several lashes.

"Ok," I started, after having had enough of his delay, "why don't we just - "

"Why couldn't you tell me?" Reggie cut me off, allowing his frustration to burst forth like a fiery geyser. He didn't care where or what the flaming edge of his words licked, an omen of what was to inevitably come between us with the passing of time. "Why the hell couldn't you have told me sooner, right up front?"

I was lost.

Not that lost is any new condition for me.

"Told you what?" I asked nervously.

Reggie was beginning to appear downright enraged, a side of him I'd never seen up until that point. He was so red-faced, and there was a shade of darkness coloring him, too, that went beyond the familiar brooding intensity.

The second angry man in my life today and it isn't even noon.

"Did Brian tell you to leave it for him to do last minute?" Reggie's questions continued.

I shook my head as though clogged ears might be the problem.

If only things in my life could be that simple.

"Brian doesn't tell me what to do. And, seriously, what the hell are you talking about?" Awareness came over me of just how small and fragile I was, and how large and capable Reggie could be by contrast. Forever firm and fit, he was a veritable mountain of a man, and in this instance the mountain happened to also be a volcano.

Then, like a flash, he went quiet and still, the volcano posing as a mountain once again. But, could I be so easily fooled? It was as though a switch had flipped once more in his brain and reversed the current.

Reggie stared at me like he'd never seen me before, or that he'd never made the full realization of my human condition. Something had suddenly manifested in front of him, and in between the two of us, only I couldn't see it. His eyes were the only ones uniquely attuned to this mirage. The specter was meant for him alone. He stared for what seemed like an eternity and considered the situation.

As unstable as I could be, as bipolar as I often allowed my moods to become, they were no match for the swings Reggie was capable of manifesting. It was an instability I'd never seen displayed before, and had hoped never to see again. But, as fate would have it, I would see it, again and again. For with the sweet also comes the sour, with the sweetness of my forbidden lust would also come the too tart price I'd have to pay.

And, then he finally emerged. "You don't know," he solemnly stated with an edge of grimness.

I didn't.

"Know what, Reggie?" I felt almost as though I were begging forgiveness from a dear friend that I'd wronged. What sin had been committed now? What other penance would I be forced to do to make amends for my life? And, what would I have to do to get myself out of this uncomfortable scenario?

"Our session today is our last one."

It might have been that my hearing was going along with all my other decayed abilities. The words seemed to take forever to sink in. My brain didn't want to process it, or maybe it was not expecting to have to process it. "Why?" It was the only word I had in the whole linguistically diverse universe. Pathetic.

"You tell me," Reggie challenged, his tone and temperament pre-heating again for another potential blowout. He seemed genuinely upset, and that was the scary silver lining. Reggie actually gave a shit about helping me and about keeping our sessions going, or at least that's what I'd entertained in my brain. Maybe it was more than just therapy, maybe it was friendship.

Maybe, if I'm lucky, there's a hidden obsession. Maybe I'm just beyond all hope.

I scratched my head and fluffed my untamed mane of haphazard blonde curls, my curls and Sonya's. It was a habit that went unchecked in moments of frustration, nervousness, and tension. And, it was a similar trait to Reggie's, a mutual sharing of body language. It was also something I did during times of sinful seduction, and it is interesting how the lines blur in my reality.

"You tell me that you're moving away, Sally. Don't just leave it for Brian to do, damn it! Tell me that he is moving you out of this apartment and this city, and that you just didn't know when it would happen," Reggie instructed, trying to clear up the whole mess and put it into a well-defined and therapeutically acceptable box, a box that could be easily dealt with.

Perhaps even labeled and put in the basement storage area.

My eyes searched his. "I can't tell you that."

"What the fuck?!" He exploded and threw up his hands, the threatening volcano once more. "You don't know that you're moving? Come on! If Brian had the balls to say something, then you'd have to be in the know."

When did I schedule an inquisition? And, can I please be tied up on the rack before we continue?

I tilted my body forward a little more, leaning into the situation gingerly, flirting with what appeared to be danger. "Reggie, I have no idea what the hell's going on, but

I can assure you I'm not going anywhere. When did you hear all of this from Brian?"

"This morning, on his way out the door."

"And, he said what, exactly?" It was my turn to play inquisitor, my turn to crack the whip a little against Reggie and Silence.

But, I will lash out gently, my darlings.

"That you're moving, and that today's session will be our last one. He said you'd appreciate it if I went about things as normally as possible..." Reggie paused, all the pieces coming into place, all of those painfully obvious pieces that were hidden by the face of seething anger. "I thought you just didn't want to have to deal with it, Sally," he now began to back pedal, another massive mood swing sliding through him.

It was practically endearing to see all that passion coursing through his veins, making his head and my heart throb in tandem.

I eyed him intensely. "I wouldn't do that." I stated. "There may be a lot of things I refuse to deal with Reggie, but this situation isn't one of them. Our arrangements aren't something I'd ever refuse to deal with." An even keel returned to the timbre of my voice to balance the mood in the room, in spite of my still fluctuating emotions. "I am not moving," I insisted. But, was it true?

What the hell is happening here?

"Good," Reggie nodded. "It would've seriously screwed with my caseload and income if this was to come up now, all of a sudden. I can't afford that." He spoke with great release and what I took to be even greater honesty. Although that perceived honesty didn't match the hungry and possessive look that stayed in his eyes, a cold but fiery fixture. It was a look that gave me great pause and great hope. It was a dangerous sizzle of an electric current that could kill or cure. I, too, felt a hunger, only it stirred amidst a curious nausea.

Once more I sat back and away, seeking refuge in plump plum cushions. "I'll talk to Brian when he gets home," I half-heartedly assured. "I'll find out what's going on."

And, with that we went straight into our routine of Thera-bands, weights, gait belts, and portable peddling stands that would leave me out of breath from an uninspired exertion. Reggie regained his typically composed form, which I now knew was a bold-faced lie. Had I not seen what lies beneath, I never would have guessed it from the veneer.

Monday and Friday afternoons were typically reserved for tea with my mother, a bookending to the mainstay of my week. And, as charming as that sounds, I can assure you it is a psychologically dangerous crapshoot. Sometimes things with her are absolutely wonderful, and other times it's as though she is determined to make me feel even more miserable in my pithy existence. It's doubtful that either of us has ever actually benefitted from the exchange of words and energies when coalesced, and I'd never quite been able to arrive at the secret of her end game in those days. What I did know was that her intensity had severely sharpened since the day Sonya died. It was barely noticeable at first, but over the months that followed, the serrated edge became undeniably pronounced and treacherous.

"So," she said as she strolled into the room from the bright sunlit hallway, "did you forget that we were spending the afternoon together?" She eyed me up and down and gave a quick glance towards the kitchen.

Of course, because my life is so very full of social engagements.

I wasn't dressed for company and the kettle wasn't on the stove. Fair enough. You would think with the somewhat regular schedule of imposed weekly activities, I would retain some sense of self in the spectrum of time, but that was often not the case. And, as the months and years rolled past, it had only gotten worse. Plus, my uncomfortable session with Reggie only a couple of hours prior had me out of sorts. I plagued myself with the question of how I would gain his friendship, and regain the fantasy of intimacy I'd woven in evolving strands around us. I'd thought it such a pity that cold, hard reality and crude cash shattered the illusion, and I'd taken to turning inward after therapy, feeling sorry for myself. I couldn't help but wonder how I would tap into that unstable passion of his again, and turn it into a fitting fantasy. All the while the phrase 'be careful what you wish for' whispered at the back of my mind, echoing in each synaptic corridor.

I looked at my well-heeled mother as I closed the door and leaned heavily on my walker; in stark contrast, I was a sweaty and emotional mess.

I suppose my walker would be the one sign of progress I'd achieved over the past year. To go from wheelchair to walker was a huge accomplishment, and I'd rejoiced inwardly when Brian had finally been able to take the wheelchair away. He'd donated it back to the hospital we'd originally gotten it from after a few weeks of consistent walker usage on my part, and I'd breathed a heavy sigh when it left.

The walker was my new challenge, my new hurdle to surmount, but I'd stalled there. I was held down in what felt like excruciatingly slow quicksand. As much as I struggled against my own limbs, as hard as I tried to break free, I only found myself sinking deeper into reliance on my shiny silver sidekick. Yet, I remembered and occasionally took solace in the strong impressions of joy that were lightly etched on my soul when Brian took the wheelchair away for good, when we all knew I wouldn't need it anymore. The rough ridges of rubber on the wheels with their unmistakable wear patterns and the hideous blue-tinged leather had been hallmarks of my own metal monstrosity, my own personal confines in hell. Now, hell had new confines placed upright on four small rolling wheels.

My mother, on the other hand, looked exceptional. Her long, fine blonde locks flowed behind her like a cascading waterfall as she strode in with the posture and balance of a ballet dancer. The years of physical work on landscapes enhanced by the prominence of management had left her with an aura of grace and a toned physique enviable of women half her age.

She, not unlike me, had always held an appreciation for place and structure. She tuned into the spirit and vibrational patterns of space on instinct and could create within the parameters something awe-inspiring. She also held a love of fitness and the movement arts, something we both used to share, a common tie that once bound us in a state resembling good health. But, I had lost my connection. She'd held on to all of it, however, even in early retirement and despite mild arthritis. And, now it was an unacknowledged wedge between us.

If I were her, I'd totally go cougar.

Between the two of us my mother might even have appeared to be the younger one. Who could say? I was no judge of time or age or beauty anymore.

"Sorry," I acquiesced to her mood and dominance. "I've had a hard morning."

She turned to face me, fine lines no match for her daring and icy blue eyes. Jeanna Dougherty was a regal woman. "Did Reggie up your physical therapy regimen?"

"Not exactly." I shrugged. "You look well." I switched topics, purposefully to her, the one subject she never tired of.

"I'm doing well, thanks, dear. The garden beds have been settled in for the winter, and I also have a new Pilates teacher. The core work has been exceptional," she casually reported and shook the brown paper bag I'd only now noticed she was clutching. "I brought you some things." She spoke with a lure that must have initially captivated my father. There were days where I wondered if it held him still. He never tried very hard to keep her satisfied, but she never tried very hard to escape. Complaisance could be a blessing, I supposed.

I smiled weakly at her and followed into the open galley kitchen. The room was a fresh field of harvest yellows with accentuating wheat wreaths and hanging pictures of fruit and wines. It held visual suggestions of small meals with close friends and family, holiday cookies, and sublime tea times. I felt that in the relatively short time I'd lived in the apartment it had come to pick up my mother's determined and decisive patterns the most. The room could almost be a representation of her. It was sunny, bright, and held within itself the rich harvest time of life, even if it was a little put on for show.

I watched as my mother set the bag down on the small table at the far end and began unpacking its contents. The smooth lacquered surface became lined with assorted teas, my favorite pumpkin oatmeal cookies, dark chocolates, and what appeared to be a couple of music CD's and a new coffee mug. "What's all that for?"

"For you!" she beamed. "I just thought someone should do something nice for you. Cheer you up."

I made my way to one of the two hand-carved wooden chairs that sat next to the table and lowered myself on to the seat's stable surface. "And, why would I need cheering up?" I asked, retrieving the box of assorted teas to see what it offered.

The Egyptian mint sounds most intriguing.

My mother smiled a little too sweetly then, and it was in the very next moment that I knew she knew.

Did everyone know?!

"You know!" I accused in the most venomous tone I could conjure, not even letting her have her undoubtedly big reveal. It was a tone direct from my childhood, from days when I would sneak out at night because of a ridiculously strict curfew and then become enraged on the few occasions when I was caught. Amazing how my mother could evoke the peeved inner child still.

She sighed. "Well, yes, I know. But, how do you know?" she now seemed exasperated with me.

The audacity!

Jeanna Dougherty was not one who liked to have her plans disrupted by the flow of life. In her reality she was the flow itself, and everyone in her sphere was merely along for the ride. It was the birthright of the beautiful. "Brian was supposed to leave it to me to discuss the move with you."

I narrowed my gaze. "Yes, I'm sure he was. Unfortunately for the two of you the plans are now changed." I spoke with as much dignity and resolve as I could muster. It wasn't easy to square my shoulders and face down my own mother, but if I wanted to stay put in this apartment and in this city I would have to win the battle with her to ultimately be victorious in the war that would soon be waged with Brian. "How lucky I am to have had Reggie pitch a fit about finances with me after Brian spoke to him in confidence this morning. And, it's startling the confidences that man chooses to keep these days."

"Now, Sally – "

"No! And, I am equally disappointed in you, mom!" I cut her off and simultaneously to the quick.

Touché!

"You know how I feel about this," I went on. "And, you had no business sticking your nose in where it doesn't belong. I'm a grown woman, goddamnit! My disabilities do not give you carte blanche to run my life. This is a matter that stays between Brian and me. So, do us all a favor and butt out!" I blurted in heated summation. There would be no mercy from me on this issue. And, it was no surprise then that Brian gave up so easily on our morning debate. He believed he'd already won.

My mother sat down across from me and found that it was her turn to calmly consider the tea. After a few minutes of what appeared to be careful consideration, she spoke. "You are so hateful."

"Gee, you are such a supportive parent." I rolled my eyes.

"Brian can't talk to you anymore," she continued. "He can't have a rational conversation with you about how he's feeling, about what he needs. He can't even get you to listen even when it's for your own benefit."

"And, who determines what is for my own benefit? Who is the judge of that? You? Him?" The ritual of inquisition still lingered in the apartment's walls from the morning's tribulations.

I watched as something within my mother's mind clicked into place. She locked her eyes on me as though she were looking through the scope of a sniper's rifle. "It obviously can't be you."

I opened my mouth to argue but instead the sum of my faculties decided it would be more appropriate for me to gape like a tired old fish. I think I might have had a witty and hotheaded rejoinder had some part of me not been in total agreement with her. There was a part of me that apparently agreed without any sort of equivocation, and within seconds I knew that it came from a place inside me that had been carved out a very long time ago. It was birthed and erected long before my accident, long before my now failing marriage, and before the full façade of who I'd chosen to become despite what would've been best for me had emerged. It had been birthed before Sally Erin Archer; it stemmed from some time ago when I was still Sally Erin Dougherty. Obviously, I could not be trusted to decide what was in my own best interest.

"It pains me to have to say these things," my mother softened.

"Does it?" I peered up at her from beneath my dampening eyelashes.

I saw a quiver of emotion pass over my mother and cloud her features ever so slightly. "Of course it does," she affirmed. Her warm and soft hand reached out and covered both of mine from across the table, bridging an expanse that felt even wider. "I'll put on some tea and we can talk about it. We can talk about all of it."

I nodded.

I'll never be able to talk about all of it.

Maybe it was hate. Maybe it was spite. Maybe it was sorrowful defeat.

I watched as my mother chose the tea we'd both been eyeing earlier, Egyptian mint. No doubt it would be soothing and exotic. All the things she was and all the things I might have been in a life let loose or even one better orchestrated. In a matter of seconds, the kettle was on. In a matter of minutes, I had been visibly reduced to tears. Jeanna Dougherty in her sporadic wisdom let me cry. It was my only way to talk about all of it.

I would've rather attempted sex with my husband than pack for the impending move. However, the decision had been made for me. As it turns out and was eventually pointed out, my name was never on the apartment lease, and I had no substantial income of my own. So, Brian had made the decision to move for us once the lease was up and before I'd even had the chance to mount a decent attack. I did win the argument over therapy and therapist, though, and was proud as a peacock to call and tell Reggie that even though I would be moving he could keep our regular appointments on this schedule. I had no idea where I was going to end up, but Brian did have to admit that it would more than likely be viable for Reggie to continue to provide services. I found it interesting that Brian saw in Reggie a confidant one moment and an undefined threat the next.

Box after box of books, clothes, yoga equipment, kitchenware, computer and tech gadgets, art, and knick-knacks began to appear. Storage containers, smelling of mold and mothballs, were brought up from the building's basement. They sat in the center of the main room, mysterious and dusty and ready to go to their new home, to move on to a new life where their contents might once again be useful. The only box for which I knew the answer to its riddle was box #5.

Brian seemed to have been revivified overnight, and in the days that followed he took on a new vigor, the likes of which I hadn't seen since our early days as a couple. His exuberance could have been that of a man packing to go away on a much-anticipated honeymoon, which was ironic since the move would be taking him further away from his unidentified mistress. He hauled objects to place them logically and lovingly into boxes and crates. He moved boxes and crates to place them in the appropriate apartment space by category. Label after label, row after row. It was like living in a warehouse of madness and memories, more than half of which I ignored.

In my usual passive aggressive manner, I refused to show interest in where we were headed. I refused to even ask if he would still be driving in to work at his local office space. It seemed more than likely at the time that he would be. Prior to preparing in earnest for the move, late nights on unspecified work projects had been the norm. Late night and early morning calls that consistently increased in frequency over the span of months had also become the norm. I'd gotten so used to hearing the very beginnings of *The Piano Sonata No.16 in C Major* by Mozart that I could have played it on the piano if I'd had the skills. As it was, I often found myself humming or whistling it to then bristle at my own ironic stupidity and entrapment. That norm, that terrible balance, would need to eventually be restored if he wanted to re-engage in his extracurricular activities.

My inner reality was the exact opposite to what I externally portrayed. I couldn't have been more curious about the goings-on. Was Brian taking me back to our old home, to a time before Sonya so that we both might magically become what we once were together? Did he believe the ghosts of those people might still live in the carpets and papered walls of that small house on the corner lot? If I stepped across the threshold once more, would I become revivified as he already was just thinking about it? Those were but a few of the many taunting questions. However, there was no point in guessing. It would only drive me crazy, and I figured I was bound to be disappointed no matter what theory I cooked up in my fevered brain.

If things did miraculously change between us in this move, it did make me wonder if he would continue his sordid affair. There was no incentive for him not to. The home life mixed with the carousing was a recipe for a win-win.

"I want you to see it," Brian said to me across the kitchen table as we had dinner late one night. The packing was almost complete and the days were growing short. Night crept up on us earlier and earlier. And, my stamina was less and less, as though I were waning in strength with the dying sun.

I placed my spoon to rest gently in my soup bowl and reached distractedly for some bread.

"I'm sure I'll see it very soon," I rebuffed, tearing the tough sourdough apart. The tear was as haphazard and messy as I knew I was in sweatpants and an adopted t-shirt from my father. Another rough day of just wandering about the apartment, and a day in which a good portion was spent in the still fully formed nursery suite.

"Let's take a drive this weekend and see it together," he said encouragingly and smiled, lighting up our dim settings a bit. "I think you'll be really happy with it, Sally. It's everything we used to say we wanted," he continued.

We used to say we wanted?

I had no idea *we* had ever declared at any point in time what we wanted in mutual terms.

"Really?" I questioned dryly.

"Really, seriously, honestly, totally..." Brian attempted to elevate my mood.

I smiled back despite myself and dipped my bread in the soup.

"Completely, terrifically – "

"Ok," I cut him off with a wave of my hand. "Ok," I caved.

Truth be told, there was something about his manner that was far more engaging than I could ever recall. I couldn't help but wonder what might be so special about this new place, and in all my subsequent imaginings I began a series of fantasies that took on a spontaneous new life as I waited for that weekend drive.

So much for not guessing or cooking up new theories.

We were travelling just a little over an hour outside of the city limits and forty-five minutes from the proper county line. And, in such a short amount of time it was startling how the landscapes could change. I'd forgotten what it was like to participate in urban sprawl. I thought of myself as a mangled half-butterfly emerging from a cocoon. I couldn't go back to being the caterpillar because I disliked what I'd become, nor could I move forward as a full-fledged butterfly. My wings were undeniably torn and tattered. I was caught in a whirlwind as Brian and I moved from the busy, bustling concrete jungle to a more sprawled suburbia, and then into what almost appeared to be pristine rural lands. This all happened in just under an hour as I watched the world go by in a blur through the lens of the passenger window.

In my mostly voluntary exile spanning the course of three years, not much seemed to change out there in the wilds of life, at least not much with the people. They still rushed about and then suddenly came to a grinding halt, waiting impatiently once they got to wherever it was they were going. There were still young women with strollers. There were still children attended by matronly caregivers. Businessmen moved along in flawlessly striped suits, while women in trendy casual dress along their daring counterparts in power suits and equally powerful heels weaved their own paths through them. And, of course, there were the other men, less striking, in denim at the parks and amid green spaces, dreamy and poetic. The societal archetypes were alive and well, and every single one of them was totally absorbed in their own little world.

They all had a web of life going that had the distinct illusion of appearing separate from every other web, and so it seemed only common sense to ignore all but the one they had built. But, to an outsider whose woven structure had been demolished in a colliding tragedy, and for whom hope of reconstruction was seemingly obsolete, it was immediately apparent that every web not only connected to but relied on every other subsequent weaving around it, and those strands branched out indefinitely, forging connections that could never be completely traceable or thoroughly understood.

I am almost outside of the web.

I felt like the spaces in between more than the substantial strands. I couldn't even faintly remember a feeling of being the nexus. It eluded me. I was not structure. I was captured and confined chaos, the butterfly effect.

Brian drove by memory and with such an instinctual ease that I was sure he must've already made this trip multiple times.

"Ella should be there already," Brian stated, and it was then I realized that he'd been talking for most of the drive as he began to make references back to information he'd already given me. "Obviously, given the situation, she's very excited to turn everything over to us today."

"Obviously," I agreed.

Our small gray sedan, the replacement vehicle purchased shortly after my accident, made one last turn onto a street with 'No Outlet' plainly advertised. We had arrived at Willow Tree Court.

I stayed in the car, attempting to take it all in as we stopped at the top of a softly sloping driveway. Sunlight spilled through the side window and coated my face in its golden, late season warmth.

How long has it been since I've basked? And, what is it about this place that suddenly makes me want to do so?

Perhaps it was the pattern of the day, given that I had already made some efforts of my own to woo life. I'd forced myself into an intricately woven, chocolate brown sweater-dress ideal for the chilly weather and accessorized with a multi-tonal brown and gold scarf. My hair was well tamed and pulled back to reveal my face to the world, spots and speckles and scars decently hidden beneath a veil of well-placed make-up. Snug and stylish ballet flats completed the ensemble, and my silver jewelry happened to match my walker perfectly.

How about that, I'm color coordinated with my metal prison!

I watched through the windshield as Brian jogged over to the front porch to greet the figure of a woman standing there.

Ella.

At least, that's what I'd assumed. It was hard to make out much other than her immaculate figure through the bright fall sunlight and the subsequent sheen on the glass. Compared to Brian she seemed somewhat tall for a woman, meeting his height with no augmented heels. Slender and contained were the best adjectives I could come up with to describe the vague and unexplainably haunting shape.

It looked like a brief exchange of pleasantries and pertinent information, and then Brian was opening my car door with walker in hand, beckoning me forth.

I stepped out somewhat boldly for a broken butterfly and was greeted by a whisper upon the breeze, rustling leaves, and the delicate scent of a moist sweetness I could not identify. I stopped in my tracks just free of the car door as it closed behind me and took in the vision I was meant to admire.

#18 Willow Tree Court.

Old, yet remarkably cared for over the years, grand and still fragile in a way that all old houses are once they have moved past their prime. Even though the grandeur of the home's structures might forever remain intact with good ownership, their insides were prone to rot and rupture. Replacements were inevitable and ongoing. The soul of the house itself, and all homes like #18, would have to accept more modern interpretations, forced or otherwise. The house was a mass of weather-hued stone and artisan-carved wood, the coolness and foreboding of the stone countered by the warmth and welcome of the interpretive wood. A wrap-around porch complete with an aged swing seemed to say to me, 'You are home.'

"Like it?" Brian inquired, his hand resting on the small of my back and pressing in to ever so gently push me forward.

I could see why he thought I would. #18 was that brilliant blend of dreams and nightmares that I had tucked away so very long ago. It was a home perfect for entertaining family and friends, a place where a large clan or even an individual couple could thrive. No doubt there would be space for everything, including my neglected dreams. There would be space for the older artworks that I'd created on canvas and paper. There would be a spot for the few remaining pieces of yoga and movement arts equipment that had belonged to me personally, that had not perished along with my dreams and the professional studio. Creatively, this house might enthrall me on stormy nights the way a manor or the moors could have done in an ancient era. In a flash I'd thought I might once again be able to create, if not with movement then without. Surrounded by tall trees that were more than likely as old as the house itself, #18 would stand shrouded in mystery once night fell.

And, night must fall, bless the darkness.

"Sally," Brian interrupted my mental flight of fancy, "do you like it?"

Brought back to my surroundings and my predicament, I merely shrugged. "Let's take a good look." That was the best I could do in my condition, and given the fact that I could hardly take in all that #18 had to offer on the outside. I hadn't even gotten the chance to really view the lot or surrounding properties. My walker and I made our way up the stone path and then wooden steps to stand beside a strange woman on the porch.

This is exhausting.

"Sally, this is Ella St. James, our realtor I've been telling you so much about," Brian introduced her to me as if I had known of the whole purchasing process from the very start. "Sally's been so eager to meet you," Brian then added as an aside to Ella.

How he treasures his logical reality and reasonable artifice!

I glanced into the face of the once mysterious figure. Ella was a grand older woman, not unlike the house itself, the chill of her steely gray hair tempered by the flush of warmth from her liberally applied rouge and coral lipstick. "Welcome home," she cooed in a subtle yet definitively final tone. "Brian said you would appreciate it if I would do the walk through with you as well, since you were not able to be present at the initial tour of the house," Ella explained her presence. "I can be entertaining, so I do understand. And, given the circumstances, it is quite natural that you would want someone with a knowledge of the history to be present in case you should have any questions or lingering buyer's remorse."

"Yes, well, that's very kind of you," I returned with a sweetly painted smile of my own.

"From what Brian tells me, Willow Tree Court and this specific house should suit your needs and unique wants. All of the homes here are all very old, of course, and your neighbors will be closer than what is common for this area due to the unplanned and organic layout of the subdivision as it was growing, not to mention the predominance of the trees for which the court is named. However, the abundance of trees and the seclusion of the court itself should prove ideal," Ella summarized. "Shall we?" And, with the flick of a wrist she indicated that Brian should do the honors and open the door.

This is the most excitement I've had in years, exhaustion aside.

Brian maneuvered past the two of us to open wide the main entrance. He beamed brightly as I made my way inside.

"You look beautiful," came words spoken in a whisper, tickling my ear. I shot a quick glance over my shoulder to see Brian wink and nod reassuringly. Was he kidding? Perhaps he was just trying to smooth the moving process with a little flattery, grease the wheels.

Once in the main hall, I couldn't maintain my aloofness or indifference any longer. I found myself positively enveloped and enraptured, though I did my best to tamp down on it. It was beyond comprehension that my life could include a place so great, or that Brian could achieve something so kind out of all of our misery.

We've both been through so much hardship. I'm not sure how we've even been able to keep up, to keep on.

Given the majesty of what was all around me, I couldn't help but reflect on all that had once been my surroundings. I thought back to the twisted metal that had encaged me when the cars collided, on the desperate attempts I'd made to have one more coherent thought or series of movements, how I'd been most like a struggling animal in those moments, a mother lioness who'd lost her cub and might lose her life. There was nothing but fight and rage and ragged edges around me then, and I had thought that in the aftermath that's all there ever would be, whether in one form or another.

But, I'd been wrong. I had no choice but to give in to the pressing decadence. The woodwork on the outside paled in comparison to the polished sheen and ornate decadence of the woodwork that lined the inside. Swirling stairways, arched doorways, glistening baseboards, and a few matching pieces of antique furniture placed strategically and sporadically were a feast for the eyes. The interior was nothing short of immaculate artwork.

How did he find this place?

That was the first question.

How could we afford it?

That was the second and more worrisome question.

Exhaustion and excitement were battling it out inside of me. My determination to be negative was losing its grip on the small part of my soul that wanted to live life again and live it to the fullest.

The budding flow of my negativity that started in the car, that kept trying to rear its head, was staunched immediately when Ella began her elaborate tour, a mixture of lilting words and luscious gestures as we moved from room to room and level to level, each revealing more extravagant surface discoveries than the last. Every room had its very own color and texture palette that were somehow both old-fashioned and impossibly vivid and fresh. Our realtor must have had a historical rehabber come in and do the work to maintain the character and at the same time make things as new as could be for potential buyers.

There's no way we can afford this. And, no way am I ever leaving once I move in!

The only spot in the house we didn't visit, to my cursory knowledge at the time, was the unfinished basement. And, it had seemed unnecessary. The only area along the tour that gave me significant pause was the two-car garage. Accessible from the inside through a doorway off the kitchen, the garage was spotlessly clean and perfect for both storage if needed and our basic sedan, yet I hated it. Bare and bland, it not only lacked any of the nuance present all throughout the rest of the structure, but it had an odd smell, an unidentified sweetness mixed in with the strong aroma of a potent cleaning agent. It immediately brought up memories of my grandmother's last days and the small amount of time she'd spent in hospice care. The hospice building had smelled just like our new garage, and my senses were flooded with the aroma and associated memories. The garage reeked of death.

Adrenaline must have temporarily remedied my usual waves of fatigue, a gift brought on by all the unusual stimuli. I found myself completing the entire tour and standing in a studio space on the third floor looking out through a cucumber-framed art window at the surrounding properties. My eyes went straight to the unbelievably massive willow tree in the center cul-de-sac that sat directly across from my new home.

My new home. What have I done to deserve this?

The willow tree was so large and gangly that its mourning branches blocked most of my view of the house across the street.

"See what I mean," Ella's voice crept up from behind me.

I turned to find her closer than she should be for not having made any perceivable sound. "What?"

"The other houses may be close at hand, but with the trees in this area they can seem well separated. Anything could happen here and go unnoticed," Ella explained. "That tree there," she said, pointing out the window to the one I was staring at, "it was planted when the first home on the court went up. "

How long do willows live? It seems like I remember my own mother bemoaning having to replace them all the time when she worked in landscaping. What had she said? 30 years... 40 years, tops. That would make the tree Ella's pointing at impossibly old.

"And willows being the way that they are, well, they sprout up like weeds." Ella gave a light chuckle as though there was something funny about that and then went on. "New trees grew everywhere since the fallen branches and roots went unchecked for a time. This whole area is a maze of intertwined roots under the houses."

"Is that a problem?" I inquired, fearful of the new home and already an issue. My mind went straight to the foundation and the dreadful cost of piering walls.

Once a homeowner, always a homeowner... or made to think like one when prompted.

The first home Brian and I had lived in, the small house on the corner lot, hadn't been anywhere near as grand or intimidating as this.

"Not so much as you might think, but then again, maybe more so. It ties everything together."

"What?"

What the hell does that mean?

"Pipes," Ella clarified. "Roots can be unpredictable. But, you shouldn't worry too much."

"Why?" I pressed. "Are the pipes for this house new or something?"

Ella tilted her head a little and smiled as she had been doing off and on since I'd met her. Before I realized what she was doing, her hand had reached out and tucked a single loose curl behind my ear. "You look tired, my dear. I think this tour has been enough for one day, don't you?"

I was unused to strangers in my personal space and couldn't help but draw back a little to reset the boundaries. "I do have a long drive back," I sort of agreed.

"Yes." Ella gave her approval.

Do I need it?

"I would like to just take a moment and look out at the other homes from here," I told her, reinforcing the boundaries of my bubble.

"Well, from what you can see. There is a better view on the front porch. But, by all means, do take your time. I will be downstairs when you are ready to go." And with that, she left me to my sacred solitude, with only a hint of her haunting presence left behind as unwelcome company.

This little adventure might have been the longest I'd spent in the company of others outside of my apartment in years. I needed the quiet and even relished the short-lived seclusion. There would be the long drive back, and I was sure Brian would want to talk all about this day trip and our upcoming move. I leaned as far forward into the window frame as I could with my walker in front of me and peered out, first to the left and then to the right. Ella was correct, as branches on all sides obstructed my vision. I could make out bits of rooftops, the side of the neighboring house to my right, and some non-descript woodwork. I did manage to catch a glimpse of a sign on one of the front lawns but couldn't make out what it said. It was time to head downstairs.

The trip from the third floor to the porch had me completely beat. I didn't even bother to stand around and talk or sightsee. Brian knew I'd reached my limit and took me immediately to the car before going back to wrap things up with Ella. While he was away I did notice the sign in the neighbor's yard —'For sale.' And, two houses further down — 'For sale.' All of the sale signs bore the name, Ella St. James, and they touted her poised picture. Our house had once contributed to three total vacancies in this very small subdivision. That information gave way to a sinking feeling, and I found myself drowning in its vortex.

Chapter 2

By the time I returned home late that Saturday afternoon, I was ready to collapse into my trusty old plum recliner and nap until dinner. Brian had stopped on the way back and rounded up groceries from a market more central to our upcoming location than the home we shared in the city. After depositing me in the main room and turning on the television, he happily went to work in the kitchen, quite the busy bee.

I must have been successful in my search for a nap because it seemed the blink of an eye and dinner was ready. Pulling myself up and out of both my chair and my slumber, I followed Brian mindlessly into the kitchen. Interesting how we had taken to eating in there instead of the dining area when it was only the two of us for a meal. It was something I rarely thought about as our routine was so second nature, but I doubt it had anything to do with cleanliness or logic on Brian's part. I suspected it had more to do with the fact that Sonya ate with us in the formal dining area. Even with the highchair removed and thrust into storage, from which it noticeably never returned, the place where it had been stationed remained unfilled. The impression of that chair lingered there as an invisible hologram. There were still scuffmarks on the hardwood from where it had been pushed and pulled so many times in a single year.

The kitchen smelled amazing from all of Brian's hard work, and I couldn't even take a stab at how long it had been since he and I shared a home-cooked meal of our own making. Takeout food and meals brought by my mother were standard fare. A shame really, for in my reflections of earlier days it dawned on me that Brian was actually quite the skilled chef. His attention to detail and penchant for planning were not lost in the kitchen.

Beef fillets, cubed sweet potatoes, late season salad greens, and hot rolls were spread before me in a veritable feast on our finest bamboo tableware. As a rule, I didn't eat much. And, if left unchecked, I tended to forget to eat at all. A meal this size looked like a sumptuous banquet.

"You didn't say what you were in the mood for..."
Brian began slowly.

I must have been staring, and who knows what I
looked like after just waking up. My expression and
demeanor could have given him reason to think anything.
"It, um, it looks and smells great," I offered meekly, giving
the best compliment I was capable of, and took a seat.

Brian quickly sat across from me and started
serving. As he reached forward to place a cut of meat on my
plate, I found my hand instantly possessed by a mind of its
own and shooting out to grab his. He froze completely
under my usually icy grip, now turned warmer than
normal, the temperature steadily climbing. Did my
instantaneous and irregular heat generate the opposite
sensation in him? His dark brown eyes looked up to meet
my blue orbs that were no doubt moist with a glaze of tears.
I allowed my hand to wander up the sleeve of his elegantly
cabled sweater. My pale skin stood out like neon against the
unrelenting charcoal of his top, and I could feel with my
frail fingers the cascading strength in his forearm, buoying
from shoulder to wrist. We were so dissimilar, and we were
so far apart. It was hard to believe I could suddenly notice
since we hadn't really been that close in the uncharted
course of our mangled marriage. It was strange that the
thought of it now should affect me so deeply, but it did. It
drew forth a torrential sadness that moved me to a steady
stream of tears. In recent years, the lengthy distance had
grown so wide so that it felt like a literal great divide,
yawning mercilessly before the two of us.

"Thank you," I spoke in a pressed gratitude, the
words coming from the deep chasm of my heart space and
then out my tight and parched throat. My thankfulness was
not to be stalled or staid.

He let the beef drop and held my hand in his. "Sally,
it all went so wrong..." his voice trailed off, and he let his
gaze slip from mine. Looking down at the yellowed
linoleum floor of our kitchen I could tell he was trying to
find composure as opposed to simply contemplating the
apartment's need for new flooring, not that the flooring
concerned us any longer. After a minute or two he looked

up at me again with red-rimmed eyes. "I just want to make it right."

I was transfixed by the sincerity and the magic in those humble and hearty words. It was a wish spoken with the fullest breath. And, after all, I wanted him to make it right, too. If not him, then someone. Anyone.

My other hand joined in on the spirit of possession, and reached out to touch the side of his face. It touched him with a gentleness I had no idea I was capable of achieving. I felt the beginnings of stubble along his jawline, a hint of tickle to tease me back. Perhaps I was completely given over to an alien life force, and not just my limbs but my whole body and mind. Maybe I suddenly held within me a kinder and more tolerant soul who was determined to give expression to that essence. "I know."

I wish I could say I love you. I almost wish I were capable of loving you, again or anew.

I didn't know which it was. I was stalled at trying to find the truth and caught up in the physical exchange of heat and what may have passed for some sort of healing, a new beginning, or none at all.

I felt hot tears trickle across the palm of my hand, and then came the tender impressions of his lips as he kissed their trails. His manner was almost timid, and the shock of such vulnerability from a man so typically certain created a hitch in my breath. It's impossible to say how long we remained in that bizarre state, but at some point my hands made it back to my side of the table, and cooling food made its way onto my plate. Whatever odd and unbidden spirit it was that had ahold of me finally let go. I was back in my body and grounded in the process of eating. The routine of our apartment's kitchen won out.

We ate with Silence as an unseated companion, and I sensed that Brian was considering me in the same way that I was considering him. I had to wonder if he felt as far removed as I tended to day in and day out. And, then I couldn't help but wonder further if the last few moments had started to build a bridge in his mind between us, between our two entirely different and often isolated worlds. His words and actions weren't necessarily out of character, but his demeanor was, to say the very least.

I admit that I was touched by the humility and caring of a man who bought me an extravagant and undeserved home we would soon enjoy, or at least make the attempt to, and who cooked me a fine meal for no apparent reason other than that he wanted to. I was nearly wooed and won over by his candid and passionate offerings. However, the viral warmth that had spread throughout my body like unchecked candle glow was snuffed when I remembered that Monday would roll around again. Brian would return to his office like a moth to the flame, and in doing so, he would return to the environment that harbored his insidious indiscretions. Ironically, I was suddenly bothered by this arrangement.

A sense of jealousy was piqued, and its frigid tendrils spread throughout my body while my heart pounded to keep circulation going against the onslaught of an inner cold snap. As I dwelled on it, I found my hands actually shaking with a sensation I couldn't even name properly. It might have been a mixture of jealousy, desire, and contempt. There may have even been more to it than that. All I knew for certain was that it was a heinously effective cocktail. The worst part was that there was nothing I could do about it other than sit in newfound misery. Who knew more misery could exist? And, as it turns out, agony is heightened after immediate ecstasy.

With as predominantly good as Saturday was, minus my fit of silent jealousy, Sunday was horrid in comparison. The start of the day was particularly unsettling as I woke right around three o'clock in the morning for no apparent reason. It was something that almost never happens to me. After all, I had learned right away to stop all liquids after eight in the evening so that I wouldn't be an unstable mess fumbling in the dark because of a bathroom run. And, due to the fact that even mild activity coupled with an early autumn sunset tended to zap my energy, I slept through the night as soundly as if I had committed no sins.

I awoke to a pitch-black room, with the only light being a splash of incandescence from the window facing the back alley and the glowing digital clock face that told me it was a little after three a.m. Opening my eyes in a cocoon, I found myself being ever the caterpillar turned tattered butterfly and unable to escape. My mind was buzzing with an energy that was incomprehensible to the deciphering powers of the brain. All I really knew was that I was wide-awake and not getting back to sleep anytime soon.

Slowly my eyes adjusted to make out varying shades of gray and numerous uninteresting shapes in the room. Familiarity gave definition to the shapes even though I couldn't visually confirm them. Then came the unmistakable sound of Brian's breathing, instantaneously intensified beside me. I turned my head to take in his sleeping form. His back was to me, and I could tell that he was loosely curled around his pillow. Even in the dark and with all the abstractness that it can bring, I found myself admiring the back of him, the line of him. He was so lean and lanky, so built for precise movements and an ease of living. Each even breath drew me in closer so that it was almost like melding into one, but I could tell that I hadn't actually moved an inch.

I was morphing into a creature more like a distant bat with honing sonar. The darkness had magnified his body so that it appeared closer to mine. I could practically feel the heat of his electromagnetic energy through my flannel nightgown, the steady rhythm of his pulse beating through me in a fascinating and attractively strong vibration, not unlike settling in close to a kettledrum.

Is this a dream?

There was a closeness emanating throughout the room, perhaps churning and mixing itself into the very fabric that ran through the entire apartment, the building, and all the nighttime could contain. It felt like it belonged to all that the darkness was able to touch. All I could distinguish in regards to it was that distance shortened of its own accord, and as it did so, there inevitably seemed to be no length and then no difference at all between Brian and myself. It made no sense to exist as one inseparable creature and also as two distinct entities. It was beyond comprehension to feel more than the body could possibly interpret.

The freedom of his bare skin began to enrage me against my own nightgown, a once protective coating now nothing more than an entrapment. It reminded me of what I had felt when I thought myself to be whole, when I felt my physical form had been admirable and not abominable. I closed my eyes to will myself to fall back asleep, and when that didn't work I attempted to change the dream, for surely that's what it was. It had to be a dream, as I couldn't recall ever feeling that way in my entire life. I was positively compelled. The dream was in control of the dreamer. The room and the night had mastery over the minds caught inside them.

Cautiously, I found myself inching my nightgown upward, tugging ever so gently until I was able to rid myself of it in one single swoop. I tossed it carelessly to the floor, peeking again at Brian to make sure he remained undisturbed. He was still sound asleep, breathing in that hypnotically even way. The softness of the blankets caressed my excruciatingly sensitive flesh as I turned onto my side and slid closer to my husband. In the dark I could be anything, wrapped in a cloak that acted as a second skin, connecting me to Brian so that a visible separation was near indistinguishable. The blackness allowed me to be all I wasn't in the light.

In the process of my unfoldment I at long last found myself pressed against Brian, my feverish skin cooled deliciously against the chilled flesh of his back that had been exposed to the night air. He had left the window in our bedroom cracked open, and I could smell the richness of the autumn earth outside, even in our urban environment. It was so alive from all of the decaying matter, holding a treasure trove of potentials.

Damn and bless my hands for the new life they found independent of my will. They felt the smooth texture of supple skin and the rippling play of muscle beneath, the tantalizing brush of hair and the decidedly wicked dew of sweat below his waistline from where Brian had been covered by the layers of blankets. They wanted more. He was oblivious to my explorations as my phantom hands touched and taunted. He was completely unaware on all levels until my left palm rested over his partially erect member, which sprang to life of its own volition beneath my coaxing.

Who does he dream of as I touch him?

It didn't matter, not in the grand scheme of things or in the presence of the surreal mania that had taken up residence and control.

I was devoid of shame, just as he was devoid of consciousness. Back and forth I rubbed slowly and surely from animal instinct more than memory. I felt him stiffen to an incredible degree, and his penis leapt up and down in my hand like an excited puppy. I, too, was excited and could feel a wetness spreading down the inside of my thighs. It was so foreign to me that at it took several moments to register the cause, and once I started I could not stop. Even if he'd woken up, I don't think I would've stopped. And, I must confess that I didn't cease until I was completely satisfied. His satisfaction was secondary.

By the time Sunday's brunch rolled around, the nursery suite was empty. I had no idea all of the items in the tiny room had been removed until I passed by it in the hallway, following my morning toilet. An unstable pit rocked from back and forth in my stomach, fluctuating between burning hot and freezing cold. Yet, I knew there was no point to wallowing in what was already a done deed, a lost battle in a failing war campaign waged for years. It was time to give it up. And, I couldn't very well take matters into my own hands and track down the items and drag them up three flights of stairs to place them where I felt they belonged. There was no way Brian packed them up to move them to the new house either. I knew very well what had happened, and I was keenly aware of why I hadn't been told ahead of time. Just one more reminder that I was a prisoner in my own life, serving a sentence in which the primary punishment was that others made many of the decisions for me.

I could hear voices coming from the main room as my father, mother, and husband were all talking and making merry over the latest developments. My captors delighted in their destructive designs. Brian and my father must have made good time clearing everything out, especially under my mother's direction. I was sure there wouldn't even be a trace of any of it in the apartment. If I stuck my head out one of the windows to see my father's sport utility vehicle on the street, those nursery items might not even be found there. It was clever of all three of them to get it done and over with so quickly, to remove all of the incriminating evidence and then dispose of it in such short order. I heard my mother's voice from years ago echoing in my head, saying 'a sharp knife cuts the quickest and hurts the least.' But, it was hardly true in the presence of painful post-surgical scars.

Or in the presence of unforgiving trauma scars...

I ran my fingers over my face and contemplated the fine lines as well as the deeper indentations left by the violent explosion of glass compacted with metal. There was nothing that could be done.

With the amount of time I spent lounging in bed and then getting myself up and ready for the day, it was easy enough a task for those three conspirators to accomplish. The cleaning out of a useless room, that was all they'd see it as; where I saw it as the desecration of a sacred tomb. But, sacred or not, a nursery is a small room filled with small things for a very small and new little person. Cleaning it out had to be simple enough. The only things that hadn't been removed were the paint patterns on the walls and the wallpaper border along the top. Smiling dogs danced and pranced near the ceiling, acting as silent yet all-knowing witnesses, while vertical yellow and brown stripes drew the eye ever upward to them. They were the judges that could not be swayed. They saw the hidden moments of woeful neglect and too late remorse. They knew what could happen when a mother just wasn't good enough.

Sonya's first word... doggie.

There was no way I would ever have a dog now.

I wandered in a dizzying haze to the main room, my mind a swirl of lingering passions from three a.m. and of mourning motherhood from three years ago.

"There she is!" my father exclaimed from his usual corner spot on the sofa. Out of comfort and consistency, he took up the exact same position every time. "Good morning, sunshine." A tip of the coffee mug in my direction, and he took a sip.

Craig Dougherty had reason to be happy with the illustrious Jeanna at his side. And, even though she was the dominant partner, Craig was not without means for getting his way. He may not put up much of a fuss for her, but he could certainly fuss for himself if the occasion called for it. His upbeat mood a proof of what was in that overly sweet pudding mixture of his personality. He would start off my morning with lightness so that I would be remiss if I made a scene over the nursery situation. He acted as though everything were as it should be, and it was.

Well played, sir.

"Good morning," I mumbled pushing past all three of them. My mother and father had taken over the sofa, the outward image of the ideal married couple, so Brian sat thoughtlessly in my recliner. "Is there any coffee left?"

"There's a cup freshly poured for you on the counter," Brian informed. "Want me to – "

"No," I overrode. "I'll get it." And with that being said so succinctly, I made my way past them to the kitchen, leaning the walker against the counter as I prepped my coffee with a hint of cinnamon and honey, after stirring in two large spoonfuls of coconut milk.

It's not like I need any help, like it would be easier for any of one of them to do this for me.

I sighed, but it was only for my own ears to hear.

Brian didn't seem any different. He acknowledged me in the same way he always had, minus the mornings during which we'd had a real tussle. This morning was no different than all the other mornings leading up to it. There was no evolution between the two of us, which only led me to the inevitable conclusion that the episode from three in the morning must've been a dream, plain and simple. It could be neatly labeled and boxed away to go with us to the new house or stay in the storage area of this building, whichever I decided. And, quite frankly, it made much more sense as a dream, for I felt there was no way all of that erotic energy could have manifested itself into such an explicitly sexual act without him being aware of it, without it staying in the bedroom and clawing for more. And, if he were aware of it, he'd most certainly be acting differently. It had been such a long time that he wouldn't be able to suppress the afterglow or the insistence for more.

If it was even that good of an experience for him.

I hoped the coffee would prove a remedy for my bout of craziness, my swing from sultry to sullen. I craved more normalcies amid the moderate insanity that was thrust upon me without explanation.

With ease of practice, I balanced the full coffee mug while manipulating my walker handles to support both the beverage and myself. It was time to head back into the belly of the beast, back into the main room to face both the brunch and the day. We'd all be forced to eat in the dining area due to space requirements, one of the many joys of a family with no recourse and no suitable escape from each other. I would sit next to the scuffmarks, as was my want.

I'd just gotten settled at the dining table and was reaching for the toast and jam when my mother started in. "So," she opened for the table, "when is the big move-in date?" She laid a crimson cloth napkin in her lap and began serving herself from a variety of trays.

I looked at my mother, then to Brian, and then back at her. She was a goddess granting us her presence and visage under such drab circumstances.

Is it any wonder I prefer the company of devils?

"So much is already packed, I assume it must be coming up quick," she continued without waiting for a response. Jeanna Dougherty wasn't really capable of waiting very long under most circumstances. She liked to have constant interaction for verifiable feedback of her position. It made her more comfortable to know that everyone was constantly supplying attention and approval.

Idol worship can be such a tedious business.

Brian finished spooning scrambled eggs onto his plate and made proper use of his napkin. I felt sorry for him in that captured instant among such a deceptively picturesque family scene. Brian's parents had passed away early in his life. His mother had been a cancer victim, and his father an alcoholic who had inadvertently killed himself with his addiction.

I am so sorry, Brian, that my parents are the best substitutes I have to offer you.

"The lease is officially up at the end of this week. Sally and I need to have everything out of here by Friday night," Brian reported to my mother. It was straightforward and factual, linear and well laid.

Well laid... were either of us?...

I snickered to myself at that thought, that double entendre I'd made for me alone, not that anyone noticed.

"I see," my mother bridged. "I just thought it would have been even sooner given the fact that you have the keys and almost everything is boxed and ready to go. I mean, it's not like you have to stay all the way through Friday. How you can resist is beyond me."

"Need some help?" my father asked Brian, as he shoveled an enormous amount of hash browns into his mouth, and I'd felt myself smile at that kindness. In reflection of the contrast Brian and I had as an identifiable couple, he also was not much like my mother. Her side of the family was what most would consider affluent, and my mother had the benefit of a solid education and impeccable examples of eloquence. She was a smart, confident woman who knew how to conduct herself, and she not only had those enviable traits, but also was fortunate enough to look the part. My father on the other hand was not so refined. He was a hard worker who could be browbeaten most of the time by someone who seemed superior. He had earned money quickly after launch through his shipping business and my mother's family, from the tidbits I'd gleaned over the years, thought it would be a prudent match for her to hitch her wagon to such an up-and-comer. Respect for entrepreneurs and self-made men ran in my family.

Brian glanced at me once again before responding, and there was a gleam in his eye.

Awkward.

I took a large bite out of a piece of toast.

"If you don't mind helping me haul some of this stuff," he accepted my father's offer. "We won't be taking a lot with us since most of our furniture isn't a good fit for the house. I have some pieces on order that will be delivered over the next two weeks, and according to Ella, some of the furnishings have already arrived early, plus some of the original furnishings and fixtures are staying with the house. But, a lot of boxes will need to go." Brian paused and shot me another unnerving glance, something with an undercurrent of emotional electricity. Our eyes locked in the jolt, and in a single second I sensed that it might not have been just a dream. "Sally has quite the book and art collection, you know, not to mention all the boxes of clothes, and some yoga and Tai Chi equipment."

Craig nodded. "Oh, I know. You say when, son. I'm between two large orders right now and can afford to be away from the warehouse more than usual this week." He polished off a disturbingly large mouthful of eggs and made a grab for the toast and then the fruit bowl.

"And, I can help Sally with her few remaining items this week, if you would like." My mother talked over me as if I were a child whose affairs were the concern of the three adults in the room.

"After therapy," I amended for her.

"What?" My mother looked genuinely confused.

I couldn't help but smile. "I said that would be fine, as long as it's after therapy. I still have sessions with Reggie on Monday, Wednesday, and Friday."

Jeanna Dougherty had her placid surface visibly shattered. "I thought therapy was cancelled for the foreseeable future due to the move." She neglected me and spoke directly to Brian.

No one was eating now. I think all of us knew what was about to transpire. Like prey, we must have thought that if we were still enough the predator would just move on.

"Is Reggie continuing on after the move as well?" my mother continued her line of questioning.

A tense Silence reigned. Silence, an enviable master of torture, the elusive pinnacle of dominants, and I its unwilling submissive... most of the time.

"Brian?" she persisted.

"Reggie is able to fit the drive in his schedule, and both he and Sally felt that it would be beneficial to continue with the program," Brian nutshelled, all the while keeping his eyes averted. I noticed his vision shifted rapidly from the fruit bowl to me, to the toast and then to me, to the eggs and then back to me. He usually got along so well with my mother, even with the relationship being based on a superficial layer of living. This conversation had to be taking a real toll on him.

My mother tossed her napkin onto her partially finished plate of food. "Well, how intriguing and misinformed," came the decree. "I thought we were all in agreement that the sessions weren't providing the results we were hoping for, and since Sally hasn't made much progress past the walker – "

"How am I ever supposed to make that progress without therapy?" I challenged, raising my voice beyond what was deemed appropriate for the dining room table.

"It's ok, Sally," Brian began.

"Is it?" I persisted. "Is it ok? How can any of you look at me and say that it's ok? Look at my face, my body, and the scars... I've lost everything! And, I wonder how any of you would feel if you were suddenly stripped of your work, your home, your ability to care for yourself... your child..." My throat threatened to close up. I swallowed hard in resistance. "How would you feel if you lost the only way of life you'd ever known?! How would you feel with glass marks permanently embedded in your skin?"

My mom reached out to touch my arm only to have me recoil and clumsily get to my feet as quickly as I could, quickly but in a pitiful shambles.

"I lost my child and my means! I lost myself! And, it's fine for you all to sit here and formulate a life around me, but it is not fine for you to sit here and formulate what is left of my life for me." I found an odd new strength in my old indignation.

"We've been over this." Jeanna was not going to tolerate being reprimanded, especially not in front of others. "Even you have to admit, as you've done in past discussions, that you cannot be allowed to make decisions for your own good." My own silent surrender in a weak moment at tea came back to haunt me through my mother's tongue. The same message she'd relayed only days ago was now revisited. "I cannot understand where all of this spiteful behavior is coming from." She coolly stated and gave a look to both her husband and mine that made her appear dumbstruck and innocent.

"It's enough," I snapped as I looked down at her from my standing position. Remarkably, I retained my balance, and with that being done, I grabbed the walker and stormed to my bedroom like a petulant child. I even slammed the door for good measure.

It wasn't supposed to be this hard, none of it was. I met the sight of my own gaze in the full-length bedroom mirror. Even with a light layer of powder and paint on my face, I could make out the lines of each fine scar, the spots and speckles, the imprints of shattered glass and a shattered shell of a shattered life. They would never heal, and I would therefore never be whole. And, with everything I'd lost, life and the people in it still seemed determined to take from me. Why couldn't they let me be?

I wanted to stay locked in place with the ghost of my child and her nursery suite with nothing to fill it. If I couldn't move forward, it would have been enough for them to let me stay locked in place. This wasn't what my life was supposed to be, whether I lived the compliant version or the vision of my own rebellion, which always went unfulfilled. And, that rebellious spirit was angry.

I tousled my blonde curls so that they fell forward over my face, hiding my ugliness from sight. My hair was all I had left of my innate femininity, the one thing that remained beautiful and willful of its own accord. It didn't need coverage or alteration. It didn't need to be hidden in shame for it covered my shame and my broken state, even when cosmetics couldn't.

My ears perked as I heard the bedroom door pop open. I whipped my head around as Brian leaned against it to bring it to a close.

"You aren't the only one who has lost, Sally," he said ever so softly and with such rational precision.

"Are they gone?"

"Yes. I thought they should leave us alone for a while."

I nodded. One point in favor of Brian.

"I think maybe you should leave me alone for a while, too," I pushed.

Why did I ever want to touch him in the first place?

Conspiring with Reggie and my parents, trying to press my life into a forward momentum behind my back. Even if he had the best of intentions, and even if part of me wanted what he was offering, I now despised him all over again — although maybe not to the same hateful depths.

"I lost my child, too, Sally. I lost the life we'd been building and the wife that had made me so happy."

"I'm real sorry for your loss, Brian," I snorted in my familiar passive aggressive manner. Old habits die hard, and some talents came naturally through heredity. It was in the blood.

Brian took a couple of steps forward, standing before me at arm's length. "I lost my ability to even try to give you another child."

I held my hand up like a stop sign. "Don't – "

"I shouldn't have done it. I know we only wanted one child, but I shouldn't have gotten the vasectomy right away."

"Brian, we both agreed – "

He didn't want to let me finish any more than I wanted to let him go on. And, it was then that I realized just how alone he was in the world. With his parents and child both gone, the only claims he had left to family were my parents and me. Not much of a bargain given the tumultuous psychology of my parents, and even I pulled away from him more often than I should have. "It doesn't matter, Sally. I've still lost the ability to give you another child. Maybe if I were able to do that, you wouldn't mourn constantly in an empty nursery."

"Don't worry. My mourning days are over now that there's no nursery."

That's low even for me.

But, I still had no desire to take those words back.

Brian sighed and dropped to his knees in front of me. He reached out to nudge my chin upward so that my eyes met his. "I have lost just as much as you have," he leveled.

"Not even close!" I spat and pulled back.

"Do you think I wanted any of this?! I never wanted our family to be torn apart or for you to lose what you worked so hard for. I never wanted to lose us – "

"We never had us." My tone and words were equally venomous. I'd fallen out of the grace of that kinder and gentler spirit from the night before, and the pity from mere seconds ago.

"We did," he insisted. "You know we did. And, I never, ever wanted to be the guy who cheats on his wife."

It was like taking a bullet to the chest. I'm really not sure why it hurt so badly. After all, this wasn't brand new information for me. His confession of it was the only thing that was groundbreaking. It wasn't like I loved him either, not fully, or that we had ever had any of the connection he was claiming. The only reason I could imagine that it hurt so very badly was the culmination of euphoria that had taken place over the last twenty-four hours. This day had made me feel as if I were being cast down from a glimmer of heaven that I'd mistakenly seen.

"I don't want this to go on, Sally. That's one of the many reasons I'm moving us to a new place. We can start over. Honestly, I didn't mean for it to ever happen. It was an accident." His explanations were probably the same as those given by most unfaithful men and with each sentence it was sort of like he was tripping over his own tongue.

"An accident? Really? How does that happen? Do you accidentally fall on top of someone with your pants off and then mistakenly start to pile-drive her?" I scrutinized his choice of words.

"Whoa!"

"Oh, gee, is my language too shocking?" I found myself laughing at him. The thought that it should be less shocking that he admit to an affair and more so that I use salty descriptions.

Brian gripped my arms hard and held me in place. I immediately began to buck against the restraint but was no match for his physical dominance. "I waited for you to heal. I waited for you to start living again, to come back to me and our marriage. I lost our child, too, and I lost you. I needed you to care for me while I was caring for you. Maybe it wouldn't have hurt so much if you had shown even a little..." his voice trembled and broke. Brian relaxed his grip on my arms only to pull me into his chest and confine me there. "I miss Sonya. I miss her every day." He spoke into my shoulder, and I felt the heat of his breath and the moistness of his tears. "I miss you, and I want you back. I'd give anything, Sally. And, I'd do anything to take away this awful thing that I did."

"I'm not an idiot, Brian, and I'm also not blind. I've known about your whoring around for months now. And, you know, it might have helped your case a little bit if it had only been a one-time thing. How does someone make the same mistake over and over again?" I refused his affection and subjugation.

How does someone make the same mistake over and over again?... The perfect question for me as well.

There was no atonement he could make that I was interested in having.

He pulled back to look at me as well as to show me his blatant remorse. "I needed something. I needed someone. But, when you touched me this morning – "

"What?!" I clumsily scrambled back on the bed and completely out of his grasp, out of his reach.

"God! It was everything it used to be, and I wanted you. I wanted more. It's always been you, and I don't want to go on with this affair anymore." Brian slammed his fists down on the mattress, shaking the whole bed. Our brown comforter gave way like loose earth. "I want my wife back."

So, it wasn't just a dream.

Validity was mine, and I wanted no part of it.

I felt my face flush with the shame of what I'd done, with the fervent fire of what we'd shared. The walls of the bedroom seemed to close in to create even more intimacy in that moment, and I felt the elixir of erotic elation make itself known. Its essence hung heavy like a thick resin perfume, a heady musk.

"Then don't," I countered, trying to shake it off. "Then don't go on with the affair."

You can't have your wife back.

"I won't. I mean, it's finished. I broke it off before I even made the down payment on the house. I wanted us to move and have that be over by the time we did so."

Like a cliché version of the typical wife I asked, "So, who is she?"

"Just a woman I worked with. Amelia."

"Worked with?" I was nit picking now. Details were everything.

I prefer devils, and they lived in the details.

He sighed, knowing he had to play the game my way at this juncture. It was part of his penance. "She resigned shortly after I broke it off with her. I was going to transfer her to another department so that we wouldn't share the same workspace, but she freaked out."

"Ah," was all I had.

"I wanted to fire her outright, but it was also my fault and – "

"Yes, you're such a good person." I rolled my eyes in the most dramatic fashion I could manage, while holding back venom, spit, and tears.

Brian sat down on the bed across from me. "I know I haven't been the best husband, Sally. Hell, I know I haven't even been a good person lately, but I just want to move us forward. I want more of what we had this morning."

"You seem to *want* an awful lot. And, I'm not even sure what you're referring to," I half-lied. Maybe his recollection would be different from my fuzzy dream state interpretation.

"God! Is it that hard to have sex with me? Or is it only hard to admit that you want to have sex with me?!" He was suddenly infuriated. Perhaps it was the loss of a sure thing coupled with the realization that I wasn't so keen on whatever had happened between us. "Fuck it all, Sally! This morning was the hottest and most unexpected thing. I fucking loved it when you stroked me. The feeling of you pressed against me, grinding against me, got me so hard!" Brian closed the distance between us on the bed. "It felt so great knowing that I could make you cum like that," he whispered.

There was no space left for further retreat. I was smashed flat against the headboard.

"Let me do it for you again," he offered.

I felt my throat go dry in the same moment that my palms got sweaty.

"What?"

"Come on, Sally," he said and leaned in to kiss me.

I turned my head away and giggled uncontrollably, a sign of my disenchantment and lack of happiness, an unexpected counterpoint to how it may have sounded to a stranger's ears. "Um, I think maybe we better put the brakes on here. You really expect me to reward you with sex for confessing an affair?"

"This has nothing to do with reward or punishment."

"No?" I asked in disbelief.

"No."

"Then what does it have to do with?"

Brian gave me a wry smile filled with conflicting hope and guilt. "Pleasure."

Pleasure. One of the few things I could still deny him.

The seething anger I had aimed at me the entire workweek of the move was almost more than I could bear, but I supposed it was better than apathy or being treated as an afterthought. The only person not angry with me was Reggie. Our appointments that week went off without a hitch. He was in an upbeat mood, and our sessions seemed to fly by. Pleasure may have been out of bounds with Brian, but not with Reggie, my object of tainted adoration.

Brian, on the other hand, would not let go of my rebuffing his advances on Sunday, and he was determined to seethe underneath a cold exterior put in place for the sole purpose of hurting my feelings.

My mother was in Brian's camp, although not for the same reasons. She must have used the words 'hateful' and 'spiteful' over a dozen times leading up to the climax of the move on Friday afternoon. She had even called me a few times just to unburden her rage and try to engage me in a conversation in which I would be demonized. I ended up turning my phone off a few times when it didn't interfere with therapy texts, and I relied on email as my main means of communication with the outside world. But, truth be told, I tended to email very little. My social circle had always been somewhat small, but it shrank to practically nonexistent after the accident. In fact, it was my own unofficial mantra to think that the fewer people there were in my life, the better.

My father was actually the hardest person to get a read on. He didn't seem particularly angry, but it was clear that he wasn't his standard jovial self either. I could only imagine the hell that was raining down on him at home in regards to my behavior, the downside of living with the picture perfect Jeanna who put so much stock in exteriors. Thursday and Friday, I spent good portions of the day watching him as he helped Brian load up the vehicles. Box after box went out the door and down three flights of stairs, due to the elevator being out of service. Both men were getting a serious workout, and I could tell Brian was trying to take his frustrations out in the activity. My father just seemed apathetic and drained.

The Salvation Army made a stop to pick up the rest of our furniture on that last day, and without those few pieces, the apartment seemed to come unhinged. There was nothing there to give it form or guidance, nothing to indicate to each room what it should be. In fact, the only room that seemed to hold any of its character was the nursery suite, but that was due to the decisive paints and paper patterns. That room knew its identity.

Every afternoon for nearly a week I'd been subjected to the unhappy ramblings of my mother, which were my own inescapable just desserts along with the few phone calls she managed to get through. I tuned in and out as she and I loaded personal belongings into boxes and the basic toiletries into an overnight bag that could be easily grabbed at the last minute. The entire workweek went by in a hectic haze. All I knew for certain by the end of it was that I had no true allies. Reggie was the closest thing to it, and he would only side with me so long as that's where the money was coming from, or so I believed. My mother and father were totally suspect at all times. And, Brian, well, I had done a bang-up job of alienating him.

I was once again in the place that no eye could see; I was the space between the threads of the web after a short reprieve. The apartment was empty and so was I.

"Ready?" Brian asked me as we stood in the doorway, surveying the apartment for the last time. So much had happened there. Most of who I had become up to that point had happened there, the defining moments post-trauma.

Am I ready? Am I ready to become someone else? Will I be able to?

There was no way to be sure. I was being ripped from my cocoon. There was no way to ever be ready for that when you lacked well-formed wings. "Yes," I lied. Brian closed the door behind me as I shifted out and into the hallway.

The trip to the car was a doozy with the elevator out, and I was grateful when Brian opened the passenger door for me to collapse onto the seat.

"Wait," he shouted, as I was getting ready to lower myself.

"What now?" I moaned dramatically.

He reached in behind me and drew forth a familiar-looking book. "Go ahead. Sit down," he instructed rather harshly.

I complied only because there was nothing else for me to do.

"Here," he said and shoved the book into my hands once I was squared away. He then promptly slammed the door shut and went around to climb in the driver's seat.

We were off.

I looked at him blankly and then down at the book. It was my well-worn copy of James Hilton's *Lost Horizon*. He must have set is aside while packing away all of my other books. "Why did you dig this out?" I asked.

"We've got an hour until we get there and then I'll be spending most of the night hauling boxes with your dad. You'll need something constructive to do." Very reasonable.

That's very thoughtful, but I'm still not having sex with you.

I laughed lightly. "I have something constructive to do. It's called unpacking with my mother."

Brian made the first form of non-hostile eye contact with me in almost a week. "That's destructive, and I think you've had about enough of that, don't you?"

I smiled. "Absolutely!"

"Let your mom do it all. She wants to anyway," he clued in.

"Yeah, I know she does, which is why I don't let her."

Then Brian smiled. "I know. But, seriously, take the rest of the day and relax. Focus on what makes you happy, even if it's a distraction. Who knows, maybe that book will be a good omen."

Maybe it will. Not that I should be reading in a moving car, bad for the eyes, but what the hell...

I had underestimated Brian... again. That chosen blindness was developing into a very bad habit. When we arrived and I made my way once more into the house that had so captivated me the first time I'd seen it, I was thrust into my fantasy full force with nothing to hang on to. And this time, the journey down the proverbial rabbit hole included massive marvels of furniture, the likes of which I never thought I'd own. It was not a slight to my measure of self so much as it was a factual summation of the type of properties in which I'd taken up residence over the years. One can't have large ornate oak and cherry wood furniture in a two-bedroom apartment that was built for mere modern minimalism and convenience. Even the small house on the corner lot that Brian and I had occupied before our move inside the city limits was styled like a cracker box and way too modern for such large and exquisite pieces. This house was built on the rule of decadence, and nothing less would do.

Brian was not shy about revealing that he'd been shopping for decent deals at estate sales and through various overseas auctions to achieve what he had and to get everything to fall in line the way that it did. It was months of secretive work that had finally paid off. And, it left me intrigued as to how he'd accomplished it all and managed a full work schedule, plus attended to the remnants of a torrid affair. On a happier note, I will never forget the way it felt to step inside such a substantial house, and to be greeted by such undeniably substantial furniture. Everything was real and there was an air of permanence about it. The air of luxury didn't hurt either.

"It's been my great big little project," Brian made light of the seriousness and the effort. "And, I am more than willing to admit that Ella helped me with some of the finishing touches. But, by and large, this was my doing."

Our few belongings in boxes seemed meager by comparison to what had awaited us. I had loved the house when it was practically empty, but I was beyond head over heels with it when it was full of the proper décor.

In between loads of boxes, I managed to motion Brian over to a small corner off the main hall. "Brian, I can't believe it. I-I just... It's really too..." I was stammering and I knew it in a heightened capacity, but my tongue would not cooperate given the large lump lodged in my throat. When words failed, I found myself tousling my hair again as if more words might be hidden there and come falling out in a smoother translation.

Brian placed a hand on my shoulder and began guiding me down the hall and to the sunken den off to our right. "Why don't you rest?"

I placed my hand over his and allowed myself to feel genuine affection for the first time in days. It was affection that went beyond the gratitude I'd experienced after my first trip out to #18, to my new home. It may have even been the first attachment I'd felt with such intensity outside of the sick stirrings I consistently nursed for Reggie. It felt deep and boiling and all-consuming in the way I hoped that it would, knew that it would. The feeling was somewhat alien, and yet there was some part of my reptilian brain remembered it. There was no preparation for the moment, though. Was it the house? Had Brian actually purchased my affection? I didn't want to believe that my emotions could be bought, that my response could be manipulated by such a fine place and placement. All I could say for sure in that moment was that I felt the ravenous flush of affection and passion and possession. I wanted to be whole, and I longed to take all of it within me and hold it there. The sharp desire was to possess, to take by a force I couldn't muster.

"Stay in here and read your book, Sally. The three of us have things covered out there," he assured. "We'll have the boxes in before dinner."

I moved my hand so that it fell over his lips, and a loud hush followed, crashing in with a deafening stillness. Something electric snapped and sparked as I moved my lips to where my hand had been. The sensation might have been better than most sex, and if not, it was at least far more intimate. It was one thing to stroke a man under black of night and bring him to orgasm and quite another to press my scarred face into his so that flesh met with molten flesh. The exploration was gentle, and I smelled the musky scent of him now that we were as close as possible to one another. I let him adjust to the sudden change between us and then kiss me back. He pressed his lips firmly into mine to forge a bond, and I felt his tongue parting my lips in a glazing lick. My tongue was not shy and met his in a white-hot dance. Two snakes in a slithering advance, rolling over each other and enjoying the glide for the sake of it. It was some sort of strange second nature for me to want to consume him, and I'm positive I would have had we not been in the middle of a move and also had familial guests to contend with.

Parental influence is a real damper to intercourse.

Reluctantly, he pulled back. "God! What are you trying to do to me, woman?!" he growled in a low tone that was both frustrated and aroused.

I pulled back a hair's breadth and whispered, "I'm not sure."

"We'll pick this up again later," he declared and made his way back out into the hall. "And, don't you even think about saying no to me tonight."

I watched Brian stride effortlessly down the hall and then trot out the front door to continue with his mission of movement and progression. He must have really wanted to evolve himself and our lives, and at that singular point in time it would have appeared that he'd done so. Although up and down, forwards and backwards, they are all relative in the vast cosmos. On an infinitely spiraling web, one direction is just as valid and misleading as another.

I'd been well engaged in the task of reading my book, and at some point in the early evening hours, the plane that bore the character of Conway and his companions crashed in the foreboding yet alluring mountain range just outside of the hidden Valley of the Blue Moon. And in the reality outside of my favored reading material, I had crashed in the alluring burgundy velvet armchair in the den of my new home. I was awakened by the scent of something delicious. It smelled like a roast.

Dinner.

I opened my eyes and they quickly adjusted to the dim lighting in the room. A floor lamp provided the most illumination, as all other lights in the den were out, but some of the brightness from the main hall spilled in to make a path.

I contemplated the den and its currently sparse decadence that I knew Brian and I would fill out over the coming weeks. There was the sumptuous burgundy armchair at the far end of the room that I occupied, and then there was another cream-colored chair in the corner closest to the door that matched mine in every conceivable way other than color. A plush sofa sat off to my left against the wall and was made up of a cream-colored base with emerald and burgundy accents, harmonizing the two extreme elements from opposite sides of the room. Apparently, Brian had come in while I was slumbering and set the television down next to the wall opposite the sofa.

Three of four walls were lined with the same books that had been there when I took the tour of the house. Obviously, the literary tomes were either long-term lodgers or the previous owners had simply not bothered to move them. Not everyone held the same high regards for literature as I did.

Literature and the arts were but a couple of the many passions that were beginning to consume me all over again. It might have been because of a dream I'd sensed I'd had there in the den, but I couldn't recall it upon awakening.

Would I regain all the others, too? Probably not.

Literature, art, and sex were all fine and dandy, but with the shape my body was in and the shape in which I assumed it would remain, there was no way I'd regain my first-hand appreciation through immersion for the movement practices of yoga, Pilates, and Tai Chi. My studio and private practice were gone. The dream I had almost achieved was torn asunder. It was one more dream to be added to the long list of all that had been vanquished in an instant. It had been three years since I'd set foot in any yoga or movement studio, let alone my own. My city practice had held such promise, and other than my daughter, it was the nearest thing to self-expression that I had achieved, my own fault, to be sure. Yes, somehow in the dimly lit den I could admit that when I hadn't been able to previously.

My resentful compliance in life was my own fault and stemmed from my own fears. My lack of true living was of my own choosing. Even in moments of frustrated youthful rebellion — both at home and in marriage — I never made the steadfast demand to be respected, to be allowed to live as I chose. And, so it should come as no shock that I ended up a prisoner to my own body. It may have even been the finest physical manifestation of what I wanted on some dark and deep level, to be manacled in such a way so that I should never have to take responsibility for living. Such a bittersweet personal revelation!

"Dinner time!" My mother called to me from the side door that I didn't even know existed. Her silhouette poured over me as she blocked the sliver of incandescence behind her.

That door wasn't part of the initial tour. Has it always been there?

I laughed at myself inwardly. How much of the house layout had I missed or forgotten about in the span of a workweek?

"Come on," she prodded. "It's a short distance to the dining room if we go through the kitchen." The stern tone of my mother brought me to a fully wakeful state.

I pulled myself out of the embracive armchair and followed her through the kitchen. That room was also full of low light, and from there we made our way in quiet observation to the dining room. The smell of the roast grew stronger and more enticing with each step of our pilgrimage. I could tell that she was still mad at me. The Silence between us had to be killing her, but she stayed devoted to it as a suitable punishment for me. Ironic that all throughout the week my punishment had been her railings, and now it should be her favor to Silence. To me it was actually blessed relief.

Crack your whip over me a few times, my quiet master, and remind me of when you can be what I desire.

Stepping across the threshold to the dining room was nothing short of stepping into a new world. It felt simultaneously like a dream and also like a very new and real life. A crystal chandelier, centered over the cherry wood dining table, glistened with promises as though fairies winked behind every facet, sparkling with light and laughter. The shimmer was reflected off of the glossy wood surfaces and the silver candleholders, which were placed at opposite ends of the flawless table for eight. Silver flatware and serving platters were in attendance and printed fine china waited for a meal to hold.

Where in the hell did all this come from?

It was unbelievably nice that we had some furniture already. It was a pleasant surprise to see that the books had stayed on the shelves. It was totally improbable that so many accessories not already owned by us could be here. Abundance and prosperity were not natural states of mind for me.

The walls were admittedly bare, except for the textured sponge paint done in a tasteful and wistful sea foam green. The paint was almost too gray to be green, and yet it was most certainly green all the same.

"Where did all of this stuff come from?" I finally managed to ask.

"Most of this was your grandmother's," my mother said matter-of-factly as she took her place to the left of my father.

"Oh," I replied, as if that cleared anything up. "Why is it here?"

"Who else has a use for it?" she answered with a rhetorical question of her own.

I shrugged off her foul mood. At the center of all the festivities of fine cuisine, I spotted a roast. I'd been right about the smell. A large beef roast was lavished upon our banquet along with cooked carrots, peas, rolls, and the colorful array of a salad. This was not the work of Brian but of Jeanna Dougherty, her way of christening a space with her preferred precepts.

I must be delirious. This is all too much!

"Are you ever going to sit?" my father asked while appearing a touch concerned about my behavior. "I'm starving."

I felt my face flush. "Sorry," I mumbled and moved over near Brian. I sat to his left to complete the symmetry of the table.

Let the merriment commence!

❖

It was only appropriate to offer a room to my parents for the night, especially since it was at least an hour's drive back, and after all the unloading and some amount of unpacking they were dog tired. It was also well past ten o'clock when everyone involved reached plausible stopping points. My mother seemed barely able to make it through dessert. And in fairness to her, I do acknowledge even now the amount of energy and dedication it must have taken to put in the day she did. The guest bedroom was a long way from being able to properly receive guests, but with a queen mattress on the floor and fresh linens it was more inviting than another drive.

Brian and I retired to the master bedroom, which welcomed us via king-sized bed, fresh linens, and fresh towels. It was basic and barren yet superbly opulent, like the rest of the house. It, too, waited to have fresh artistic and symbolic musculature added to those gorgeous bones. A reddened earth accent wall framed the headboard and silky salmon-colored wallpaper adorned the rest of the room. Upon closer inspection, I noticed woven brocade to the paper that added a false hint of lacey fabric.

"I still can't believe you did all of this," I told Brian as he stripped down and prepared for a quick shower in the adjoining bath.

"You know," he replied, standing naked in the center of the room, "I can't either. It was something I really wanted to do, but I'm astonished at how much I was able to get done so quickly. And, there's a lot to be said for a good agent."

"Really?" I was mildly intrigued. And, even though I hadn't done the bulk of the moving or any of the cooking, I was already starting to wane. But, to my credit, it was very late for me. Seeing the witching hour was a rarity, and one that was approaching quickly.

"For sure," he affirmed. "Ella knows a lot about this area and the history of the homes, and I think she cares about them beyond what her job entails. She was very knowledgeable about the furniture. Good quality and good deals. I'll tell you, that is beyond me. I'm a tech guy. What do I know about it?..."

I chuckled at that. "Yeah, we should send her a thank you note and maybe even have her out once we get settled so she can see the fruits of her labors. She's sort of odd that one, but if she had a hand in all of this then she must be a real sweetheart underneath it," I confirmed, basking in the glow of internal gratitude that was aimed outwardly to all those who contributed to this momentous movement.

"I'm going to hop in the shower." And with that, Brian disappeared around the corner, leaving me alone to determine my night's attire. There was a box in the far right corner labeled 'Bedroom-Clothes-Sally's: 1 of 5.' He was a tech guy all right, a giant geek with logic and order leaking out his ears and onto the boxes. But, that's what ran the world these days, and many would consider me fortunate to marry one who not only had the hard technical skills but also the wherewithal to run his own software company. We weren't wealthy, but he did do well for himself, and by default he did well for me, too. It was in that category, too, that our marriage mimicked my parent's.

With the tiniest aid from my walker, I made my way over to the box and got down on the floor to inspect its contents. Nightgowns and panties sat at the very top, as expected. I sighed. Suddenly I felt very cumbersome and encumbered. I began digging to see just how many gowns he'd been able to stuff into the box. About three layers down or so I felt something cool and pulled my hand back from the strange sensation. What could be cool in this box? I gingerly reached back in again. It was slippery enough to feel almost wet, but it wasn't wet. I grasped the unknown object firmly and pulled to find myself clutching the most adorable beige and black silk lingerie top. I reached in again and found the same sensation greeting my fingertips once more at about three layers down. I grabbed and pulled to find a matching pair of flirty bottoms.

Who was he expecting to come over tonight? Amelia?

I gaped at the flirtatious objects and contemplated their arrival in my home. As my eyes adjusted through the glare of stunned uncertainty, I noticed a small slip of paper attached to the top. It was a price tag. The matching bottoms also had one. Brian had bought these and probably not that long ago. Was I meant to find them, or had he packed them away hoping to do the surprising himself? Were these originally meant for me or were they now mine by default?

Mine because the other woman had been removed...

I shook the emerging images of Brian and some mystery woman from the forefront of my mind. I didn't need to conjure that up. It would only result in never-ending torment, mine and then his. I reconciled with the part of myself that knew that no matter what her age or physical stature, she'd be better looking than me. I needed to accept that fact, or so I had deluded my mind into thinking.

I gathered up the seductive materials and made my way over to the bed to begin my transformation. It took a little thought, a lot of effort, and the blessed lack of a mirror to bring it all about. But by the time Brian came out of the bath, I was draped in silk and sitting rigidly on the edge of the bed.

Brian stopped dead in his tracks when he saw me, his only covering a thick terry cloth towel wrapped securely around his waist. Time hung between us in a densely compressed format. I allowed him to look at me even though I refused to meet his eyes directly, a defense against being completely seen. Instead, I focused on the lean structure that made up the length of him. I took in the delectable sight of his long and muscular legs, his taut midsection that was not common for desk jockeys, and the broadness of his shoulders. His shoulder-to-hip ratio resulted in an enviable V-shape, and had been a sexy silhouette I'd super-imposed the images of other men on occasionally in our early days together. His lanky build was one made up of tightly wound, sinewy strength, a package gift-wrapped in terry cloth. It was admirable to see someone from office life work so hard on their appearance. Nature had been gracious to Brian, and he had owned the innate wisdom to maintain the gift. I also admit to taking in the growing bulge beneath his towel. Modesty be damned.

"You found my other present," he said in a husky tone I knew he couldn't control. In fact, that tone let me know just how close he was to being out of control.

"I did."

With a mellow shyness, I watched him take a couple of steps in towards me. "Do you like it?"

My hands roamed the surface of the silk in continual contemplation. "It feels awkward," I admitted with great candor. "But, yes, I do like it," I confessed.

My ears perked at the almost inaudible moan that escaped his lips in a breathy flourish. He was standing directly in front of me, making sure that I had a full view of what was growing between us. "I know you won't believe me when I say this, and frankly, I don't care. I have to say it."

My eyes met his. The lighting in the room was low enough that it would hide most minor imperfections and let me keep an air of mystery. "Go ahead," I encouraged.

"You look beautiful," he said with all the breath his lungs could provide. The declaration rolled out of him like a storm front.

Another wish? Was he only saying what he wished I could be? Did I wish it, too?

I felt myself smile and then quiver.

"You always have. And, I know you think your scars make you appear less than, but you don't to me. You are still so incredibly beautiful, and there is nothing that could change that." Brian placed his hands cautiously at the top of my head and began to stroke my unruly and undeniably feminine mane. He made his way down to the nape of my neck and then my shoulders, the smooth glide of his warm skin over my furious curls and heated hide.

I found myself wantonly removing his towel to let it drop carelessly to the floor. He sprang forth, indulgently erect and impatiently bobbing.

We've had sex before. This shouldn't be so difficult.

But, it was for me. I suddenly had this fear of disappointing him somehow. If he wasn't pleased with me would the new dream I lived in quickly vanish, never to be retrieved? Would he go back to Amelia or forward to someone else?

All the fear and questioning began to melt in my mind as my eyes were drawn to his intensely erect shaft. He didn't speak and remained content stroking me as I beheld what was a sultry proposition. I could do whatever I liked to him, and he wouldn't have to see my face. Even the scars on my body would be far removed, especially in the barely lit bedchamber. I could do whatever I wanted and be whoever I imagined myself to be, a sexy siren luring him in for limitless amounts of pleasure, mine and his.

I reached out and touched his cock with my fingers at first, slowly gliding up and then down the soft skin of his member, letting the slick surface become more familiar to me as I regained fragments of memories from previous liaisons with my husband. As I traced the length and width of him, I heard low moans from above me.

Then came the haunted call of my name. "Sally." Deep in the recesses of my womanhood I knew that hushed call dangled at the edge of the precipice of begging.

I felt like begging, too. I longed to taste him, to find a measure of contentment in the hidden abode of our newly sanctioned bedroom. Reverently, as though I were about to say a sacred vow, I lowered my mouth so that my lips encircled the head of his cock. In swift reaction, Brian's fingers dug into my shoulder blades. He had locked me into place while simultaneously bracing himself. I twirled my tongue around, licking and lapping at the very tip of him before consuming more, going further, taking him inch by inch until I had swallowed him whole. As I consumed him, he concealed me.

"Oh, god, yes!" he cried out in a raspy tone. "Suck me you little witch!" he demanded.

I was suddenly transported to more than three years ago, to a time and place in our apartment where we had made love on the sofa. I could remember sucking on him then and hearing the exact same phrase. That memory then led to another one, an older one in the previous house we'd shared. He'd said the same thing to me there as well. It had been so long since I'd heard it that I'd simply forgotten what he would say in the throes of passion and how he would say it. He was responding the same now as he had then, the same now as he did before the condemnation of my scars and the shambling shame of my body.

Renewed! I did as instructed and began to relish my work, sucking and licking and enjoying the feel of being a devouring whore. I licked and lapped for who knows how long, until I heard a quick intake of breath, and then he pulled back from me.

I glanced up at him to see his flushed and flustered appearance. "Not yet," he said with a naughty smile I hadn't seen in years. In fact, I'm not sure even to this day if I'd ever seen him smile quite that wickedly before that night. "Lay back on the bed," he instructed and nudged my shoulders gently to beguile me into doing so, not that I needed much beguiling.

I lay back against the yielding linens, the top quilt surrendering its thickness to my weight, enveloping me on all sides. I felt hands caressing the inside of my thighs, stroking up and down in a rhythm that suggested nothing short of worship. I closed my eyes tight and let the feeling take over so that nothing existed for me outside of pure sensation. I felt the stroking stop at the juncture of my legs for a brief moment and then Brian began to caress the very center of my long-denied bliss, only to find that I was already wet and waiting for him. I gasped and sighed appreciatively under his ministrations. I lifted my hips in tempting approval as he slid a finger inside and began to drive me crazy with desire. I delighted in what he was doing with his hands but wanted more, much more. After a considerable time of torturous ecstasy, Brian crawled over top of me on the bed.

I glanced up at him through my eyelashes.

"I want you, Sally." I felt him run his immense cock along the silk the cloaked my belly in expectation.

I lifted an arm to draw his face nearer to mine and we kissed. Our kisses grew from fluttery to gluttonous; and as we continued, I felt him pressing his hardened shaft against my belly more and more. This went on until longing deranged us both. Brian hesitantly pulled back once again and then slid into me with erotic slowness so that we both might feel me stretching to take him in. I dug my fingernails into his back as he started to move inside me, both of us cresting at lightning speed.

I heard Brian growl from somewhere far away as I shattered into a million pieces, into a countless number of flecks of pure stardust.

Maybe I won't ever be put back together again. I feel so surreal, so completely spent. Maybe if I am put back together again, I'll find a better form.

My husband lay on top of me, sweaty and heavy and panting. His face was smashed into the bed linens right next to me. I stroked his back until his breathing began to take up a normal rhythm, hypnotic and balanced. I reached higher and stroked his hair, too. His locks were a thick, dark pelt that was hardly ever as polished as he would prefer. The positioning was a little uncomfortable, but I wanted to reveal the tenderness that I felt, a compassion that went beyond words.

"Brian," I finally broke our intoxicating companion, Silence.

He spoke into the blankets. "Yeah?"

"I love you."

In some way, some manner that I can't quite understand, I love you.

It was an exposition I'd made, as much to myself as to him, and it would have to be enough since we were so many years behind the curve.

Chapter 3

My parents seemed more than ready to leave and get back to their lives after Sunday morning's breakfast, which turned out to be a simple and quiet affair of cereal and coconut milk. In fact, the tide with them managed to turn in my favor as my mother decided to do our obligatory tea once a week, on Fridays, due to the lengthy drive. Whether her decision was based on pragmatism or pettiness made no difference to me. I came out ahead. After they drove off, Brian set to work on more unpacking and arranging. I offered to help, as it seemed the very least I could do, but I'm not too proud to admit that I was downright thrilled when he told me he'd see to it all. He was a man on a mission, and I was happy to let him have his glorious evolutionary settlement. Many aspects of our lives seemed to be quite suddenly settling, even in just a day's time. It was like ash falling towards the earth from an abnormally clouded sky. It was there to enrich the land and provide new growth from absolute destruction, which only begged the question, 'Was any form of destruction an unsurpassable absolute?'

Left to my own devices I fell back into the den that I was already staking out as my territory and the book that Brian had set aside for me the day before. By lunchtime I was at the start of Chapter 6 and the fictional party had settled themselves into something of a daily routine within the auspices of Shangri-La.

Settlement.

The similarity in theme was not lost on me. The concept spoke for the very first time without the overtones of hideous boredom. It seemed more like a promise and a welcomed relief, more like an escape hatch into a lifestyle far more pleasing. Of course, it might have been the excitement and stimulation of so much newness and so many fineries. Only time would tell. Only the passing of days, weeks, and months would reveal the ultimate truth in its grotesque and gregarious nature. The dichotomy of deception and the cohesion of clarity would eventually become more than abstracts for me to mentally play with.

Brian was proud of the turkey sandwiches I'd made and the small side of field greens that went with them. Making lunch was a task that in the apartment would've proven too tedious and tiresome for me to attempt. In this house, within the walls of #18 Willow Tree Court, it was a joyous chore quickly accomplished.

I was able to find my way to the kitchen, although not by way of the den.

Where was that door?

And in the kitchen, I made use of the few things that were there already to whip together a quick and light lunch.

"It's coming together," Brian broke the invigorating reign of Silence about half way through his sandwich.

"Mmm…" was all I had to say. Words can be such paltry things, falling short when the blessings of peace are on one's shoulders.

The rest of the meal was spent in a contented quiet, and afterwards, Brian helped me take the plates and glasses back into the kitchen and place them in the sink.

"Just leave them," I instructed as he made movements to denote the start of dishes being done. There was no dishwasher in our historically immaculate kitchen.

"You sure? It'll only take me a minute – "

"It'll only take me a minute, too. I can stand that long and lean against the counter." I laughed in an unwontedly breezy way and shook my head to indicate that he was being silly.

Brian shrugged. "Ok." And with a quick kiss on top of my head, he was off to continue his quest of finding a place for everything and then putting everything in its place.

I wasn't in the mood to return to reading after the meal, so I decided to have an adventure. There were facets of the house that felt unfamiliar, even with having been on a walk-through with Ella. There were aspects that were still a complete mystery to me. There were cracks and crevices to explore and secrets to be ferretted out, and I was just the woman for the job. In fact, I was the only woman for the job, and it was time to get intimate with my new abode…
although not the garage. I'd felt as though I already knew all I needed to about that area of my new space. There was no

need for me to go there and no want either. I knew enough to stay away.

With my trusty walker as an aid, I decided to start at the staged beginning in the main hallway. It was nothing short of due diligence to become even more familiar. The house itself was expressed only in generality to me, and I had no idea where certain key features might be. Even with the deceptively open floor plan, the house seemed to harbor all sorts of additional spaces and features that to some might appear to be hidden in plain sight. A perfect example of that was the cloakroom that was the first door to my left from the main entrance. I more than likely missed seeing it before because an open front door would initially block its view as I moved past. Holding it in my awareness now, I grasped the cool gold-toned metal knob and pulled the door open to see just how enveloping the small space could be. There was room for a couple of dozen coats in there along with top tier shelving for shoes and light storage. The wooden shelves gleamed brightly just as all the woodwork in the house seemed to do. I wondered how long it would stay in such prime condition before I would be forced to hire someone to keep up with it.

Brian must not have considered the amount of regular maintenance that would be needed for a place like this.

Again to my left and immediately next to the cloakroom was another door.

And, I wonder what is behind Door #2...

I opened it slowly and found a dense, void-inducing blackness. It was so dark that the inky shade spilled upwards and onto the edges of the hardwood, unable to be contained once there was a breach. I felt the inside walls for a light switch and finally stumbled upon one. Dim, yellow light revealed stairs going down at an extremely steep angle.

Basement.

The one area Ella said she'd skip on the tour, since Brian had already seen it and there was nothing in that space for me to see.

Basement.

The word felt as dark as the space, and as curious as I was, there was no way I'd attempt to go down that narrow stairwell, especially not knowing what all might be down there and whether or not willow tree roots were pressing in the walls. I also smelled a faint musty odor.

Great. I bet there's mold.

I shut the door in modest disgust, hoping that would be my worst discovery of the day. However, it paled in comparison.

To my right were the double pocket doors that led to the dining room, and beyond that was the doorway to the den which stood wide open. Those were two rooms I was already intimately familiar with, although I would've very much liked to know where the door to the kitchen was in the den that then met with a back entrance to the dining room. But, I could find that out later. With the kitchen behind the dining room, I was satisfied with my cursory knowledge of the first floor layout. Time to climb the shiny stairs up to the second floor landing.

The climb was easier than I'd remembered, and I found it more convenient to actually pull my walker up behind me and use the railing for support rather than attempt to make any sort of productive use out of my ambulatory sidekick. Once I was securely on the landing, I looked down over the railing to survey the main hallway from aloft. It was beyond scenic. For the first time I really noticed the dusty rose tones enmeshed in the walls. The palette like petals was almost a salmon color but had been neutralized by the sponge-style application. The texture folded in on itself to hide what might lie at the bottom of those spectacular petals, a bottom that was reached by traversing tremendous depths. I loved how the artisan who applied the paint had been able to give the wall texture a sense of movement. If a strong breeze blew by, would the petals scatter?

At the end of the hall was a large double-paned window that took up most of the far wall. Through the gauzy white curtains that were left hanging as minimal decoration, I could spy portions of the backyard. It looked like a sea of green and gold out there, alive with waves of tree branches.

I eventually turned my attention to the second floor landing and the rooms that grew off of it. The landing itself was dark, sort of resembling the gaping mouth of a cave. The only light forthcoming was what poured from the rooms with their doors left open. I peered closely at the walls to see if I could spot a light switch, but there wasn't one. I looked up for a pull chain, but again there was nothing. I did see the outline of what was probably a light fixture directly above me, but there was no way to be sure. To my left were two doors to guest bedrooms, with the first door being the room my parents had occupied during their brief stay. I approached the doorway and stopped to see the mattress still on the floor with the linens neatly folded on top.

My mother the neat freak. No wonder she and Brian get along so well, and so superficially. Order and design. Logic and pragmatism. A match made in hell.

The walls were a periwinkle blue that reminded me of my grandmother's house and the spare bedroom I used to sleep in as a child during my visits. The memory came back to me in a flood of color and then with a heady lavender scent. Lastly, the tinkling sound of wind chimes stirred dormant portions of my gray matter. It was something I hadn't thought of in years and might not have ever recalled again, had it not been for the choice of paint in the guest bedroom. I stepped inside and examined the walls closer to see little white flowers painted in an alternating pattern all over the room. The work of a stencil, most likely.

I tore myself away and continued on to the adjacent room, feeling as though my grandmother might be peeking over my shoulder the whole time. It's funny how the slightest thing can conjure up such sustainable and near tangible energies. It was another bedroom and would most likely act as either another guestroom or become a workspace for Brian. For the moment it was vacant and hadn't taken on any form. The only things definitive about the area were the plain white curtains, heavy and drawn back on either side by white metallic leaves, and the paint colors. This time it was primarily a sunny yellow palette, but there were thin brown stripes running vertically in between all the sunshine.

Sonya.

Had I thought her name or heard it in a hushed whisper? There was no way to be sure.

I backed away slowly from the room whose colors and patterns too closely mimicked a vacant nursery suite I'd left behind only a couple of days ago, finding comfort in the shadowy landing. I desired the shrouded space and the fact that it could hold me in a way no human arms could ever do. It is easy to be embraced by blackness and impossibly addictive to be consumed by burning light that throws the failures of your life into a brilliant high contrast. Brian would have to repaint that or I would once again be swept into a state of mourning. It was disturbing how much I was drawn towards it already. It was even more disturbing how frightened I was by my own tendencies. The visage of yellow and brown haunted me at the opposite end of the spectrum from the periwinkle blue, and I was caught in between.

I felt a tremor shake down my entire body and then the shackles holding me to the yellow and brown room released with an almost audible click. I felt my feet reassuringly ground in the floor and my head then focused on the physical reality before my eyes.

On the other side of the landing was the bedchamber with accompanying bath that Brian and I occupied, and at the very far end of the landing was a common bathroom. The only thing really sensational about the common bathroom was the claw-footed tub. I had always wanted one as a girl, that and a window seat. So far it seemed this house did not have the window seat.

I turned away from the bathroom and was getting ready to head towards the stairs to make my way to the third floor when a figment caught my eye, an innocuous shape so small and simultaneously prominent. There was something soft and brown sitting in the far corner of the faux nursery. A blob-like object that I knew hadn't been there before and couldn't be there now. In hindsight, I realize I should've just let it roll off my back and out of consideration. I should have proceeded with my plans to explore the third floor. If I had been in better control the entire time, and right from the very beginning, the story created might have been a different one, a better one. But, that's not what happened and that's not the course this story took. That's not the path I chose to take at every alterable turn. And, to be fair, if things had gone dramatically different there might not be a tale to tell.

I hesitantly made my way back to that dishonestly upbeat room with the horrifically coincidental paint patterns. I stopped at the doorway and tried to make out what was lying in wait in the far corner diagonal from the entrance. The only additional detailing that emerged was a sense of soft fuzz and discoloration. Something small and soft slept in the corner. It didn't seem to be moving, and as I walked in and got a little closer, I noticed that it also didn't seem to be breathing. Whatever it was, it wasn't alive.

Great. I found a dead animal that somehow got into the house while it was vacant.

If only it had been that. A dead animal can be disposed of easily enough.

I knelt down in front of the obscure object, and when I worked up the nerve to touch it, it all became clear. It was a toy, a plush toy. Old and discarded and discolored. Worn and stained and battered... and wet...

Fido!

I wanted to scream, and I think I did. All at once I was out of breath and out of the room. I found myself turned about on the landing, my head spinning like a top. It was Fido in that faux-nursery!

"Brian!" I yelled with the fullest amount of breath I could muster. "Brian! Where are you?!"

I called up the stairs to the third floor. I panicked and screamed out to the first floor.

Nothing. I was met with the faintest echo of my own emotional terror and then stony Silence. I looked back to the faux nursery, and as my eyes scanned the horizon, I stopped dead in my frantic tracks. Fido was not in the corner.

What the hell? If I whistle and call to him, as though he were a real dog, would he reappear? Come running?

I was frozen, rooted to the spot as though I had sprouted to life from the wooden floor slats of that ancient plane. The floors and the walls were a part of me, my bones. The paint and the polish were my skin. We seemed to exist as one, and I couldn't find myself outside of the structure. Part of me wanted to move forward and check the entire room for a trace of what my eyes had beheld only seconds ago. Part of me wanted to get the hell away fast. Finally, I decided to take a step forward only to fall flat on my face. I saw my walker go flying and smash into the wall just next to the bathroom. I'd managed to catch myself with my hands and not do any further damage to my face. And, from my unconventional vantage point on the floor, I could see just how clean the woodwork was, and just how empty the yellow and brown room remained. There was nothing there.

It took a few minutes but then I began to think that in my panic I must have tripped, literally tripped, over my own feet. In my emotional excitement turned triggered agony over the second guestroom, I must have imagined my dead daughter's stuffed toy, the toy she clutched during the car accident. I was dismayed at my own ability to recall that small item with such remarkable clarity. I stayed on the floor for who knows how long, crying at my own guilt and insanity, sobbing uncontrollably for my daughter and the chance at a life I'd had years ago. It was a chance I never felt I deserved to take.

Eventually, like digging my way out of a shallow grave, I pulled myself to all fours and from there upright to my wobbly knees. But before I could problem solve how to best retrieve my walker, I suddenly noticed I was kneeling on something... something spongy and soft.

"Oh, god – " I breathed hopelessly. I knew. In my core, I knew.

Scrambling backwards, I saw it. I saw him. I saw Fido. It was Fido who had tripped me! He looked up at me with black, lifeless button-eyes and an accusatory stare that would never blink. His visage donned the blood of my victim for the world to see, and he seemed to whisper without a voice, "Murderer."

"Sally?" someone called my name into question. Were they calling me into question? Had the house intoned my name? "Sally." It was more insistent now, like a statement of my being and my fault.

I began to shake at the experience, and in response something outside of myself began to shake me in fevered agreement.

"Sally!"

I opened my eyes to see Brian standing over me, his face a potential mirror of my own concern and confusion.

"Brian?" I squeaked out my question, reaching up to touch the side of his face. It was warm and solid and delightfully stubbled. It felt definite and fleshy and real, but so had everything else just seconds ago. I felt hot tears streak down my cheeks and renew salty trails already present. I looked around me to see the familiar book-lined walls of the den, to see the sofa and accenting chairs, to see the television and the stark modern-day sanity that it imposed. It all looked as it should. I sat in the burgundy armchair I had picked out as a favorite; my book was left open in my lap. It was all harmless and normal enough, but the tears wouldn't stop their flow.

"Did you have a bad dream?" Brian pressed with his question and his hands on my bobbing shoulders.

"I don't understand," I replied ridiculously. That didn't answer anything. "Where were you?" I accused with my inquiry.

Brian stepped back and removed his hands. He peered down at me, looking a little dazed himself. "Where do you think? I've been upstairs putting things away."

"That's not possible," I dismissed, sounding all the more ludicrous.

He laughed at me a little. "Sally, you were having a bad dream," he affirmed, dictating my reality and my mind's sick fantasy, neatly sorting out one from the other.

"I was just up there. I yelled and yelled. You were nowhere!" I insisted, knowing how crazy it all was, as my waking state took a firmer hold. The emotional fog of what surely must have been a dream began to lift even as I stared at my husband as though he were the world's worst liar.

Brian sighed and shook his head. He gave me a quirky smile and then explained further, even though he didn't have to. "Sally, after lunch I went back to the unpacking upstairs. You did the dishes. Then afterwards you must've fallen asleep here. I heard you screaming and came downstairs to find you in the throes of some sort of nightmare. I'm really glad you didn't hurt yourself, thrashing around like that. Do you remember what you were dreaming about?"

"Brian, the upstairs... there are two guest bedrooms?" I evaded and avoided.

"Yes," he reluctantly replied, not sure where my question was leading.

"One is blue and one is... one is yellow," I swallowed a large lump, "yellow with small brown stripes?"

"No," Brian answered solidly. "One is blue and one is white," he corrected.

I wiped at my drying tears furiously. "Show me."

The humiliating trip to the second floor tainted what was left of the day. My mood was sullen upon discovering that one guest bedroom was indeed that comforting periwinkle blue and the other was a simple and indeterminate white. Brian tried to stabilize the mood and find a sense of normalcy by changing topics and informing me that he planned to turn the white room into his own home office. It had all been too mundane for me. No lavender or wind chime reminiscence greeted me when I looked in at the blue room. And, there were no terrors or accusing toys to be found in the white room either. I then skipped dinner and Brian ate alone.

By the time night fell I was completely spent and took a quick bath before curling up in the dense and enveloping bed linens.

Brian joined me some time later in the master bedchamber and the ambiance became instantly disjointed.

I listened as he undressed and then went to brush his teeth. When he sat down on the far side of the bed I sat up.

"Why wasn't my name ever on the apartment lease?"

He looked over his shoulder at me. "What?"

"Why wasn't – "

"I heard you," he snapped. Brian ran a hand through his hair and it became disheveled, as was its tendency. "Why are you bringing this up now?" he wearily asked.

"I don't know," I shrugged. "I just need to know."

He sighed. "When we went through the process of renting the apartment, it was simply better to have it under my name only. I mean, you didn't really have a job. You were opening up a new studio for future expansion, and there was no income to calculate. And, if we're being frank, there was only risk and initial debt to calculate."

Reasonable.

"Plus," Brian continued, "your credit score wasn't doing us any favors."

"Ok."

Enough.

"Ok, Brian. I get it." I averted my eyes and took an interest in my fingernails. I wasn't now nor had I ever been the traditional, responsible adult. I may have been reasonably compliant and resentful because of it, but I was generally not responsible, not fully. "I know I'm not the most stable person. Even when things were good, they weren't ever really stable."

Brian smiled at me then, probably out of pity. "Were they supposed to be stable?"

I gave a light snort and a weak smile. "Things are always that way with you."

"Yeah, I guess so." He acknowledged my point. "But, if both of us are really stable and constant, where does anything new come from?"

"This house is new, and it came from you."

He nodded. "But, you inspired it."

My heart leapt and my breath caught in something close to a hiccup. "What?"

Brian turned around and leaned in close to me. "And, your name is on the title," he whispered seductively. "This house is as much mine as it is yours. It might be yours even more."

I dipped my head so that blonde curls covered my face, hiding my scars from close inspection. "How could it be more mine?" my voice wavered as I asked helplessly, praying to be worthy of such adoration and of such a generous gift.

"It seems more like your style. We moved because we needed a fresh start and because you belong here." He exhaled the words right into my ear, rustling my ringlets.

I pulled back. "I have another question," I warned.

"What?" Brian seemed willing to meet it, a man with nothing to hide anymore.

Is there any way to really be sure of that?

"How the hell can we afford this place? It's huge! And, it's not like the house is falling apart either. From what I can tell, it's in more than decent shape and the area is pretty freaking nice, too. A house like this would have to costs hundreds of thousands of dollars, Brian," I leveled. I didn't want to disrupt the possible joys of living there with an ugly fact, but there it was.

"I'm glad you have an eye for value," he complimented.

"You forget that I did manage to run a successful business practice before we moved to the city."

Unconventional, but moderately successful, I suppose.

"I haven't forgotten," he assured. "And, it's quite true that most houses like this do cost more than we can afford."

"So?..." I prompted.

"So, even though the area is nice, it's far removed. The remote location brings prices in this court down a bit. Couple that with the fact that this is an old house that's been vacant for a while and it needs some repairs, and you start to see the bigger picture."

"What kind of repairs?" I dug deeper.

Brian kissed me gently on the lips. "We can go over the laundry list of things when I get home tomorrow."

"Oh, god!" I groaned.

"It's not that bad," he dismissed my dramatic outcry.

"Well, if it's not that bad then why was the price low enough for – "

"You want to do this now?" Brian threw out the rhetorical question. "Fine," he answered himself. "The main reason we can afford this house is because the previous owners died here. They died of purely natural causes, so there's no need to get all creeped out now that I've told you. But, as I'm sure you can imagine, it makes a house a little harder to sell, especially in a market that is already rough. Now, let's get some sleep. I have a long drive into the office tomorrow, and you have therapy." And with that, Brian got under the covers, gave me an obligatory kiss, and clicked off the bedside light.

"Um, goodnight," I concluded and attempted to go to sleep myself, not knowing what I might dream about after that bombshell. I need not have worried, as all I remember about retiring that night was descending into a sea of blackness.

Brian was gone before I even stirred the next morning, but it wasn't that strange a circumstance since I had slept in much later than usual. And, being in the house alone was a touch too unsettling for me after the icy grips of the previous afternoon's nightmare, so following my morning coffee, I made my way outside and across the street to the gigantic willow in the cul-de-sac.

I figured I had about an hour or so before Reggie would arrive, enough time to really take in the front yard and the sentinel that stood guard over it. The sun was removed from view, tucked behind a great gray blanket that stretched across the mid-autumn sky. The air was crisp and cool, and I reveled in it. Lower temperatures meant that my scars wouldn't become overly inflamed and angry. They would remain their sullen pale silver selves, only a shade or two off from my regular skin tone. With a little makeup and the proper clothes, I could almost pass for pretty, except that in certain lights it was impossible to miss the indentation marks and superficial streaks.

I found I was able to completely disappear under the mourning branches that hung all the way to the ground, burdened with the weight of passing years and the many sorrows that must have happened in the willow's expansive lifetime. People had passed away in my brand new home, under the merciful auspices of this terribly poignant tree. There were people who had apparently breathed their last within walls that now housed me. I could only hope that the passings had been peaceful and that there would be no lingering ill effects. Maybe a window had been opened during those instances and the souls of the departed had found their way out with ease. Mirrors covered and inner doors shut so as not to create any confusion, a quick and seamless transition to the other side.

Was that something my grandmother had taught me? Was it something from a random storybook?

I comforted myself with thoughts of serene and even happy passings, spirits heaven-bound. My mind sought comfort in the imagery and mostly found it there. A cold pit in my gut spoke otherwise, but I largely ignored it.

This willow is so impossibly old and impossibly beautiful.

Hidden beneath the boughs of such an incredibly old tree, I felt like a voyeur and a native predator. I could see through and make out my surroundings clearly, but others would not notice me, of that I was certain. It was a powerful position.

After some time, I peered upwards to take in the millions of leaves and the burdensome branches cascading down. There was something so ironic about a tree growing ever taller and then sinking its branches by degrees and layers forever lower. The dense depression I found to be evident there was balanced by a sense of renewal springing forth from the buried decay. I leaned my back against the tree and thrust my walker aside. It was such an old tree, the bark all twisted and gnarled. There were spots where branches had rotted all the way through and fallen off; scars from weather and what-have-you were highly visible. Many animals had obviously made their homes in this tree as well, and I could hear birds call from overhead even though I barely made out their flighted forms.

I know what it means to be old and scarred and to look out at a world that values surface beauty and grandeur, to see a world moving all around you while you stay stuck in a single spot.

I was unable to move beyond it, and this tree was the only being that seemed to represent that in fullest context. In representing it, this tree might even on some level understand all that it meant. All of the anguish in me, could it give birth to some outward vision of beauty? It was in that category that the willow had me beat. It had found a way to be of service and to be beautiful, despite its imperfections and marked sadness.

I took in a deep breath and allowed my nose and lungs to find that unmistakable moist sweetness on the wind. It was the same scent that had greeted me the very first time I laid eyes on this willow and #18.

Invigorating.

There seemed very little going on in the court today. Most driveways were free of cars, and I assumed everyone was out and about at work or busy with some other early weekday engagements.

Solitude.

Upon further inspection I noticed that of the two 'For Sale' signs that had been present when Brian and I took over the house, only one remained. Another house on the court, the one nearest to ours, had sold.

That was quick...

This gave me a feeling of great relief, to the point where I actually physically sighed. My shoulders relaxed, and I sensed that I must have been carrying around a yolk of worry with me ever since we moved, worry that the house and all its needs and the undefined issues of its location would bury us. But, if another house sold, then perhaps my fears were largely unfounded and a few minor repairs and some scheduled maintenance would see to everything, and keep Brian and I moving along with our regularly scheduled program.

I squinted and bent forward a tad to see if I could glean any more information about who might be moving in and at what stage of the process they were in, but the windows were all dark and there were no clean up dumpsters or moving vans to give away clues. I'd have to walk over to the property and peek through the windows to gain any more knowledge, and that just wasn't on the agenda.

Instead, I turned to face the tree and contemplated the grooves of time carved by the elements into its bark. Ridges and swirls played roughly under my fingertips as I traced lines this way and that. Up, down, and around. In some spots, the grooves almost seemed to create patterns and images like an optical illusion while in other areas I could create words if I looked at the bark from a certain angle and maybe even squinted a bit. I wondered if lovers had ever carved each other's names or initials into this tree, praying their love would grow along with it. A weeping willow wouldn't have been my preferred symbolic choice of all the types of trees available. One of the local oaks or maples would have done better.

I couldn't say how long I continued my tracings or my contemplations. I was engrossed in the still movements of the bark, encapsulated by the act of tracing age marks and scars. I found myself moving around the base of the tree over and over again as I sought to understand it, and I didn't stop until my fingers traced one simple word – 'doggie'.

Doggie.

I stopped and stared with the word echoing in my overly imaginative brain, and as I did so, the carved word absorbed itself into the bark so that my eyes adjusted to see nothing but ancient wood with its natural indentations. I saw what one expected to see.

Sonya.

I thought of her and her first word even though the visible representation I had manifested from repressed recesses no longer remained.

Two questions immediately leapt to the forefront of my mind. Why couldn't I stop torturing myself and move beyond the accident and the mourning? Why did I allow myself to be worse off than I had to be?

The second question came down on me like a ton of bricks when it formed, for I realized that in my moody contemplations I had walked around the base of the tree countless times with very little reliance on it for support. I had walked around it because I had wanted to. All of a sudden I had decided to get better because it was convenient for me to do so. Had I been holding myself back all this time? Granted, I wasn't about to run a marathon anytime soon, but this feat of walking in small, consistent circles without assistance was tantamount to my first full on footrace in three years. I made my way slowly back around to my walker and from there to my house. I sought the den, my book, and the normalcy of my morning appointment with Reggie. And, thankfully, that appointment's basic vibration set the tone for days and weeks to come.

Not much about life seemed to change other than me, and aspects of me. Brian kept his usual work schedule, Reggie kept his usual therapy schedule, and my mother stopped by on Friday afternoons for our now weekly teatime. Pieces of furniture filtered into the house, filling it out. Old possessions and tiny new luxuries got placed here and there; but by and large, the rhythm of life seemed to regain its basic composure, and everyone went back to moving about in the same fashion as they had before.

I moved differently, though. I moved through life with an increasingly slippery grasp on a standard sense of time, and oddly enough, I became all right with that, much more so than I had ever been before the move or after the accident. It used to throw me to keep track of days that looked primarily the same, even with a solid sense of biological time in place of the chronological. And, being thrown used to frustrate me. But, being out of time and out of bounds in the auspices of Willow Tree Court suited me, and I didn't fight against the flow.

Other things about me and around me changed, too, behaved differently. First of all, my therapy sessions over the course of even a single week were seeing dramatic improvements in the form of heavier weights, longer walks, and better balance. I attempted to get out of my own way, to let myself go. It was highly unusual for me, but the payoff was worthwhile in its gradual upward gradient and I persisted, moving my innate stubbornness to an open field. I moved differently about the house, too, taking my walker for assistance but attempting to rely on it less and less. The house and the court seemed to miniaturize themselves in response without altering a perceivable distance, and I chalked it up to a build in personal stamina. By the time my mother arrived for our most recent Friday tea, I dared to go from the den to the front door without the walker to let her in.

Jeanna Dougherty gaped in a most unattractive manner before finding her composure and her words along with it. "What do you think you are doing?" she demanded from the bright backlight of my front porch.

"Are you coming in?" I asked, laughing at her a little before catching myself.

She brushed past me as I closed the door and then turned to face her.

"Here," she said and grabbed at my arm while wrapping herself around my waist. "Let's get you seated."

I wriggled myself free of her clinging grip in as courteous a manner as possible and took a step or two back. "I can get myself to the kitchen. It's ok. Let me have your jacket," I instructed like a well-polished hostess.

Now it was my mother's turn to laugh. "It's not ok," she insisted and kept her jacket on. "You could fall and hurt yourself," she pointed out what seemed to be the blatantly obvious.

"Mom, relax. It's all right. I've been doing much better. And, both Reggie and Brian are aware that I'm walking about the house unassisted from time to time. Based on my most recent therapy sessions, we all think it's time that I tried," I informed her.

I took note of her tight-lipped expression and knew this didn't sit well with her. "And, what great strides could you have possibly made in the course of this past week that would make this a wise decision? What if you fall when no one is around? You could hit your head and – "

"Mom," I stopped her flow. "It's time," I said with great finality. "Now, give me your jacket, and let's go have some tea. The kettle is on." And, with that I placed her jacket in the cloakroom and began my awkward, independent walk through the dining room to the kitchen, hearing my mother's graceful steps following fluidly behind me.

Once we were seated at the small kitchen table, tea before us, she started in again. "I still don't think this unassisted walking while you're alone is a good idea." She eyed me critically while dipping her teabag with flawless precision. "And, Reggie said nothing about any of it to me," my mother further noted as she blew across the surface of her steeping brew.

"Why should he say anything to you?" came my defiant rebuttal.

"Because I'm your mother." That was her universal trump card, and she always played it so well. "I do keep tabs on your therapy, you know. It's not like Brian can do everything by himself, and your situation requires a lot of effort from family members."

Had I been a rabid dog I would've bit her, froth and foam flying. Instead, I sipped my tea cautiously and considered my next move like a strategic homosapien with a well-developed frontal lobe. "Isn't there some sort of therapist-patient confidentiality at play here? I would think that my medical records and progress reports would be off limits to anyone I haven't designated as a recipient." I spoke in a tone that I knew she would perceive as a veiled threat. And, who knows, with all of the changes in me, it might have been.

She dismissed my words with a wave of her hand as though they were no more than a smudge of smoke on the wind. "Don't cause such a fuss."

I shrugged, letting my words hang there between the two of us.

"So, Reggie has been keeping his appointments with you since the move then?" she inquired and tactfully switched the subject focus ever so delicately.

"Yes, of course. And, it's been going really well. I hate to admit it because I fought against it so hard, but I think the move has been good for me. It's been difficult and unsettling at times, but I feel better overall," I summarized. And, it made sense in the clear light of day and with reasonably sane company to be able to admit in a roundabout way that my nightmare and the odd moment with the tree were only a manifestation of the unsettling prospect of moving, the shock of massive upheaval. Other than those two instances, my life had seen its fair share of improvements.

"Huh." It was the dismissive response my words were met with by maternal authority.

I put my foggy mug down on the table and reached out for my mother's hands, drawing her in. "I guess what I am trying to say to you is thanks. Thank you for helping Brian and for forcing my hand in this."

My mother stared at me with an indecipherable expression. "I only want what's best for you," she confirmed.

"I know, mom. I know you do. And, even though I don't want you sticking your nose into all of my affairs, I know why you do it and in this instance you were right to do it. I needed to get out of that apartment and start over. It's been hard putting all that's happened behind me, but I think I might be ready to try and do that now." I allowed my feelings to pour forth into a semblance of what they meant in a spoken language.

"Well," she eased, "you do look better." A token.

"Do I?" I hadn't even thought to contemplate my looks. Mirrors were something I avoided being too close to. I typically kept my eyes averted during face washing and teeth brushing, mostly viewing myself from afar before meeting the day. It made sense that increased exercise would affect my appearance, though. But, even if my physique improved, my skin and scars would not. No, close-up days with mirrors were long gone, except on special occasions, no matter what gains I managed to make.

My mother nodded and took in a large mouthful of tea, swallowing it in several gulps. "You do. I think you stand up straighter," she explained. "And, I guess that's due to you doing better in therapy."

"Probably."

"How did therapy go this morning?" she asked with a forced casualness.

"Good. It went very good. I'm walking so much more now," I was pleased to report.

"Is your appointment length increasing?"

"Not so much. I just need fewer breaks, so we get more done," I clarified.

"And, what time did Reggie leave?" My mother took a small mouthful of tea for less of a break in our exchange.

"Noon. As usual."

You ask an awful lot of questions. Had that slipped my mind?

It didn't seem likely that a habit such as that would, a strong trait belonging to a woman I'd known my whole life, and yet her line of questioning and the number of sequential inquiries seemed out of character.

She took in the standard information I provided her, but I also couldn't help thinking that she seemed distracted, despite her ability to carry on our conversation and probe so well. "All of this is rather sudden," she finally focused on me.

"It is," I agreed. "I'm not sure what's provoking what. All the change, I think it's causing some sort of inner momentum."

"It makes you want a new life?" she asked another question, an unusual one, and I sensed intrinsic honesty in her continued probing.

My eyes locked with her great blue orbs, dancing like slightly melted ice. "I do." I spoke in a hushed tone, and with fullest breath, as if an evil entity might hear and thwart my plans if I spoke even a decibel louder. That's how it often happened in fairy tales, at any rate. I replied in a tamped whisper to convey the essence of a wish to her, to any that would benevolently listen. Would my wish be granted?

Her hands clutched at mine. "Me too," she exhaled in desperation, and in the contracted time that followed, I caught the whiff of that scent.

I drew back as though I'd been slapped. "What?"
How dare you squat on my wish!

She didn't say anything else and finished off her tea. As she went to set her cup in the sink, I tried again.

"What did you mean by that?"

"Oh, what woman hasn't wanted a new life a time or two? You know, as the years go by," she casually clarified, her back still to me as she peered out the window just above the sink. "I had no idea the backyard was so big. Has Brian hired a gardener?"

"Mom…" I stopped myself. It was immediately apparent that she had let something slip, her perfect mask slid down to reveal the imperfections of her life for a moment, and I had seen something I wasn't meant to see. In a fraction of a second her discontent was concealed again, and I could tell that she wanted it to remain that way. I had only seen a surface glimmer, and she would let me see no more. Curious how my sudden outburst had connected with something in her that had simply reacted to my own emotions. Were we not that dissimilar?

Now that her composure was refortified, there was no way she would confide in me why she wanted a new life. Perhaps that desire was why she felt the need to meddle so much in mine. "Are you hungry?" I moved on.

She turned and gave me her glorious and glamorous signature smile as she leaned back against the sink and into an elegant pose. "Yes, I am actually. I skipped lunch and came straight over. I'm famished."

"I'll fix us something to nibble on."

As it turned out, I nibbled. She devoured.

Days and even weeks passed, spinning in a great spiral of near homogeny, and it wasn't until close to

Thanksgiving that anything of tangible or intangible note took place. In the period that resided between, life was in the little things. Brian and I were doing great as a couple by my estimation. Slowly but surely, like the tortoise outpacing the hare due to exhilarating determination, Brian and I had found a rhythm that allowed us to have a sex life. We reached a new milestone of three times a week and the razor's edge that often sat between us dulled until it practically dissolved.

My mother did wind up making our Friday teatimes a little earlier as the weeks peeled off the calendar so that she arrived right around the same time Reggie was leaving, giving me no break in between. It was a little strange, but I assumed that with the physical distance caused by our move, it made her feel better to keep track of me. I didn't know whether or not she had Reggie's phone number, but apparently phone calls were becoming insufficient even if she did have it. Every once in a while, I would spy her talking to Reggie by his car before she came in, if she managed to catch him outside. I doubted highly that I would ever be able to get her to let me live my life in total independence.

I did even more spying as I watched our newest neighbors emerge during the same time frame. I never really noticed a whole lot of moving though, so it must have gone on later in the evening and probably past my bedtime. Brian at one point had said he'd spoken with them briefly as he was heading to the car to go to work one morning. "A nice family unit," was how he had described the retired doctor and his ripe young daughter, Annabelle, who couldn't have been more than twenty-two or twenty-three years old, tops.

I'd caught sight of her on a couple of occasions and felt a mixture of being intensely threatened and instinctually maternal. She was undeniably attractive with her raven's black hair sweeping down to her waist and creamy complexion presented in flawless fashion. Her ember eyes had trapped mine in an instant as we glimpsed each other through corresponding second floor windows. She seemed both delicately young and cumbersomely old.

There was a part of her that could be a devouring predator towards any man she set her sights on, but then there seemed to be something amiss that needed protecting, as though she were the most fragile of fledglings. I really wasn't that much older or stronger than her with my current condition, despite its improvements and my ability to finally give up the walker.

Only seven years ago, I had been her age and wasn't even close to getting pregnant yet. My body had been thin and supple. I'd possessed the youthful glow of healthy skin untouched by time or tribulation, and in my ignorance, I'd squandered nature's blessing. I still had my long blonde curls that spoke of feminine elegance and a whisper of a wild side, but I was far removed from her graceful expression and jaded by the realities that can come crashing in on untapped possibilities, making them wither into near lifeless husks.

Mornings during that period were typically spent underneath the willow in the cul-de-sac, and on the days that I had therapy, I was sure to get out there early enough to find my zone. I'd become intrigued by what appeared to be ever changing and perpetually moving bark, even though no movement and no definite changes could be readily detected or proven by documentation. I just sensed the evolution made possible by the tree and was drawn to it as though I kept a secret with a very close friend. I might have been the only person to have ever noticed the miraculous taking place in our everyday lives, and that made me feel good about myself in a delightfully mischievous and cunning way.

Thanksgiving was an unmistakable time marker that plucked me from my blend of days, and it gave both Brian and me the chance to celebrate our good fortune in moving to the new house with what little family we could claim. It also gave us a chance to get to know the neighbors, the ones who were available to stop by for a drink and a bite of dinner, anyway. Brian and I hadn't received large amounts of visitors or opened our home to the outside world in years, but we felt as ready as we ever would be. I felt as ready as I ever could be.

My mother and father had come over in the early part of the afternoon on Thanksgiving Day to help get all of the food preparations done and the house into its finest festive array. It was then that I noticed the peculiar habit that was already developing of no one bothering to park in the garage. The garage was totally empty and ready to receive cars, and my father and Brian still continued to park side by side in the driveway. I considered asking each of them why, or at the very least Brian, but I decided to skip over the issue in deference to the holiday focus.

Brian and my father busied themselves with decorations, beginning outside on the front lawn and porch overhang and then eventually working their way in to trim the main hallway and dining room. It took a combination of our old decorations that had been used in the apartment and some of the boxed up delights that my parents had kept for us from our first house to properly christen the new home with the holiday spirit, but it all worked out just fine.

The house took to us, the new furnishings, and the symbols of merriment as if they were the most natural things in the world to be bestowed. I felt as though #18 had waited years for touches like the ones we were suddenly providing, and a spike in its vibration shivered under my skin to confirm it. It was interesting to see how the long, braided holly wrap made its way perfectly along the banister from first floor to second, as though it had been premeasured to fit exact specifications.

In the kitchen was all the cooking and refreshment preparation, the domain of my mother and I. Jeanna Dougherty had seen her fair share of parties over the years and knew just how many bottles of wine and assorted spirits to set out for the impending arrival of our guests. She knew just what was needed for finger foods and in what amounts, just how long to cook the turkey and how much stuffing would be supplied by it once it cooked down. Linen napkins for a formal dinner and red and green paper napkins for more casual libations were placed in the most convenient slots in a dining room that was filled to overflowing by the time she was through with it. I considered myself her lovely assistant and was thrilled to be having a span of time with my mother that could be counted as productive.

In the throes of planning and arranging, she didn't stop to comment on or criticize my lack of walker or the fact that I chose to wear a low heel with my daring red and black plaid skirt that swished about me as I walked. The skirt moved a bit like a Christmas bell ringing in the Yuletide season. By the time I noticed that we were nearing the home stretch in our set up, I slipped away from her to head upstairs and put on my face. As I walked into the main hall, I heard my phone beep from inside the cloakroom. I entered the room, pulled down my purse, and retrieved the phone to see a text message: 'On my way.' Apparently, Reggie had felt the need to text that to me even though we weren't meeting for therapy. I chuckled at his compulsion to send me a message as a wave of longing and melancholy rushed over me in the very next second. I felt the surge of a sickening heat twist itself up inside me at the thought of him drawing closer with every passing minute. The only recourse I had was to let my mind and body have a moment of running wild before I surrendered to the tasks at hand and went upstairs.

Fucking makeup.

It was a double-edged sword, a blessing and a curse. On the one hand, I felt grateful to have the option to hide my unsightly features. On the other hand, I despised myself for relying on it for important occasions and delving into polite society. Deep down, I really wanted to be seen for who I was underneath it and to have that image be acceptable as well. And, putting on makeup meant that I had to bring my face in close to the mirror a time or two and focus on every last scar, speckle, and spot so that I could then do my best to correct them. I had to get intimate with my deformities and could deny them no longer as I often attempted to do each day, seeing my reflection only from a distance. The entirety of my hide was an aspect of self that I preferred to shun indefinitely, especially since all the scar creams used over the years had turned out to be colossal flops.

With a heavy sigh that only met my own ears, I went into the master bathroom, closed the door, dug out my bag of cosmetics from below the sink, and set to work. The bright and unforgiving lights of the room mocked me even before I drew close; the mirror's sheen intimidated me.

Psychological bullying.

I had no choice but to endure it. I pulled out a foundation compact from my bag of trickery and wily feminine deception, opened it up, and brought my face in towards the surface of unfortunate truths.

I immediately dropped the compact and heard it clatter loudly in the porcelain basin of the snowy white sink.

There's no way!

It was my face, but not as I remembered it, not as it had been for three whole years. My features were all there as they should have been, as genetics had dictated them to be, but the scars that had plagued me so vehemently were nothing more than faint scratches on a well-filled surface. The gouges and the anger, the embedded prints of shattered glass were nothing more than mere shadows of themselves with a hint of a scratch to prove they had ever been there at all.

I ran trembling hands over my confused and rejuvenated flesh, feeling for the marks with closed eyes that were suddenly weeping tears, tears which sprang from an unknown source. I wept from a cool pool of personal proliferation. I searched for what plagued me, and could not find it. I feared opening my eyes once again in case the scars and the mars would return to, but I did open them to be greeted with the faintest trace of what once was. It was as though I had already applied makeup... but I hadn't. Had no one else noticed this? Had it happened somewhere in between the first and second floors?

I might have been in the bathroom for minutes or hours, crying at the joy of what befell me. Was it a holiday miracle? A textbook example of mind over matter? An offering in return for my very soul? I didn't care. I would've bartered my soul if that's what it would have taken to keep this gift. Whatever was going on, I wanted it to continue.

And as the stream of tears slowly dried, I hurriedly washed my face and applied a light layer of powder. The powder was there not to hide but to highlight my features. From that point on, it was all fun and games with the cosmetics, and I could choose to be the belle of the ball, to accentuate instead of conceal.

Once my face was made ready for the festivities of the day, I stopped to admire my strengthening form and near flawless skin. The jet-black of my sweater met the creamy tone of my face and the whorish red of my lips. My blonde curls kissed my shoulders as they spiraled past on their way down my back. If pulled up my skirt would my angry scars still be there? I kept my scars hidden so well they were not only kept out of the line of sight of others but frequently from me, too. How long had I been free and not known about it? How long had this all been building?

I sucked in a deep breath and slowly inched my skirt higher and higher, inch by torturous inch. I closely examined the skin that lay over the developing muscle tissue; something I almost never did, focusing on fine details over form. They weren't there! Dear, gods! They weren't there! Even now, my heart beats fast as I recall that inexorably insane moment and that wondrously unreal realization. I had been liberated from the hell my body and my past had kept me chained to. I was free of the cycle I'd been trapped in, of the piteous drama I'd relived over and over every time I saw myself for all that I actually was. My hands rubbed up and down the sumptuous flesh, rosy again with the promise of life and the zenith of womanhood.

Am I dreaming? This has got to be a dream. It's got to be!

That thought did occur to me, as it wouldn't be the first time a near life-like dream had taken hold of me within the walls of #18. I felt a quake ripple through my body, a tremor that told me in no uncertain terms that this was a definite waking reality. Even so, I prayed. I prayed to anything that would hear me. I prayed that if it was a dream I'd never wake up.

"Sally," came a distant voice from the floor below. "We have visitors." It was my mother's voice. I indeed had visitors, as I could hear strange voices trickling up from the rooms beneath my feet.

I turned once more to the mirror to see the image of a woman who was both stunned and stunning.

Chapter 4

I don't really recall leaving the bathroom, tearing myself away from the miracle in the mirror. The walk downstairs eludes me, too, as queer as it is to have a blatant lapse of memory after such startling and imprinted detail. But, I do remember Annabelle as I surfaced from the ethers at the bottom of the stairs. I stood so far away from her, but it seemed as though the entrails of her core energetics were wrapped around me, bending the space that separated us like a lens, bringing us closer than we should have been. My hand gripped the solid and shimmering wood of the railing at the base pillar as I anchored the whirling room that whipped around with wild fun and flirtatious intentions. Food, liquor, and pleasant conversation blurred the lines of reality so that they mingled with a pure fantasy backdrop, and Annabelle was at the center of the fairytale foreground for me. She was at the very epicenter and acted as the epitome of desire.

Annabelle's eyes caught me first, as they would prove to do without fail from then on. Every time we'd meet, in every encounter we'd have, it would be her eyes that chained me to her. I found myself floating in those black pools, twisted round like I was caught in a maelstrom and not caring if I drowned. As I look back on it all now, I think I wanted to drown. I wanted to sink down all the way, be submerged in her eyes and in her depths. I didn't long for forgiveness or have any hope of reaching the safety of the shore again. In the same space, with no walls or windows between us, I felt the keen heat with which she radiated, resplendent like a white-hot sun. She smoldered in a way no man, and quite sincerely, no human had ever done when set before me. I was drawn inexorably to the poisonous fruit of her lips and wanted to suck the sweet nectar that undoubtedly oozed from them, the dew of her fragrant and indulgent youth. Her decidedly blatant stare roamed my silhouette slowly so that there was no mistake in the communication that she wanted me too, to feel the curves of my flesh and the tremble of my musculature beneath her eager and albeit unskilled applications.

Against part of my will, the more refined part, I stared back at her and allowed myself the guilty pleasure of appraising her physique. She was so young and primal, so perfect for any and every ministration that I might lavish on her, if only the fates would allow it to be so.

She wore a seductively short white skirt that was almost see through and totally uncalled for in the late November weather, letting me glimpse the curve of her legs as they climbed high up her ensemble. The outline of her lean and lanky haunches was evident and pristine. She may never have known a female lover's touch, but she should. It felt like a waste for her not to. As I glanced upward past her flat midsection, I took in the tempting outline of her barely noticeable breasts riding high up on her ribcage. And, I finished our seductive dance of distance where I began, in her eyes.

"You look amazing!" It was an exclaimed whisper in my ear, shattering a mutually woven spell. I glanced to my right to see Brian standing ever so close and taking my arm in his. "Whatever it was you did upstairs to bring all of this out, it was worth the wait."

I tore my gaze away from Annabelle in social obedience, and in an instant she was gone, having flown away from my vision, a startled raven shaken from hypnotic involvement taking off for safer treetops.

Am I an evil sorceress, a seductress, a siren? Am I a "little witch," as Brian is so fond of calling me?

"You really think so?" I engaged Brian's attempt to rouse me into conversation and moved away from troubling and ego-stroking questions.

"It's as though I've never seen you before. You're like a new woman!" he continued and then suddenly backtracked, as all uncertain men who have stepped on a few landmines of discussion in their day are prone to do. "Not that you haven't always been beautiful, Sally."

I nodded and let him trip over his tongue a bit more and wonder what I might be thinking in return or retaliation.

"You've always been the most beautiful woman I've ever seen. It's just that you look great... I mean, you look different great."

I let out a lilting laugh as the lovely are allowed to do without reproach. "I know what you mean, Brian," I assured and touched his forearm. "Thank you. It's nice to know you see a change in me. Therapy and liberally applied cosmetics are paying off-finally." I brought about a swift end to our awkward exchange. "So many people!" I acknowledged our guests in an upbeat whisper.

"Neighbors mostly," Brian explained unnecessarily.

I gently fluffed my bouncy curls for a hint more body, set my shoulders with the mantle of determination, and let myself be led by my husband into the friendly fray for a carousel of introductions.

Ella needed no formal introduction, of course. And as she readily approached, I had a brief moment of worry due to the fact that Brian and I hadn't managed to have her out to the house sooner than the Thanksgiving bacchanalia that was well under way.

"Sally, my dear," Ella cooed and swept me into her waiting arms. A kiss on each cheek and she resumed. "It is so good to see you up and about this way! You have such grace and poise. I guess a more rural setting agrees with you."

As I pulled back from her tighter than should be embrace, I noticed Brian had left me to mingle with our other guests. "I guess it does," I concurred, taken up in the encompassing aura of Ella, whether I wanted to be or not.

"It is both incredible and gratifying what a change of environment can do for the body and the soul," she reinforced her point from a perspective of musing and then locked onto me in an inclusive way. "I'm sure you know what I mean." It was almost ominous, and as I look back on it, I know just how completely ominous it was and still remains. I should have grasped the gist, but I was too caught up in my own revival and haunting essence.

"I am feeling much better," I gave in to her impressed nuances, "much more like myself, I suppose."

"Oh, yes, I can see that. And, let me assure you that it is only natural to become your own self over time and with exposure to things that can't help but reveal who that person might be." She let a long pause hang. "But, perhaps I am giving in to my theatrical tendencies once more. The world is better with a bit of grandeur though, don't you think? It allows for a sense of completion, even when there might be none. And, completion is where the deepest satisfaction lies; it's what people really want."

I'll never entirely understand you, Ella. I'm not sure it's even possible.

"And, I love what you and your other half have done with the place," she persisted in holding on to our conversation, even as I took another step back in preparation to move around her and meet new people. "This house needs someone who can appreciate all its antiquity and eccentricities, someone who can put in the time and connect with the elegance, care for it as it should be cared for. All the older, finer houses need that."

"I think we have it just about where we'd like it." I smiled.

"It seems less and less that people attempt to see their homes, their lands, and themselves as living in harmony with one another. It is important to take into account the age and style of a home when choosing items to bring into it. And, it's equally important to care for the natural and intrinsic needs of the land and plants that reside there as well. The spirits and desires of a place are just as important as the preferences of the inhabitants. One should decorate and alter for personal tastes, of course, but it is also prudent to decorate in honor of energy and preferences of the home space as well." As she spoke so eloquently about things I'd never taken the time to consider, and certainly didn't judge, Ella moved about me in a small circle, taking in the décor and spatial layout, no doubt with a critical eye. Taking me in, too, for appraisal. Arriving once more in front of me she took my hands in hers. "You've done remarkably well with it thus far, an admirable job."

"Thanks." I felt so transparent and lacking in thoughts and words to match her articulations. In my substantial outer being, now stronger than it had been in years, I sensed my own inner being and found I was undeniably insubstantial in a more mental and emotional sense. I may have gained body, but was I lacking a little spirit?

Had I ever stopped to take an inventory of that after my accident?

"There is no need for me to visit the rest of the house, I am sure of it." Ella grinned a thick line of lipstick and gave her official seal of approval, declining an invitation that hadn't been sent. "You have it all furnished and finished?"

"I'd say we do," I affirmed. "Although, I haven't really spent any time in the third floor space or even ventured into the basement. The steps seem really steep going down, and there's a smell. And, while I'm talking about this, there's a smell in the garage, too."

Ella offered nothing, and her sudden devotion to Silence quickly irritated me. It sat like a splinter under my healing skin. For a woman of so many words to offer nothing but devotion to Silence all at once couldn't be a good sign.

"Do you know if there is mold in the basement? Or, is there something that happened in the garage to make it smell that way?" I pressed, hoping a clue or more might pop out of her in lyrical prose.

"Oh, I wouldn't worry. Brian did have a home inspection done. And, a house that's well cared for, a home that's at the center of a happy family, offers very few issues to its occupants." She patted my hand as though I were a fretful child. "Oh, and in the spirit of holidays and homecomings, good cheer and good neighbors, I am so pleased to report that all of the homes in this court are now sold. You have new neighbors." And on the note of that news, I saw Ella beam. The coolness of her natural tones and the balance of her warm makeup shifted so that she made it completely to the warmer end of the spectrum. She'd shifted in the same way our house had shifted after we added all of the festive decorations to honor the holiday season and the opening of our home to others.

"Well, I guess that means a happy holidays for you," I said, doing my best to appear supportive as my eyes began an unrestrained and unashamed scan of the room, betraying my true intentions. I really wanted to get something to drink and eat and then move on to other attendees. It wasn't that Ella had ever done anything wrong, but something about her just wasn't right. Her mimicry of her surroundings was a little too chameleon for my tastes, and her ostentatious verbiage was hard to digest. It wasn't normal for people to act as though they had just stepped out of *Wuthering Heights*.

"I feel quite accomplished, although I can't take all the credit. The final house practically sold itself, what with the previous owners simply moving back into it and all," she sighed in contentment. "This place is positively magical. It makes selling easy as pie... and sweet as pie, too. And speaking of which, I should let you eat and drink and make merry today."

You read my mind.

"This is your day, your time, my dear. Be sure to enjoy it while you are able." Bestowing another quick kiss that spread across my cheek, leaving a trail of lipstick for me to wipe off, Ella gave her best wishes to the hostess and glided across the hallway to the den. And, that made it impossible for me to address or decipher what was likely a cryptic and backhanded compliment.

Then I'll head into the dining room for contrast.

Not only was that where the food was, but it was also where Ella was not. I remember thinking a tolerant 'I'm sure she means well,' but there was just something off about a person that felt the need to be that involved and over the top.

Annabelle was nowhere in the dining room. Strike one. My mother was doing her best imitation of a younger woman in the dining room. Strike two. Not to mention that the man she seemed to be so precocious with gave me the creeps. Luckily, there was an abundance of food and liquor to make up for the lack of what I considered quality company. I set about loading a plate with items from the veggie tray and poured myself a sizable glass of a promising red wine that smelled like blackberries, oak, and autumn.

After a long sip from my glass, I insisted that my petulant self be social whether I wanted to be or not, given my mother's disgusting display. I'd seen her mildly flirtatious before, and that was hard enough. Seeing her act like an enraptured schoolgirl around one of my new neighbors was gut churning.

And, where the hell is my dad?

Jeanna Dougherty motioned like a fluid wave of untamed water for me to join her as I came within range. I made my way under her arm and let her hold me close as though we had one of the healthiest relationships going. It made for great and comfortable theatre. "I don't know if you two have officially met or not, but Sally, this is Dr. Gregory Taylor. He's your new neighbor right next door. He recently moved in with his daughter, Annabelle. Gregory, this is my daughter, Sally," she introduced in a loose but acceptable manner.

I shook his cold and clammy hand, a suited match for his unhealthy pallor and sickly sweet stench. I couldn't fathom how my own mother missed the aroma emanating from him, as she was standing so near. It was like a mixture of cheap candy and cigars. And, if she did smell it, how could she abide it?

"Welcome," I lied with a silken tongue that was an exact duplicate of my mother's.

We have things in common after all. Maybe more than I will ever admit.

"As I was telling you, Sally and Brian moved in several weeks ago and this place has been a haven for them both, but especially for my daughter here." My mother looked to me for agreement, and I gave a quick grin. "Oh, Sally, you look lovely tonight," her words wobbled, and I watched as she teared up at the sight of her own daughter's rebirth. She had noticed, too.

I hugged her carefully, my hands still full of assorted libations. "Thanks, mom." I received her response with all the gratitude I could summon as I bounced back and forth between disgust and delight. Why was it so hard? "Well, I really should mingle and meet everyone else."

"It's a pleasure, Sally," Dr. Gregory Taylor finally spoke, his gravel-filled voice giving him away as a smoker.

Cigars.

"Yeah," I said and appeared purposefully distracted as I wandered into the kitchen.

I found Brian there, along with my dad, and three other people I'd never seen before. There was an older couple that reminded me of an aged version of Ozzie and Harriet and a middle-aged woman who seemed to have been ridden hard and put away wet by life. Her dulled skin and wrinkled expressions were lined with kindness, however, and I was drawn into the capricious circle.

"This is my wife, Sally," Brian announced as he pulled me in to their loosely formed presence.

Everyone nodded a quick acknowledgement before Brian continued. "And, Sally, these are more of our neighbors from three doors down in #24, Lyle and Margaret Hastings. They just moved in also."

Handshakes and the standard 'nice to meet you' and 'thank you for having us' were exchanged. Margaret and Lyle were sweet, sincere, and incredibly typical. Margaret wore a smart if slightly dated gray pantsuit that had accenting shoulder pads in it while her husband Lyle donned beige slacks, a blue and red themed argyle sweater, and penny loafers complete with shiny new pennies. The only thing missing was a pipe for him to hold as a prop and an antique brooch for her.

"And, this is their friend, Cynthia," Brian presented the worn woman with the undeniable lines of kindness.

"Cynthia isn't a neighbor exactly," Margaret jumped right in before the elusive Cynthia could speak a word. "She doesn't live on the court but passes through it regularly on her hikes."

Well, how ordinary, Harriet. Is everything in your life that way? Or is it all a bunch of cover stories?

I had a hard time believing in that amount of ordinary.

"It's a pleasure to meet you, Cynthia." I extended my hand and was met with a hesitant and then flimsy handshake as Cynthia cracked a creased smile. Of all of us, Cynthia was by far the worst dressed, wearing nothing more than worn blue jeans and a plain green turtleneck that had also seen better days. She also seemed a little chilled and slightly hollow.

Margaret drew near to me and spoke just above a whisper. "She's a little shy, but once you get to know her, you'll love her."

I looked to Cynthia who seemed unfazed by the fact that we were obviously talking about her without also talking to her. "I know how overwhelming it can be around so many people," I empathized. "As a matter of fact, and I don't know if Brian told you this, but this is the first time in three years that we've opened our home to company outside of family."

"Really?" came Cynthia's incredibly strained question.

Is it that great a burden to speak?

It seemed to me that she'd rather have been standing there in quiet observation, sucking up what it meant to be in our midst rather than actively a part of it. Bittersweet.

"Yes," I continued my conversation with her, seeking a natural dovetail to let her off the social hook. "And, that's primarily because I felt so strongly the need to hide, as I was in a slow recovery – "

Did I just say 'was'?

"From an automobile accident," my father explained without provocation.

"Oh my!" the Hastings exclaimed in unison. It was satirically comical and made me wonder how long they'd been together to have such attuned personal radars and shared expressions. I pondered for a split second whether or not Brian and I would be like that someday. Probably.

"But, these are better days," Craig moved on for us all, and came between me and Brian to plant a quick kiss on top of my head. "You look terrific, pumpkin."

"Thanks, dad," I accepted and even encouraged his hardy embrace about my waist while I turned to Margaret and Lyle. "So, you recently moved in to #24?" I opened while casually leaning on my father to allow him to help support some of my weight. I was doing much better, but the muscle strain of prolonged standing continued to have a hold on me.

"We recently moved back in to #24. We lived there for about eight years before we moved out last spring. We went back to the city for some time to be closer to social contacts, but this place just calls you back," Margaret explained vaguely. "Folks come and go around here, sometimes the same people more than once, but for us it's home."

"It sure is," Lyle echoed her sentiment and put an arm around his wife's shoulders, emphasizing just how much they belonged together. Behind closed doors though, who knew what they were really like. From all outward appearances my mother and father were a charming couple, but behind the façade lurked a darker actuality.

Casual pleasantries and what some might consider witty banter moved about the kitchen circle with a whirlpool spin. Without contributing hardly a thing to the discussion, I allowed myself to be swept up in the elated engagements of it and smiled and laughed when the moments warranted. Brian seemed in his element as the entire scene was rational and regular, and I enjoyed seeing him that way just as much as I enjoyed seeing him totally thrown from his safe zone now and then. It wasn't until I noticed with my peripheral vision that the doorway from the kitchen into the den was open that I pried myself loose from the vortex of inclusion and moved on to supposedly say hello to still more guests. I had been waiting a long time to walk though that doorway.

As I stepped across the threshold and into the sunken den, I immediately set eyes on Annabelle relaxing in my favorite burgundy armchair and considering my current reading material.

She glanced up at me, and I felt the hook sink in deep. "I've never heard of this book before. Is it any good?"

Her voice was absolutely musical, and it was then that I thought she might be the siren in disguise much more so than I.

"It's one of my favorite stories," I confessed, "and the first paperback ever published."

"The back cover of the book makes it sound intriguing. Do you think it's true?" Her eyes grew wide with anticipation and possibilities.

"Well, it's fiction..." I trailed off. There weren't words for a second time that night.

She grinned like a Cheshire cat and stood up. "That's not what I meant," she said as she approached me, and within seconds she was less than an inch away, moving up on me with the speedy and silent stalk of a predator. And, I was now within takedown range. "I mean, do you think it's true that some places are so enchanted that they can actually heal a person? Do you think a place all by itself can bring out either the best or worse in people?"

Those were the very questions I'd always held in my soul and the very philosophy and beliefs my life had been founded upon. And, Annabelle had hit the nail on the head the first time we'd officially met. She looked into me and found a soul there, found longing there. Even with my recent life improvements, there was still a longing... for her, for completion.

"Personally..." I stalled, "I do." Those last two words were spoken in a heated rush, in fullest breath, and in an almost inaudible whisper so that I could bring my lips as close to hers as I dared and still have an excusable reason for doing so.

"I do, too," she whispered back and moved in close enough that I could feel the brush of her silky ebony locks against the sides of my face. I shivered against the heat of her flesh.

I shut my eyes tight. Could this amorous swim of the spirit really be happening right in my own den with my husband in the next room and a house full of people? It was so unseemly, so bizarre. It was a total diversion from the life I'd led in broad daylight and the tarnish of the years past. When I opened my eyes again, Annabelle was a couple of steps back and contemplating me.

"I'd like to come over and see the rest of the house some time, when there's more time." She placed the ball in my court.

"I'm home most days, so anytime," I returned with a predatory smile of my own.

She stretched forth her arm and extended her hand. "I'm Annabelle, by the way."

My hand melted into hers. "Sally."

"I know." And with that, she waltzed out of the main doorway to the den as Reggie walked in.

"Hey!" I greeted cheerfully, feeling the excitement tinge with embarrassment as a strange juxtaposition occurred. Annabelle leaving and Reggie arriving had caused the fire in my belly to go from satisfactorily devouring to hungrily nauseating. The fire quelled itself from healthy blaze to flickering flame that could not be stilled. It was a tedious shift, but one that I felt compelled to make.

Reggie is so addictive...

"Wow! Look at you," Reggie announced as he strode towards me. "I never really noticed during each therapy session just how far you've come, but all dressed up now, it's pretty damn impressive." He polished off what was left in his glass.

"That means a lot coming from you," I said with great candor, and with the flickering of a flame inside that had been pre-lit by Annabelle only moments before.

"Does it?" he asked.

"Yes, it does, and I've been meaning to talk to you about something that's been on my mind since the move."

"And, what would that be?" Reggie looked relaxed enough to have the discussion I'd wanted to. A few drinks were more than likely to thank.

"Well," I began with trepidation due to the fantastic fear of impending closeness, the tentative delight of a possible twist of fate. "You had seemed so upset by the move and not so much by me moving, that I wanted to address it at some point. You seemed really disturbed by it, but only by the lack of income that it would create – "

"That's not entirely true – " he cut in.

And, I cut right back. "Just let me finish what I have to say. It won't take long."

Just let me speak to you from this new position, and we'll see where it goes.

Reggie bowed his head slightly, roughed up his short, red tinged mane and then plopped down on the sofa, letting me proceed.

"I might have been overstepping my bounds and the whole patient-therapist relationship thing, but I had thought of us as friends, Reggie, at least I did up until then. And when you lashed out and said what you said about the money, it made me recalculate what we might actually be to each other. Maybe I should've brought all this up sooner, instead of waiting until now. And, I'm not even sure why I'm dredging it all up." I paused to reclaim focus and amorous intent. My loins ached… but was that for Reggie or Annabelle?... "All I know is that we have a professional arrangement, but I really wanted us to be friends, too." I let out a breath I didn't even realize I'd been holding. "I guess I just wanted you to know that."

I guess all I really care about is making myself feel better.

"Are you done clearing the air?" Reggie tested the boundary I'd laid down for him, while also adding his own brooding energetic to the mix, to the lure, to the bait that had been placed for me and stemmed from his very being. But, was the bait also poison?

"Yes."

"Now I'd like to say something," he started his own confessional moment, although it was nothing so forthcoming as my own. I'd gone way out on a limb, and at that time it might have been asking too much of him to do the same. "We are friends, Sally, and I do care about you. That day at your apartment was a mistake, and it was one mistake in a whole long line of mistakes." Reggie leaned forward to place his head in his hands.

"What does that mean?" I prompted. Something juicy, I'd hoped. My heart beat fast at the thought of him being my confidant again, at bare minimum; a confidant who had the unfortunate habit of always keeping secrets from me. I simply wanted to keep him near, keep him tied to me, no matter what happened. The urge to have him surging through my system in any capacity was so great; it had grown teeth over the years and dug in under the hunkers.

"I need to talk to you," he murmured into his hands.

"Ok. Go ahead," I offered.

He glanced up at me and it was then I noticed how bloodshot his eyes were, and I nervously ruminated over how much he'd probably had to drink while he got his own thoughts together in what felt like a haphazard format. "Not now. I need to talk to you privately, not with all these people around. There's something you need to know."

I'm sure there are many things I'd like to be privy to.

"It's just us in here. If you'd like I can shut the doors."

"Monday. I'll come over early on Monday," he informed, with an edge of insistence that had me flashing back to that explosive day in the apartment when he'd tried to place everything into his theoretically desired box.

I eyed him cautiously and chose my next words carefully, ever conscious of how large he was in comparison to me. The entire discrepancy seemed to distort in his favor whenever we were alone and especially on the very few occasions that he'd been particularly brooding or angry. There was both an alluring and dangerous tension there, like the thrill of the prospect of walking across a bed of hot coals. "I sort of have a morning routine, Reggie. I'm not sure I have time to – "

"Make time," he insisted and stood up to full height. "Make time for it." And with that being said, he left both the room and the house without another forceful utterance that my ears could detect.

What've I gotten myself into? How many torches can one person carry?...

The flame had been there for Reggie a very long time, but I felt inside me that it was being pitted against the new and emblazoning fire that I willfully fanned for Annabelle.

I really should be more careful of what I wish for.

By the time all of the guests had left, the notable and the not so notable, it was far too late for my parents to drive back to their place, so they once again retired for the night in the periwinkle guest bedroom. Only this time, there was an actual bed and supplemental furnishings for them to enjoy, not just a mattress on the floor. And, really, that periwinkle room had been the only viable option left for guests, as Brian had already started the process of turning the white room into his own office.

Brian and I showered quickly together and then lay on top of our earth-toned bed linens naked and ready to do more than talk, even though we definitely needed to talk, too.

It was becoming a regular pleasure and a guilt-free indulgence for me to touch my husband in whatever manner I pleased. He was so plaint and open to me, so ready for anything that crossed my mind and made me wet. I took my sweet time stroking his cock, feeling it swell and jerk in a grateful bob as I meditated on both him and Annabelle.

Annabelle.

It was sort of a trade-off in my mind, a tag team of one and then the other, and I hoped that he might be more receptive to some of my musings about her after sex. I continued my erotic work so long and thoroughly that he finished before I had ever really begun to have my way with him. Fortunately for me, Brian has always been a people pleaser at heart.

"That was fantastic," I sighed as he moved from between my legs to join me once more near the headboard.

He gave a husky laugh in response, "I do try."

"Yeah."

"This has been a full day," he continued, leading me to believe that the mood was right for discourse after intercourse.

"The fullest I can recall," I agreed.

Brian laid half across me and rested one hand possessively yet compassionately on my breast. "And, I thought for sure with everything going on you'd be too tired for anything else tonight."

It is way past my bedtime.

In an odd twist of fate, it seemed that as the days were waning, instead of me waning with them as per usual, I was waxing. "I'm full of surprises," I spoke mischievously.

"Uh-huh," was Brian's response to that.

"Do you like surprises?" I went on. It felt to be as good a time as any, even though there was great trepidation in my roundabout approach. After all, it's not every day that a spouse brings up such a topic in the bedroom before the sheets have even cooled.

"Sure. Who doesn't?" he was always so logical. And, what was the harm in that response? The odds appeared to be in his favor that night.

"Then I'd like to talk about Annabelle."

And talk we did, for she was the summit of surprises. And, I have to give Brian and myself credit, for we were honest with each other about her and about our mutual interest. Neither of us seemed shocked by the other or dismissive.

"I think you should see how things pan out with her first," came Brian's conclusion after more than an hour of unfathomable discussion. I could barely contain the concept of his unplumbed abyss and felt shallow in my own depths.

"Really? Why?"

Brian looked away from me then, and his next word revealed why he didn't want to visually connect. "Amelia."

I swallowed a sickly little lump. It was a phantom that hadn't made her presence known in our bedroom since we took up residence on the court. #18 had shielded me from her self-created mirage, but I might have known it would only be a matter of time before she found me, my unknowable nemesis. In one single incantation she was made energetically and magnificently manifest, like a blazing phoenix at the crest, and her aura engulfed the room. I could feel her, the personally perceived perfection that I gave to her in my mind, the haunting horror in what she might have that eluded me, despite my reclamation.

"Excuse me?!" my voice broke in trembling terror at the mere mention of her name. She had such power, held such sway.

"I cheated on you, Sally. And, no matter how much I want to… and believe me I want to… I can never take that back. I can never take that hurt away from you, not entirely. So, let me give you Annabelle."

Annabelle. Her name is like a soothing balm.

In direct contrast to the ilk that had filled the room at the mention of Amelia, it was remedied straightaway by the gentle and intoxicating charm of Annabelle.

"You should have the chance to be with her, since that's what you want. And, when you are ready, when and if both of you are ready, I will come to you."

It was an offer I couldn't refuse.

The rest of the holiday weekend, I never spied Annabelle. My parents left Friday afternoon following a decadent tea supplemented by party leftovers, and I found myself regularly peeking out windows, taking unnecessary walks in the back yard, and moving out to be with the willow tree in the front cul-de-sac. It was all to no avail, as she never showed herself. In fact, her house was perpetually dark with no movement to be detected inside. By Sunday afternoon, I assumed she and her nauseating father had gone to visit relatives or something similarly boring and gave up hope. It was then that I was met by the anxious anticipation, both good and bad, of having to speak with Reggie on Monday morning about whatever it was he felt was so pressing.

Bundled up in my warmest cardigan sweater, I sat underneath the willow as the sun set on Sunday evening and felt the bark move beneath my back. There was no pretense of delicate swirling any longer. It was real and palpable. The tree reconfigured itself at will, showing me and perhaps me alone its secrets. I saw words and patterns every so often that as of yet made no sense to me, but I kept watching. I would keep watching. I watched through the remorseful branches as the day put up one last fiery fight before the night overtook it, burying the sun in a grave of hibernating earth and giving the gift of rebirth to the moon and stars overhead.

As I continued my transcendent watch, I heard the high-pitched laugh of a child from somewhere nearby. My uterus skipped at the sound, as it is a thing of joy and longing for any parent or one-time parent. I could not help but feel the pull, and turned to try to see where it was coming from. I looked all around, my head on a swivel and didn't see anything or anyone. It wasn't until I came back to staring straight ahead that I saw her, the platinum imp who owned that laugh. She dashed about the front lawns of several homes back and forth, running for the sake of it and hiding in bushes and flowerbeds now and then as she went along. I took in the bounce of her glistening blonde curls and the hardy youth of her frame. She couldn't have been more than four or five years old and looked like one of the fairies of so many culturally diverse legends. As she came to a quick halt in my front yard, my eyes adjusted to not only see her, but to see what it was she had paused to view.

Brian was in the front dining room window, and he was staring at her just as she seemed to be staring back at him.

What the fuck is wrong with my husband? He must be freaking her out.

I never thought of my husband as disturbing, but even I felt a little unhinged by his unwavering line of sight. Fearing that he might be labeled a pervert, or worse, if this eerie exchange kept up, I got to my feet and made my way across the street, closing in on the little girl in my front yard. As I got within a few feet of her and she still hadn't turned to recognize my presence in her sphere, I spoke. "Hello there," I began in my most nurturing tone.

She turned and I found myself staring into the bluest eyes I'd ever seen. They were my mother's blue, my blue, Sonya's blue.

"Hi, mommy."

Sonya?! Sonya!

"Sonya," I whispered into the wind, and in a blink she was no longer before me. I looked up at the dining room window and Brian was gone. "I'm dreaming."

How many times will I try to convince myself I'm dreaming?

"I'm dreaming," I demanded and fell to my knees on the dying grass gone golden with the shades of the season, as if she had shed her ringlets there to make it so. I touched the earth underneath me, so cool and solid and real. I smelled the sweetness of the crisp night air and heard the faint sounds of nocturnal creatures as they stirred. My tears met the barren land and a current moved through my barren womb.

"Are you all right?" A rich and feminine voice tickled my ears and stirred me from the downward spiral I had thrown myself into. "Sally?" I felt a bracing hand on my shoulder and looked over to see slender fingers well-worn with age and ability. I followed the flow of an arm up to a shoulder and then to a face turned pink with the chill. Margaret Hastings had come to rouse me from my point of grief. With so much going right, I was suddenly reminded how everything was still wrong. How could I even think I would get beyond her?

"Margaret," I replied at long last and got to my feet with whatever shreds of dignity were left hanging.

"Have you been crying?" she asked in a tone that I wished my own mother had possessed. Even in moments when Jeanna Dougherty meant to be kind and caring, she still lacked the genuine affection of an accomplished mother with well-adjusted children. Jeanna Dougherty was much more a daunting woman than a strict maternal figure.

I wiped at my eyes ferociously with the backs of my hands and avoided the question as well as her gaze.

Margaret wrapped an arm around my shaking shoulders and began to lead me away. "Come with me," she spoke with gentle authority, and I was in no mental state to refuse. I went along pliantly, mindlessly, crossing three lawns and a driveway to enter with her into the hearty abode of her house.

I felt as well as saw the lustrous gold light that glowed from her windows as we went through the back door that led into her cozy kitchen. The smell of fragrant herbs greeted me upon arrival, along with three demanding cats that curled about my ankles before being shoved aside, and it made me think of the days when I would go with my grandmother to the market for fresh-baked rosemary bread and cinnamon sweet rolls. It was that same mixture of savory and sweet that could make someone feel complete and balanced. Once inside I was deposited at the kitchen table while Margaret flitted about to make preparations for her impromptu guest. She would pause every so often to smooth away any wrinkles or unsettling in her dapper gray pantsuit, and I had to laugh quietly to myself at the seeming absurdity in those actions.

As I was dazed and distracted, it would be fair to say she might have went on about her business for any reasonable length of time, but when she did at long last join me at her table, she brought with her chocolate chip cookies and tiny little cakes that looked too finely detailed to ever eat. She also brought piping hot cups of coffee. The smell enticed me, my favorite aroma.

"It's decaf," she assured as I looked quizzically at it. "It's a bit too late in the day for regular."

I let my bleary eyes meet hers, and with a matching vibration I found the beginnings of stability. I looked around the room to find three other sets of eyes considering me, probably even judging me. Margaret's cats. There was a large black male with green saucer eyes who had plopped his rear end on the counter and proceeded to bathe a tail while also pausing every so often to glance at me. Then there was an indeterminate fluff ball of a smoky gray cat, which seemed perfectly contented to lay in front of the stove and take in my visage with complacency. And, finally there was a very petite and sleek female calico, who despite having been rebuffed, refused to take no for an answer and wound her way about my legs to settle in on top of my feet.

"Did he hit you?" she asked uneasily, knowing it was not her place but testing the turbulent waters of my emotional realm just the same, and drawing my attention away from her furry and fussy housemates.

I shook my head vehemently. "No, of course not."

"Well, I wouldn't have thought it of him. He seems so sweet and caring from the little bit I've seen, but you never know..." She let the concept trail off to die a swift and natural death.

I blew on my coffee and did the best I could to compose myself. Deep, even breaths and a purring cat on my shoes were slowly but surely doing the trick, along with Margaret's emblazoned kitchen and earthy demeanor.

"Try one of the spice cakes," Margaret urged. "They go great with coffee." She smiled as a unilateral sign of encouragement while helping herself to one. "I'll feel guilty if you let me indulge alone."

I reached out and brought one over to a small dessert plate she'd set before me. The fine china was rimmed with violets that had gone faint from years of washing. Glancing around the room, I noticed just how much of a hearth space her kitchen was. Drying herbs hung from wooden ceiling beams, jars of preserves and spiced oils sat on window ledges, and a large copper kettle that must have been in regular use gleamed from the center of the stove as though it were lit with the pride of purpose.

"I lost my daughter," I finally confessed to find my own words were quickly absorbed by the drying plants in the room and went unacknowledged by the cats.

Margaret nodded and then looked at me with a blank and neutral expression.

I took a bite of the cake, which was somehow both delicious and then suddenly as tasteless as sawmill shavings. I swallowed the huge lump of a bite with a swig of coffee as my throat was going dry from feelings unexpressed and sentiments never spoken. "The car accident," I added. "I was not the only person in the car."

"Oh, dear girl," she cooed and stroked the backs of my hands and then gave them a pat. "I am so sorry. I had no idea."

"It was three years ago," I said as if that should somehow make it less painful. It gave me distance, but that was all it did. And, there were still times where the barrier of compoundable years was breached by the sharp pangs of loss. "She's been gone for three years."

Margaret continued her sympathetic nod. "It must feel like an eternity since you've been able to see her, to hold her in your arms. A mother's love... family..." Margaret trailed off again.

"I saw her tonight." I let go, figuring that if nothing else, I'd at least be able to swallow better after that admission.

I didn't expect sympathy and certainly not empathy. I expected a reaction of shock, horror, disbelief, or even pity towards a crazy woman. All of those types of responses would have been understandable and oddly ideal if they came from the nurturingly normal Margaret Hastings. But, what I got was that same sympathetic nod and the look of an empathic inner knowing.

"Well?" I finally pressed her into speaking.

"How did she seem?" Margaret's voice was very even keel, too even keel.

This was incredulous! "What do you mean how did she seem? I'm telling you I saw my dead child and you want to know how she seemed?!"

Margaret took a good drink of her coffee. The liquid heat seemed to steady her. The bitterness appeared to ground her. "It's a fair question, my dear. Did she seem angry, upset, happy, vague, distant, close?..."

"What the hell is wrong with you?!" I leapt to my feet with such speed and force that I knocked the chair back and heard it crash loudly onto the tile floor. The three cats scattered in all directions and were instantly gone from sight.

Margaret stood and slowly made her way over to my side. She placed a hand on each shoulder to hold me and impart some strange exchange of somber energy. "There, there. It's all right," she said with firm guidance. "Go home to your husband and give it some time. Things will be as they are meant to be."

Nothing is as it was meant to be!
"What – "

"No," she held up a finger to bring Silence down on me, as though I were her child, their child, or at the very least, their subordinate. "Go home now. Calm yourself and have a good night's sleep. It will be all right in the morning." And with that being pretty much the end of it, Margaret led me back to the door we'd come in through. "Give it some time, and give it some thought," she advised again as I stepped back out into the cold night air. She shut the door behind me and clicked a lock.

The residue of warmth at my back pushed me out into the darkness, across three lawns, and up to the porch of my own home. But, before I dared to go inside and try to put things back in place in my mind, back to a way I thought they belonged, I peered out into the darkness of the night and the stillness of the court. I opened my eyes and my heart to the greatest degree I'd been capable of. I opened my senses and my soul so that I might be sure of what was really there. Only a few houses had any sort of lights on now, and directly next door was the unforgivable pitch blackness. I heard and saw the central willow sway in the breeze, a rustle of near dead leaves speaking in a language as old as time. I understood it. In the core of my being and at the crux of my soul, I understood it.

"Sonya," I whispered shyly out into the night. "Sonya," I called again, to be answered by the rush of the wind through the willows and then through the oaks. Then came the stillness that had no answer because it didn't need to provide one.

I went inside.

Brian was fast asleep by the time I reached our bedroom. After quickly washing my face and barely bothering to glance at the luminous skin that was remaking itself day by day into an ever more enviable image, I slipped into a long nightshirt and crawled into bed. This time, none of it was a dream and there was no person to safely wake me. There was no one who could.

Brian was also gone before I woke on Monday morning, which was unusual given the fact that I was up early enough and we always had coffee together before he headed out to the office. The only times our routine varied was when I was feeling decadent or depressed and dared to sleep in. It was all very strange behavior, which led me to believe that he had been standing in that dining room window looking out, and he had seen what I'd seen. He was a witness to the madness, and it could only be avoided as a topic for so long. His being a part and party to it made me feel less mad and more manageable.

In the great and steely gray light of day, I found the courage and wherewithal to think on last night's happenings. And when I did so, Margaret's words vexed me further until I remembered that Reggie was planning to arrive early to talk to me about a subject he deemed urgent.

The summoning of Reggie into the mental sphere smashed my ability to reflect any further, to try and sort it all out by lunch. I'd have to deal with him and his issues, our issues, first before I could properly tend to what was mine alone. My stomach twisted itself into knots at the thought, and my heart would occasionally skip a beat. I alternated between happy and sad, riding the waves of elation and then smashing down on the rock-lined shores of depression. I wanted a confession of desire, but I feared something far more detrimental and volatile was at play.

As a means of distraction, I grabbed a portable cup of coffee and made my way to the willow in the cul-de-sac to explore. Would new words and patterns be etched in the bark from last night's phantom visit? Would I see specters or hear voices? What would await me?

And, why was it all beginning to seem somewhat commonplace?

The bark yielded nothing new as I allowed myself to be sheltered beneath the swaying branches and breathe the crisp morning air. It was sobering and disheartening. No new patterns or images, although the etching of the word 'doggie' had re-emerged and seemed unbelievably deep to not have drawn sap, the blood of the tree. There was no denying the presence of this word, and there was no stopping what was to come.

The day was heavily overcast, and I knew the unrelenting frosts would arrive soon and bring insects to a timely demise, followed by early winter snows to chill us all as the nights grew longer and the sun lost its strength. Each day it rose lower and lower in its arc above the horizon and in its unceasing travels from east to west. Soon, it would be too cold for me to stand for very long under the auspices of this tree. Most of the leaves were gone already, and I was sure I could be seen plainly beneath the boughs. The predator had become the prey. There would be days in the not too distant future where I'd be forced to hibernate in my dwelling, sparing myself the biting winds and heavy snows, but becoming prisoner to both my past and the present moments. Those would be lean times, hard times. Those wintery moments would individually weave the web of my future, an ensnarement.

The one glimmer of hope that the morning offered was the illumination and movement coming sporadically from the Taylor house next door to my own. I couldn't make out who was roaming about through the gauzy curtains that haplessly shielded each window, but the lights were on and someone was definitely home.

I wondered if Annabelle was home, and if I would see her today. Our first and only encounter had been far more than cordial, and even with the shrinking shards of motherhood distantly sobbing inside me, I held an inferno that would not be so easily extinguished.

Moody musings did little to boost my spirit, and soon enough, my stormy mood had produced raindrops and Reggie. I felt the cold clap of water on my head and shoulders as I watched Reggie's vehicle pull into the driveway and his short rusty mane pop out of the car. He jogged up the steps to my porch and paused before ringing the bell as I yelled, "I'm over here!"

Other than staring at me, Reggie offered no welcoming gesture to my approach. I made my way up the steps and to the shelter of the wood and stone encased porch. The swing swayed with the strengthening winds.

"You're wet. How long have you been out here?" Reggie probed plainly enough.

"I've been out for a bit, but it only just started raining here. Did the rains follow you in on your drive?" I returned with a question of my own as I opened the door and allowed him to follow me inside my not-so-humble abode.

"Yeah, kinda." He was casual in his remarks and posture, but I couldn't shake the sense that there was a disturbed undercurrent beneath him, a power riding him that was not so friendly or so humble either.

Will it pin me down? Will he?

"You're a whole hour early," I pointed out the obvious.

Reggie shrugged and removed his jacket, hanging it in the cloakroom off of the hallway. When he stepped back into the open format of the hall, he locked in on me with pinpoint accuracy. "I said I would be."

I cleared my throat, as it seemed a flem was welling up there. Could it be the coconut milk in my morning coffee or something more sinister? "Well, to be clear, you said you were going to be early. You didn't say exactly how early."

"Didn't you get my text?" he asked.

"No, and you shouldn't have assumed I would."

He has every reason to assume I would.

Of all the phone calls, texts, and emails I often let drop, I couldn't recall having ever let one of his slide.

Reggie closed the physical gap between us. "Why do you feel the need to criticize this?"

"Did you want to go get the equipment for our session?" I switched the subject to something more mundane and less offensive.

"After."

I escorted us into the den.

From there, Reggie's words seemed to twist and turn as the room did so around us, mimicking his vulgar verbiage with an accentuating and bawdy dance of its own. From my burgundy armchair, I watched the walls pivot and thrust like a husky harlot as books moved up and down and then side to side, until finally settling for a stunning spiral maneuver that did nothing to ease my stomach. I knew that I was alone in seeing and sensing all of it. It had nothing to do with Reggie and everything to do with me and my interpretations.

Reggie had planted himself on the sofa for the big reveal of his dirty little secret and roughed his hair as was customary when he found himself flustered or furious. I made a mental note that out of the entire time I'd known him, he'd been given over to excesses of mood and peculiarities of temperament more and more. He'd lost his temper at least three times in the last few months, and prior to that it had been hardly at all. As a matter of fact, prior to the initial outburst when he'd found out I was moving, I couldn't think of another time he'd shown any kind of deep or severe emotion. And, with as much as I wanted to periodically scream 'how dare you' and 'how could you' as he went on with his confessions, I became far more interested and alarmed by the dancing delirium of my den.

"I shouldn't have slept with her, Sally. It was a huge mistake, but she was so like you and so available. I guess I wasn't in the best place." Reggie's excuses went on and on, leading to, "Please, say something!" as a final insistence.

I knew that feeling, as I no longer liked too much Silence either. The tone in my voice was far more cool and collected than I was beginning to feel, as a fever pitch rose within me in direct contrast to my outward projection. "I can't believe you fucked my mother," I spat with muted disgust.

Now, it all made a new sort of sense. The timing and turning over of the garden beds when I lived at the apartment, the constant therapy updates my mother was privy to, and lastly the insistence and interest on her part in Reggie's schedule. Every logical link and newfound realization that in hindsight was so blatantly obvious was like a shotgun blast to my psyche. The image of her and him talking right outside my home by his car flashed again in my brain, and I stopped my mental processes from flowing under their own volition before the thought train could go any further.

I am way too imaginative for my own good.

"I didn't really want her. I mean, I did want her in a way, but that's just because I couldn't have you," he blurted.

"What kind of a sick twist does that shit? Really, what would make you think that's a fine idea or that anything could be an acceptable excuse for it?" I grilled from the solitary benefit of my morally superior position. "And, why in the world would you ever want to confess that to me? It's disgusting!" I ridiculed as I felt the strong urge to vomit.

Reggie rose to tower above me. "Because you got better, and I thought that with our connection, with our friendship, you might consider..." his eyes roamed over my seated form leaving no room for miscommunication. "And, I knew Jeanna would eventually tell you."

He is out of his perverted mind.

Attempting to quell the nausea with action, I stood and squared off in front of him, despite the sway and swirl of the room. "You've got to be out of your mind," I verbalized a fragment of my thoughts and threw up my hands as I pushed past him. "What is it with the men in my life anyway?"

"The men in your life?" Reggie zeroed in. I felt his hand on my shoulder as he spun me around with almost no effort. "What does that mean? Did Brian – "

"You know what?" I hissed hatefully as I brought my face in close enough to bite off his nose. "Get out of my house."

Get out of my heart.

"Wait, Sally, let's talk about this. It doesn't have to be this way." He ran his hands up and down my arms in what he probably thought would be a calming motion. "I care about you. You know that."

I shook him off with as much force as I could rally. "I said get the fuck out of my house!" And with the release of pent-up hostility that spewed like molten lava from the liquid core of my being, my insides matched my outsides.

I hate them both, and it feels so good!

I saw Reggie's jaw twitch as he clenched it in consideration of what to do next, and even though I felt a cold tremor move through me at what the options might be,

I held my ground. The other possibilities he mulled over inevitably passed, and he left the room. I heard the door of the cloakroom open and close and then the front door followed suit.

I exhaled a long breath I didn't even know I was holding, and just as I was about to collapse into my comforting burgundy recliner, the doorway to the kitchen popped open from its hiding place within the den's bookshelves.

I could use a drink.

And, that thought was followed by the cliché... *It's five o'clock somewhere.*

I crossed the threshold into the kitchen with naïve ease, but would I be able to take the heat?

As I stepped into the darkened kitchen, the lights stayed off. I'd kept them off in an effort to ease my surely spiking blood pressure. The only illumination I had to go by as I made my way to the refrigerator was coming from the outside window directly above the sink.

The sky was growing consistently darker, and moment by moment it sent an ominous message that the steady rains were only a precursor to the storm that would arrive on their heels. I reveled in the darkness as spiteful and hurtful words and images ravaged my synapses. I was a woman on fire, and my mother was the next most likely victim of my wrath. I would cut Reggie from my heart and from my life like a reaper wielding a scythe over a field of beckoning grain. Whatever spark of attraction I might have felt or connection I might have once wanted was over. I would will it to be over, no matter how much most of me couldn't bear to let it go, to let him go.

Was everyone in my life severely jacked up? I knew that there were issues, but for quite some time I had entertained the notion that of everyone in my sphere I was the most damaged. Apparently, I had underestimated my entourage.

I seized a clover and honey ale from the fridge, twisted the cap off with vigor, and flung it into the sink. After a couple of steadying swigs I made my way over to lean on the countertop and peek out the windows into my backyard. The rains had dappled the landscape and bent the natural light this way and that so that all manner of possibilities were visible whether they existed or not. I could pretend that anything or anyone was out there, but what my own eyes and what my mind's eye actually saw at the final forefront was Annabelle standing in the ground cover of lamb's ear that decorated the west fence line. The tall wooden privacy fence that snaked around my backyard protected her from prying eyes and curious seeking. As she stood there admiring the velvety softness of the plants around her ankles and the raw feel of the rain on her shoulders splashing down from the leaves of the witnessing oaks, she was the essence of my ideal prey.

I have been preyed upon enough.

I watched as the rain shower increased in strength and plastered her clothes against her body. Her great gray sweater top and rose-toned bohemian skirt held enough cold water to create muscle shivers in the subject of my voyeurism.

How long will I let the poor little thing suffer before I have the heart to sacrifice her?

With half the beer gone, I felt loose enough to make my way to the back door off the kitchen. I opened it wide and yelled into the drumming rains. "There's a storm coming in fast!" I pointed to the dark clouds on the horizon, and I signaled with a wave of my arm that she should make her way inside the waiting shelter of my house.

Annabelle didn't need much coaxing and immediately followed my advice, prancing through the wet grass to meet me under the overhang. "Thanks!" she said as I held the door for her. She stepped beyond me and then only a couple of feet into the kitchen before stopping.

I shut and latched the door behind her and turned to my rain-slicked visitor.

"I'm soaked through!" she laughed and then met my intense stare with a more somber attitude. "You must think I'm very silly and maybe a little stupid, huh?"

"I'll get you a towel." I avoided the question and the fact that she was in my yard and not her own. We didn't know each other well enough for that not to be considered trespassing. With relative swiftness and ease, emblems of my improving condition, I made my way through the house to the second floor bath and back. But by the time I arrived in the kitchen, she was in the middle of stripping off her top and had already removed her cumbersome skirt.

Admittedly, I was at a loss, for as she turned about to see me standing there with the large terrycloth towel she made no attempts to cover her bare breasts and simply stood like a statue waiting to be admired in only her panties.

I didn't hand her the towel. I couldn't. I felt unable to move and unable to speak. My throat had gone unbearably dry. Eventually, Annabelle decided to approach and retrieve the towel offered from my clutches. She patted her skin reasonably dry and then started a conversation without even covering herself. "I guess we're the only ones here?"

I nodded. Transfixed.

Annabelle wrung out her long raven locks into the towel and then shook them free so that they fell like tendrils over her budding breasts. She was Venus birthed from the oceanic depths. Clean and perfect.

"Lucky me," she smiled, and with that unnatural speed I'd experienced at the Thanksgiving gathering, she glided up to me.

She was close enough that the heat of her flesh registered on the surface of my own, and I felt myself flush. I smelled rain and earth on her, and there was a hint of the sweet crispness of fresh apple. It was predominant and nubile and fitting.

Annabelle dropped the towel to the floor. "Don't you want to?" she asked simplistically and brushed a bevy of curls over my shoulder so that she had access to run her innocent fingers along the curve of my neck. "I've always wanted to."

Why do others always touch me first?

I cracked a sideways smile. She could be predatory, but there was a feeling within me that pushed back against her allure and let me know that between the two of us, I was the consummate predator. I only had to let myself be.

It's my turn to touch.

My hands made their way along the plane of her abdomen and then cupped each tender breast, carefully stimulating her nipples ever so gently before letting go completely. I then allowed one hand to stroke across the smooth surface of her clavicles while the other traveled ever lower until it reached the boundary of her elastic panty line. Annabelle had thrown her head back and gone sublimely submissive.

So much for being a predator, sweetness.

I slid underneath the boundary and found her hot, wet, and waiting. Just a finger gliding along her excruciatingly aroused and swollen surface was enough to solicit a whimper from my delicate afternoon delight. So, I pulled back totally after that taunting turn.

It took a minute or two, but Annabelle came back around and looked at me in utter confusion and abandon. The storm struck around us as the sky went black outside, and I realized I could now only see her vague outline. "Let's go upstairs." It was less of a suggestion and more of a command. I knew I had her caught in my trap, a slave seduced in my welcoming web, as she had thought I'd been caught in hers.

My prey went willingly, like a little lamb to the slaughter.

Chapter 5

The overhead lights in the bedchamber stayed off, but I did turn on one of the bedside lamps to give enough of a glow to enhance the gratitude that flowed between us for one another. As I drew Annabelle further and further into the room, she seemed less and less certain but paradoxically more and more determined. An alien electricity wound its way about us as Mother Nature cracked and sparked outside in her own display of a wet fury and passion.

I placed Annabelle carefully on the edge of the bed as though she might shatter if I set her down too hard, even if it was on a definitively soft surface. There was a breakable quality about her, despite the fact that her sturdy flesh was so young and supple, so hardy and rose-tinged. Once she had her designated spot, I stepped back and wantonly tossed my curls from side to side to get them away from my face. I laughed inwardly at the irony of that, as there was a time when all I wanted to do was toss them around to get them to cover my face. But, that was before I had been reborn. That was before I was unashamed to be wholly and physically Sally. After mesmerizing with a dance of cascading ringlets, I drew my chunky sweater off and over my head in an effortless glide, letting it then settle to the floor in a woolen pool. There was still dampness to the fabric from when I'd met the coming rains under the willow, and that moisture had cooled to a point where it chilled my skin ever so erotically. I felt my nipples become erect from dampness and desire. My own breasts were a perfect match for hers, perky and pronounced; they sat well atop my ribs and accentuated the subtle curve that merged across my long torso to meet flared and flirty hips. My manner of dress hadn't been as sensual or stylish as hers, but the manner in which I removed my clothes was far more intrinsic and captivating. I felt like a snake slowly slithering out of its skin as I stripped away my stretch pants. Once my pants were abandoned on the floor, I stroked the smooth surface of each leg as I made my way back up to full standing height, enjoying the body that had once betrayed me.

I stood before Annabelle as her equal in every physical way; only I was the light to her dark, I was the knowledge to her naivety. My coarse blonde curls were in direct contrast to her silken ebony mane. My blue eyes met her black orbs with a cold and consuming fire. I saw her watch the entire process of my unfoldment with rapt attention, and I knew the power I held over her. I knew it inside and out, for it was the same power she held over me.

As I slithered along to stand before her, Annabelle opened her mouth as though to speak but then thought better of it. Perhaps she couldn't.

What more is there to say, really?

I let her taken me all in, visually at first, and then her hands explored my nude form in the faint way that I suspected they would. There was the tiniest of trembles in her touch, but it was invigorating to have her touch me nonetheless. She made her way from my aching breasts to my sensitive abdomen in a series of hypnotic swirls, pausing several times as she considered moving her hand even lower. She balked enough that I knew I'd have to take control if we were to ever arrive anywhere near where we wanted to be.

I knelt in front of her and pressed my lips into hers in a searing kiss that made molten metal of us both. We were so loose and liquid, so pliant and in the pliancy I understood that I would have to be the one to hold some sort of solid shape as we intertwined. I would have to become solid and liquid, gentle and strong, nurturing and nuanced for she wanted to lose herself, and I was done being lost. I was done being prey. It had never been my natural state, my truest guise.

It's so strange to realize in hindsight how during that time I had regained my physical strength but was still losing something else. I didn't even know a different avenue of loss was presenting itself, opening up, and I was walking down it. I may have gained my body, but I was losing my sense of self, in her, in the house, in my own earthy essence.

The more I became wholly and physically Sally, the less I became the self that I needed to be. And, I didn't care.

My tongue looped around hers in friendly persuasion, and I proceeded to draw her forth, to take what she had to give me. I felt her tremble and quake as I stroked the inside of her thighs and began to rub through the only barrier that remained wedged between us, her white satin panties. I used that barrier to my advantage, allowing her moisture to completely soak through until it was weeping as I glided around the nexus of her sex. I wickedly applied a mildly increasing pressure with each passing circle that I made.

Annabelle's hips started to buck against my hand, wanting more, craving more. But I held back, for it would not be on her timetable. I would devour her at a pace that was pleasing to me. From cobra to lioness, humane killers both, I weaved my spell of shifting back and forth between the two. She laced her fingers through my hair and gripped the sides of my head, deepening our kiss until it turned ravenous and almost uncontrollable.

I have to take control.

She was like a hurricane, a maelstrom and the dark bird that was caught up in it, and I was about to get sucked in to winds and wings that were beyond me, beyond my navigation skills. I had to take charge and keep us from crashing into the rocky beach.

I wriggled myself free of her tenacious grasp, and was given an instant facial expression that revealed her disappointment. Not subtle. I brought my mouth close once more and kissed her swiftly in an act of assurance. "Lay back," I instructed firmly.

Annabelle smiled coyly and pulled herself all the way onto the bed and then laid flat against it, as per my command. I stood up and then over her, as she made herself ready for whatever ministrations I would lavish next. I placed one hand over her practically purring pussy and then another. I moved my fingers underneath the waistband of her silken undergarment to remove the final veil at last. I pulled her panties down and off and tossed them unceremoniously across the room.

She seems so small and so vulnerable.

I would have to be careful, take my time. For as much as she wanted it, I could also see that there was a part of her that actively feared it, and in response, also feared me. I brought myself up on the bed with her and onto all fours. My body hovered above as I bent my head low to whisper into her ear. "Relax," I breathed huskily. "Enjoy," I suggested and nuzzled her neck on my way down with a processional of kisses that appeared to set her free and into a fervent frenzy. Her hands grabbed and then stroked my curls as I made my way ever closer to her overheated center.

"Oh, Sally," she sighed so sadly that it nearly broke my heart, and I would have stopped to comfort her were it not also for the undertones of longing and need.

I arrived at her dewy and beautifully bare sex and kissed the skin there that shielded her clit from me, for the moment. I then brought my tongue around for lap after lap as I made my passage inward, until I finally parted her and began to indulge in the sweet and heady nectar that she was creating from my exquisite efforts. I licked and kissed and swirled until she started getting out of control again and insistent, bucking against the tension and begging for me to do more.

"Sally! Sally, please!" Annabelle cried my name and called for me to release her from the cage she had built around herself, and around her own erogenous nature. I could sense the wild bird beating within her chest. It wasn't heartbeats that I heard and felt but the furious flap of caged wings demanding to be set free from the imprisoning bones of her ribs. They were strong wings, dark wings. She held inside the spirit of a raven that wanted to be set out in the wild.

I brought my mouth over her clit, and took it in as far as I could. I started to suckle her. Slow and easy at first, letting her adjust to the change in applied pressure, and then with more force, a harder suction. I slid a finger inside her to find her muscles immediately gripping around me, contracting. I glanced up at her at the same second that she attempted to look down at me. She was beyond comprehension and existing nearly outside of herself. She wanted to be let out. I could hear the call in my head. Her begging to no longer be a prisoner to whatever demon it was that possessed her.

The walls of the bedchamber pulsed in response. I wondered then if it was simply the pulsing of my own blood throughout my body that made it appear that way, or if the walls actually moved and mimicked with a slick beat all their own. Knowing #18 as I do now, as well as the court and the trees, I realize the beat belonged to those walls and it coaxed me into an erotic embryo. I slid in a second finger and heard her gasp. I felt her twist and convulse around me, surrounding me.

"Don't stop!" she screamed. "Don't...don't stop!" Her voice was strangled by sexual sensation, the invisible hands of Silence that conspired with me.

I pumped my fingers in and out of her as I continued my lapping and sucking of her clit in a rhythmic act of ritualized worship. We went on until I was drunk off her nectar, and she was tottering on the edge of what was left of her sanity. Finally, I heard Annabelle let out a carnal moan and felt every muscle in her body clench in perfect sequence. She had shattered around me even as her body tightened into cohesion. Her orgasm drew one from somewhere inside myself, and I hadn't even been aware of how close to the edge I was until I went hurdling over it.

Several sobering breaths later, I quasi-came to my senses and saw Annabelle shivering in a languid mass on top of my bed, her legs still spread wide before me, her form a bundle of confusion and chaos. I brought my mouth in again and began to lick her clean, drink up every last drop in a nurturing and oddly maternal effort. Then, I brought my body onto the bed with the last ounce of energy I had. In an act of pure instinct, Annabelle curled up around me and promptly went to sleep, leaving me to follow suit once she was out.

❖

When I woke, the storm had passed, and Annabelle was no longer next to me. A strong stream of daylight lit the room, and as I sat up, I noticed her retrieving her panties from the floor. As she turned, we made awkward eye contact. Neither of us could be sure what the other was thinking.

"I really should get home. My dad will be worried," she explained without provocation.

I got to my feet. "Of course. I think the rest of your clothes are in the kitchen. And, they're probably still sopping wet. Do you want to borrow – "

"No," she stated strongly, as strongly as she had probably ever stated anything in her life.

I looked at her as quizzically as I could to relay how out of place her response seemed.

"I mean, no thank you," she corrected herself and walked hesitantly over to me. "I'm not sure what it is I'm supposed to say here."

I touched the side of her face, and she turned to rest her head in the palm of my hand. "That's because you aren't supposed to say anything." We held the pose for as long as we could, and while we did so I noticed something in the stronger daylight, something that I hadn't seen in the muted glints of the storm. Bruises. Old, healing, and ever so faint in their lingering outlines. Annabelle had bruises all along her upper arms and parts of her torso. They were yellowed and near gone, but they were there enough for me to take note of their undeniable and inexcusable existence. I removed my hand and stroked her hair so that it laid in a more presentable mass. "It's ok, Annabelle. Let's get your things, and you can hurry on home."

Her skirt and top were still cold and wet, a heavy bundle to put back on, but Annabelle was determined to don them, and once she dressed, she quickly scurried out my back door and ran across the lawn to her own home. She was swallowed up by the house that held her and done damage by whatever was within.

It got to be late in the day, and then it got later, as it always does. It wasn't until well after the sun went down and the rains started again that I realized Brian hadn't come home, as he always does. I'd never heard him arrive, and so I hadn't started making dinner or thought to look for him in other parts of the house. My stomach growled and my heart beat hard. With all the tempestuous weather, I thought something might have happened to him. A car accident leapt to the forefront of my mind, as it was prone to do from my own past experience. I made my way to the cloakroom and pulled down my current choice in purses to retrieve my cell phone. I stepped back out into the hall and quickly dialed his digits.

What if he's not home because he's with Amelia?

I banished the thought as expeditiously as I could and tried to focus my attention on him being just fine. Had my amorous affair with Annabelle led me to think of his dealings with Amelia?

There's always a price to be paid, I suppose.

Classical music rose up from below my feet, the sound soothing and nerve-wracking in tandem. It was interesting that such a cocktail of extremes could be possible, and then I recognized the tune. It was Mozart, the song that was Brian's ringtone, *The Piano Sonata No.16 in C Major*, and it was coming from a place in the basement that was directly below my feet. The musical atmosphere was hauntingly cheerful, given its emanating location.

I paused, my hand hovering above the knob to the basement door. I'd never ventured down there. At first it was because the steps were so steep, and I was physically unable to do so with a walker without risking life and limb. Then, it became about the moldy smell and inky blackness that might stain me in some permanent way.

Now it is about a cold fear.

It dawned on me then, before I turned the handle in defiance of my instincts, that I was afraid of the basement in and of itself. I didn't fear that something was down there; it was more that I feared the space of the basement and all that it might contain of its own accord. Over two months of avoidance reared its ugly head, but I turned the knob anyway and overrode the fear that seemed so ridiculously real.

The blackness spilled upwards to reach me and covered the tops of my bare feet. I wore nothing but a loose sweater dress after my interlude with Annabelle and instantaneously wished I'd worn full body armor.

One of my heavy nightgowns from my rehabilitation days would be perfect.

I flipped on the light switch at the top of the stairs and made my way with calculated caution down the painted gray wooden steps. My feet landed flat on cold, hard concrete, and I breathed in the scent of mold and must.

That can't be a good sign.

"Brian?" I whispered and then felt silly for doing so. "Brian?" I called a notch louder.

"Sally," he answered vaguely from somewhere off to my left. The light from the stairway down did little to illuminate the entire basement; and so even though I could hear him, I still could not see him.

There must be another light source down here somewhere.

I squinted into the void. "Where are you? And, what on earth are you doing down here?" Taking another step to the left, I felt something brush across my face. I jolted back and almost fell from the force of my retreat. Gingerly I reached a hand out to try to determine just what it was that had touched me. Within seconds I knew. It was a pull chord for an overhead bulb. I was obliged to pull and did so to then be rewarded with a golden glow that filled up the rest of my area of the basement. It was still dark and dense, even with the additional light on. And, it seemed as though the basement ran the entire length and width of the house. Other than the main area of it that I was standing in, it appeared to have corridors and chambers honeycombed and hiving off on all sides.

The enveloping blackness reached forth for the edges of the glow and was barely constrained from the brush of yellow dimness. I could see a couple walls and felt fortunate that I didn't also see willow tree roots, or for that matter, the roots of any of the other massive species of trees, busting through them. The stones, placed so artistically and architecturally many years ago, seemed sturdy and well maintained.

Brian sat cross-legged on the dusty floor, still in his upscale office attire, and held an unobtrusive piece of cream-colored paper in his hand. He wasn't even looking at the paper, not that he'd have been able to read it in the dark anyway.

I knelt in front of him. "Brian, what's going on?"

He thrust the paper forward, and I took hold of it. In my hands I received the heavier weight of cardstock and the texture of finery and finesse. As I inspected it, a brocade pattern became clear around the border with crimson flowers coming into focus in the center, and there were words written in a printed script along the top. It was a greeting card. I read the front flap, 'For Someone Special.'

Nothing so sinister there.

But, looks and words can be deceiving. I opened the front flap and read the pre-printed red script on the right. 'There's no special reason to send this card, for you are more than special enough. You have captured my mind and my heart. Thinking of you.'

I smiled.

How lovely.

It was indeed a beautiful sentiment, if only a little drugstore typical.

Then I noticed the hand written passage on the left inner flap. 'Amelia — I am always thinking of you. Always. You are the most special person in my life. Thank you for being there.'

Amelia.

Her name was a familiar and repetitive bullet, a burning chunk of lead that ripped through my insides.

I dropped the card as though it had scalded me. Holding the fire of his once simmering passions for another woman was a feat beyond my feeble limitations. A well of grief opened up with a silent lion's roar in my gut. It was more than I could bear to see these things, even if only hours ago I had brought another woman into my bedroom and made love to her. It wasn't the same. Brian had betrayed me, and here was the elegant and emotionally charged spirit of his indiscretions written by his own hand and not to be denied.

I'd never have thought of myself as someone prone to the dramatic act of hand wringing, but apparently, I was wrong because in that moment it seemed to be the only thing I was able to do. I could not speak, and I could not leave. But, I could and did wring my hands to purge the invisible imprints of that declaration.

"It won't go away. It just won't go away." Brian's pathetic incantation jarred me from my yawning well of spousal grief.

"Why would you do this? Why would you keep this here?" I asked for closure if for nothing else. "Why would you keep it at all?" That was the better and more poignant question.

Why would you show it to me?

Brian raised his head and wearily glanced at me. He was disheveled, despite his well-draped work clothes. He appeared older and bitter. There was despair in his hazy eyes. "I didn't."

"What?" I wasn't even aware that I'd spoken a response until I heard the echo of my own voice. I was moving outside of myself and feeling the walls of the basement moving in to contain me, control me, contort me.

"Oh, god," Brian sighed into a prolonged exhale. "What the hell is happening to me?" He brought his hands to his face and buried it in them. Seconds later I heard him weep in a most piteous fashion. My primal urge was one of comfort, but unlike with Annabelle, I was not stopped by another's longing and needs. This time I was stopped from latent maternal influence by my own longing and needs. I needed this to end, and I longed to know the truth. What was happening to him? What was happening to me, to us?

I stood to full height, towering over Brian and felt the great flame of my cool and sadistic wrath. Amelia resided in this basement and held sway over him still. Amelia held me captive, too, and I would no longer tolerate that. I felt the strength in my limbs and the pulse of my own rhythmic heartbeat. I was healed, and I was worthy... or so I led myself to believe. In actuality, I was probably very much like my mother.

"You better have more to say than that." I was also exacting.

"I gave it to Amelia a long time ago. I never saw it again until we moved in here, until I started bringing stuff down to the basement for storage," he began talking into his lap. "When I found it the first time I tore it up and threw it away, but a few days later it was down here again. I don't understand." The helplessness in his revelations irritated me to the point where I felt like lashing out in some overtly venomous way, but I held my tongue until the venom was safely swallowed.

His story seemed incredible and unbelievable, and yet I knew it to be true. And, that was all the more disturbing. I would have rather believed he still loved Amelia in some small measure than to believe we were the victims of some sort of curse. As short and simple and insane as his explanation was, I knew it was true.

"And, then there was Sonya – "

"What?!" It was a conversation I'd wanted to have, and then all at once I wanted anything but. Not then and not there.

He met my eyes with an alarming and disarming look of his own. "I saw her last night, and I know you did, too. I've been seeing her. And, I found this down here as well." Brian brought forth one face I never wanted to see again from behind his back, the fallen and fluffy face of Fido.

It was Fido as he had been in my dream. Old, discarded, and discolored. Worn and stained and battered... and wet... He looked up at me then as he had done in my dream, with black, lifeless button-eyes and an accusatory stare that would never blink. He would not go away either. I knew if I tore him to shreds in the same way Brian had done with his inexcusable card, Fido would only come back to haunt me once more, materialize in perhaps an even more malicious guise.

Brian dropped the stuffed dog at my feet. "I don't know what to do with it. I don't know what to do about any of it."

I let out my own exasperated sigh. It was all too much. Had the blessing of our new house turned into a curse? And, if so, why? What had either of us done to bring it on? I shook my head incessantly and tossed about the fringe of my curls so that they whipped the skin on my face like lashing tongues. It was just painful enough to be sobering. "Brian, get up. Just get up off the floor," I said, tired of his submissive and subverted display.

He did my bidding and stood in front of me mentally battered but not really that much worse for wear. The aging and the bitterness, it was temporary. It would wear off.

"Is there anything else down here that I should know about?"

He shook his head. "I don't know. Other than the stuff I already brought down in boxes, I have no idea what else might be down here," he confessed his ignorance.

I did a quick one hundred and eighty degree pivot. "Great," I said sarcastically.

I let out a long breath as though I were about to walk a tight rope. My nerves were frayed to the extent that I felt completely frazzled, but compared to Brian I was holding it together better. It felt ironic to admit that, as he had been the stable one throughout our entire marriage. Even before the auto accident and the condition I found myself in after, Brian had been the strong, assertive, and stable one. He was the one providing the bulk of the household support, in every conceivable way. I only brought what I absolutely had to in a slovenly attempt to make the best out of what was an admittedly bland situation. My life had been lackluster because I had allowed it to become that, and I had blamed Brian for it. Brian, as was instinctual for him, bore the load. He was not without fault, but he was with unfathomable resilience.

It was my turn in that basement and in that position to do what I could, even with the bullet wound of Amelia still weeping a spiritual blood. It was in the basement of

#18 that night that the roles started to reverse, or at least reverse enough to give some semblance of balance.

"Well, I guess we ought to see what else is down here. I'm not sure we can take any more surprises popping up," I reasoned.

"I'll get a flashlight," Brian offered and bolted out of the basement with the speed of a hare.

Gee, I hope he comes back.

Not that I would've blamed him if he hadn't, as not only did the basement give off an unpleasant smell, but there settled in it was a peculiar cold, a cold that was no mere matter of degrees Fahrenheit. It was more of a draining of warmth from the vitality of the living. I shivered against it as a visceral reaction. But, soon enough he did come back, and he came just as rapidly as he left. Brian had the common sense to bring with him two flashlights; although they were so old they must have been in storage since we left the first house we lived in on the corner lot. It was a miracle that they worked.

"I put them in the junk drawer in the kitchen," Brian reported, an unnecessary and all too regular tidbit of information given the circumstances.

I turned my flashlight on and began to explore the main area I was standing in. Familiar boxes from the move and previous storage made their way into my inquisitive beam immediately, followed by my walker that was already growing dusty from disuse. I made my way back through an archway to an area that must've run under both the dining room and the kitchen, as Brian went off through the archway to explore the space that sat underneath the rest of the main hall. There I found nothing out of what may be the ordinary — empty shelving in some spots and shelves filled with very old canning and clutter in others. I also discovered a tarp covering several paintings that more than likely belonged to a previous owner. I didn't even bother with examining the subjects on the canvases and covered them back up without expending any extraneous energy. The space I followed then veered off to the left in an L-shape and went under the sunken den, my favorite spot. The basement ceiling naturally lowered a little to compensate for the flooring. The den had truly taken on my vibratory patterns, and the claim I staked had been fulfilled as the weeks passed.

Following the layout all the way back, I arrived at the far wall to be greeted by the sheen of colored leather, the rough ridges of rubber, and a glint of metal. Waiting for me in the darkest recesses of the basement, right under the den, was the wheelchair. I stared in horror at my old confines. The wear patterns on the wheels and the blue tinge of the leather were unmistakable, and I couldn't take my eyes off it. Part of me wanted to tear it to pieces with sharp claws that I did not possess, while at the same time another part of me wanted to pretend I'd never seen it.

If I don't see it, it can't hurt me. If I switch out the light it will fade into the darkness and become the past. It will dissolve.

But, that was ludicrous. Even as I tried it with the simple flick of a switch, I was positive it would not be so easily dissuaded. When the beam came back on, the chair was there waiting.

"Did you find anything?" Brian asked as he made the left turn to meet me where I stood. I heard him stop dead in his tracks and watched as the beam of his flashlight danced uneasily about my own.

"You took this away. I remember," I told him, and hoped for confirmation.

"Yeah, I donated it back to the hospital several months ago," he corroborated.

The Silence between us merged with the encroaching blackness so that we were cloaked in our own unwavering inner hysteria pressed outwards. Two words finally surface in summation, "Oh shit," I murmured. I didn't want anything to do with any of it. The wheelchair, the walker, Fido, Brian's unmentionable card... it was all a heinous collage of a manifestation that highlighted the uglier portions of my life, aspects that should've had the decency to remain buried. And, it might've been that what resided in the basement would never entirely go away no matter how hard we tried to expunge it, but we did have another option. "Let's lock this place up."

"Huh?" Brian's brain was slower on the uptake than mine in that insidious space.

"Let's lock the basement up tight, and keep it locked."

"For how long?" Pragmatism was returning in a glimmer.

"Forever."

Brian shook his head back and forth and gave an odd and off kilter grin. "That's crazy."

"Why? Why is it crazy? Just because this stuff is down here doesn't mean we have to see it. We don't have to torture ourselves with it," I said steadfastly and in the deliriously determined spirit of self-defense.

"I think we should move," he concluded.

"Move where? Back to the apartment?" I spoke out in shrill alarm.

"No, I'm sure that's already gone. It was rent controlled." Logical. I watched as Brian attempted to enforce logic in a space that had never known it, that existed outside of it.

"Then move where, Brian?" I pressed mercilessly. "Can we even afford to move? This place won't be easy to sell."

It wasn't easy to sell when we bought it.

I felt like such a fool. I should've asked more questions and done so sooner instead of wallowing in my own misery at the time. I should've put up more of a fight, or at the very least more of an initial investigation.

I should have sensed this coming.

Brian ran fingers through his hair until it stood on end. That style looked far more natural for the basement dwelling. Add it in with the dust and dirt on his otherwise immaculately normal clothes, and he was the embodiment of the angst found in that place. "I guess we can move in with your folks until we do manage to sell this place." An olive branch offering of a possible solution.

"Forget it! That is not an option," I dismissed.

"But, Sally – "

"Forget it, Brian! Hell no!" I fought.

"Why not?" He weakly fought back.

Because of what it will do to me. Because if I leave here I might once again wither into that dreadful husk of a person that I was before. Because Annabelle is next door and my parents are a whole blessed hour away. Because I can't even imagine being near my mother now that she's slept with Reggie.

"Because I'm not ready!"

"Ready for what?"

"I'm not leaving." It was more than defiance. It was determination within the solid utterance of my words. "We are not leaving." I turned and made my way back to the main area of the basement, where I could at least see the steps leading up and knew there was an easy way out. "There is nothing wrong with this house that the click of a lock can't fix," I told him as we gathered more safely near the steps.

Brian held disbelief in his eyes. Whether or not he refused to believe in me, the solution, or both was not readily apparent, but in the end it didn't seem to matter. It was my chore now to make him believe.

"Oh, Brian," I sighed, "we came here to make our lives better. I want things to continue to grow between us, and I want to continue to get better, too. I can't do that back in the city, and you were right all along when you tried to convince me of it. And, nothing will ever get better for either of us if we live with my parents, no matter how short-lived that arrangement might turn out to be." I brought my body in close to his. If logic and rationale couldn't persuade him, perhaps the promise of sex could. "Please," I moaned ever so softly in his ear. "You gave this house to me. Don't take it away now."

Brian wrapped me in his arms and held me tight, so tight the constriction made it a tad bit difficult to breathe properly, but I suffered thorough and let him have his ensnaring embrace. "Ok," he conceded, "ok. I guess we can just lock the door for now. There really isn't anything down here that we're going to need access to any time soon."

But, there was. I'd seen it in passing as I made my way through my half of the basement. It was a box that Brian hadn't even considered bringing up into the main portion of the house and mingling in with all the others. It was *the* box in my mind. It was the box that held countless camis and dress tops, skirts of varying lengths, dress slacks, tight jeans, and the rare item made from spandex. Some of the lingerie I'd bought myself a long time ago was also in there, along with my favorite pair of shameless and salacious red snakeskin stilettos. In that box, innocuous box #5, were all the things I'd once promised myself I would become but then relinquished to life's fervent and inescapable pull, to the time and the tides. It was time to reclaim the flow from the ebb.

"Actually," I said and pulled back slightly, "there is one thing I'd like to take back up with us before we do this." I escorted Brian over to box #5 that sat against the far outside wall and pointed. "That one."

Brian handed off his flashlight and proceeded to pry open the top flaps of the box to have a peek inside. He reached in and retrieved the stilettos that had been set ever so lovingly on top, and turned to hold them up. "I don't think you've ever worn these for me."

"Haul that box upstairs, and we'll see what happens." With a wink and a nod between us, we both brushed off the shock and the horror that had come before and decided to plow through. It was easier at that point in time to move on and lock the door, thinking that nothing would ever come of what rested beneath our feet every single day.

Sex can be a healing balm, a powerful weapon, or an amazing distraction. And, then there are those fleeting and finite instances when it is all of those things rolled into an alluring and elusive whirlwind of an encounter. Perhaps that was why I longed to return to my finest physical form all those years. Did I sense the loss of power and prominence? Was it more than healing and wellness related? I was starting to suspect I had deeply desired to make use of the power I wielded over Brian and Annabelle. I donned my red snakeskin stilettos for Brian and chose to wear nothing else with them, letting him have his way with me on the bed that was still mussed from my romp with

Annabelle. I felt alive and artificially enhanced in those shoes. They made me feel like someone else. They made me feel glamorous and glorious and beyond the comprehension of a mortal man's mind. I relished the sensation. The spirit of who I once was almost revivified me. I longed to become her again, to let the lioness loose from her familiar and self-imposed den, for there was nothing to stop me from becoming what I had shoved aside.

Once Brian was sated and the contents of my box were unpacked and neatly placed in drawers and closets, I brought up Annabelle. And, shortly thereafter, I brought up Reggie. My situation with Annabelle I recounted in great and beguiling detail. All I had to say about Reggie was, "I think he'd let therapy go on indefinitely, whether I need it or not. He needs the money and I understand how that's a prime motivation. But, I don't need the therapy anymore, and I don't want it. It'll be hard for him to hear, and it may be worse coming from me. Will you tell him?"

I kept the scandalous acts of my mother and Reggie, and the role that played in my pleadings, from my husband. I feared that the icing of that information on our massively layered and not always appealing cake would be too much to digest. Brian was capable of putting up with a lot, but the limits had been stretched practically every day since we had moved into #18. It made me uncertain as to where the boundary would be for him, where he held his own event horizon, his breaking point. Brian could be decisive, despite the fact that there were long intervals of time where he let me forget and have my way. The move itself was proof of his ability to take action. There was no way to tell him about it all that would make the information more palatable. The news that my mother had slept with Reggie only to have Reggie then turn around and want to sleep with me was reprehensible at best, and at worst the product of a diseased mind and derelict soul.

Mine or Reggie's?

The fact that I was caught up in the vortex, that I was to be found in an unwieldy center, did not reflect well on me either. It was best to keep the skeletons in their closets. It was best to click as many locks into place as I could, or so

I was prone to thinking. However, out of sight and out of mind does not also mean out of reach.

"I'll give him a call from the office tomorrow and cancel your future sessions. If we need him again, we can make a new schedule at a later date," Brian accepted and began his reasonable plans for execution the next day. "I'm sure he'll handle it well, even if he doesn't like it."

"Thanks," I relaxed back into his arms as we kept the bed and each other warm. The drain that we both experienced from the basement was slowly wearing off. I was quickly enlivening once more within the walls and energetic patterns of my bedchamber. "It would be so awkward for me if I had to tell him."

"That's understandable," Brian soothed, and with that I had fooled myself into thinking all of the pieces were in place for the ugly and uncomfortable to be shut away from my life. I was resolved to make the attempt at normalcy, at least until I had tea with my mother on Friday.

I knew almost immediately when Brian must've called Reggie because it was early that next afternoon when my phone started blowing up with text messages and voicemails. I knew it was Reggie calling before I ever glanced at the caller ID, and for that very reason I never answered and promptly deleted the voicemails without listening and the texts with only a small peek at them. I figured I could handle looking at texts without feeling compelled, as there was something about both text and email that provided a natural barrier between communicators, most likely why they were my favorite forms of communication with the outside word.

The texts were overtly typical and astonishingly shocking all at once, given the massive mess of a situation lying right in front of me, and the manipulative mess of a man that I'd been dealing with. He'd hidden it well for quite a time, but I knew what kind of man it really was that lurked behind the curtain. Still, I was given to random bouts of surprise when I attempted to bestow the benefit of the doubt. What was most alarming about the texts was the blatant loss of control and emotional outpouring.

Who is this person? This can't be Reggie.

It wasn't the Reggie I'd thought I knew for a span of just under three years. Had he been this person all along? Had he always danced along the precipice of instability and simply masked it with persuasion?

Of course. The mask has been ripped off recently. That's all there is to it.

Even without the benefit of body language and vocal queues, I could feel and grasp the desperation in his tightly typed texts. And, even though I loathed myself for it, I was a little turned on.

'Please, don't do this,' was the first message I received. It was followed shortly thereafter by, 'I'm really sorry for doing this to you' and 'I know there can be more for us.' I finally turned my phone off after reading, 'I think I love you.'

That was too far; so far that it killed my sexual buzz, the only good thing about the entire scenario.

I wanted to scream at my phone, 'No, you don't!' I wanted to type back in a harsh roar of a response, 'Stop it!' But, I didn't do either of those things. It was maddening to hold it in beyond that point. For a little less than three years, I had fantasized about Reggie with his fit form and strawberry blonde hair, toyed with the concept of the two of us and played with the outcomes in my mind. But, it had only been engaging to me when the entire prospect didn't seem real, or at the utmost, secret and in no way permanent. Having him declare such feelings for me and act out in the way that he did only served to freak me out. It wasn't hot and sexy and forbidden. It was frightening and a complete cluster-fuck.

Be careful what you wish for...

I wanted to ask how long he'd been having an affair with my mother. I wanted to inquire as to how long he'd thought himself to be in love with me. But, those were questions that would have to go unanswered, because I felt so strongly that if I responded to him in that heightened state, it would've only made things worse. Of course, quite often things get worse on their very own. It doesn't take interference; it takes time and consistent pressure.

I didn't visit the willow in the front cul-de-sac for meditation for a couple of days as the rains continued steadily, and my mood was as chilled and damp as the weather. I'd attempted to read only to find myself interrupted over and over by my own thoughts and outer disturbances.

Annabelle had knocked on the door one morning right around the middle of the week, but I refused to answer even that tempting treat. I let her stand on the front porch with dear degrading Silence for over an hour, as she would sporadically try both the bell and then subsequent knocking. And, then I watched as she left looking dejected. I told myself that it wasn't that I wanted to hurt her. I tried to convince myself that I was just too unpleasant to be around company. But somewhere deep down, I knew that in her pangs of disillusionment I took a sick delight. If she hurt then I seemed to hurt less. If I inflicted pain on her, then it seemed as though my pain eased, albeit temporarily. After some time spent thinking on all these things, I'd resolved to speak with her the following day and patch it all up, soothe the mental wounds that my Silence and obvious ignoring had caused.

Later that same day, *Lost Horizon* had been shoved onto a shelf in the den. I'd gotten bored with it for the first time in my life and sighed wistfully as I stuffed it between a couple of books the previous owners had left. I didn't seem well suited for it all of a sudden, as the plot and the play out were a little too beautiful and a touch too perfect. The simplicity and the harmony between those pages were at loggerheads with the reality that had charged into my life.

As I'd scanned the shelves that were full to overflowing, in the hopes of reading again uninterrupted, it seemed that nothing sounded good. I felt like I'd been doomed to listen and watch the rain as my singular form of amusement. Nothing seemed to delight my soul as the pressures from outside were building. I couldn't get the thoughts of that wheelchair out of my mind, and was tempted on more than one occasion to go down those steps and see if it remained in its dark abode. But, fear created a barrier before the lock.

Brian bought a latch, screws, and a discretely sized padlock on his way home from the office the night before, but hadn't yet installed it. That was on his to do list for after dinner. I also couldn't get the thoughts of Reggie and my mother out of my mind either, and I'd tried hard. I hadn't heard from my mother since the Friday after Thanksgiving, and if she had tried to call, my phone was off. Of course, she could have reached Brian if she were all that concerned, so obviously she wasn't.

I was alone, isolated, and dejected, much like Annabelle. And, I thought boredom would finally have its way with me when my eyes spotted the thick black spine of a book that would hold my interest. The title jumped out at me with its impressive gold lettering. *Edgar Allan Poe: Complete Tales & Poems.* That was much closer in vibe to my murky mood and provided mild entertainment on a rainy day.

The tense boredom from the middle of the week came to a turbulent end by Friday. And, it wasn't just because of my mother, but also because of the house. Brian had installed the basic lock for the basement door and tossed the key into the junk drawer, thinking that would be the end of all our strangeness, but the mild alteration made way for larger changes.

It rained the whole rest of the week as November began to morph into December, keeping me from my usual self-imposed outdoor appointments, the markers of chronological time in my day, although I had a growing difficulty of marking the days of the week. I began to rely partially on Brian's work schedule and mostly on Friday teas to give me a halfway decent estimate. I had started to learn in those detrimental and drenching days that I didn't like my routine messed with, and had also discovered that I'd actually created one in the first place. My mornings spent outside and under the branches of the willow were sort of like a silent ritual of awareness, a vigil I held over my house and the court in the nurturing morning light. But, the weather was cold and growing colder, and the rains, although gentle and soaking, were also bitterly biting.

I was lonely and only partially absorbed in my new readings. With Brian's work schedule at a fever pitch, he worked as much when he was home as he probably did at the office. Annabelle didn't make another attempt that week to see me, and the few times I did decide to turn my phone on, I wound up having to turn it off shortly thereafter due to the texts. 'Don't make me do this,' one had warned ominously, and I couldn't even imagine what that might refer to. 'Sally, I love you,' declared another with such heat and reverence that I could hardly bare to see it. It resonated within me and struck a chord of truth I definitely wasn't ready to deal with. I hadn't known how to block a number and although I'd made a mental note to ask Brian, I never got around to it. That question might have led to a lot of other and more embarrassing questions. Besides, there was something addictive about being intensely present in another person's heart and mind. It was becoming strangely and privately intoxicating to know that I could have that kind of effect on someone else, chords aside. I held in my devoted pantheon of followers Brian, Annabelle, and Reggie. It was more than I ever dreamed I'd have. It's an appalling admission to be sure, but I can admit that now, again an olive branch of honesty.

By Friday morning, I think I had gone officially stir crazy, even with poetic Poe as a current read. I looked out my kitchen window at the backyard as the rain pelted against the glass. Trees were rapidly losing what was left of their leaves, and the hardier ground cover was also beginning to turn brown with surrender. It was a dismal view of a world going inward, of a land going to sleep under the knell of impending hibernation. I walked through the kitchen and into the dining room to peer out the front window at the court. I could see the dead foliage in my front yard and the skeletal apparition of the willow across from it. In its raw starkness, the willow held even more power; it drew my eye ever stronger to it until I wasn't sure I'd be able to walk away. Like I had once yearned for my red snakeskin stiletto shoes, I yearned for that willow. I yearned for it more. But, the sky kept getting darker until it seemed that all the morning light was gone, and I did finally get myself to move on and into the hall.

I glanced at the shiny new lock Brian had put into place on the basement door as I made my way towards the stairs. It winked at me with its pristine stainless steel surface. Petite and powerful, the lock held the unkeepable promise of keeping everything in its place. I made my way to the second floor, not knowing why I was doing laps around the house. I suppose I was searching for something to do, some sort of project or fun proposal to jump out at me. One did.

I caught a glimpse of the stairs leading up to the third floor out of the corner of my eye.

That's right. I've been meaning to go up there.

Other than when Brian and I had taken that tour of the house together with Ella, I'd never seen the third floor space. I had no idea what was up there now that we'd been unpacked for a good two months. Had Brian taken anything up there for storage? Or did the space remain as vacant and ready for decorating decisions as it had been upon initial inspection?

I made my way up the steps, anxious to see it and feeling increasingly elated with each step that brought me closer. What little light there was from the foreboding sky poured through the massive cucumber-framed art window. The window seemed bigger than I remembered and gave a sort of heavenly quality to the space, as though it existed ethereally amidst the clouds. And, despite the fact that I was looking out through the window from the last step, the window seemed to be looking back at me like a giant universal eye. The exchange was so pleasing that I allowed myself to be absorbed in it for an indeterminable amount of time.

My hand had a mind of its own though, which acted unilaterally now and then. Prior to the trip to the third floor studio, unilateral decision-making tended to happen around Brian, and in response to my hidden and not so hidden affections for him. Now, it was simply happening. I found a light switch I hadn't known was there and flipped it on. The bright overhead light flooded the room and transformed the large window into a mirror. I saw a reflection of myself clad in the eggshell white raiment I'd chosen that morning against a rough outline of a cloud-covered sky. I appeared as an angel in my gingham skirt and peasant top. But, did I deserve heaven? If nothing else, I deserved the clothes and shoes that had once been in box #5.

I wasn't sure I was worthy of the miracle I'd found. An easel had been set up to the right hand side of the window with a fresh canvas and was situated to catch most of the natural light throughout the span of a day. There were shelves with paints and paintbrushes, various adhesives, and jars full of mixed media possibilities; there were neatly stacked sketchpads and an assortment of pens, pencils, and charcoal. To my left hand side, and taking up half of the entire space, was all of my old movement arts equipment, meager as it was. It was a compilation of scraps compared to all I once owned for my professional studio. But, what I still had available to me had been cleaned and positioned to provide a warm welcome. Two bright green yoga mats with matching blocks caught my eye first, and then I adjusted to see the creamy yoga straps and pale white, translucent stability ball that I'd bought when I'd the inkling of larger endeavors. Foam rollers, sculpting balls, and toning rings of all colors hung from hooks on walls and sat on shelves just waiting to be used again. It wasn't much, only perfection.

It was more than I had ever hoped to have again in my life. And, I figured Brian must've had the foresight to set up all of my old equipment, knowing I would gravitate towards it when I was ready.

Am I ready?

I walked around the area, gliding my hands over smooth and stable surfaces, touching tentatively the items that had been given a proper place so lovingly. It was everything to me, and it was all I ever have been or could be.

It's not a professional endeavor. It's more. It's me.

The doorbell rang, breaking the scene and tearing me away from my reverie. There was no clock anywhere on the third floor, and I hadn't brought my cell phone with me, so I'd had absolutely no idea what time it was. More than likely it was my mother, and it was time for tea.

But, what if it's Reggie?

That thought stopped me dead in my tracks and kept me from going directly downstairs to answer it. Instead, I made my way over to the cucumber-framed art window and looked down, which was not useful at all considering my porch was covered and there was no way to tell who was on it. I did manage to make out the shape of a car in the driveway. Due to the darkness outside and the reflective surface of the window, I had to assume it was my mother's. She would've brought her own car, as she did almost every week, and not my dad's sport utility vehicle. So, at least I knew what I should be looking for. She was as much a creature of habit as Brian was, and as I used to be, sort of.

The car looked similar enough to allay any additional fears. But, once the fear subsided, the anger began to emerge. The doorbell rang again and was followed by knocking, yet I remained frozen in place. I didn't want to leave the harmony of what was certainly my new studio, and I didn't want to deal with her. I also didn't care for the sensation of holding a hot poker in my guts as my anger grew to fury.

After several minutes and once the front door had gone quiet, I began to make my way downstairs. I left my studio to sit and wait for a more opportune moment with me. I couldn't leave my own mother outside in the rains forever, even if she did stand under a covered porch. And, I also couldn't avoid the inevitable conversation we were to have, even if it was temporarily easier not to have it. I held a glimmer of hope that the willful yet superficially concerned Jeanna Dougherty would see to reason and return to an appropriate and presentable life, that she would be sorry for her actions and act as she should.

By the time I reached the front porch, there was no one there. I opened the door to welcome winds and rains. I shivered against the chilling onslaught of the coming cold and soon to be winter season. Stepping out onto the porch, I looked to my left. It was definitely my mother's car, but she wasn't in it, nor was she on the porch. It was when I looked over my shoulder and to my right that I found her. She was standing on my neighbor's porch, on Annabelle's porch. Only she wasn't talking to Annabelle. I saw the unforgettable and unforgiving outline of Dr. Gregory Taylor, the man who smelled of cheap candy and cigars, a sickly sweet stench. I felt myself bristle at the mere sight of him. And, as my mother continued her shameless and hapless fawning from Thanksgiving, my hackles rose and a predator's unrelenting territoriality churned within me. This man was a predator of some sort, too, and I knew it instinctively. Not only that, but based on his daughter's bruises and his obsession with my mother, he was the worst kind. And, he was hunting on my grounds, which was an unforgivable breach.

"Mom!" I called out, but she didn't seem to hear me. My cry was covered by the sounds of rain hitting an overhang. I raced down the steps and half way across the front lawn. "Mom!" I yelled again and with more vigor, adding in an arm wave. I let the rains beat against me, cooling my internal heat by a few degrees.

Dr. Gregory Taylor just smiled and waved back all too knowingly, which caused my mother to turn her head and acknowledge my existence. I saw her lean in and whisper to him before departing and joining me as she should, and as we both sought the shelter of my home.

"These rains are becoming a bit much," my mother complained, as she stepped into the main hall and I shut the door behind us.

"That's not all that's a bit much," I murmured so low that she didn't register my disapproval. Or if she did, she'd chosen to ignore it.

I didn't help her with her coat and instead walked through the dining room to the kitchen, where I immediately put on a kettle out of habit and the need for random activity. My mother wasn't as quick on her feet, for she must have sensed that something about me was out of the ordinary, something about the both of us and between the both of us was amiss, askew. Many minutes raced by as my heart beat to a gallop within the confines of my ribcage, before I felt her break the plane of the room.

"Need any help?" she inquired, but it was only to attempt a comforting conversation, a litmus test to see where I was on her gradient scale.

I'm absolutely acidic.

I was in no mood to give her comfort or to play her games. "Just have a seat," I said way more abruptly than I'd intended. I'd really meant to ease into things as this was not going to be easy on anyone, and if I was to keep this from both Brian and my father, I'd need her cooperation.

When did my life get this jacked up?

It was shocking that my mother complied with my command.

Cooperation or no, I still want to strike at her, and she knows.

Of course she knew. How could she not? It was more than likely that Reggie had called her, too. In his emotional outpourings and total loss of control over the past few days, he probably didn't have the good sense to keep his mouth shut. He'd acted like a wild animal caught in a trap, lashing out and spewing sounds, thrashing at his prison and source of pain, only to make matters worse. I'd have pitied him if I weren't so busy hating them both.

Silence, my tormentor and taskmaster, bit his whip into her and me, as I stood in quiet condemnation and stared. I could take it. I was used to the hush and the hardships. She needed to be the one to speak first, to break under the pressure of Silence, to seek out my words and my replies. It took much longer than I'd imagined.

"What's this all about, Sally?" she questioned in a stern tone as the kettle on the stove had begun to whistle at me for release. I shut the flame off and moved the kettle to a cool burner.

Pressed by years of childhood habits, I responded to her out of obedience and instinct. I was like a Pavlovian dog answering a bell, but my words were my own at least. "I would give anything to not have this conversation."

My mother waved her hand in dismissal. "Oh, don't be so dramatic."

"Why not? It seems to me that you like drama in your life." I'd found a hard and witty rejoinder.

"And, just what is that supposed to mean?" she feigned innocence, letting the process go on for longer than it should. It felt as though our relationship had hit an all-time low, and as it sank to the bottom, it knotted in a nauseating pit in my stomach.

"I know about you and Reggie," it sounded like a threat, and I'd been so grateful it came out that way. Deep down, I realize now that I'd meant it as a one. It was a blow to her character and a death strike I would have had no trouble delivering by spilling it all to my father if she forced my hand, not that I wanted to, for I understood then that there is no way to spill blood without getting splashes of it on yourself.

Silence.

"And, as if that weren't sickening enough, now you're throwing yourself at my neighbor!" The cork was out of the bottle then. "What the fuck is wrong with you?!"

My mother rose to full height and made a physical display that reminded me of the disciplinary measures of my early years. "Watch your mouth," she hissed, her voice trembling only slightly, but enough that it was noticeable. "How dare you even presume that you know anything at all?!" She was beyond her mask of composure in a split second. The mask had shattered and lay in ruins at our feet, and Reggie was the hammer. "You think I wanted my life to become like this? Do you?!"

I'd made attempts to swallow the growing lump in my throat that had migrated up from my stomach, to no avail. It was all too raw and real. Would I eventually vomit the cancerous hate that sat inside me? The sickness that had consumed me for Reggie, and that I had basked in, and that now included my mother?

"How could you do this to dad?" I asked softly, a hurt tone slipping in with the mixture of disillusionment and barely restrained disgust.

My mother looked at me in reproach and then gave a bitter smile. "I didn't do this to your father. He's done this to me. He doesn't care about me or about the things I do. He cares about how it appears. And, after years of trying to find some meaning and some purpose, I've had to go outside the bounds. And, now that Reggie has left me, too, I'm looking for companionship... Sally, I don't deserve to be alone – "

"Look elsewhere," I said mercilessly. "I don't want to see or know about any of it. And, I don't want Brian to ever know either."

"Is that all you can think about? Yourself? You are so hateful!" She stopped half way across the kitchen as though I had placed an invisible wall between us, built it with my seething hostility as the mortar.

"You've made a colossal mess! You've fucked up my life!" I bit back at her.

"You fucked up mine!" she shouted in a grandiose release, coming to her greatest expression of truth. It had to have been a feeling that existed within her from the very start.

I was catapulted in memory back to my childhood, back to a single capsule trapped in time. And, as my mother railed on, whether in apology or continuity, I hadn't been able to hear her. I was ravaged by a sensation of neglect and of loneliness.

I don't deserve to be alone.

Her words and somehow also mine. I remembered the end of a school day when I was in kindergarten. I could smell the autumn air and feel the exhilaration of the children around me as they ran to their bus or parents' car. It was time to go home at the end of the day. I stood under a large flagpole in the middle of the schoolyard and looked up, watching the colors billow in the breeze. I wanted to go home, too, and so I waited. I leaned against the cold metal of the pole and felt the temperature seep through the fabric of my jacket and shirt.

The buses all pulled out and away, one by one. Cars left the parking lot until it appeared as a field of fallen leaves, and I'd begun to cry. I wanted to go home.

"It's ok, Sally," I'd heard a voice from above me speak, and I looked into the face of my teacher. She had looked a lot like my own mother then, with her blonde hair and brilliant blue eyes, only her eyes were warm like summer skies, and I knew my own mother's would only look at me with a hint of slightly melted ice.

I'd wrapped my arms about her legs and squeezed tightly, and the tighter I squeezed the more my tears fell like rain.

I wanna go home.

Had I thought it or said it then? I couldn't be sure.

"Your mom is on her way," my teacher assured, but I didn't let her go. At some point I pulled my head from the fabric of her slacks and looked out at the lot of leaves, the field of forgetfulness, to see my mother's car, and her inside it. She had been staring at me, considering me. And, I knew in a second that the thoughts were not good ones. She'd been a young woman, and I was an anchor her family had asked her to bare. She had complied. The result was a sapping of energy, a perpetual drain that kept her from being what she might have become.

I'd known then, in that moment, I'd somehow wrecked my mother's life.

As I surfaced from my earliest memory of the pattern of neglect and then strict concern that was my childhood, I noticed my mother had left the kitchen and I stood alone in the room with a tepid teakettle. Upon further inspection, it was revealed that my mother wasn't even in the house. I stepped outside to see that her car was gone and the hour was late. Based on the low light in the sky that came from behind clouds, clouds that still gave us an unrelenting rain, Brian would be home soon.

The rains couldn't keep me at bay any longer, and with the time that I had left to myself, however long that may be, I approached the willow tree in the cul-de-sac. As I got close, stepping above the concrete curb to the grass, I saw just how much the bark had changed in only a few days. New and painfully revealing words were etched in its surface for the world to see. The words 'heaven' and 'hell' intersected each other like a T-square in a crossword puzzle, making them mutually dependent on the letter 'h.' They swirled in the mix of natural grooves and practically disappeared only to have the word 'lovers' grow off of an 'l.' Had I spun a web I didn't intend to weave by taking on a lover? Or were my mother's lovers my own personal hell? I couldn't believe I was thinking like that, thinking of those things, as I stood drenched to the skin in rain that showed no sign of letting up.

I worked my way around that unbiased tree, following spirals and scars that led to a cascade of ebony hair and the tufts of a russet mane. I saw the face of a cat, too. It was a very petite and sleek female calico. Perhaps the one that had wound its way about my legs and came to rest on the tops of my feet at Margaret's house?

Margaret knows more than she's letting on, more than she's willing to tell.

As I continued circling, my hand came to rest over the word 'doggie.' That word was etched even deeper now; it went into the tree so deeply that the red sap of the willow flowed freely. Mixing with the water that ran down its trunk from the frigid rains, the sap took on the color and consistency of blood, and that blood gushed through my fingers and down my arms. The word wept its victim's blood at me, for me, to me. And that blood was the same as my own, as the blood that began to weep freely from my heart. I cried because of a childhood wound that I'd then inflicted on my own daughter. My wound was her wound.

Did she weep now? Do the dead cry themselves to sleep?

I smeared the sap on myself, covering my arms, face, and neck. I longed for the guilt to be seen and for the freedom to come. It would be a freedom beyond what my body could offer. I felt feral and forgettable, just another wounded animal in a world full of so many. I kept going until I was entirely saturated, and then I placed my hands back on the tree to cover that word.

"Sonya," I breathed her name with all the air I had left in my frigid lungs.

It was then that a small sappy hand appeared and touched my own, resting there as though it belonged. Sonya stood beside me draped in the bright purple plaid of a dress I recalled from the accident. But, she was aged now and old enough that if she had been living I could have put her on a bus to go to school. She was drenched by rain and red plant sap.

"I wanna go home," she said plainly, unblinking in the rains and preternaturally still.

I knelt before her, meeting her on her own level. My hands touched her wet and matted ringlets, the cool skin of her cheeks as she stood there like any child would. She was completely at ease with the forlorn affection of her parent. Finally, I smiled at her through tears that were inseparable from the downpour. "Let's go home."

Chapter 6

Hearing the sound of my own daughter's feet running through the house and slapping against the hardwoods as she laughed and played was a joy beyond compare. I held that sound close to my heart, and I closed my eyes so that the sensory perception of hearing might be enhanced and I'd be able to commit the sound perfectly to memory. I wanted to remember all of it and to hold it in, never letting Sonya go again. My guilt was melting. As she ran all the way around the first floor, through the den, into the kitchen, and finally out the dining room to meet me in the hall, I rejoiced quietly.

I've brought us both home!

And, I was a fool.

Sonya stopped and stood unblinking before me, her hair and clothes immaculate and totally dry. It was impossible and beautiful as I stood there, rain-soaked and shivering. "Mommy," she called out to coax me from my inner adhesions.

I smiled down at her. "Yes, baby?"

"Can I go up to my room and play now?" It was such a natural request coming from an unnatural source.

Up to your room?

"Of course," I whispered, as a sound any louder from me would have elicited a spring of bittersweet and unchecked happiness. "But, first give me a hug."

I knelt down and she flowed into my arms, wrapping me in her cold and unbreathing embrace. I knew instinctively that I should feel the rhythmic inhale and exhale of her lungs, but I didn't. I had sensed then that everything was wrong with the scenario that played out before and all around me, but I shoved it aside in favor of my daughter's presence.

"I love you," I sighed into her ear.

Her tiny hands gripped me tight. "I love you, Mommy." And with that, she dashed up the steps to the second floor landing and disappeared. Shortly thereafter, I heard the ambivalent noise of her moving around. I walked as quietly as I could up the stairs so as not to disturb her play, and found her roaming Brian's office. She was playing with the familiar stuffed figure of Fido, only now he was spotless and as plush and lush as the day Brian had brought him home for her.

The white walls in the office seemed so out of place in that moment, and I'd made up my mind to paint them in the days to come. I would paint them with yellow and brown vertical stripes.

The remains of Friday and whatever became of Saturday eludes me. It is just one more lapse in a series of so many. Time seemed to become liquid around me, and the tighter I attempted to grasp it, on the few occasions it seemed pertinent to do so, the more the shrinking sands of that proverbial hourglass slipped through my fingers. I know Brian was home during that period, but he'd shown no discernable signs of awareness towards our ghostly occupant, and I let myself believe that Sonya's influence was over me alone. I do remember that it was late Sunday morning before the rains stopped. I'd spotted Sonya waiting for me in the kitchen as I came out of my den and my current read, looking for a drink of water.

"Will you take me outside to play?" she asked, the daylight from the window above the sink giving her curls a silken gleam with a hazy edge that could have been a halo.

"Sure," I said and reached for her hand to feel icy fingers clutch my own.

As we headed for the front door, she stopped me. "I want to play in the backyard."

I realized then that it was out of habit that I headed towards the willow in the cul-de-sac, and I'd actually spent no substantial of time in the backyard up until then.

"Oh," I said blankly. "Oh, ok." And, we headed for the kitchen door that led into my mostly sumptuous and only slightly barren backyard.

It makes more sense for a child to want to play back here.

The thick brown grass was still moist from the abundance of rain that we'd received, and the limbs of the trees were soaked so as to be a shade of dark brown that was almost black. They stood out vividly against the blue-gray skies. I sat on the steps and watched Sonya run around and then disappear amid a thicket of trees. There were oak, maple, and even a willow in my backyard, most of them acting as a wall against the far fence line.

"Stay close," I called out to my daughter and heard only the mischievous sound of her laughter as assurance. After a few carefree moments, I saw something moving ever so faintly out of the corner of my eye and off to my left. I turned to see an outline emerge. It was Annabelle. I quickly got to my feet and waved cordially.

Annabelle with her long raven's mane and loose fitting clothes made her way across my lawn to stand before me, although not too near I noticed.

"Hello," I started for the both of us, bridging the gap. "Isn't it nice to see some sun again?" I let my rhetorical question hang there as she collected her thoughts and emotions.

"I came by a few days ago," she insisted, refusing to let the recent past rest.

I felt myself give a sympathetic head tilt and I softened my expression. "I know. I'm sorry. I've been out of sorts." I'm still not sure why being vague was the best I could do.

"Is it because of me?... Because of what we did?" she carefully inquired, looking down at her feet and the dead grass all around them.

I reached out and stroked her hair gingerly. "Certainly not," I cooed.

What is it about Annabelle that makes me both predatory and docile all at once?

She took a couple of steps towards me to the point where I was warmed by her body heat. "I guess I just thought it might be."

"Shhh..." I stilled her and brought a finger to her lips as my body closed what little space was still between us. The fabric of my form-fitting coral cashmere sweater made a dance of friction happen along the surface of her satin top.

"I've missed you," I confessed, even though I found a part of my mind flitting off in mental search of my child.

Annabelle's black eyes held glowing embers as her gaze locked onto my own. "I've missed you, too." Her cautious and capable energy nudged me towards the back door and instinctually made me want to draw her up to my bedroom. Then my rational side kicked in, and it reminded me that Brian was working from home and was up in the studio. At best we would disturb him and at worst he would interfere before either of us was ready for him to do so.

"Wait," I said starkly as she started to follow me up the back steps. "I'm not alone today," I'd informed her.

"Oh," was all she had to come back with, aside from backing away slowly as though she'd done something wrong and was about to be punished.

"It's all right. It's just that I don't want to disturb Brian. He's working," I explained simply enough for her to take a step back in towards me.

I strode past her and well onto the lawn, a grassy carpet, before turning around to see her holding as still as a statue. I held my hand out and motioned for her to take it. "Come on," I said with a wink and a smile.

Annabelle took my hand and followed me into the swallowing tree line, our legs decadently rubbed by the soft surface of the lamb's ear that decorated the base. Although most of the branches were nearly bare, there was such a density to them and an interwoven quality that it was easy to become lost in the mass and the maze. I pulled her close for an indulgent kiss and then pressed her back against a solid oak tree so that I stood between her and the fence.

We met with insatiable voracity. Her lips against mine, our tongues intertwined, and our very souls intermingled. There was some indescribable quality about her that sank an undeniable hook into my sternum, and it caught about the bones. We writhed together like two wild animals amongst the tree limbs, and I heard before I felt my fingernails clawing at the bark of the sublime and supportive oak. I had been so caught up in her and the moment that I'd felt like I was going to chuff in appreciation. Her scent was heady with a light apple essence. She was earthy and yet sweet and I couldn't get enough of the taste in my mouth. Annabelle came to my aid, her hands guiding mine, as I slid her satin top off and over her head to set free her bare breasts. Her nipples became erect in the cool air, and I saw a shiver pass over her flesh that allowed it to take on goose bumps. It wasn't until I felt her hand slide down and into my skin tight black stretch pants that I tore myself away from the erotic ensnarement.

I laughed lightly at her sudden boldness and my willingness to let go. "Not now," I put the brakes on and eyed the temptation placed before me, if only to torture myself for the pain I had put her through the other day. But, then my eyes caught sight of something else amid her dewy beauty, and my torment increased a thousand fold. Annabelle's entire right arm was a mess of bruises, fresh and bright and blue with tinges of a highlighting purple around the edges where they'd just begun to heal. If looked at by an uneducated eye, they could almost pass for pretty in the way the color of them bloomed forth like exotic flowers. "Oh my god! Annabelle!" I exclaimed loudly and ran a hand gently along the surface of her arm.

Annabelle turned her head away and let me run my fingers over the surface of her damaged flesh again and again as I took it all in. "Don't say anything, ok?" she asked of me in a muted voice that sounded like the plea of a prisoner. I heard as well as felt the incessant beat of the raven's wings within her chest.

"What the hell do you mean don't say anything?" I challenged. "Annabelle, look at me." I touched the side of her face and brought her back around so that her eyes would engage with mine. "Annabelle, there's no way I'm letting this go on."

"There's nothing you can do about it," she resigned. "Please, Sally, don't make trouble. Don't make it worse. I really want us to be together, and if you say something..." Her voice trailed off and pleading in its place came her tears. "Please," she finally spoke again and then melted into my arms in a softly sobbing semi-solid heap.

I held her until she became quiet, and then I whispered into her ear. "Come over tomorrow. We'll have the house to ourselves, and we can sort all this out then." It was the best I could offer her under the circumstances.

Annabelle nodded in agreement and then the two of us began getting ourselves presentable for the world once more. After she flitted out from amid the trees and left me alone, I began to notice other things happening in the space we'd shared with our mutual tears and sighs.

I noticed my own claw marks in the bark first, and they were so fierce and forceful that if I hadn't known better I would've thought it to be the work of an animal, a large-scale predator. I ran my fingertips along the rough ridges I created in what seemed to be the oak's otherwise unblemished surface. But, as I stood there fantasizing about my mistress, an emblem began to appear beneath the scratches. 'OMW.'

I drew my fingers back slowly and brought my eyes in for closer examination. There was no doubt about it now, as pale marks emerged in the dark bark of the oak. 'OMW.'

Reggie.

I felt him to be so very near to me in that instant. The wind picked up enough to whip my hair about my face, and then I felt a warm breath tickle my ear in a word. The wind whispered to me, "Sally." It whispered my name, only in his voice.

Then as quickly and innocently as those letters surfaced, they dissolved and were absorbed back into the tree, leaving only my marks of territoriality and passion. I tried to shake it off and dismiss it as out of hand, but as more and more of the bizarre and unusual happened around me every day, the less able I had been to do so at each new occurrence.

The willow in the cul-de-sac.

My mind had gone there immediately. Would there be a change to its ever evolving and revealing bark?

"Sonya," I'd called for my daughter as normally as I could. "Sonya!" I called in a stern, matronly tone.

She seeped into my vision from between the trees.

I knelt in front of her. "Honey, I want you to stay in the yard. I've got to go out front for a minute and check on something. Ok?"

Sonya nodded and then dashed away from me again to happily wander through what was left of the late season foliage.

I made my way past the house and out to the front cul-de-sac, my mind a swirl of thoughts, and my feet barely touching the ground by the time I arrived at the willow. I searched the bark of the tree for manifestations, and there initially appeared to be nothing new. The word 'doggie' was still etched deeply, but the bleeding of the sap had stopped, and the wound seemed to heal over in some strange way. There were still tufts of a russet mane and the flow of ebony locks made apparent in the swirls along with the face of a familiar calico cat. Angry hands presented themselves only to the well-trained eye adept at looking, as they attempted to remain undiscovered in the natural grooves of the willow's surface.

It was just as I thought I'd head back to the house and my own yard that I happened to look down at my feet. And, it was then that I saw something etched at the base of the tree. The carving in the exposed root looked so very fresh. 'OMW.'

I sensed Sonya in the house often, more often than I actually saw her. I also heard her more than I saw her, but her essence was everywhere. The walls breathed for her still lungs, and the basement took to eliciting soft moans and occasional whimpers. I shrugged it off. I was fond of spending time with Sonya in my third floor studio space where we could look out the large art window and play with paints and sketch pads without having to be disturbed by what might be going on below us.

In losing track of my hours and then even whole days as a week managed to work its way past, I also had begun to lose track of Brian and the evolution of the willow tree. Brian had seemed to want to become enmeshed in his work. First, it was due to a couple of large software projects and then that quickly turned into a lifestyle.

When Brian was home, he was in his studio most times, and he didn't even seem to notice the changes going on in there as I'd painted the walls with vertical yellow and brown stripes. I'd also added plush throw pillows and a beanbag chair so that Sonya could feel it was her place as well as his. Whether Brian noticed her use of the space or not was a mystery to me at the time. As for the willow, I avoided it mostly because of the disturbing emergence of the letters 'OMW' and also because I'd gotten so wrapped up in the return of my child.

Annabelle had visited me the Monday following our lusty adventure in the trees and had persuaded me to let the situation with her father drop. I could recall that much due to the distinctness of our conversation. Of course, I had been in the mood to be persuaded that day. She either pretended or believed that he was trying to be a better man, and for my own sake as well as hers, I let her go on as I pretended to believe her. She'd said that they were trying to have a better relationship and that she wanted desperately to pursue that and to make him love her. As much as I doubted that was ever going to happen, I could see the love that was restrained in her eyes and held my tongue. I did warn her outright that if I ever caught him hitting her I would step in with no holding back, and she seemed both uncomfortable and partially comforted by that.

The rest of the week spun around like a top, and it wasn't until the weekend was upon me again that I realized I'd lost a sense of days, and even the time within each day, during the throng of my personal jubilee. I couldn't specifically demarcate where one ended and the other began. Some nights I dreamed and others I didn't. Had I even slept? At times I couldn't be sure, and I'm not positive even now. I can say that I was made all the more happy and then unnerved by the fact that my mother hadn't shown up for our regular Friday tea, which dawned on me at some point along the spectrum of the weekend. The peace and quiet were nice, but I was put off also by fears of what may lurk in corners of my life that I could not see. My cell phone was kept off both because I didn't want to know if Reggie was still calling and texting, and because I didn't want to be bothered by anyone during the day while I fornicated with

Annabelle and played and taught various arts and crafts to my dead child. I suppose I had just figured that if my mother or anyone else needed to reach me, they could do it through Brian.

It was all very odd and made to seem even more so as I reflect on it. I used to despise Brian for acting as my caretaker and gatekeeper, and then suddenly I found myself relishing having him in that role. It felt as though he kept the rational and day-to-day mundane world at bay while I was free to wander about a more ethereal realm.

At some early point in time during the week that followed, it had appeared things were settling down yet again, and I finally considered turning my phone back on. But, I have to admit that it was when things got quiet that I felt the most unsettled inside #18 and Willow Tree Court. Quiet and peace often preceded whole new levels of unearthing, evolution, chaos, and possible destruction.

I remembered having dreamt of my grandmother the night before, having found her in my house and in the periwinkle guest bedroom sitting on the edge of the bed. On each windowsill in that room she had arranged fresh and pungent lavender plants. On the bedside table she had a plate of rosemary bread and cinnamon sweet rolls. She looked at me as I entered and began to cry.

"Why are you crying?" I'd asked without vocalizing.

And, she responded in a warbled and watery voice that only my soul heard, "Why are you diminished? I have shown you so much, given so much. Why are you diminished?"

I reached out and took her hands in my own, kneeling before her and feeling as though I needed her forgiveness. I'd been so concerned at seeing her in such a state of unrest. "What do you mean?" I quizzed, but still I had no voice to recognize as Silence sat at the seat of my questioning.

"You have everything now and yet you throw it all away, you spend yourself on ventures and endeavors that have no future. You take from the living and give to the dead. The more I attempt to heal the more you wound yourself." And, then she wept so piteously and uncontrollably that I became lost in the rhythm of her anguish. It made me feel as if I were on a boat, being tossed back and forth by the rolling waves of the sea. "There should be nothing to distract you, and you are all the more distracted," she cried out to me and to the room.

As I held on to her hands, I noticed her arms aging and darkening, her skin hardening and twisting. Her fingers morphed into twigs, and I was thrown back and away as those twigs furiously grew green leaves. She continued to contort and transform until before me stood the image of the grand and great weeping willow in full glory, as though it were the middle of summer and from the front cul-de-sac, only it had taken up residence in my house and had crashed through the floors in a quest to find soil for its roots. As the limbs moved like animal appendages and reached out to drag me into what seemed a threatening embrace, I'd awakened in Brian's clutches and in our own bedroom.

I might have lost time and some memories of my waking moments during the course of a week. I might have lost nights to wakefulness mixed with dreams I couldn't recall when I did sleep. But, I could not shake the vivid imagery of that dream.

I had just finished making lunch for myself and playing with my daughter in the backyard when the doorbell rang. Our play sessions grew shorter and shorter like the days as the weather dropped into further degrees of cold. There was the lengthening of each night to contend with, and the entrenchment of the winter season. Soon it would be too cold to spend any measureable time outside. I motioned to Sonya to keep playing as I went into the house and made my way to the front door.

I threw the door open, not sure who might be standing there to find a tiny slip of a woman and her two young children. I could sense immediately that the children were hers. Perhaps it was the way they clutched at her hands or even the fact that all three shared the same unique brown eye color. That honey brown shade should have been warm and soothing, but instead, it held a chill and hinted at a tangled surface I couldn't quite appreciate. They looked up at me like screech owls from the branch of a low shrub, their ocular orbs immensely large. "Yes?" I asked sharply, sharper than I'd intended.

The woman smiled up at me, and I saw a tremor pass through her, maybe it was from the cold weather or maybe it was because something had moved inside her independent of her will. "I apologize for bothering you," she squeaked softly, a mousy voice for a mousy hoot owl being. "I'm Trina, and this is Sam and Mary," she introduced herself and her kids. "We used to live here, and I was hoping that you might allow us to take a tour of our former home."

I eyed her and her two children a little more thoroughly as I considered what she was saying. I'd had no intention of opening my world up any further than it already had been since the move, and yet there stood more people seeking entrance. They were all so very young, beautiful, and yet somehow sorrowful. They were frail and yet conversely enormous of spirit. I can recall feeling the sorrow emanating off of them. Perhaps it was broadcast through those amazing eyes that they all shared, or it might have been the pale pallor of their skins made even whiter by the cold. They were so chilled and so perfect that they might have been sad little porcelain statues placed on my front porch in very old-fashioned seasonal clothing, clothing that reminded me of black and white movies or an art nouveau picture postcard bringing season's greetings.

"Umm... sure. Come on in," I welcomed awkwardly and stood aside as Trina ushered her children forward and into the auspices of my abode. Shutting the door, I promptly turned and extended my hand. "I'm Sally Archer," I introduced.

"Catrina Casey, but please feel free to call me Trina. It's a pleasure," she said more formally, and took my warm hand into the grips of her cold one for a quick shake. "Thank you for allowing us into your home," she gushed through her intrinsic mellow quiet and gave me a tender albeit bittersweet smile.

"May I take your hats and coats?" I offered as normally as I could, considering the impromptu visit by strangers.

Trina shook her head and rubbed the shoulders of her children gently as they both stood very still and gazed up at me. "Oh, we won't be keeping you that long," she said. And then, something caught her eye. I saw her and her children both glance past me in unison. "Well, well," Trina spoke a touch louder, "Who is this?"

I turned to follow her line of sight, and saw my own daughter standing several feet away in the main hall.

They can see her?

I had never stopped to wonder if others would be able to see her the way Brian and I did. I knew Brian had spied her in days past, and he might have even been aware of her presence in the house more recently, although he'd never said anything. But, I had always assumed that other than the two of us, no one else would be able to see her. After all, even Annabelle had never acknowledged Sonya's existence. She belonged to Brian and I alone, so that made the assumption seem reasonable.

What about this place or anything that's happened here has been reasonable so far?

"Hello," Trina spoke as a kindly and unmothered mother to the child not hers.

Sonya just stared at her and her children, acting much shyer than I'd ever thought she'd grow up to be. I could sense that she wanted to go to the young, pretty, and sweet woman. I also knew as any mother would that she longed to play with other children. But, she was denying her natural inclinations, as natural as they could be for someone not living. "Oh, Sonya, don't be so silly," I corrected my child, acting as if there was nothing wrong with the entire situation. "Come here to me," I instructed.

Sonya complied with my wishes and wrapped herself tightly around my leg as she continued to peer out at our visitors with an uncertainty and wistful longing.

"This is my daughter, Sonya. I guess she's just a little shy around new people," I explained.

"Oh, that's all right, Sonya," Trina cooed. "Sam and Mary are a little shy too, and they are a few years older than you."

I stroked Sonya's curls reassuringly and then turned my attention back to my guests. "Would you like to see the house now?"

"Oh, yes. Thank you."

As I began to escort Trina and her two flawlessly behaved imps throughout the first floor, Sonya had made a mad dash for the upstairs landing to escape our alluring visitors and flow into the energetic web of the house. I knew her so well, our vibrational patterns synced like two close clocks, that I could tell she had made herself unobtainable. I walked the unexpected guests carefully throughout the dining room, kitchen, den and main hall, explaining all our new furnishings and their placements, how we'd felt about the house, and also our choice in holiday decorations. I tried very hard to keep it superficial and upbeat, in spite of the fact that my gut felt as though the situation warranted an entirely different reaction.

I, of course, walked right past the doors that led to the garage and the basement. There wasn't any way I'd take outsiders into those spaces, not knowing what to expect myself.

Trina said little and her children spoke not a word. As we made our way up to the second floor, she seemed content to just peek into each room briefly and then meet me back on the landing.

"The third floor is my art studio, and it really isn't a space to take the kids. I hope you don't think me rude for not inviting you up," I blocked as she made her way for the stairs.

That's my space, sacred space.

Trina took an obligatory step back and nodded. "Certainly. It's just so strange to see the house like this. Some of it is exactly the same while other facets have changed completely."

"Everyone decorates differently," I summed.

"Yes. That's obvious."

I led my guests back down the stairs to the first floor, elated that the impromptu tour was drawing to an end. As we all made our way towards the front door, Trina stopped short and spoke steadfastly. "What about the basement?"

"What about it?" I returned.

"Have you been down there since you've moved in?"

Her question had seemed both unusual and prying. "Yes, naturally. We use it for storage."

"What's down there?" she persisted.

I cocked my head to suggest that she couldn't be serious with a question like that, but Trina was not influenced by my body language. "Personal possessions. That's all," I shot her down.

"Have you made use of the garage? It's very large and can hold a good amount of items, and at least two vehicles." She hit on both sore spots with a precision that couldn't be purely coincidental.

I merely shook my head in response. That was all the answer she was going to get. I felt as though she was leading me along a predetermined course now, and I didn't like it. I didn't like being led in such a blind way, especially since I didn't know where this stranger intended to go.

I strode past Trina and her children with a strong sense of purpose, getting them out of my house. But, as I reached the door and placed my hand on the knob, a flash of memory hit me. Brian had said that the previous owners of #18 had died in the house and had passed away from purely natural causes. And, that little tidbit begged the question of when Trina and her children would have lived there. Prior to the previous owners? That seemed highly unlikely given the fact that she was in what appeared to be her mid to late twenties and her children were probably about six and eight years old, respectively.

"Excuse me," I turned away from the door to face my guests. "But, I'm curious. Just how long ago did you live here?" An inquiry of my own for her, a predetermined course, a straight line.

"Oh, it was a long time ago. And, time certainly does fly, does it not?" Trina asked as though she were presenting me with the riddle of the sphinx. She gave me an indecipherable smile and then ushered her children around and out the door, not waiting for my hospitality any longer.

I didn't even turn to say goodbye or to watch the three mousy owls leave.

When would they have lived here?

Eventually, a cold wind snapped me from my pondering, and I turned to shut the door. But, as I glanced outside, I caught sight of someone moving through the empty street. I stepped out on the front porch for a closer look. It was Cynthia. I remembered the sad and well-worn guest from my Thanksgiving gathering and waved to be polite. There had been something so genuine about her, so involved, that I felt drawn in by it. I hadn't been sure she'd seen me then, as she didn't wave back.

I couldn't get Trina and her children out of my mind. Their claims of having lived in the house didn't seem to fit with their ages or the order of events as I knew them.

Maybe there's a piece of information missing, something I'm not privy to.

Even after everything that had happened in that house and the surrounding area, I was still stubborn enough to insist upon rational explanations, when and if were available. I avoided the willow in the cul-de-sac following that visit and went to Brian to report what had happened while he'd been at the office. I'd found him consumed by work in his studio almost immediately after he'd gotten home.

"So, call Ella and ask. I'm sure she can explain everything. Maybe Trina is the daughter of the people that owned the house, and she and her children moved out after her parents died," Brian offered sensibly in response to my disturbing tale and my more disturbing spin on it. He didn't even turn to face me; he sat with his back towards me, face to computer screen, nose to the grindstone.

That makes sense, except that she said she'd lived here a long time ago. Not that the term isn't subjective...

I looked over to the beanbag chair in the opposite corner from where his desk stood sentinel to see Sonya sitting there with a dejected and agitated demeanor. She shook her head disapprovingly of his possible solution.

"I think I will call her. Something about it doesn't seem right," I replied resolutely.

Brian sighed and turned his chair around to actually face me. "What specifically doesn't seem right, Sally? I've gotten a lot of information about your feelings on it but nothing concrete about what may be wrong."

Eventually I felt my mouth gaping and shut it, before opening it again to blurt, "How can you say that? After some of the things we've seen – "

"No," Brian overrode me, a rare occasion. "No, I'm not going to go there. I'm not going to discuss it. Things have been fine ever since that door was locked, and I'm not revisiting any of it. Now, please, I have a lot of work." And, with that Brian stood to escort me out of the room, with Sonya dashing to make it out of there in front of me.

"But, Brian – "

What about Sonya?!

"Later," he said flatly, and closed the door with me staring at its smooth wooden sheen in disbelief.

I had underestimated Brian... yet again. That chosen blindness had definitely developed into a very bad habit over the years we'd been together. Just when I thought I'd had him and our relationship back under control, it slipped out of my grasp and went rogue, rogue in a very linear, logical, rational and sudden fashion.

I knew then that Brian had buried himself in his work, and wouldn't emerge again unless he was dramatically lured or horrendously shaken out of that deep and indulgent grave. In the morning I'd call Ella. That would either shake the dirt from around him with discoveries, or I'd use the shiny shovel of Annabelle as a lure. One way or another, he was going to get involved, he was going to pay attention.

The very moment Brian was out of the house the next morning, I grabbed my cell phone and made my way to his office to retrieve Ella's phone number. I hadn't slept well the night before. Tossing and turning, I was sure I'd kept Brian up half the night, too. There was an uneasy feeling in the house and in my own core, as if I were being invaded. I had dreams that shook me, and yet I couldn't recall their details upon awakening. I was as frail and brittle as the frozen branches of the trees outside. I shook with the onslaught of the winter that drew nigh and the solstice that would soon come and take much light from me.

It was ridiculous and perhaps pointless to drag Ella into my probably delusional charade that rode the border of mundane and magical, but still I dialed her digits and drug her in anyway.

I wasn't sure what I was asking for specifically, other than a history of ownership for the house, which was how I began the conversation, with that request.

"That shouldn't be so difficult to get together for you," Ella had said in her stylistically lyrical lilt. "Actually, with just a pinch of initiative on your part, you could dig the buyer, owner, and occupant histories up for yourself online. These types of records are readily available to the public."

I hadn't been quite sure how to take that remark, but I had certainly felt insulted. Ella was doing me a favor by putting it all together for me though, so I decided to play nice. "I'm sure I could, but if you could just help me. You know this area so well, and I'd appreciate your insights."

"Yes, of course, my dear. And, I must admit, you won't get the sort of detail from those online sites like what I can provide you with. I have files for each of the homes in your court, and a thorough knowledge of the history that can be made available for each one at a glance. However, some of the records are old and haven't been scanned into digital files." Ella was being both agreeable and off-putting, her usual temperament of warm and cool, cat and mouse. It was unnerving every time.

"Oh," I said hesitantly and then gave a gentle push, "well, could you make photocopies and mail me a packet? I'd be happy to send you a check for your time, trouble, and the postage?"

Ella laughed lightly into the phone and then replied with her characteristic cooing. "Oh, my dear, that is so unnecessary. I'll be more than happy to get that out in the mail by the end of the week. You should have it by the middle of next week at the latest."

"Thanks so much," I said, feeling both grateful and relieved, and not sure why I should feel either one of those things so strongly.

"It's a pleasure, and to be quite frank with you, I am thrilled that you have taken such a deep and abiding interest in the house. Have you had a chance to go to the third floor or basement yet?"

"I've done a bit of both of those things," I said vaguely.

"Ah, good," she approved. "You should get to know all aspects. And, how are things coming along?"

What things?

"Fine. Everything's fine," I spoke as lightly as I could, attempting to harmonize with her tone to mask my unsettled state.

"Very good. Well, I won't keep you then. Give my best to Brian." Then I heard the click of the call disconnecting.

With that disconnect came something else though, the knowledge that I had five new text messages.

No voicemails though. That's encouraging.

That was deceiving.

Every text was exactly the same and all sent within the span of the last day or so… 'OMW.' I quickly deleted them all. My phone must have been silent for days on end. No missed calls, no voice messages, and until a day ago, no texts. Then suddenly with the cloud of my inner disturbance rose an outer storm of disquieting voicemails from Reggie that were days old and from the proverbial personal storm himself. The screen on my phone registered them from out of nowhere — a long delayed reaction. I turned my phone back off, unwilling to deal with a second wave of absurdity. Also absurd in my mind was the fact that I hadn't heard from my mother or father at all. Their unusual involvement with Silence was starting to make me nervous, and the whip of my perpetual tormentor bit my flesh as I debated about whether to turn my phone back on again, to call and end the lengthy sentence between them and me.

I wandered downstairs and shoved my phone back into my purse without giving in to the pressure to turn it on and make the call. My mother had wronged me; she had committed a sin against her own daughter and an even greater betrayal of her husband. As far as I was concerned, there were no excuses, no reasons that were good enough. She should be the one to seek me out first and want to mend what she had broken.

I felt myself mentally dig in my heels, like a donkey that refused to go further. My actual feet however were given to pacing. I made lap after lap around the first floor of my home, from the hall through the den, to the kitchen, into the dining room, and back to the hall. Over and over I did this, as I took in my surroundings with a blind eye. I was lost in a bottomless well. It felt like a dark hole with unscalable walls. I'd come so far and had gotten everything I'd hoped for, only to find other tormentors hiding behind those wishes, dashing my dreams to bits. My familial situation would never be as I felt it should, I knew that in the death knell of an instant as I thought on my mother and what had happened between her and Reggie, what might inevitably happen between her and my fucked up neighbor. And, even though I had Annabelle and my delightful dalliances with her, I also had her problems and her baggage.

I was snapped from the preponderance of my pacing and piteous thoughts when I felt Sonya's stare from the edge of the landing. She seemed as disturbed as I was when I met her gaze. I couldn't hold her look for long and turned to go back into the dining room. I found myself drawn to the window and compelled to look out at the barren willow tree. I knew if I drew the curtains back, its visage would take in the length of my own lithe frame, and I would feel as fragile and simultaneously steadfast and landlocked as it did. Those weren't feelings I wanted to seek out, but I drew back the curtain anyway.

In abject horror, I confess that it wasn't only the willow that I saw. It wasn't only the ancient tree that beckoned me. It was Reggie. Amid the late morning cloud cover and the strengthening winds, stood his unmistakable form and the draw of his roughed and russet colored mane. It was a shock of color against the starkly subdued background contrast.

"Mommy!" called Sonya from a floor above me.

My body was flash frozen with palpable fear. I became still as stone, and I was unable to answer her. There was something foreboding about his expression, a hint of explosiveness under the placid surface. There was a tendency towards cruelty and violence in the lines of his face that I hadn't registered before but was keenly aware of then. There was no hiding it.

"Mommy?" Sonya called out again, uncertain as I always answered her.

"Go to your room!" I bellowed in response, ripping myself free from his cloying vibrational grasp. I'd known in an instant that he was sure I'd seen him.

"Mommy?" an unsteady Sonya began to make her way down the stairs.

I tore my gaze away from our lingering intruder in the court. "Sonya, I said go to your room!" I insisted in a furious backlash, a threatened lioness seeking viable defense for herself and her cub, her long dead cub.

Sonya froze in place, and for an elongated instant, I thought I'd seen her flash in and out of existence before my very eyes.

My eyes, are they playing tricks?...

As that question rattled around my brain, I was simultaneously reminded of the pulsating bedchamber walls and my unearthly experience the first time I'd made love to Annabelle. There was a movement present even though nothing seemed to actually move. I couldn't prove that anything had shifted, and it might have been partly because I myself refused to move along with the surroundings.

As Sonya's image finally steadied, the room then began to come unhinged. The sea foam green walls thrashed about as though the dining room were in the midst of its own torrential tidal wave. I heard cutlery rattle, and plates and cups clinked from their precarious positions. The chandelier trembled above me. I'd held my hands over my ears in an effort to make the roaring of the sea and the rattling of the accessories stop but was brought to my knees by the overwhelming sounds. As I looked up from my submissive position, I saw the paint on the far wall part as though it were drawing back its oceanic head in preparation to eat me, a yawning chasm of a mouth splitting open to swallow me whole and drag me away to the depths.

Stop!

The walls shook with an unknown energy and an unbearable noise.

Stop!

I closed my eyes tightly as I felt the room compress and contract in anticipation.

"Stop!" I wailed in a last-ditch effort and fell flat to the floor, waiting.

I waited for a terror that never came. I waited for a fate that drew back and away to bide its time. The walls were then still but well textured, with a sponge paint done in a tasteful and wistful sea foam green. The paint was as it had been the first time I saw it, almost too gray to be green, and yet it was most certainly green all the same. There was no noise, audible or otherwise, and Sonya was gone.

I'm not sure how long I laid on the floor, moving only to go from flat on my face to a curled up fetal position. All I can remember from those morphing moments, that episodic interlude, is the sound of water. It sounded as though water were slapping against the sides of a boat, a dingy that I floated around in amidst the newly calm waves of my dining room. From out of the Silence that followed the storm came the sedation of waves, and I let them wash over me and then around me until I was no more and then was again. I remember waking up from a dream I can't recall and having the rocking settle to a solid floor beneath my body weight.

I pulled myself to all fours, and then when I felt steady enough, I got to my feet. "Oh my god," I whispered into the void of my home, meaning to give it a sane substance. I brought my hands to my face to give myself verifiable form. "Oh my god," I said a little louder and walked out to the hall in search of a clock.

Do we even own a clock?

I didn't remember.

I ran my hands along the warm fabric of my sweater top, taking comfort in the irritating itch of the fabric. I smoothed out my black stretch pants and brushed at dirt I didn't see but assumed was there from my time on the floor. I was just starting to feel somewhat put back together again and was in the process of getting my bearings, when I heard it.

"Sally," a familiar voice called my name, and with it came the beginnings of the rape of my soul.

I shook my head as though the sound might be in my ears and nothing more.

The voice called again, "Sally." It spoke to me from directly on the other side of the locked basement door.

"No," I spoke firmly, but my spirit wavered. "No, please," I pleaded, a portion of myself willfully surrendering to the formidable predator that wanted to devour me. I shivered against the chill of my own defenselessness against him.

And, as it should have been, my words only served to enrage the voice. "Sally!" It screamed at me through the boundary of the basement door. "Sally!" It screamed over and over again, as fists from the other side pounded against the wood.

"Stop it! Go away!" I screeched in return and in distress.

The attack from the other side increased in ferocity, and I instinctually backed up as I heard the wooden boundary begin to splinter.

"Reggie, stop!" I roared and then turned to flee, to run out the front door and into the sobering cold, but instead as I whisked the front door open I ran right into a pair of grounding and shielding arms.

"What the hell?!" Brian sputtered, as he fought to contain me in his embrace. "Sally, Sally, calm down!" he insisted, and with each newly repeated command I came that much closer to doing so.

"Brian!" I exclaimed and threw my arms around his neck, burying my face in the solid mass of his chest.

"You're a wreck," he stated frankly. "Did your mom just call?"

That statement and then question posed one right after the other should've made me laugh, but I hadn't been able to say or express anything then, as in my gratitude I'd wanted only to cling to him. I wanted his logic and rationale to bring me back to a world I could understand and possibly feel safe in again. I desired so much to take all the blessings and leave the curses.

"I'm so sorry, sweetie," he whispered into my ear and rocked me gently as I grew nearer to tame.

Standing there in the doorway, I breathed in the cool December air and felt the stinging cold of each gust of wind. I hoped the winds would pick up and then beat down upon me so that I'd be made to occupy my physical body, to pay attention to it alone and vacate my fevered mind. As my muscles shivered against the onslaught of Mother Nature, I found myself coming back to earth, coming back to my own senses and sense of self.

"I know it's been a little while since you've seen him, but you two were close. It's ok to be upset. I'm sure whatever you're feeling is perfectly normal," Brian said with a tone of reason. "I'm here, Sally."

I pulled away from him while still managing to clutch at his forearms, so that I could collect myself further and indulge in more of that cold and clarifying wind.

"Let's get you inside," Brian guided, and against my better judgment, I let him lead me into the house. "I'm so sorry, Sally. I know this type of thing is probably the last situation you need to deal with right now. These last couple of months would take a toll on anyone," Brian said as he closed the door behind us and wrapped an arm about my weary shoulders.

"Why are you sorry?" I asked, able to speak a whole sentence to him at last.

Brian brought me to the sanctuary of the den and deposited me in my burgundy armchair. "I guess there's no reason for me to feel personally sorry, other than for your loss."

"My loss?" I was indeed at a loss.

Brian knelt down in front of me, looking slightly perplexed. "Yeah, your loss. Didn't your mom call?"

I shook my head, vigorously tossing my curls about so that they whipped the skin on my face. "My phone's been off," I said with a sudden burst of anger and frustration.

Where did that come from?

Brian brought his hands to the sides of my face to steady me and to have my eyes meet his gaze. "Sally, I don't know what's going on with you right now, but I have some potentially disturbing news, and I need you to focus. We need to move through this."

I didn't want to hear it. Somewhere inside me I'd already known, and I'd already decided that I didn't want to have confirmation of my terrible knowledge.

"Sally," Brian started with a deep breath and graduated firmness, "Reggie's dead."

I know.

Brian stood to full height and attempted to gauge my reaction, or lack thereof. "He was found in his apartment on Sunday, and his sister came into town yesterday to make arrangements," Brian persisted with relaying his message. He then took another calculated break to gaze at me as though I were a curiosity.

Sunday. It was the day I'd taken Annabelle in amongst the trees and had spotted his text emblem imbedded in the surface of the oak beneath my feral scratches.

Was that Sunday?

I'd gotten to the point where I doubted my own recollections, the timeline of my memories.

I'd heard him whisper to me on the wind that day, and I'd even seen the same marks in the willow's exposed root bark. "He has a sister?" came my unrelated question.

"He had a sister," Brian corrected my tense. "As it turns out, and from what tidbits your mom's been able to glean, he was kind of estranged from what family he had, and it wasn't much. The funeral is – "

"How did my mom find out?" I went on, sounding a touch more alarmed than I'd wanted to. I remained resolute in not tipping my hand or hers, but the unfolding of events didn't bode well for keeping secrets.

"Reggie's sister, I believe her name is Sarah, went through his phone and started calling people. She didn't know him very well, so I guess the phone and a few papers were all she had to go off of for initial contacts."

"But, why did she call my mom? His relationship was with me, as my therapist. Why the hell would her number be in his phone?" I persisted, even at the risk of tipping my own hand.

"Those details aren't really important right now, are they? And besides, you know that your mom liked to keep tabs on your therapy. There's nothing so unusual about it." Brian let out a loud sigh to signify his growing annoyance with my nit picking, with my finding fault and flaw in everything lately. "Sally, I don't think you're registering what I'm trying to tell you – "

"Why didn't I get a call?" The question was said so that it demanded an explanation, and for added emphasis I got myself to my feet, knowing full well that I was being petulant and outlandish, but I didn't care. Anger had sprouted in the pit of my gut and was sending out shoots in all directions, little hot pangs of rage.

Brian threw up his hands. "This is only a guess on my part, but maybe because your phone was off." He was getting a bit peeved, too. As my temperature rose, Brian's seemed to do likewise.

"I can't do this now." I knew I had to back away, get away for a while and get a grip on myself. I was better than I had been during my episode in the dining room, but I still found myself feeling fragmented on the inside. And with each new external pressure Brian applied with his latest news, I felt those fragments fissure and fracture a little bit more.

As gracefully as I could manage in the heat of the moment, I maneuvered past him and made my way out of the den.

I heard Brian follow me into the hall as I headed for the cloakroom.

"The viewing starts tomorrow and goes for three days, and the funeral is Saturday..." Brian continued to spew details as I grabbed my heavy brown coat lined with tufts of rabbit fur that had been placed around the hems of the sleeves and hood.

I opened the front door wide to the wild winds and a sky that spoke of an impending winter storm. All the better, as I'd prayed for it. My soul spoke out to the heavens and asked them to break open and cover all the hideousness with a blanket of white. Had I been able to talk coherently, to trust myself to speak the proper words, I would've wished it out loud and with the fullest breath.

"We have to talk about this!" Brian insisted and was answered by my door slam.

I made my way down the porch steps and across the vacant street to the cul-de-sac. I almost flew into the waiting wooden arms of the willow and began examining the roots for traces of Reggie's presence. The roots were all flawless, and other than the natural grooves that would be found in the bark of any tree, there was nothing to see. I circled the willow, bringing my eyes higher and higher with each pass as I took in the familiar terrain, the usual omens, and the weathered surface. It was getting harder minute by minute to see properly as the sky darkened at an unnatural pace.

I was roused from my incomplete inspection by the sound of footsteps on the pavement close by. I looked up to see Margaret Hastings crossing the street and heading straight towards me, her blonde and gray hair immovable in its signature flip style and perfect preparation. I wondered how many times she'd seen me circle the willow, and then I wondered if I could even come up with a plausible explanation for it. With it being Margaret, would I have to? Our last conversation hadn't been exactly typical.

"Your timing is good," she spoke joyously as she made a strong and striding approach. "I was just on my way over to see you." Unlike the first couple of times we'd met, Margaret hadn't donned a pantsuit, which would've been appropriate in the weather we were having and were about to have. Instead, she wore a full-length brown and black plaid skirt with black flats that were straight out of vintage stock and obviously cotton based. Her black pea coat covered the rest of her ensemble, but I was certain it would be just as dated and darling.

"Now really isn't a good time," I warned and gave her a bedraggled look to bring credence to my claim.

"Oh, nonsense," she said and made a grab for my hand. "Now is the only time we have," and with that being said, she tugged encouragingly, and I followed across the street and up her driveway. We went in through the side door that led to the familiar and cozy sight of her kitchen. Even in daylight hours, whether comparatively dark or light, her kitchen gleamed with a golden glow.

Margaret shut the door behind us and took her coat and mine to hang them succinctly on well-placed hooks. I took note of her brown and black short-sleeved sweater that featured a bright white knit bow on one shoulder. It fit so well with her dated look and dream-prepped hair bob.

"I'm really hoping you'll like my surprise," she beamed and walked a few paces over to a nondescript box that sat on the floor in front of her stove. In the box laid the petite and sleek female calico. I saw here peer up at me with her illustrious yellow eyes and a glimmer of recognition.

Yes, they were my feet that you curled up on.

Margaret waved her hand in a signal to me that I should come closer to the calico in the box. I made my way next to her and looked down again to see that the calico was not alone; she'd had kittens, a whole squirming mess of kittens.

"Wow," I said at long last, but my tone fell short of true excitement. "I didn't even know she was pregnant."

"Neither did we," came Lyle's voice as he joined us in the kitchen, argyle sweater and penny loafers setting the tone for his persona.

"So, you see our predicament," Margaret summarized.

"I do?" I reflected the assumed summation and accepted a mug of something hot that Lyle poured from a kettle on the stove and then handed to me.

"They need good homes," Margaret announced and retrieved a squirming ball of squalling orange fluff from the box.

The little fluff ball with baby blue eyes cried softly as Margaret pressed it into my arms. I carefully set my mug down on the stove to make both hands available to the new life I'd held. "Oh," I sighed despite a sullen mood, "so tiny." I spoke more to the cat than to Margaret or Lyle, and in an instant I'd felt my heart turn over as the kitten clung on to my sweater with its mother glancing up in approval. The calico closed her eyes, contented.

"That one's a little boy," Margaret told me and then bent low to pluck another from the box. "And, this one's a little girl." Margaret thrust a mostly black kitten into my clutches. She was the same size as her brother and just as fuzzy. I was intrigued by the blackness of her pelt that was interrupted only by a delirious splotch of white on her chin that didn't seem to belong.

Both babies were adorable with their bright blue eyes and wide with wonder expressions. Both clung tenaciously to the being that held them with their tiny, razor sharp claws. Both cried out initially and then relaxed into my loving embrace. I hadn't been able to help myself.

"We were really hoping you and Brian would be able to take at least one," Margaret admitted with an edge of guilt and indulged in her own mug of the heated beverage.

"We've never had cats before," I said, unsure.

"There's not much to it. Food bowl, water bowl, and litter box. That's pretty much it," Lyle nutshelled.

"Well..." I stalled, "What about your friend Cynthia? Is she taking any?"

"She can't," Margaret said definitively and took the little orange boy from me and then the crying black girl. She placed them both back in the box with their mother, who appeared to have fallen asleep even with babies hanging from her teats.

"Ok." I didn't press. I hadn't possessed the energy all of a sudden. "By the way, I saw her. I believe it was yesterday that she was walking through the court. I waved, but I don't think she saw me."

"She saw you," Margaret said and then took a seat at the kitchen table and gestured to indicate that I should join her.

I grabbed my mug off the side of the stove and took a seat.

"You've had quite a lot of visitors lately, haven't you?" Margaret posed the question.

The inquiry was strange, but it was a small neighborhood and I'd thought perhaps folks were prone to prying. "More than I'm used to. I hardly ever had visitors when I lived in the city, especially after the accident. And, for such a rural location there seems to be a lot going on."

"Oh, sure, you could certainly say there's a lot going on," Margaret replied and blew steam from the top of her mug before taking a hardy swig.

"I'll leave you two ladies to it," Lyle excused himself from the room. "But, Sally, think some more on taking a kitten. They're worth the effort." With a nod to indicate goodwill, Lyle Hasting exited the room, leaving me to Margaret.

I sipped at my tea and found it very sedating and delightful. It was obviously a lavender brew with a blend of a few other flavors I couldn't quite place. The combination was delicious and happened to accomplish just what I'd hoped to do by going outside. I was calming down. I was becoming very sedate.

"Sally, I don't mean to pry – "

"But, you will," I finished for Margaret, and she smiled patiently at me for doing so.

"Yes," she confirmed. "And, I hope you won't take my meddling the wrong way, because I mean well. Lyle and I both mean well."

I shrugged and indulged in the tea even more, taking a longer drink from the dregs.

"It's just that we're worried about you," she spoke so serenely and with such good intentions that I was captivated by her kindness. Her emotions and intentions were in direct contrast to what I'd experienced less than an hour ago in my own home.

"Why?" I asked plainly.

"We've seen some of what's been going on, and today had me especially worried, what with that man standing outside your house – "

"What man?!" I shot back in shrill denial.

"Let's not do this," Margaret said, moving past my pretense. I felt her look straight through me like an x-ray machine, and I'd immediately felt significantly more naked before her than I had standing bare in front of Annabelle, although with Annabelle it had been far more pleasurable. Being under Margaret's scrutiny was very uncomfortable, and for all her efforts at surface impressions, it was impossible to miss how much depth she actually had. "I know about your daughter, and I know about Trina showing up out of the blue with her children. I know that you've gotten yourself in a tangle with Annabelle, and that it's only a matter of time before her father intervenes in some unfortunate way. And, I know about your therapist showing up today. I believe his name was Reggie."

I believe his name was Reggie.

Margaret's referral to him in past tense echoed throughout my mind until it was all there was in that instantly cavernous space.

"I know all of these things because I pay attention," she admitted and sounded as though she believed herself to be just in the cause. "And, I pay attention because I know this place. I know this court. I know what can go on here, Sally, and I'm willing to tell you far more than Ella is."

I finished my tea, not sure what to say to her or how to even begin responding. She spoke the truth to me, and she knew that I knew it. It also appeared that she knew way too much about my habits and contacts. My state was startled even with the benefit of lavender tea, and there was no hiding or assuaging that.

"I would have told you all this sooner, but I didn't feel it was my place right off the bat. And, I didn't realize things could go so awry so quickly. You have to take control of it. You need to pull yourself together and put things into their proper place, or they will fall apart completely. Even though you think you are healthy and you feel whole, it is easy enough to see that you are diminished. You take from the living and give to the dead."

My grandmother's words.

Her words and her voice from my dreams rolled over Margaret's as she spoke to me in kind counsel. I wasn't exactly sure what she wanted or what she was advising, but it was in that moment that I shifted from uncomfortably tangled to someone who paid her rapt attention.

"Why are these things happening?" I eventually spoke.

"Because that's what happens here. This court and all the houses in it are different, and who can say why? All I can really tell you is that they reflect who you are, layer by layer, and you will change as they change. They change as you change. Who knows what the deeper reason is, or even if there is one." Margaret placed her hands over mine, and I felt the heat transfer from her to me as it must have transferred from the tea mug to her. "Maybe it's the effect of all the tree roots being so old and tangled together. Maybe the trees and the homes hold the memories through their unbreakable bonds. Maybe there's something in the land or in the water source underneath it. I don't know. And, I'm not even saying some of these elements aren't present everywhere and in everything, it's just that they are more at work and more tangible here."

Margaret gave my hands a light squeeze and looked to me for a response. When there was none, she went on as she had to. "Maybe we're just extremely blessed and cursed to have so much potential all around us every day. Or it could be that things are that way around here because that's just how it is." There was no more in the realm of explanation, and I knew it when she withdrew her hands and sat back. Margaret's candor was disturbing as I had been expecting a solid answer, but it was the one thing she couldn't give me. "I've searched for causes and reasons, and even though there are many possible, I've never been able to determine one absolute."

"None of this makes any sense," I said sadly, wishing for a split second that Brian were in the room with us to give a rational interpretation of it all.

Margaret got up and went to the stove to refill our mugs with more of the steeping tea, and then she promptly found snack cakes on the counter to go with it and brought those over as well before sitting down again.

"I know. Anything can happen here, and it always does. We are fortunate to have homes and lands... trees... that are able to inform us so adeptly, to have dead loved ones so close, and to be able to communicate in a way that most people would only dream of. But, they can curse us, too, the dead, with their needs and wants. And, our lives are the only lives they have now. We bring the dead with us, and in a place like this where sentience is predominant and physical, those ties become unimaginably magnified." Margaret's tone had taken on an edge of foreboding, so much so that I expected the sky to crack apart with lightening and then rumble with thunder. But, it didn't. Silence punctuated the severity in her message.

I chewed on a snack cake distractedly, not sure what to do with everything I was being told. The conversation itself seemed so surreal, and I was starting to learn that conversations with Margaret might naturally be of that slant.

"It is important to know when to hold on, when to have space, and when to separate all together. Sometimes you have to let go completely and other times things seem to work out ok, unnatural but ok. But, no matter what choice is made in a given situation, one thing is always certain... the dead should never hold too much sway over the living."

A splinter of recall lodged at the forefront of my brain. It was something Ella had said and then something Lyle and Margaret had told me at the Thanksgiving gathering. I'd felt prompted by the sliver. "You moved away from here once and then came back. Why?"

"Why did I come back?" she made the attempt to clarify, thrown by the lateral progression of my inquiry.

"Why did you move away in the first place? And, why did you come back?" I cleanly sliced my one question into two.

Margaret bent her head, and it was the first time in our conversation that she hadn't looked directly at me. I could tell that meant something momentous. "I moved away because I was losing myself and my life to this place, but the moving didn't help. I knew I had to come back and take control of it, because once you've been here you never really leave, at least not entirely. It is home and it is a part of you, and you can't run away from yourself, Sally, or what you are allowing yourself to become."

"So, what is it you think I should do?" I asked after several moments had passed.

Margaret drank her tea and started eating cake along with me. "Take a kitten," she said simply. "Take two, they're small."

I snickered at that a little, and Margaret smiled at her own levity. "Thanks, but I'm being serious," I reminded her.

"I am, too, in a way. Cats can be more of a help than you realize in situations such as these," Margaret continued her sales pitch.

"If nothing else, I guess they're really cute."

"That they are, and quite comforting." Margaret polished off her snack cake, took a long drink of her tea, and then focused on me. "I'm sorry. I'm sure once I started telling you these things you expected more from me. And, it might be that I'll be able to give more in time. But, let me be clear, the only answers I have are my own. You have your answers. And, this much I can tell you, places are more haunted by the living than they are by the dead."

Chapter 7

Returning home with two kittens and a bag of temporary supplies in tow seemed the least risky thing I could do at that juncture in my life. As Margaret had been packing them up, she'd mentioned more curious things that to anyone else might have sounded eccentric at best and slightly mad at worst. The fact that she'd said it all in that crystal clear, pragmatically wise, and well-adjusted tone didn't even help. But, my background and recent events served to temper my judgments; it made them more tolerant and increasingly fluid. Brief snippets of conversation that may have been equally to herself as well as to me about cats having a long and global history as guardians, as well as their understanding the balance between life and death stuck in my mind as I crossed three yards to reach my own.

By the time I'd left her house, the skies had gone very dark with a late evening storm's hue and had even opened up to produce the snow I'd been hoping for. It came down in big flakes all around me and the kittens, who seemed uninterested, preferring to curl up against it in the folds of my coat. I remember how I couldn't help thinking that they were so very different from dogs. It seems silly to reveal that now, as obviously they would be different, but the energetic quality of the cats were in direct and perhaps even conflicting contrast to one dog's cosmology in particular, and I'd known it the moment I'd walked back into the house — Fido. I thought on him and his unblinking button eyes, holding his image in my mind's eye until the thought evaporated like steam from my fevered brain, which felt as though it were slowly cooling.

All I can say in reflection of those initial days where the two new little life forms joined my world is that everything around them seemed to suddenly lighten. It was impossible for anyone to come into the kitten's sphere and not shed their burdens. The basement had settled down so that there were no more noises emanating from behind the locked door since the first encounter I'd had with Reggie through it, and Sonya had taken to contented isolation in my third floor studio space. As a mother of a dead child, I'd naturally felt the pangs of guilt associated with her chosen withdrawal, but I am even now startled to confess that a strange magnetic pull had created itself between me and the two new calico offspring, and it happened quickly.

The kittens were even magical enough to lure Brian out of his office a couple of times. And, when Annabelle had visited on Thursday morning, the morning of the winter solstice, she too, was drawn to the fluff balls that hardly ever left my side.

The solstice had eclipsed my ability to lose myself in the fabric of twisted time, in the parade of days and weeks that pretty much looked all the same. The dawn felt different that day, and a pressure began building up with every passing second that clicked us closer to nightfall.

Annabelle and I relaxed in the den, undisturbed by the outer and inner worlds, only influenced by that strange pressure. She sat on the sofa and held the small black female just above her face, as I reclined in my burgundy armchair with the little orange male.

"Have you named them yet?" she inquired, settling the girl into her embrace from being held aloft.

"Not yet. Brian brought home more permanent supplies last night, including collars, which then brought up the subject of tags and names," I informed her. "But, to be honest, even with these guys in the house, we've had other things on our minds."

I could tell that Annabelle sensed my mood change, even though nothing about me, including my tone, had altered on the surface. Without saying anything, she just stared at me with those impossibly black ember eyes of hers and sat patiently.

"A friend recently passed away, and his funeral is this Saturday," I opened up.

Annabelle nodded receptively, and I took that as my cue to continue.

"My therapist, Reggie. I think you might have seen him at Thanksgiving. Anyway, he died earlier this week, and the viewing is tonight and tomorrow at a chapel in the city. Brian and I didn't go last night, and I'm already feeling bad enough about that."

Reggie, have I betrayed you in some nameless, ethereal way? Is that why you haunt me now?

"What happened?" she asked easily enough.

"With the kittens coming into the house and his workload, we just didn't go last night," I explained.

"No, I mean, how did Reggie die? What happened? Was he sick or..." Annabelle prompted gently and adjusted the black female kitten that was taking to climbing up her soft robin's egg blue sweater with its sharp needle fine claws.

"Oh," I said, embarrassed at missing her meaning. "Oh, I, um, I'm actually not sure." It was beyond humiliating. I had claimed he was a friend as well as my therapist and I had no idea what happened to him. I then wondered if my mother knew and bristled at the thought that she should be privy to and sitting on that information when I was not. I grew angry at the thought of all she'd achieved with him that I had not.

Reggie, my dearest. My darkest.

The thought whispered from a part of me that betrayed all the rest.

"I'm so sorry for your loss," she said meekly and averted her eyes to contemplate the kitten, not out of curiosity but more out of what seemed an unsure state. I could tell she didn't know what to do or say next. Once condolences are given, conversation beyond that point can become riddled with problems.

"Thanks," I replied as warmly as I could to indicate that I was all right with everything, even though I was very far from it. "And, actually, I have a favor to ask of you."

Annabelle looked at me once more, and I felt that undeniable hook that held us together. It was that same hook into my sternum, and it consistently got caught about the bones.

"Would you be willing to come to the viewing and maybe even the funeral with me and Brian? It would mean a lot to me to have you there," I extended myself in that moment. I'd known it was a lot to ask of someone, especially someone I'd been keeping as a secret lover. It wasn't like I'd ever presented Annabelle to the world as someone significant in my life, and she and I had certainly never discussed such things. Yet, there I was in the midst of a conversation mingled with grief and guilt and adorable kittens, asking her to step out with me in a supportive role. Perhaps I had planned it that way in the back of my mind. I might have even planned it in an instant, seeing the advantage of my position and forcing her into the uncomfortable scenario. I don't recall ever thinking on it that way, but it did seem sort of like the type of manipulations I'd been prone to conducting over the years.

And if she's with me, maybe I won't hurt for Reggie so badly, long for him in this new and deeper way.

Reggie seemed incredibly close to me after death, closer than he had ever been in life.

Annabelle placed the kitten slowly and carefully on the floor in front of her and then reached out to touch my arm. The heat of her touch sizzled up and through me like a pleasant and vibrating electrical shock. "Sally, I am really very sorry, and I want to be there for you, but I can't." And with that having been said so succinctly, she pulled away from me entirely and sank back into the cushions of the sofa.

Her answer had caught me off guard. "What?"

I saw her lower lip quiver, but just barely. "I can't. I just can't go with you tonight."

I'd felt both hurt and stunned, and I hadn't even been sure what the dominating sensation was. Rejection from Annabelle was something new and all together unfounded in my reality.

"It's not that I don't want to be there," Annabelle began as she took notice of my expression, which I'm sure was not the nicest. "It's just that I can't be gone like that. We would be out most of the night."

And, suddenly I knew exactly what she was referring to through her vague explanations. Her father wouldn't allow her to be gone like that. If she went to the city with Brian and me, she'd be out for hours, in fact most of the night. There was something dangerous about that proposition in her world.

I gave an exasperated sigh. "It's ok. I understand." I resigned myself to not interfering, as she had requested of me when I first became aware of the situation she was choosing to live in. She was an adult, and it was her choice. I knew that if there was any boundary with her that I had to respect, it was that one.

Annabelle pulled herself off the sofa and flowed across the floor until she was kneeling in front of me. Her lips were only a breath's length away from my own, and I closed my eyes and my heart to her attempted affections as she remained in that excruciating space.

Neither of us spoke for the longest time until Annabelle decided to be the one to break the Silence that had come into the room like a sadistic voyeur. "Sally, I don't want you to think that it's because I don't love you enough."

I opened my eyes in a flash, eyes that matched her sweater and complimented by contrast the embers in her own sockets. My eyes scanned her face and form for additional message cues and found nothing other than a docile yet steadfast resolution. "I beg your pardon," was all I had as a retort.

Annabelle pressed her forehead into mine, and I heard as well as felt the flutter of her breath and heartbeats, the undeniable presence of imprisoned raven's wings beating for release. "I love you, Sally," she whispered.

Just not enough to outright defy your father for me.

Of course, that was unfair, as she might not have had anywhere else to go. And, that nasty thought had dissolved quickly enough in the warmth of the situation.

"I love you, too," I found myself telling her, against my own drives for emotional self-preservation.

"It seems like it's been so long since we've been together," Annabelle exclaimed in a frustrated whisper. "I've longed for you, and I've longed to tell you how I feel."

I ran my hand along her shoulders and up and down her arms delicately, not sure what wounds might be hidden beneath the flawless feminine surface of her unbelievably soft sweater. "My life has sort of been coming undone," I said to make amends.

"I want to bring it and us back together," she said and swept her sweater up and over her head to toss it behind her. She stayed on her knees in front of me, topless and tantalizing, ready to give herself over to me, ready to let me lose myself in her. It was a decadent offering, and I felt like a starving animal ready to devour a gourmet meal.

In no time, I had showered her with kisses and caresses and had shed my clothes to sit totally bare on the burgundy armchair, just as she had stripped down to nothing and stayed in her position on the floor. My body hummed in anticipation, as the walls of the den hummed with a throng of their own and with the life that flowed through the room. But, with life also comes death, and even though there seemed to be growth and interaction all around us, I felt an icy pit forming at the base of my spine. It stemmed from something that sat directly below me, directly below the floor.

The kittens had left us both to use their sharp little claws and climb high up on the sofa. They sought solace in each other and rest from a morning of exertions. Annabelle and I were seeking solace, too, but as she drew in close to me once more, I sensed that she was seeking something else as well, something far more elusive and valuable — unity.

I pressed back into the chair, ignoring the icy pit and giving her access to me in the way I'd had access to her. Under her ministrations, I found myself unfolding like a lotus, petal by petal. I was undone in the luminous rays of a foreign sun hanging low in the proverbial sky. I opened in front of her in a sacred act of surrender, so that she might worship me in the ways I'd been able to worship and enjoy her. I submitted, as was not in my nature to do, so that someone might once do it for her.

Annabelle's breath caught as she took me all in, and her gaze grew hungry until she could no longer deny herself the satisfaction of indulgence. I felt her lips do a slow crawl up the inside of my legs, first one and then the other. And, with each journey she took, I felt myself growing hot and moist and ready. I even began to undulate gently, beckoning her to lap at my shores. But, as she came near my overheated center, she glided past and pressed her body into mine so that her head came to rest on my breasts where she chose to remain and suckle for a time. It felt instinctual and maternal and erotic. She might have been there for quite a while as I let go and lapsed in and out of awareness, only knowing the sensations that were happening all throughout my body. Eventually, I became hyper-aware of the sensation stemming from between my legs, as Annabelle sought to shatter me completely so that the pieces of myself would be loose and ready to be placed back together in a better and happier pattern.

I shattered.

Morning melted into afternoon, and a solid blanket of white renewed the landscape all around me. I peeked out through the kitchen window at my backyard drenched in snow. The trees there were all leafless and sleeping, and I wondered if the willow in the front ever really slept. The night that came would be the longest and darkest of the entire year, and if it were to ever slumber, it would most likely be under such circumstances.

Alone again and contented and confused beyond any state of being I had ever known. Other than obligatory expressions of love that I'd given to my parents over the years, I was not someone who said those words often and I meant them even less. Other than Brian and Sonya, Annabelle may have truly been the only other person I'd ever known and also come to love.

Reggie?...

I pushed the thought of him and his forceful image from my mind.

I loved Annabelle without resentments attached. A new ability. A new feat.

I went to the refrigerator and pulled out a beer. It was time to unwind further, to clear my mind. I thought I might even grab a nap before Brian got home and we had to get ready to attend the viewing. I continued to watch the snow as I finished my beverage, and then I wandered back through the den, avoiding the dining room, to the hall. The kittens were nowhere in sight, and I thought about going to find them when I heard the footfalls. Someone was coming up the basement steps.

I wanted to run outside. I wanted to bolt upstairs. But, instead I stood frozen in place, waiting to see what would happen next and dreading it.

Did I think about him too much? Have I summoned Reggie? Brought him even closer to me?

"Sally," came the whisper from the other side of the door. "I know you're there, Sally. I can feel you," Reggie said with a tinge of sorrow and yet a more placid tone than what had been presented to me a few days ago. "Why won't you talk to me?"

What is there to say? I drew you in unknowingly with my own lust and then rejected you? I can't say that, not out loud. I don't want it to be true, or any more true.

"Reggie, please, stop. You're scaring me," I implored weakly, feeling more kindly towards him now than I had in quite some time but trembling at his presence.

What if it is wholly true and stands on its own?

"Don't be scared. I just need you to talk to me," he said in that reasonable way that had been so signature of him during our early sessions, that persuasive undercurrent that made me feel like agreeing to anything. It was the voice of the man I'd thought I'd known, the man I'd once envisioned as my confidant and even fantasized about as my secret lover.

I took a couple of steps more, coming further into the hall and nearer to the locked basement door.

"I tried, Sally. I tried so hard to reach you, but you shut me out right as I needed your friendship the most." Reggie drug up the old argument we'd had right before I put him from my life.

"It didn't seem like only friendship that you wanted," I said warily.

A hush came between us, and just like when he was alive and in front of me in a room, I could feel him thinking. He was contemplating his next move, mulling over the possibilities. "It wasn't only friendship I wanted. I wanted more. I still want more."

Do I?

"I know, and that's not ok," I'd said succinctly, hardly believing I could have the same discourse with him dead as when he was alive and fearing that he still might be able to do something about his wants. "And, what you did with my mother is not ok," I reaffirmed, reinforced.

I have to keep focusing on that.

"In my eyes it was always us, Sally. When I first met you, I felt sorry for you and then as time went on I saw who you were before I'd met you. And, I thought you'd never be that person again. The trouble was, I fell in love with the person you used to be. I wanted to be with the woman you were before the accident." Reggie revealed to me the sympathetic plight of an unstable mind, and my mind, stable or not, was drawn to the horrific beauty of it. "And, Jeanna is so much like the person you used to be... isn't she?..."

I swallowed a large lump. I actually liked what he was saying prior to my mother's name being thrown in there. "I don't want to hear any more about that."

I felt a cold tremor move through me, as I knew Reggie's hush in response to my request was simply to consider options.

"You got better," Reggie stated with a torrent of restrained emotion that ran the full spectrum between hot and cold, light and dark. "You got better, and I knew I was losing you. I was losing my chance with you, and so I made the only move I could."

It was a demented sort of logic, and I had no comeback for it. I was flattered, lured, and repulsed all at the same time. I felt Reggie's desire heating me at the same moment that I was disgusted by how he'd chosen to express it all along, and even in that very moment there sat the element of probabilities pregnant with remote potentials between us.

It's as if we are both slipping into the cold dark of the solstice's spell.

"And, you turned away from me!" he roared into the quiet after several minutes and started his banging away at the basement door.

"Reggie, don't!" I yelled in response. "Reggie, I'm here now!" I screamed at the shivering wood barrier and the spirit trapped on the other side. I dashed over to the door and placed my meager body weight against it, both to reinforce the structure and to bring myself as near to him as I could, in the hopes that it would ease his rage. "I'm here," I spoke softly into the oak grains. "I'm here," I said again with a hint of tenderness as the banging ceased and the sounds of a caress made themselves heard from the other side.

"Don't make me do this," he said cryptically, echoing a sentiment he'd expressed in a previous text during his lifetime.

"I won't," I assured, while unsure what it was I'd agreed to.

"Sally, I love you," Reggie spoke more evenly once again with the tattered remains of a broken heart and a wounded spirit. I sensed that brokenness and that wounding stemmed from a source that was created long before Reggie met me. I was just the most recent outlet he'd found. I was the outlet of choice at the time of his demise.

"Be still, Reggie," I begged. "Please, be still."

But, the house wasn't still. It wasn't as empty or as quiet or as settled as I had secretly prayed it would become. The areas and the occupants in and around it apparently weren't still either. I'd allowed myself to think that the addition of a couple new and tiny lives would be enough to right a situation that I didn't entirely understand. I was dead wrong.

The evening started out as I'd imagined it would, with the sun setting very early. Brian came home, we had a simple dinner of chicken and curried rice, and then we began to get ourselves ready to attend the viewing.

"Have you heard from your mother?" Brian asked from inside our bedroom closet.

Is my phone even on?

"No," I let it go at that.

"I talked to her at lunch, and she said she was going to call you," Brian informed.

I guess it's off.

"Is there a point to this?" I questioned back as I slid into a long maroon skirt that went over black hosiery and accented mildly the beige and maroon blouse I'd selected. Black matte flats completed the ensemble. I was elegant yet muted. Somehow I thought Reggie would've liked that. I looked good, but not too good. I seemed attainable.

Brian stepped out from around the corner and made his way into the main area of the room, carrying dark slacks and a navy blue button down dress shirt. "Well, aren't you a little snappy tonight," he'd felt the need to mention. "My point is that she wanted us to know that this is probably going to be a very simple and quiet affair. His sister said that only a handful of people showed up last night, and that there wasn't any reason to think tonight, Friday, or the funeral would be any different."

"Ok then," I attempted to put an end to it, and headed for the bathroom.

"If we aren't really expected to be there tomorrow, then I'd like to just make this a one-time thing before the funeral. I've got a lot of work to do before Monday." Brian arrived at his ultimate point.

I turned to consider him and his forced blank expression. "I can't say what would be expected any more than you can, but I intend to go tonight and tomorrow. What you do is on you."

I saw Brian give me a purposefully defeated posture. "If you feel the need to go both nights, then we'll go. "

"Thank you," I let my mounting temper subside as I made my way to the bathroom. I'd been feeling edgy ever since he'd come home late that afternoon and there was no reason for it that I could tell. Brian hadn't done anything differently. He even went to the trouble of throwing together our meal and cleaning up as I started the primping process prior to dressing. I was just on edge. Perhaps it was the prospect of the viewing itself, or it might have been the high probability of running into my mother. Also, in the back of my mind rumbled thoughts of Annabelle's polite decline to go with us.

It was just as Brian and I were retrieving our coats and my purse from the cloakroom that the doorbell rang.

"Who on earth could that be?" Brian asked to no one in particular.

I shrugged as an answer anyway. Who could it be?... If previous experiences had taught me anything, it was that it could be anyone or anything.

Brian opened wide the door.

"Hello," said Margaret cheerfully. "I hope this isn't a bad time."

"We're going to be heading out in a few minutes, but, please, come in," Brian replied as cordially as he was able.

Margaret slid past him and laid eyes on me, and in that exchange we both generated genuine smiles for each other. I also noticed she was carrying a small package, a brown paper gift bag. "I won't keep you," she assured. "But, I did want to come by and say thank you again for taking those kittens and for giving them a good home. I know you will grow to love them."

"We already do," I told her with the utmost sincerity.

"Good, good. I never had a doubt. And, this is just a little something for you and for them. It isn't much," she spoke as though she were bracing us for a letdown at the same time that she prepped us for liking her surprise.

Out of the brown paper bag, Margaret pulled two hand-painted food dishes, appropriately sized for adult cats. One was orange with black writing and artsy paw prints, and one was black with corresponding white accents.

"Oh, those are really nice!" I said upon seeing them, and Brian nodded and gave a general 'uh-huh.'

"Have you named them yet?" she inquired.

"No," I said a little sadly, "not yet."

"Then maybe this will help?" She turned the food bowls around and handed the black one to Brian and the orange one to myself.

"Helios," I read aloud.

"Selene," Brian responded and held the food dish aloft to display the name for me to see.

Helios and Selene.

The names were as dignified, old-fashioned, and unusual as the source. And, I couldn't help but admit that I liked them. They seemed a perfect fit for our two furry adoptees. One glance at Brian and I saw that he obviously liked them, too, and was equally surprised.

Margaret looked as though she were waiting with baited breath for our determinations. "Too much?" she finally asked.

I reached out and grabbed her hand with a gentle squeeze. "They're a perfect fit," I announced and handed off Helios' food bowl to Brian so that he could take the two into the kitchen.

"Oh, I'm so relieved!" Margaret let out a dramatic breath. "You two enjoy those babies, and I'll get out of your hair," she said, making a dash for the front door. "Take care," she called and made her way back out into the night and the snow.

Brian returned not a minute later. "That was unexpected."

"Yeah."

"Well, let's get a move on," he said, "and turn on your phone." Pragmatic and resuming the course our evening was destined to take. But, destiny is one of those odd things that has an indefinable nature, and even now I wonder if fate ever really changes, or if all paths inevitably lead to the same outcome. It's impossible to say with any sort of certainty.

I turned on my phone and ignored the message on the brightly lit screen that there were three voicemails from my mother. I deleted them in rapid succession without listening, knowing I'd most likely see her very soon.

We made our way out and onto the crunchy snow-covered grounds of our front yard, then to the driveway where our small gray sedan was parked. The hood was still fairly warm from Brian driving it home, and there was next to no snow covering the top of it. It would've been in even better shape against the weather if Brian had parked it in the garage, but that space must've repelled him as much as it did me. I was curious if he sensed and smelled the same things emanating from that space. The first time I'd set foot in it, I knew I'd never want to do so again. Who needed those smells or the memories associated with them?

"Do you still have room for one more?" came a voice more like the coo of a dove than the caw of a raven or crow. And beyond Brian, I spied Annabelle's unmistakable shape emerging from the inky blackness of evening and the sparkling whiteness of snow. She'd donned a long, black woolen coat that seemed both trendy and somber.

I smiled from the far side of the car. "Yes, yes, of course." I signaled to Brian to unlock the rear door on his side.

Annabelle made her way over and slid in with ease.

I then grinned at Brian awkwardly. "Ok. Let's go." What more was there to say? My demeanor and words were no reflection of the elation I felt riding atop of the nervous dread in my gut, nor could they be.

It wasn't until Brian backed the car out of the driveway and into the street that I saw a sliver of light coming from one of the front windows of Annabelle's house. And, in that window was the unmistakable silhouette of Dr. Gregory Taylor. It was then that the nervous dread sat astride my feelings of elation.

We rode for almost an hour with Silence. That specter may as well have been sitting in palpable shadow beside Annabelle in our back seat. I could read Brian like a book, especially since he was too unnerved to put up a mask of any sort. He was a bag of mixed emotions. He hadn't expected Annabelle, and due to his recent plunge into work and withdrawal from the tedious and tiresome stress of home life, he'd all but forgotten about my relationship with her. He'd been left driving and wondering where things stood or laid, as the case may be. Like any red-blooded, heterosexual male, he seemed to have a spark of lust about the whole situation being nursed within him, and I didn't blame him one bit. In fact, I had wanted that lust there. It made the environment safer for me and Annabelle and also made Brian far easier to manipulate.

I felt Annabelle keenly as she sat directly behind me in our mid-level metal chariot. I could even spy glimpses of her in the passenger side rearview mirror. The darker the night sky got, the brighter her skin glowed in defiance. Every so often her eyes would meet mine and I would see in reflection the embers that burned there.

She defied her father's wishes for me.

That was how I saw it then.

She may have even defied veiled or unveiled threats as well. Those realizations and the stark remembrance of Dr. Gregory in the window made me feel even more bonded to her. I probably loved her more than Brian, loved her with a ferocity that rivaled my love for self-preservation.

"Well, ladies, we've officially reached the city limits," Brian announced, as if there were something especially important about that.

Neither of us spoke, but a mutual smile was shared through that rearview mirror.

"Annabelle, are you from the city?" Brian was attempting to make small talk. It was eerily similar to how he would behave when we were dating. I was at once smitten with his polite intentions towards my lover and also colored by a tinge of jealousy.

"No," Annabelle replied lightly, unsure of herself in his social sphere.

"So, you've always lived more out in the country?" Brian continued to prompt.

"I've always lived in the house I live in now, except for when I went off to college," she explained, attempting to shift into a more natural tone of voice.

But, didn't you both just move back in? Did he go off to college with you?

That concept was startling but not at all surprising. Possessive.

"You like living there with your dad?" Brian glossed past the glaring discrepancy to pose a normal enough question, but I could instantly tell that it set both Annabelle and me on edge. There were no normal questions anymore.

"Sure. Why wouldn't I?" she challenged. It might have been the most venomous I'd ever heard Annabelle's voice get, and what made it all the more alarming was how cool and calculated she could be in her sting.

"No reason you shouldn't," Brian diffused. "I think it's nice that you have such a good relationship and that you keep him company."

Dear Brian, are you hoping that flattery will get you everywhere?

And, that was where the conversation died. Brian didn't even try to revive it, and I was grateful for that. No one bothered to speak another word until we pulled into the parking lot for the funeral home.

I was surprised to see the lot so full. Row after row of cars partially covered in snow, their exposed metal glistening under the shower of light from the lot's lamps. "I thought this was going to be a simple and quiet affair," I threw Brian's previous description of the viewing back at him.

"That's what I was told," was Brian's only defense.

We'd found a spot near the back of the lot, behind the building, and parked. All three of us in uneasy determination, walked up to the front entrance and then into the overly done welcome of the foyer. It felt good to get out of the external cold of the night, but it was then replaced by an internal cold that seemed to be a natural characteristic of the building. I was reluctant to give up my coat, but with everyone else doing so, it was only proper.

Off of the foyer were doors that led to several different chapels, and above each door was the emblazoned name held by that specific space. Trinity, Hope, and Blessings were the names above the doorways to the chapels off to my right. And, in front of each doorway were also stanchions with signs bearing the last name of the families using the chapels. Peace, Spirit, and Eternity were the names of the chapels to my left. But, Brian, Annabelle, and I weren't being guided to any of those doorways, to any of those chapels. One of the funeral directors was escorting us all the way to the end of the long and detailed foyer to a memorial space with double doors, and the chapel was named Resurrection.

Of course! It couldn't possibly be named anything else.

Reggie was as good at torture as he was physical therapy, and even though he may not have had an outer hand in the worldly funeral arrangements, I couldn't help but feel that he'd had some sort of metaphysical hand in the bizarre and divine alignment. Was it an inside joke shared by the two of us from beyond the grave? If so, then I'd felt the joke was on me.

The stanchion in front of the double doors read McPherson-Fields, and that was sobering. It had been years since I'd heard or even thought about Reggie as having a last name. Reggie McPherson had simply been Reggie to me. He'd been the Reggie I'd fantasized about, the Reggie I'd confided in, and the Reggie I'd eventually come to fear.

When I entered the Resurrection chapel, I quickly realized that all of the cars outside must have belonged to the mourners of other departed souls, not that Reggie had departed to go very far.

"Simple and quiet," Brian leaned over and whispered into my ear.

"Is now the time?" I bristled as I took in the handful of people milling about. Brian, Annabelle, and I had almost doubled the room's population.

My mother and father were in attendance as well as a couple of other people I'd never seen before. Due to both of my parents being occupied with a conversation, I hadn't been spotted right away.

It was easy enough to determine who Sarah was. She stood at the focal point of the room near the casket and slightly off to the right with a gaze that was far away. As I made my way further into the room and closer to her, I was both touched and astounded by how much she resembled Reggie. She had been endowed with the same bright strawberry blonde hair color, similar robust build, and the tone of her skin could have been taken directly from his hide. She looked older, though, and tired; and as I pitied her, I also felt a kinship with Reggie, a kindness creeping up on me again for him since he had passed. It didn't diminish much in that moment, despite the fact that he was haunting me. I left Annabelle and Brian to join Sarah, unable to resist the morbid pull.

"You have my deepest sympathies," I opened and extended my hand.

Sarah took my hand in hers for a brief shake and then met me with Reggie's eyes. "Thank you," she returned flatly.

"I'm Sally Archer," I introduced. "Your brother was my therapist."

Sarah nodded to signify that she'd heard me and understood.

"I'm sure this must be so hard for you – "

"Not really," she cut me off. "I didn't know my brother that well. We hadn't talked in years," Sarah revealed matter-of-factly, to which I just stood there. "Reggie wasn't a part of what was left of our family, but he was still my brother. So, I guess I owe him a decent Catholic funeral."

Reggie was Catholic and a black sheep?

It had started to dawn on me then how much he'd known about me and how very little I'd known about him. It was a reoccurring dawn that had happened several times over the period of the last few months. Reggie was practically a stranger in my midst, an unknowable visitor I'd let into my home three times a week.

"Listen," Sarah interrupted my thoughts, "I know you expected more weeping from me or something, but I can't give you that. If you want to cry for him, be my guest."

It was obvious that from there on the conversation was over. And, it felt a shame that she hadn't shared more with her brother in his lifetime, considering how alike they'd looked and sounded. It was also obvious why no one else was standing around her conveying condolences. Sarah wanted the whole obligation to her dead brother done and over with, and she had no intentions of getting to know anyone who had been in his life.

As I moved towards the casket and closer to Brian and Annabelle, I got intercepted on my route. My mother threw her arms around me. "Sally, I've been calling you," she wavered in a faulty tone directly into my ear. "I wanted to see you before this." She spoke with great sorrow and finally pulled back a little so that our eyes might meet. There was suddenly no façade for Jeanna Dougherty. Her red-rimmed eyes and speckled cheeks let everyone know that she had been crying for some time. Her expression was one of total and immense grief. I would have been afraid of a collapse from a lesser woman, but she could hold her own no matter what.

"This is hard for me..." I started, but my words trailed off into Silence's hands.

"For me, too. And, I know you might not be able to forgive me just yet, but we need to move on. You need to set this aside." She was riding a fence between counseling and flat instruction in her grief cycle, which apparently included me in the process. "Reggie is gone," she said solemnly and placed a hand on the base of the mahogany box that held the remains of my interloper.

Reggie is not gone.

I didn't find any kindness in my heart for her until she began to cry freely. Her whole body became involved in the expression, and I saw the tattered remains of my own mother, a woman who in some way had cared for another, and that person was irretrievably removed from her life. I pulled my mother in close to me and held her. I held her for the grief I felt, too, even though it seemed far more natural for that grief to come from her. "I'm so sorry for your loss." They were my words to her, and an echo of Annabelle's words to me.

Once my mother had pulled herself somewhat back together and stood apart and on her own again, I addressed another matter in the spirit of moving on. "Tea on Friday? Tomorrow?"

She nodded.

"Noon?"

She nodded again and then retreated into the arms of my father as he came over to join us.

"Hey, pumpkin," my dad said in a gentle greeting to me. "How are you holding up?"

"I'm fine. I don't think it's really hit me yet," I confessed and only afterwards realized that what I'd said was true. My mother had much more time to come to grips with the reality of Reggie's passing than I had. Although, I still had him harassing me from beyond the veil.

"Give it time. I know you and your mother were much closer to him, being involved in the therapy regimen for years. Even though it was business, I'm sure it can feel like friendship. We'd like to come over for brunch this weekend and talk about plans for the holidays." My father made a segue into more practical matters, taking our minds off of the emotional turmoil.

"Sure," I agreed.

"Do you think Sunday would work for you and Brian? It's Christmas Eve, after all."

"It works for me, but you might want to check that with Brian. He's been very busy with work lately," I informed and my father hugged me diligently before walking on to guide my mother towards Brian. But, where was Annabelle?... I did a quick scan of the room and didn't see her, and she had been with Brian only moments ago.

As my eyes made their way back to the casket, I noticed that most of the people had stepped away from it to talk once more among themselves. Reggie and I were alone. I walked slowly from the foot of the casket up, and as I moved in, I spied the tufts of his strawberry blonde hair and then finally the vision of his familiar face. He looked like he was simply sleeping, and in that sleep he might even have been dreaming. It made me think of him and wonder what he was like as a little boy. Had he appeared this contented and innocent in his youth? I was left wondering.

"Reggie," I said his name so quietly it almost wasn't audible. "I feel like I never really knew you," I stated honestly.

I didn't know that your own family had abandoned you. I didn't understand your way of reaching out to me.

"I wonder if I'll start to know you now." My remorse was great, and as it settled in my heart began breaking. "Rest in peace," came my warbled whisper as I pressed on to avoid being consumed by tears.

Rest in peace... even though I know you won't.

I'd found Annabelle right outside the chapel doors as Brian and I prepared to go. It was immediately apparent that she was worried about something, unnerved and almost undone. She attempted to hide it, but I knew where the caged raven lurked. At first I thought it might have been her own internal reaction to the overwhelming presence of death and the prospect of dying. Viewings and funerals are never easy. But, then I began to consider the possibility that the hour was very late, and she'd soon have to contend with arriving back home.

As Brian made last-minute arrangements for Sunday with my parents, I fetched Annabelle from a plush crimson chair that sat off to the side.

"Everything all right?" I checked in with her.

She met my gaze with a fluttered disturbance. "Yes, everything's fine," she lied to me.

A whirlwind of quick goodbyes, the gathering of coats, and then a frigid walk back to the car all preceded the frigid prospect of our long drive back. Silence weighed far more than it had when we'd driven out for the viewing. If it had been palpable then, it was downright penetrating as we exited the city and made for our homes. We were all left to our own thoughts, and that wasn't good.

By the time Brian had pulled into the driveway, I could see Annabelle's panic in the rearview mirror just before she stepped outside. It had been etched all over her face. And, as I stepped out into the night, I spotted the same silhouette in one of the front windows of her house. Her father was watching us. Had he been standing there the entire time we were gone? I doubted it, but it had been an eerie contemplation. At the very least, he must have been regularly checking for her, waiting for her to appear, waiting for her to come into the house where no one would see or hear what went on in there.

I heard Annabelle's feet crunch down into the frozen layer of snow as she started to cross our yard.

"Goodnight," Brian said to her retreating form, as she'd already made movements to leave without saying anything further to us.

"Annabelle!" I exclaimed in a shrill pitch and dashed around the car to stand in front of Brian.

Annabelle turned and smiled, but it was when her smile faltered that I knew I had to do something. I walked up to her and brought my face in very close. It didn't matter who was watching. "Annabelle, please, stay the night," I offered. It was my second massive step with her in less than twenty-four hours.

"Sally-Sally, I can't," she shivered.

I grabbed her forearms tightly, knowing that we both sensed terror at the thought of her returning to her house. "Yes, you can. You absolutely can," I insisted. I feared for her, and in the back of my mind I also feared for myself. I feared her father, the basement, the garage, Reggie's pleas, and Brian returning to his work immersion and aloof ways. I feared that I was falling apart and that everything I'd built up around myself in my newfound physical vigor would soon be shattered. I feared that if all of it continued in the way that it looked like it was going, I'd have nothing left but a dead child in my disregarded studio space and a dead man in the basement. I felt consistently stronger on the outside but increasingly diminished on the inside.

I was desperate for Annabelle to continue to quicken me, and I deeply and sincerely wanted to quicken and shelter her as well.

I saw Annabelle glance over my shoulder to where Brian stood. I knew she was considering him and what all he might entail. Then when she looked back to the silhouette in the window and finally at me, I knew I'd had her decision. "I'll stay the night," she proclaimed and followed me into the house with Brian behind her.

To his credit, Brian didn't say much of anything about it. He allowed Annabelle to come home with us as if it were the most natural and casual thing in the world. I was simultaneously proud of him and a tad bit disappointed. He set about making tea as Annabelle and I made small talk to ward off the dread that had found a seat in both of us. I soon found Brian joining in on our conversation, and as we all finished our tea and met with the wee small hours of the morning, the vibrations changed. I think I sensed the switch in mood first, for I was used to Annabelle and the manner in which she would become molten and fluid like a pool of flowing lava. Shortly after she'd begun snuggling up to me and becoming very clingy, Brian began to take more notice of the quiet and the arousal that came on its heels. There wasn't a need for further talking between the three of us, as what came next had been a preconceived dream I was sure we'd all had a hand in creating. It was a dream manifested from independence and achieved through interdependence.

As I was the interconnecting link in our lovely and loving trio, it was me who had to make the decisive move that would determine the course of events that morning-night in #18 in the dark of the solstice. Sunrise was still many hours away.

"Let's go upstairs," I said huskily to both my partners and slipped off the sofa to head to the second floor. I'd made my move. Brian and Annabelle both followed suit.

As I slipped out of my clothes in the darkness of the bedchamber that was only disrupted by a single bedside lamp, I knew that this would be the very first time I'd actually see my husband with another woman. It was one thing to conjure up those images in my own imagination, but conjurations were subject to doubt and could therefore ultimately be dismissed. What happened between the three of us would be fact and would be memory and would never be removed or subject to doubt and reinterpretation.

Standing naked in front of the bed I had both of their attentions, and I felt that incredible surge of power that came from what felt like reverent worship for me from my acolytes. I felt alive and powerful.

Brian stood back and away and seemed contented in his place to watch what would unfold between Annabelle and me. She drew near to me, as was her tendency to do, and delighted in my efforts to undress her, to engage with her in heated passion play, and to display her before my very own husband. As I had my way with Annabelle, I realized that I was sharing with her something and someone that was from my life prior to her and to this place. I was letting her share in something personal and private with me that no one else would ever see or do. The bond grew deeper; it grew intertwining roots.

I marveled at how well Annabelle could please me, and at how patient Brian could be merely watching us. I sensed the pulsating heat in his blood as the bedchamber walls grew slippery and sleek with a throbbing pulsation all their own. There I was again, contained in a chamber of erotica. The walls indulged in the pleasure as much as I did. They stiffened and contracted like Annabelle had done around my fingers. And, eventually, they sighed with Brian's voice as I signaled that he should indeed join us.

With Annabelle satisfied and relaxed from her writhing, she lay sprawled out on the bed, and I had the pleasant chore of undressing my husband. A fount of kisses and caresses flowed between us as I stripped him bare and released his erection. I was wanton enough to fondle him so that he was as hard as I'd ever felt. I'd even placed him between my legs and let his shaft rub up against the moist center he'd found there, until I was sure I had to step away or simply finish him off.

I stepped aside and nudged him towards Annabelle, who laid in wait before his hungry gaze. I wanted to watch as much as I didn't. Well, maybe I wanted to watch just a little bit more. As Brian climbed on top of her and held himself directly above her languid form on all fours, I made my way around to the far side of the bed to be near her as well. I kissed her from aloft and then whispered into her ear, "Enjoy him."

Annabelle kissed me back with a fervor I'd never felt from her. She wanted to be set free, that same vague and wordless pleading, and I kissed her vigorously as though that might hold the key. As our lips parted ways from each other, each of us made room for Brian. I stroked her hair as he kissed her gingerly at first. I remembered Brian as a new lover and how he would take his time to get to know someone, go slowly so that he would be sure to please the other person. Brian made his way down her neck and to her petite and perky breasts, stimulating her so that the energy in her arousal was as good as new. I watched as he ran his hands over every inch of her skin, which glistened with sweat.

Was he like this with Amelia?

And, as quickly as that thought had come, I banished it to where it belonged. The basement.

As he placed a hand between her legs, Annabelle suddenly bolted upright to a sitting position and Brian ceased all movements. She seemed startled and unable to relax again. I moved to sit beside her on the bed and spoke with soft words. I caressed with gentle strokes, assuring her that everything was perfectly all right. "No one is going to hurt you," I promised as her black orbs met mine, searching for an answer, seeking reassurance and temperance for her trembling. "Enjoy him," I instructed again, bringing a hypnotic hiss to my voice like the essence of a snake about to uncoil. Brian was gentle and kind, and in my mind she should feel as though she could enjoy him without fear. I eased her back down to lying on the bed and started stroking her myself, until she was coming undone with longing. Slowly I replaced my hands with Brian's and let him apply loving ministrations to her. The transition was slower, but she took to it better, finally spreading her legs and allowing him to finger her until I could tell that both of them were ready for more.

I stepped away from Annabelle then and let Brian take her completely. He thrust within her with caring and precision, as I knew he would. I watched the two of them tangled together in a primal dance, undulating back and forth, riding a wave in rhythmic time. There was a quality about it that was both beautiful and alien. As I continued to take in the sight and become as much of a voyeur as Silence could be, I noticed how easily Brian had been able to finish her off, bringing her to a shattering climax so that the room broke with her into a million pieces and I followed, too, even against my own will. I stood still but was in absolute oblivion, until Brian beckoned me home from the void.

"Sally," he called to me, more aroused with each breath, with every moment that passed between the three of us.

I awoke from my void-induced stupor and stared at the two of them. Annabelle had moved up towards the headboard to sit on the pillows, and Brian was kneeling in the center of the bed, hard and ready for me, ready to finish his night and his hunger with me.

A wound opened up inside me, one that was still filled with the remnants of a potent poison, and I took note of how it had started to drain away. Brian was hungry for me. Even in giving him another woman, and a woman as tantalizing as Annabelle, when it was all said and done, he called to me. The wound inflicted by Amelia, and the tiniest bit of poison that remained within purged itself. And, the scar healed over. I crawled up on the bed to join my husband and to allow Annabelle the coveted position of voyeur.

Our mouths met in raw hunger, and he was far more forceful with me than he'd been with Annabelle. His caresses turned to clawing as mine did likewise. As he slid into me, my nails dug deep into his hips so that he was locked in and committed to each thrust, committed to me and my pleasure.

"Fuck it, Sally! You little witch! You're going to make me cum!" he roared from his perched position.

"I sure hope so," I said back in a low growl.

Seconds later, both of us went over the edge of abandon. He'd climaxed first, jerking me right along with him for an epic ride. I shook and the room shook. I felt Brian trembling on top of me, too. Annabelle was all a shiver sitting against the headboard.

And, then came Silence. The bedside lamp was clicked out, and all of us curled into a ball to spend what was left of the darkened solstice hours together.

❖

All traces of Annabelle were gone when I stirred. Brian wasn't in the bed with me either. I pulled myself together and into some brown stretch pants and a honey-colored V-neck top, then made my way downstairs and towards the alluring smell of coffee.

As I reached the kitchen, I saw Brian in a pair of boxer shorts making eggs as our coffee pot gurgled, letting me know it was nearly done with its morning chore. I also spied two ravenous and happy kittens at their new food bowls positioned right beside the stove. Helios and Selene were chowing down on their dry food like we hadn't fed them in days, when it had only been a matter of hours. What was more amusing was that they were each eating out of their appropriate dishes. I'd made a mental note to invite Margaret over in the coming days to see them.

"It must have snowed a shit ton after we fell asleep," Brian reported over his shoulder. He must have heard my footfalls, and assumed he should start talking to engage in some sense of normalcy.

I didn't need normalcy, but I was willing to go along. "Really?" I allowed for his preference of conversation, as I reached for a mug and grabbed the pot from the coffeemaker to fill my cup.

"Yeah, so I'm going to work from home today."

"My mom's planning to come over for tea at noon." I offered my own piece of normal information in the exchange as I went to the refrigerator to dig out a container of coconut milk.

"You might want to give her a call after breakfast to see if she's planning to make the trip. I don't know what the roads look like in the city, but right outside our door, they're pretty rugged," he said and spooned eggs onto a platter.

Once both of us had coffee, we made our way into the dining room to sit down to a simple breakfast of eggs and a bowl of mixed fruit.

"Did you sleep well?" I asked spryly, with a touch of pixie dust in my voice.

Brian smiled at me and then actually blushed. I couldn't repress the giggle that escaped me as I sat back looking at him. He looked like a virgin on prom night. "Stop," he said lightly and brushed off my laughter. "Yes, I slept well. God!" And, it was then he started eating his eggs with a voracious appetite. "You know, you never cease to amaze me," he managed to say between bites.

I leaned in across the table and planted a large kiss on his forehead. "I slept well, too. Did you see Annabelle at all this morning?"

"Nope."

That meant she must've left before either of us woke and gone home. There was nowhere else for her to go. And, it was then the dread returned to its seated position within my core.

"I'll check on her later today," I said more to myself than Brian, which must've been evident, given the fact that he didn't respond to my decree.

"Oh, and before I forget, there's an idea for the house that I'd like to run by you," Brian made an ungraceful topic switch.

I sighed and placed the issues surrounding my mistress hesitantly on the back burner. "Yes?..."

"I was toying with the idea of turning the upstairs space, the third floor, into an art studio for you," he beamed brightly at me over the last mouthful of eggs. "Would you like that?"

I shook my head. "I'm sorry. I should've told you and then thanked you a long time ago... but, I've already seen the third floor space," I admitted reluctantly. I'd thought about acting surprised, but opted for full disclosure instead.

"What?"

"It's beautiful, really. I love it. You did a great job displaying all my remaining movement equipment and craft materials," I gushed forth, proving to him that I really did admire his efforts.

Brian pushed back from the table. "What the hell are you talking about, Sally?"

"Are you angry?" I asked as I was taken aback.

"I'm not angry," he said a little slower and softer. "I'm just confused. I haven't done anything to the third floor space."

With Silence accompanying us, we both made our way up to the third floor studio space to unravel the latest mystery that had plopped itself down among us. I led the way up the last flight of stairs, flipped on the main overheard light switch, and revealed to Brian the handiwork that had gone on up there. Everything was just as it had been the last time I visited, which had been way too long ago.

An easel sat to the right of the window with a played upon canvas. There were the friendly shelves with paints and paintbrushes, various adhesives, and jars full of mixed media; there were neatly stacked sketchpads and an assortment of pens, pencils, and charcoal. And, as remembered, the left half of the space contained all of my old movement arts equipment. Two bright green yoga mats with matching blocks, creamy yoga straps and a pale white, translucent stability ball. Foam rollers, sculpting balls, and toning rings of all colors hung from their hooks on walls and sat on their shelves... still waiting, unlike the art supplies.

"See," I said proudly, like I was vindicated.

"I see," said Brian cautiously as he stepped into the space and wandered around a bit. "I see a lot of things, but I'm telling you right now, Sally, I didn't do any of this."

A pregnant pause situated itself between us, until I finally burst the bubble. "So, you're telling me that all of this stuff, this entire set up must have just appeared, arranged itself on its own?"

Like the basement.

"Like the basement," Brian's words echoed my thoughts not a second later.

"But, this is a lot nicer than what is in the basement," I argued as if I'd had a leg to stand on with those flimsy and dismissive words.

"Yes, it is, but it still must have managed to manifest itself..." Brian was at a loss. He shook his head in disbelief and brushed past me on his way down the stairs, leaving me alone to peer out the large art window at a light gray sky continuing to provide snow flurries.

Then, out of the corner of my eye, I saw movement in the far left corner. I took a few steps further into the studio space.

"Sonya?" I called out with a mother's voice.

I saw her sitting down in the far back corner looking dejected.

"Mommy, when are you gonna come back and play with me?" she asked with a child's plea, impossible to deny.

I knelt in front of her and brushed at her blonde ringlets. "Soon, sweetie. I promise." I kissed the top of her head and then made my way downstairs, for the first time feeling very uncertain of my own child and then guilty for it. I knew on some primal level that I'd been actively avoiding her.

Brian had gone straight into his office and closed the door; the sanity of the workday had begun. I knew he was done discussing the studio, just as he was done discussing the basement.

My mother had braved the weather and was punctual in keeping our tea date that Friday afternoon. It had helped that the sun came out and melted a lot of the snow and ice on the country roads and along our court. I spent a portion of the morning glancing out windows towards Annabelle's house as I absently wondered what Brian was thinking as he shut himself up in his office. I also took time to watch drips of water from melted snow and ice fall off the willow.

Are you awake once more? What would you reveal to me now if I walked out there?

Once the tea was poured, I opened the conversation with a potentially controversial piece of decision-making.

"I'm not going back to the viewing tonight," I announced with a hint of defiance.

"I'm not either," my mother said vacantly and sipped at her chamomile concoction.

"Oh, well, I'll admit that I'm surprised. I guess I assumed you'd go," I told her.

"It's over, Sally. Reggie's gone, and there is no salvaging anything there. I'll go to the funeral on Saturday." They were cold words, and I would've been disgusted had they not been said with a tremor of underlying emotion. There seemed to be a see-saw effect happening to my mother all of a sudden, as if she were still intent on carrying the burden of her outward appearances, but it also seemed that the burden was starting to become far too heavy.

We are all such damaged people, such broken people.

"Mom, what happened?" I asked. "I never did hear how he died. Was it a car accident or something? He wasn't sick, was he?" I pressed for more details, figuring that she could endure the pressure and somehow held the truth. There was a part of me that needed to know, that needed to understand what had happened to him so that the swell of nausea that was so characteristic of my tie to Reggie could begin the be staid, heal over.

Will it ever?

My mother then reached for a napkin to dab at her eyes, signaling to me that what was to come next would not be pretty. "Reggie killed himself," she blurted out and blew her nose. I'd never seen that woman in such a shambles, buoying between done and undone. Whatever Reggie had been to her, he'd meant a lot. It started to hit me there over tea that he was more than just a toy on the side of a marriage that had its failings. He must have truly convinced her of some deep caring, and she had cared for him in return.

Don't make me do this.

Reggie had warned me in those words in his text.

Don't make me do this.

He had said it again from behind the basement door.

"Why?" I couldn't stop seeking, even though I knew the answers, or at least bits and pieces of them, and even though I didn't want the answers.

"Who knows?..." Jeanna threw up her hands in abandon. "He didn't leave a note, and from what I can tell he didn't say anything to anyone about what was going on. And, in those last days we weren't close or even communicating. His sister didn't know anything either, not like that's an indicator. I never suspected he was suffering..." My mother broke down again into freely sobbing. Reggie might have rejected her at some point, but one thing about that whole situation was crystal clear, she had never rejected him.

I've done this.

I condemned myself with a huge heap of guilt and thought back to Fido's unspoken label for me — Murderer.

It took a while for me to pull myself out of the hole of my guilt and disgrace, and for my mother to stop crying, but once we both had ourselves well in hand we decided to talk about the Sunday brunch in the spirit of moving on. It was just easier that way. We talked about having her and my father stay all day Sunday and into Monday for the Christmas holiday, and we'd even tentatively planned a New Year's Eve together.

Having people in the house and events to think about might give me a better grasp on time as it flies by. But, is that what I want? To measure out my life in coffee spoons?

My mother looked somewhat happy above the distress, as she placed her mug in the sink and brought a package of cookies to the table for us to munch on. I was sure she felt she had her daughter back, and perhaps for the most part that was true. But, with a dead child waiting in the attic and a restless spirit in the basement, I was fragmented at best and greatly diminished at worst. There was simply no way she could have or know all of me. Plus, I was consistently preoccupied with thoughts of Annabelle, and what may or may not be going on inside the house next door.

"Oh my god!" My mother had suddenly squealed in a pitch I hardly ever heard, and got to her feet.

I'd been jarred from my thoughts on the splintered nature of my existence. "What? What?" I said shooting up to turn and see her dash into the dining room.

She'd bent down to retrieve something from off the floor, a little orange fluff ball. "Where did you come from?" she asked as though the kitten would answer.

"Oh, I meant to tell you, we have cats now," I said and chuckled a bit at the ironically late timing of my news.

She didn't take her eyes off of Helios. "Cats?"

"Yes. One of the neighbor's cats had kittens, and Brian and I took two. The one you're holding is Helios. And, his sister Selene is around here somewhere." I glanced about briefly, scanning the nearby area, but I didn't see her.

"My, my, aren't those big and unusual names for such sweet and tiny babies." My mother fussed over the little bundle. "Things do seem to keep changing around here," she said blankly as she scrunched a kitten into her chest and made her way back to the table.

"They certainly do," I breathed to the walls of the house and through the dining room curtains, all the way to the outline of the willow in the snow.

Chapter 8

After my mother left late in the afternoon, I went about feeding both Helios and Selene. Their bowls were empty and they'd corralled me in the kitchen, demanding to be fed with plaintive mews. It was amusing to me how they'd each taken to their own bowl and had made the right choices according to Margaret's labels. I noticed then how hardy they both looked, and how much they were already starting to grow. It was as if with each new day they made another giant leap in their developments. Soon, even that baby blue in their eyes would be gone for permanent colors.

If only human children grew that fast.

And with that thought, I cast a glance up to the ceiling, as if I might spy Sonya through the barrier. I sighed and left the kitchen to head upstairs. Brian might finish up with work very soon. But then again, he might just as easily decide to work well into the evening hours. As I made my way around to the hall, I heard what I assumed was breathing. It was a lot like a rustling at first, and I almost mistook the sound for a wind picking up outside. But, it was also like the breaths rustled about behind my ears. I felt a nudge towards the basement door, something both gentle and unexpectedly internal.

I placed an ear to the wooden boundary and the rustling got louder, only it wasn't from breathing. It was from someone crying. "Reggie," I called, as quietly as I could.

There was no immediate reply.

"Reggie," I said again, more like a prayer than an inquiry. I spoke so tenderly then and realized that a chasm had opened up within me. There was nowhere to go with the knowledge I held of his situation, of what he had done and possibly why.

With no response from the other side of the door, I moved away and back to the kitchen to retrieve a key and flashlight from the junk drawer. What had happened may not have been all my fault, but I'd certainly had a hand in it. Harming Reggie and my mother may have been unintentional, but it was not without its karmic toll. I had to see him.

Removing the padlock, I hoped that Brian would remain occupied upstairs for a while. I swung the door open and was met by that signature musty smell. There may not have been mold or tree roots down there, but foulness lurked and gave off an aroma. I fought back the inky blackness right away with the flip of a switch, illuminating the stairway down. "Reggie," I called out again, only to be answered by a heightened sob.

I hesitantly descended the stairs into so much stagnancy and grief. Waves of it hit me with such force that I was immediately fighting nausea, which increased with each step until my feet hit the cool concrete floor. I turned on the flashlight to aid me in my search. "It's ok," I continued talking. "It's just me."

A couple of minutes later I watched as Reggie slowly emerged from the darkness of a basement corner. He'd looked exactly as I'd remembered him from life, from our sessions together, from a time that was ours whether we realized it or not. He was alluringly large and strong and carried his weight with a good deal of self-confidence. His russet mane and fair complexion stood out against the blackness. The only thing that seemed changed about him was the slouch in his shoulders. He appeared bowed.

I took a step forward and then cautiously took another. "Reggie," I gave credence to his form carefully and spoke more for my benefit than in an effort to reach out to him. It bothered me greatly that he wasn't talking back and didn't even try to move. Silence stood between us in a macabre invisibility that had feeling but no substance, and bore down on my soul with a tightening of screws.

'Be careful,' Silence seemed to say. 'Pay attention. Take your time.'

I took a few more steps until I was standing directly in front of him, until I was close enough to touch him had I wanted to. I defied Silence and my own better judgment.

I searched Reggie's frame for answers and then his face. Tear marks were the only clue to his state of being. He had been crying, but why?...

Why not? If anyone had a reason...

"My mother was here today," I offered. "Were you crying for her?" It hurt so much to ask, and I wasn't even sure he'd answer. But, if there was pain in the asking and possibly in the answering, I was hopeful that there might be a sweetness, too. And, in an unattached part of me, I'd wished for him to mourn for her, to grieve for their lost connection. It would've been redemptive for their very natures, for their souls.

It was then that he looked at me with total abandon and personal obliteration in his eyes. They were the eyes of a man that had nothing, eyes of the dead.

"I fell in love with you," Reggie said to me at last, "the real you."

I couldn't help but touch him. I reached out and placed a hand on the side of his face and was surprised by the solid surface and warmth I'd found. If it weren't for his lack of breath I would've sworn he was still alive. Reggie turned into my hand so that he rested serenely there. It was a moment I captured in a mental image click, for it might have been the closest we would ever get to what we might have been together. Even to this day, I look back on that encapsulated instant fondly; remembering it tenderly, for it was the best we would ever be with one another.

"I'm so sorry," I said to him, as if that could ever be enough. "I'm so sorry for abandoning you. I didn't understand, and still don't..." my voice failed as he touched me, his hands stroking the sides of my face and then running the length of my unruly hair.

"I fell in love with the person you were before the accident," Reggie went on with the exposé I'd denied him in life. "Not the wife or mother or business owner, but even before that," he clarified. "Before all of it happened to you. I know who and what you must've been."

I felt myself coming undone in his transfixed and unforgivingly dead gaze. He had nothing to lose, and I had everything to gain by hearing what he had to say. In my soul I sensed that something primal was about to be unleashed.

"It was who you were and who you're becoming now," Reggie told me. "I didn't want to lose you," he whispered, and I could tell that it was to avoid moaning.

And, in that moment, and in that space, I had tears for him. The weeping I wished I could've done so appropriately at the viewing arrived in the solitude of the basement. Like my own mother, I wept from a veritable ocean of sadness. I'd only been lying to myself when I'd thought out of fear that I didn't in some way love him. For nearly three years he'd been everything to me, and despite appearances, perhaps I'd been practically everything to him. I'd sensed our intertwining lock without knowing it and made moves without consciousness. We'd led each other on ignorantly, like the blind leading the blind, and this was the result. In the end, when things were going so badly, I'd tossed away all that had been good in an effort to rid myself of fear and disgust. I'd discarded more than a life; I'd killed a love.

"You were all that I had," he finally said through my tears and his own, which I reached forward to touch, to see if they were real. And, to my astonishment, they were as real as any tears shed by a living being — hot, wet, and salty.

"I didn't know," came my pathetic response. The flashlight and key clattered on the concrete floor and I flowed into his embrace, clutching him tightly as if to will him back into a cohesive existence. The tentacles of his agony and anger wrapped around the center of my chest, putting pressure on my heart so that it sobbed with every beat.

"I don't see what everyone else sees, Sally," Reggie revealed as his hands roamed the plane of my back and nestled into the hollow above my hips.

"What do you see?"

"Something in you that is wild and mysterious..."

I clutched him even tighter.

What if he had been the only one to ever see it?

"... and dangerous. Like me," he added.

I didn't know how to respond to that. The truth hurt, and it stung even more that I'd lost the one person who would've been able to identify it without harsh criticisms attached. I'd done wrong by so many people in my life, even those that stayed by my side and cared for me in spite of it. And, I was a murderer, even if I hadn't dealt fatal blows with my own hand. That's what I was. I was a predator who'd been trapped and had been willing to do anything to get out, and the only one who had seen me and loved me for that very heinous and selfish trait had been Reggie. Reggie, who had been a trapped predator himself, even if I wasn't aware of his exact confines.

Did he have a past like mine?

He must have, especially to have been forsaken by so many, including those in his own family. The sparseness of his viewing paid tribute to who he had really been, and there would be a vigil that Silence would hold beyond that in perpetual testament.

"Like you," I agreed without question and stretched on tiptoe to kiss his cheek.

Reggie swept me up into his arms and kissed me with a diseased passion that sparked a delirious fever in us both. I grew hot, nauseated, and famished. I wanted to devour him into myself and preserve him there, all the while uncertain whether or not I'd be able to keep him down. The urge to consume and the urge to vomit were at odds with each other inside me. I knew instinctually that I was capable of the types of depravity he was, and that I was as torrential as he could be. There was an aspect of that realization that was liberating but also threatening. Our own natures could very well be our undoing, an undoing he'd found with my mother first. We were equally disastrous.

In my musings and subterranean passions, I had this strange sensation of being tossed about, slapped by waves and also floating amongst them in a hardened and scratchy bliss. I was in that same dingy that had floated around amidst the waves after my unreal assault in the dining room. I sensed movement and didn't care where I was going or how far he'd take me.

Very carefully, with almost holy reverence, Reggie set me down. We were alone in the dark, and only a glow from the far away basement light source reminded me that there was the distant hope of a way out, should I want it.

I'm being placed on an altar.

"I wish you had never left it," Reggie whispered into my ear and then vanished like smoke on the wind, and I was alone.

Blue tinged leather surrounded me, although I could not see it in the blackness that grew denser with each breath I gave to it. I felt the unmistakable patterns of the hide at my back and to my sides, along with the cool metal of the monstrous altar that held me. But, it wasn't really an altar at all. Once again I felt like vomiting but held the contents of my stomach in, as I became a quivering mass of memory in my wheelchair. I feared that my desires and Reggie's were not that far apart, and that I also had a wish to return to the confines of my chair, to a time where I'd had the perfect excuse for my life and everything that happened in it. Reggie had been close and my world had been small. I hadn't known then all the things that came to light in the aftermath. And, if I hadn't gotten better I would've also retained the perfect punishment for my dead child and withering marriage. Life would've stayed just.

Everything was in its place when I was set in that chair, and there was no need to look further down the spiral path of living.

I stroked the metal sidebars and stoked the fevered flames that licked at my brain. Then I ran my fingers along the rubber of the wheels and heated the surfaces I found there. I'd been in this wheelchair when I'd first met Reggie and had experienced that instant connect. And, he'd had me to himself with no hope of escape. He'd been able to live his life without worrying about me slipping through his fingers like the rest of the shifting sand.

Had I really been more stable here?

I questioned myself from the imprisonment of the leather and metal. I felt my limbs wither and my soul age in its grasp. The tears that flowed were cold, and from a well of bottomless regret that sent a chill through my being. The fever and its delirium that I'd relished were taken from me, and I was left in the cold and dank. I remembered what it felt like to be a prisoner in my own flesh and recalled each and every scar that had marked me with vivid clarity. Horror ran through my veins and pummeled my chest until it escaped out my mouth in a very dry and brittle cry.

With what strength I had left in my limbs, I leapt from the chair and scrambled for the dimming light source at the other side of the basement. With a vague recollection of how the basement laid out and where I was, I scrambled, hitting walls and shelves and items on my way.

Do I want to run away? Should I stay?

I threw up clouds of dust in my wake, even with conflicting thoughts and actions, and finally tripped and fell in a sudden stop over the tarped canvases near the archway. I lay there drawing in one sickening breath after another, the foul odor, arising from the dirty floor. Seeing my flashlight only a few feet in front of me and the key to the padlock shimmering near it, I relaxed a bit and attempted to let some of the sadness and sickness subside, which it did very, very slowly. The light was sobering and sane, and I focused on it with startling desperation.

Several breaths later, I got myself up to a sitting position and began to check the surface of my face for scars. After more passes over my skin than I can count, I came to the conclusion that there were none and let out a huge sigh. I ran my hands over my legs and arms for further confirmation of my physical wholeness, only to be once again assured by my senses that everything was as it had been before I entered the basement, before I'd sat in that wheelchair. I went to work untangling the tarp from my feet, and as I did so I noticed a familiar face staring back at me with large owl eyes from the canvas on top.

I drew in closer to the canvas and had a sudden sinking feeling but couldn't be sure in the low light. Instead of bolting out of the basement and putting the whole horrible mess behind me, I'd decided to retrieve the flashlight and bring it to shine on the pile of canvases.

When the warm yellow light hit the artist's outline of her face, I recognized her instantly. Young, beautiful, and yet somehow sorrowful — it was Trina. Her owl eyes shone up at me from a time long gone by, a time before the coldness had settled in her. But, to replace the coldness, that artist had captured a hint of sadness, which was the burden of a living creature with a breaking heart. Her pale skin loomed largest, showing a grand essence behind those hoot owl eyes and mousy features. Her clothing choice in the painting mirrored the style of clothes she'd been wearing when I'd seen her, and she appeared consistently flawless. I wondered when the work was rendered.

As I shone my light all around the surface of the canvas, a small copper plaque secured to the bottom with some sort of adhesive caught a glimmer and my eye. It read — 'Catrina Casey, 1945.'

1945.

The year rattled around my head until it hit a sane pool and created a splash. I flipped immediately to the canvas behind Trina's image. Sam and Mary were the subjects of the next rendering, and at the bottom was another small plaque — 'Sam & Mary Casey, 1945.'

I proceeded to the third and final canvas in the stack and was met with the face of a man I'd never seen before, and I was thankful for that. Outwardly and initially, the man in the portrait appeared quite handsome, with a dark and brooding quality that had never been lost on me. He reminded me of my own interpretation of Edward Rochester from *Jane Eyre* with his tall, prominent, and hardened features. He looked positively chiseled and also absolutely ruthless. There was a cruelty about the mouth and eyes, lines that suggested a sinister being lurking behind the fine façade. I shivered at the mere sight of him and then glanced quickly to the bottom of the canvas for a name — 'Lionel Casey, 1945.'

Who the fuck are you?

My first impulse was to drag Brian out of his pristinely logical office and down the basement steps, so that he'd stand in front of the canvases while I shouted 'ah-ha!' It was tempting as he'd been so ready to dismiss my feelings on the matter when Trina had showed up at the house with her two children. I still hadn't received the paperwork from Ella to add more ammunition to my arsenal, but I no longer felt I'd needed it. However, before I took Brian down to the basement, I knew I had to get more information. I didn't necessarily need records and files, but I needed knowledge and understanding.

Unlike prior instances, I had learned enough about #18 and the court to realize that going off half-cocked would solve nothing. My situation was not ideal for that, if any situation could be. No, I may have had awareness in the beginning when we'd moved in, which may be more than can be said for most people, but I'd lacked knowledge. At that point in the spiraling spectrum, as I sat with the revelations of a veil lifted, I'd had knowledge but lacked a thorough understanding. All of that lead to one inevitable conclusion — the quest for more knowledge. I was learning. I was a viable strand in the web of life again, and not merely a space in between.

I padlocked the basement door shut and returned the key and flashlight to the junk drawer. Wasting no time whatsoever, and not even stopping to tell Brian where I was headed, I donned my coat and dashed out the front door. The sky was lit up with furious shades of red, magenta, orange, and yellow. It was as though the world were on fire, as if the sun were putting up the largest fight of its life to not have to dip below the horizon and accept its period of prolonged rest, an abdication to the rising moon and shimmering stars. It wasn't really that late in the day as we were still so near the solstice, albeit on the other side. But, it felt late as sunset was happening swiftly and with savage outcry.

My feet crunched down into the deep bed of snow as I went from my yard to Annabelle's. The lights were off in the house and all the windows remained dark, as they'd been all day. Staring at her house, and even more so at the front door, was a lot like looking into the gaping maw of an unfathomable monster. Something malevolent dwelled there, but was it home?

I shook off my yoke of loyalty to Annabelle briefly; resolving to take it up again as soon as I could, as soon as it was pragmatic and I could do more than bang on a door. At the first noticeable sign of life in that house, I was going to act. And, if that first noticeable sign didn't happen by the following night, I swore I'd break and enter to get at the truth. It was a vow, a solemn pledge made with the heartbeat of a healthier love.

I journeyed across two more lawns to reach the side door of Margaret's house. The lights were on and I prayed she was home.

My prayers were answered, and they paved the way for a confessional in her hearth space. With no time spent on an easier transition, I sat down and launched into what was happening to me and around me and did so right in front of Lyle and the three inquisitive faces of wildly different housecats. I told her about Annabelle and even Reggie, to which Margaret didn't even produce a blip on the radar of surprise, she merely turned to make eye contact with her husband and convey some unspoken message. In fact, it wasn't until I had started in on the portraits of Trina, her children, and Lionel that she showed any stirrings of deeper interest, of stormy questions forming behind her perfectly placid surface.

"I just don't know what to think anymore," I finally said in total subjugation to circumstance, a sign of near defeat. "A person can't possibly go on living this way, with these things."

"Not well, at any rate," Margaret acknowledged.

"Look, I get this feeling that you know a whole lot more about all of this and that you can help me," I leveled." So, please, help me."

"Have you called Ella?" Margaret asked.

"Yes, yes, I called to get files on the history of the house, ownership records mostly. But, I'm not sure that's what I need. I mean, that's not what's confusing me," I clarified. "I know Trina used to live in my house, at least, according to her," I laid one of my cards on the table as a good faith gesture, in addition to the cards I'd laid out with Reggie and Annabelle.

"She lived there," Margaret confirmed, "but I didn't know her then," she said with a wry smile. "I may be getting older, dear, but I'm not that old."

I gave a small smile of my own. "I wasn't suggesting that you were."

"I met Trina when I moved into this house the first time, after having passed by #18 on my way home. I met her and her children... and Lionel."

"Who was he?" I pressed on.

"Lionel was Trina's husband. He bought the house late in 1939, before the war started to loom too large. They were very well off and seemed to have nothing to fear from the outside world either way. And after what happened, the house remained vacant for a very long time and fell into a state of disrepair, until it was purchased again in the early eighties by Tom and Ellen Sedgwick. And, yes, I knew the Sedgwicks... very nice and sensible people. They were good neighbors," Margaret reminisced. I could see in her face a flash of poignant memory and an encapsulated sense of old and dear friends lost.

"Wait, you said the Sedgwicks bought the house 'after what happened.' So, what happened?" My wits were suddenly razor sharp, and I was honing in on important details with pinpoint accuracy, as it was quite obvious to me then and now that it's the little things that most often matter, that so often ensnare you. It's not so much the threat you initially see, but the threat you don't.

Margaret opened her mouth to speak and then thought better of it. She gave a nod to Lyle, and he joined us at the table for an unparalleled conversation.

"Trina and the children died," Lyle summed up.

"When?"

"In the spring of 1949," he said sympathetically, as if he held some connection to the events. Although I didn't believe Lyle could possibly be that old either. "You see, Sally, it was a ghastly affair, and that along with a whole list of other things that went on before, created a taint to the court. Reports started to twist into crazy rumors and local tales, until Willow Tree Court and all the houses in it only seemed to draw outsiders and certain types of people. There's simply no denying that wild, extraordinary, and sometimes heinous things have happened here." He let his words have space so that they could hover between the three of us, and then finally sink in with me.

"How did Trina and her children die?"

Do I really want to know that? I've lost my own child.

"Trina and her two children, Sam and Mary, died of carbon monoxide poisoning. She set them in the back seat, started the car, turned on the radio, and never opened the garage door."

The garage! The terrible, hospice-like atmosphere and that sickeningly sweet aroma mingled with the whiffs of a strong, astringent cleaner. Of course, that smell was familiar. The garage looked and smelled of death after what had happened there, even after all these years.

I knew I was gaping, lost in my own incredulous thoughts, and they weren't only about the garage but about the woman and her offspring. Trina had seemed so mousy and delicate and kind. It was plain to see that she loved her children, and they seemed to cling affectionately to her even after death. How could it be possible?

"Mary was eight and Sam was six, I believe. Is that right, dear?" Margaret asked Lyle.

To which he casually responded, "Yes." Giving me a few more moments to digest, Lyle then went on. "Trina was a good mother, Sally, but Lionel was not the ideal husband or father by any stretch. They quarreled regularly, and though there may have been love between them, he was oftentimes cruel to her and the children. And, then when Trina found out he was having an affair... I think that was what did it. I think Lionel taking on a mistress put her over the edge."

"But, the children..." I returned to the most central point of the story for me.

Lyle displayed both a somber and soft expression, one of understanding. I may have even seen something similar on my father a time or two. "I don't think Trina ever meant to hurt her children."

"Of course not," Margaret chimed in, rallying to Trina's defense. "And, times were different then. For women it was harder. There were fewer options, fewer avenues of escape."

"And, that one incident succeeded in severely tainting Willow Tree Court to such an extent?"

Don't things like this happen all over the world? Aren't cases of temporary insanity and blinding grief fairly common? It's part of the human condition.

"After it happened," Margaret picked up the tale from her husband, "it was reported that the willow in the cul-de-sac wept a bloody sap for days. The heavy spring rains came through the area and began to wash away the bright red tree sap so that it looked as if the street itself was running red with blood."

The willow seeped a red sap that looked like blood droplets in the rain the night I took Sonya home to #18. It wept over my dead child and another incident of maternal betrayal brought into the court's history. It wept by extension.

A chill passed through me, and I couldn't resist the shudder that followed.

"What about Lionel?"

"What about him?" Margaret asked.

"Well, I've seen Trina and the children. Is he still... around?" It was hard finding the proper words. In fact, the entire discourse seemed strained for all parties due to the topic being one that went beyond linguistics.

Margaret gave a heavy sigh, stood up, and went to retrieve the indeterminate fluff ball of a smoky gray cat that hovered around the stove. Scooping the bountiful animal up into her arms, she leaned back and appeared obliged to continue. "Thankfully, Lionel was dispatched years ago."

"And, the Sedgwicks?"

"I think they've moved on," was the best Margaret could do.

"We haven't seen them since their passing," Lyle offered as a means of expansion on his wife's words.

"And, that's it?"

Isn't that enough?

"No, that's part of it," Margaret answered. "This place has a long, diverse, and colorful history, but we don't need to go into all of that. You asked about Trina and her family, and we told you."

"You told me a horror story about my house and some of the people that used to live there. You haven't really told me what's going on. How can any of this help me?" I persisted, forgetting my manners and that I was a guest in their home needing their help. I kept blindly pushing.

"We've had similar conversations about all of this before. I think you know what's happening. And, I feel as though you've let things get out of control all around you." Margaret made the effort to correct me.

I'd opened my mouth to snap back at her, but she held up her hand.

"I'm not really blaming you, dear... only giving you my opinion. You see, Lyle and I have been where you are now. We've had loved ones and strangers encroach, and we've had to make decisions around that, take steps. "

Margaret and Lyle shared another exclusive glance, and in the time it took to do so another piece of the puzzle fell into place. "Cynthia," I announced, to which they both nodded. "She's more than a friend?"

"She's my baby sister," Margaret informed wistfully. "And, I can't let go of her, not completely."

"Can't or won't?" I asked brazenly.

"Take your choice," was Margaret's comeback.

"So, then how is your situation any different from mine?" I countered rather harshly.

"I have control of my situation," Margaret said abruptly. "I have a life. Remember what I told you before; the dead should never hold too much sway over the living. You're giving your life to them, Sally, and that's not going to end well. Sometimes complete separation is the only healthy, salvageable thing you can do."

"But, what if they won't go," I thought about Reggie, and then inevitably about Sonya.

"Those we bring with us are only here because we won't let them go."

"But, what about Brian? I'm worried about what he might be experiencing, holding onto."

Even hiding.

Was the beautiful card he'd given to Amelia still in my basement? And, if so, was it there because he wasn't letting go? He may not have been able to drag a living, breathing, and autonomous woman into our basement, but he'd certainly been able to drag his ardent memory of their time together, his own ghost of her.

"I'm not saying Brian isn't a part of the issues, but you need to worry about yourself — fix yourself and your situations," Margaret hardened, making me think of a tough aunt I'd never had.

"Once you clean up your mess, it'll be easy enough to see where Brian stands," Lyle chimed in with an encouraging catalyst for me to do the work they advised.

Do they share a brain?

I was in awe and slightly disturbed by their similarities and synchronicities.

"What's going on in your house, in your attic and basement... and to some degree in the garage as well... is what you can't let go of and what can't let go of you. Perhaps someone needs to let go," Margaret summarized as best she could. It wasn't easy. Words did oftentimes fail, such paltry things.

"Completely?"

Sonya.

"Sometimes you have to let go completely. Other times you only need to make a certain amount of space, space that allows you to maintain the connection you cherish but also lets you have a life. It's important to know what's best in each situation."

"How will I know?" I just couldn't help but push.

"Whatever clings to you the tightest is usually the most harmful, holds the most sway, and must be done away with completely."

Sounds simple enough... I suppose.

When I left Margaret's house it was pitch-black out, except for the couple of street lamps in the court and the reflected light off the snow. It seemed impossibly dark. As I looked around I noticed only a handful of houses were lit from within, and Annabelle's wasn't one of them.

I instinctually made my way to the barren willow tree to kneel in the snow and examine the bark. Margaret and Lyle had given me a great deal of information, and yet it had still felt as though so much was missing. I'd thought perhaps there might be so much information involved that only time and due diligence would fill in the gaps. But, did I have the time?

I made my rudimentary examination of the willow's surface, seeing some familiar etchings right away. The word 'doggie,' which always drew me first, was beginning to look hollowed out and thin, as though the scar were fading in on itself and becoming brittle and dry. I sensed that there was a greater truth in this process, but I hadn't been unable to decipher it. The russet mane tufts had disappeared, but the long ebony locks that swirled into the natural grooves remained prominent. Also prominent on one of the raised and exposed roots was the carving 'OMW,' refusing to be dismissed. It was deeper now and highly suspect. Would it also take to bleeding? Or could it heal over in time with no need for such dramatics? I hoped against hope for the latter but feared the former. Where the calico face had been cat's claws, outstretched and feral, had come to surface and they gave the distinct impression of some sort of defensive posturing. My thoughts went to Helios, who was the more outgoing of the two cats I kept and had made his presence felt right away, but he was still so very tiny.

I continued my vigilant circling of the tree, running my hands over the bark for a second pass. And, it was then that even more imagery revealed itself with remarkable clarity. I saw the angry hands that had been there before, but they led me directly to what looked like an artistic rendering of a frightened raven in a gilded cage. The carving was absolutely exquisite, beautiful enough to be stripped and placed in a museum on display. The raven looked convincingly terrified in the handiwork, fallen from the sky and possibly attempting to get up again only to find broken wings that would not serve and impenetrable imprisonment. The scene was horribly beautiful and done with such reverence that I nearly let the message slip past my conscious mind amid the fineries.

Annabelle.

Had that been a whisper on the wind or my own original thought? There was no way to be sure, even if it had mattered. The winds were picking up, and I shivered against their onslaught. As I moved to go, to head back to the warmth and questionable sanctuary of my home, I felt a gust of wind shoving me, pushing me away from my house and towards the solid, mutable surface of the willow tree. Another gust gave me a great shove, and I was up against it in alarm. I thought to struggle further, but that was when I heard it — the wailing.

The winds had picked up and whistled through the branches to create the unnatural sound of a wailing woman. It was sad and somber and unmistakable. It held a distinct aura like the mourning of the dead, tattered remnants of lost life. As I closed my eyes it was almost possible to see the detailed outline of a sobbing woman, her own flesh withered and gone blue with decay. I tossed my curls about as I made the effort to shake those visions away, to get them off me. But, when I opened my eyes, the imagery waiting there was far more intense. Droplets of water from melted ice and snow dripped from the willow's branches and dotted the snow below with their moist heat. It was as if the tree itself had grown warm and was melting all the cold that touched its cracked and creviced skin, it was as if the tree were weeping and wailing.

Is this a dream?

It sort of felt like one, but a nagging voice in the back of my mind shouted, 'You're awake!' And, I knew I was.

I closed my eyes again and ducked my head against the wind's angry resurgence that pressed me flat against the trunk. As I raised my head to look out once more and contemplate home, I saw hands, thousands of hands. There might have been a million, as it was impossible to count. Touching, rubbing, scratching mercilessly at my skin, at the bark of the tree I'd instantaneously morphed into. People, so many people touching me, manipulating me, and in the process manipulating themselves. The hands went round and then round again, until they grew into the bodies of animals that scurried up and down and flitted from branch to branch, leaving their own unique marks. They made their homes in me and abandoned them, too. They sought refuge and resource and change.

And, then there were the trees, other trees. Their leaves, bark, and roots all touched and taunted mine, causing just as much damage as they did rejuvenation. They fed me and kept me alive, and in that same way I encouraged their growth and unusual connections. However, there was no way of telling where the destruction started and the renewal stopped, as it seemed to ebb and flow and twist in a spiral pattern to match the grooves inherent in my own skin, my own bark, my intrinsic layers that sat upon layers, moving forever outward in concentric rings. All of it whirled about me and seemed too much, far too much to take in.

The winds began their relentless assault yet again, tossing me this way and that, until I only knew direction from the bent that they provided. I had no choice but to bow down to their merciless will and surrender myself. To resist would've broken me clean in two. I cried out my joys and my anguish into the wind as I was riddled with both, I wept and I danced. And then with the winds, came the sound of a sudden gut-wrenching crash. Ravens and crows took flight, startled away by the sound and the causative destruction. A scorching blaze that roared up like a lion seized me then, a fire that was lit all around me, turning me to ash and cinders and a more purified state.

And, then everything was normal.

I stood flush up against the willow tree, in my own body once more. I felt the whip of an occasional wind and the cold emanating off the snow. Silence kept close company with me, and I found that I was actually grateful. Instead of lashing my skin with a whip of his own, he soothed me with the brush of a hand against my back, and then a stroking that reached into and calmed my core.

What new and sweet torture is this?

I wondered how it was that I had grown to appreciate Silence's companionship again. It was as though

I'd gone around in a circle to find myself coming back to the place and beings I'd left behind. It was all far too much for one day, and I needed to go home. I had a funeral and more of the dead to face tomorrow.

I consistently ignored the urge to drag Brian downstairs and show him the canvases. Instead, I heeded Margaret and Lyle's advice and decided to work on clearing up my own issues, cleaning up my own mess. Brian wasn't blind, I'd told myself. He'd seen and experienced many of the same things I had and would soon have his own issues to deal with, of that I was certain. Bringing up the issue with the canvases and the court history would've been the equivalent of a headache to a drowning man, hardly noticeable.

I also ignored the impulse to go bang on Annabelle's door. The house was dark and vacant looking, sure, but that didn't mean I couldn't have gone over there and started something, or at the very least made some goddamn noise. But, I didn't. I reigned myself in, and decided to adhere to the minimum twenty-four hour stipulation I'd given myself. It hurt a little to think of her not being present at Reggie's funeral and burial with me, but some things have to be faced even with imperfect circumstances.

Brian and I got ourselves all put together in proper funeral attire, piled into the gray sedan that matched seamlessly with the somber, gray morning, and went.

Somehow, and even though the funeral was a quiet one, I thought it would be easier. I thought it would be simple to hear a few words and see the shell of a coffin lowered into the ground with the vacant remains and some final goodbyes from onlookers, but it wasn't as straightforward as that. Watching my mother continue to weep at his graveside was agonizing, and it didn't matter that her tears were softer and fewer in number than they had been just a couple days ago. Watching my father provide what little comfort he could was even worse. Reggie's sister was stoic while Brian was merely detached, and those points were the highlight for me.

It was difficult to care about the feelings of the few other mourners that I didn't know. My biggest challenge was holding back the few tears that rimmed my own eyes. Every so often, one tear would make the breach of my eyelid and trickle down my cheek like broken poetry. I had the dichotomous comfort and plague of knowing Reggie was not in the ground, and that made me both contained but not contained enough.

Sunlight was breaking through the thinning layer of clouds as the service concluded and everyone started to depart. My father and Brian exchanged a few words about the Sunday brunch and Christmas day, an efficient discourse and making the most of our trip to the city, while I took the opportunity to break away and wander back to the gravesite.

"Reggie," I spoke into the hole and towards the coffin, as though he could hear me, as if his earthly remains might call his spirit back by force, by an invisible strand in the web that none of the living could see or sense. "I want you to rest, be at peace." The words were edged with a cavernous love that I could not deny, and tinged with grief that would not be staid. "Be at peace, Reggie," I said, making the first attempts to let go from my end. "Move on to your rest and your reclamation." The last words made their way out of my body in a breathy rush, and I saw snow flurries shimmer in sunlight and then mingle with the puff of visible air I produced. The area around me felt tranquil, as did a portion of my own self, but that was more than likely only because Reggie wasn't there.

❖

An intention may have been set in motion at the gravesite, but the moment I set foot back inside the house, I knew nothing much had really changed other that the slightest inklings within me.

"Would you like me to make us some lunch?" Brian asked as we hung up our coats.

"That'd be nice," I said, trying to quell whatever mild tension was hovering between us. We were buoying lately from passionate caring and fondness all the way to a tense denial of our interconnected spheres. A middle of the road with regular, everyday occurrences sounded like reprieve.

"I think I might have to make a run to the local market. It didn't look like there was much left in the fridge last night when I went to grab a beer," Brian reported.

Did you even notice that I wasn't in the house?

"That's fine. I'm not starving yet anyway."

"Then I'm gonna change before I go," he announced, which sounded like a good idea. I followed him upstairs where we both changed out of our dirge of attire. I slid into a soft pair of black stretch pants and ample pink sweater that I must admit was circa 1985, while he opted for jeans and a sensible button-down polo.

In what seemed like a heartbeat, Brian was giving me a quick kiss and darting out the front door to round up a meal, and I was alone. But, I wasn't really alone. It wasn't long before the sound of footfalls was heard from the other side of the basement door.

I stood stock still in the hall and simply listened. Part of me was actually elated by the fact that Reggie was still so near, but most of my soul was filled with a sadness that went beyond any measurable degree of severity. I loved him. There was nowhere to go with that, no place to hide the feeling anymore so that I could live in denial. That unhealthy, tempestuous, feverish love boiled up inside me until it needed release in a sticky sap of sweat. I was stuck on him and he remained stuck to that glistening sap of my spirit. But, it was wrong for me to hold him there, no matter how much my arms ached to hold him.

"Sally," he called after many minutes had passed.

I crossed the rest of the hall and stood directly in front of the door. "It's all done, Reggie," I confirmed. "Your funeral was today."

"Was it?" he asked with too much innocence for him to truly be unaware.

"Yes. And, the burial was beautiful," I half-lied. "Very touching."

In many ways.

"Did you cry for me?"

"Yes."

"Were you the only one?"

"No. Most of the people there were crying. Your sister, Sarah, cried the most, I think," A bold-faced, full-fledged lie that I sensed would give him a measure of happiness.

Silence spoke with non-words. 'Be careful.'

"That surprises me."

I said nothing, being careful.

"Sally, I don't know where we go from here," he admitted with the timbre of a young boy who had gotten lost.

We aren't going anywhere.

I felt my eyes tearing up again, and I placed a hand on the hard wood as if that might give him solace. "Reggie," I said through free falling tears, "this is all my fault. I am so sorry for what I've done to you."

"I wish I had died in your arms." It was such a forlorn and dark regret, and one through which I also suspected there was manipulation.

My heart betrayed me and contorted it into what I considered a sign of his affections.

"I wish none of this had ever happened," I countered. "I wish you hadn't... done what you did. I wish you'd never left me."

And, yet, I could never have kept you.

"I didn't leave you," he insisted, and I felt the sharp blade edge on the scythe of his temper ready to reap me.

"No, you're right," I partially agreed with him.

But, I guess it really is completely true.

"Sally, I want to see you," came his dangerous and all too alluring request.

The feeling inside me then, I had to wonder if it was close to what a junkie felt when they were seeking their next spike. I wanted to see him, too. I was desperate to see him, but terrified of how it might turn out. I wanted to give him whatever it was he needed to move on, to let go. And, the longer I thought about it, the longer I stayed in that intense space with him, the more I grew to understand that one of us definitely needed to let go. If we didn't, I feared that the undying fire of our fervent emotions would consume us both and nothing would be left of either.

"Of course," I acquiesced and went to get a flashlight and the key.

When I opened the basement door, Reggie was waiting right at the top of the steps. At first I thought he'd just step blithely into the hall, but he held his place. The inky blackness spilled up ahead of him, making me apprehensive about my impending descent. But, as Reggie turned to go down the stairs, I felt compelled to flip on the light switch and follow him.

When we reached the concrete floor he turned to consider me. "Why are you still crying, Sally?"

Because it's not over yet, and because there is this part of me that never wants it to be over, not all the way.

"It hurts," was all I could come back with.

When I was finally able to see through my tears and make eye contact with him again, I could tell that he already knew. I saw that twitch in his jaw and the contemplation of options rattling around behind his consistently and deceptively stony surface. Reggie was always calmest before the storm. "It hurts that we have to end this," I brought myself around to saying.

"Sally," he closed the physical gap between us, and I felt that nauseating fever begin to take hold. Reggie placed his hands on my shoulders. "Don't do this to me. Not again."

His words were like arrows through my heart.

"Reggie, you were right, I am a lot like you. I am dangerous. But, I'm also not a monster, and neither are you. We don't have to destroy each other." It was the very beginnings of my campaign.

"Sally, I love you," he insisted, and as I looked into the lines of his face and heard the sincerity of his voice I knew that feeling, that love was at the heart of our destruction. No matter how much a portion of me might have wanted to, there was nowhere the two of us could go together from that launching point or any other.

"I know," I assured. "I know you do. And, I feel exactly the same way you feel. But, Reggie, we aren't good for each other. We're too much when we're together. And, I sense that you know it, too, despite any other feelings you may be having. Two wounded and dangerous people can't heal each other, or at least we can't." I kissed him gently and simultaneously felt and heard his sigh in response.

So there is some breath left somewhere in you, an energetic current that is not dissipated after death, that can make wishes come true.

"I have to let go, and so do you. You're dead and you can't stay here," I spoke with firm resolve.

By the time I'd pulled away and took a step back out of his once capable hands, he was already starting to disassemble. It wasn't something I could initially see from a visual perspective. It was more that he seemed to be hollowing out, losing the tenacity to be who he once was.

"But, where will I go?" he asked when there was only the faintest outline of him left to hold on, to hold the space.

"I don't know," I spoke the truth then, all of it. "But, I'm sure it will be better than here, and I'm sure you will be better off."

Let yourself transform, Reggie.

It was my unspoken wish for him, released in an exhale.

Let yourself transform.

It was my unsung wish for myself.

"You aren't the only one with unresolved ties," Reggie said, as the flame within him seemed to be flickering out, unable to hold its light against the natural encroachment of an energetic cold and dark. And with one last effort, he pressed a piece of fine cardstock into my hands, cardstock with a brocade pattern around the border and crimson flowers in the center. Coming into focus were words written in a printed script along the top — 'For Someone Special.'

Reggie was gone.

Brian came home with an armload of groceries to find me coming up the basements steps.

"What the hell?" he asked softly, shutting the front door behind him. "I thought we were keeping that door locked." The tone denoted a definite yet gentle reprimand.

"Reggie was down there," I said without missing a beat or even pausing to consider if I should've said anything at all. I merely let it out.

Brian shook his head in frustration and walked to the dining room table to set the groceries down before turning on his heels to face me. "If we're going to keep on living here, that door has to stay locked," he insisted.

"If we're going to keep on living here, we can't do it like this," I returned and stepped brazenly into the hallway.

"Where is he?" Brian asked, softening his tone once again but not by much.

"Gone."

"Gone where?" he continued to prod.

"Just gone. That's why I went down there in the first place."

Brian ran a hand through his hair in exasperation, and I could tell he was confused about how to proceed. "I thought someone was down there. I kept hearing sounds, but I assumed..." he trailed off before finishing his thought. "Are you ok? You look like you've been crying again."

That's because I have been crying again. Damn! How many times will I mourn the passing of one person?

"I'm fine. I took care of it. Now, you need to clean up your own mess." I strode forward and shoved the declaration of inappropriate love and spousal betrayal that he'd had for another into his empty hands. That deceptively innocuous greeting card.

Brian looked down at it and then back at me. "Why are you bringing this up here?"

"Why is it still down there? Why is it with us at all?"

"I don't know," he said defensively.

"Well, I do. You still have feelings for her. Hell, for all I know you might still be fucking her!"

"Sally – "

"Spare me!" I shouted over him in a ferocious roar. "It doesn't matter to me which one it is. You take care of this baggage yourself. It's yours. I took care of Reggie." I'd felt so proud and self-righteous in that space, but I had been too proud.

"Oh, yes?... And, whose baggage is Sonya? Is she part of our mess, too?"

It was as though Silence laughed at the both of us then in that hall. Brian had held the trump card, but by playing it, the bloodletting of victory splashed back to color him as well. Neither of us was clean, and maybe we never would be.

"How dare you! I love my daughter! I love her! Do your hear me?!" I found myself suddenly near and shoving hard to press him backwards into the table, to somehow make him submit and apologize, by force if necessary.

By force. He's almost twice my size.

"And, is that why you brought her into this house and then put her to the side? How many times are you going to be guilty of neglecting your own child?" Brian fought back verbally, although not physically. He may have thoughts of rage time and again, but Brian was never one to act out in violence.

And just like that, every sin I'd ever committed against Sonya, whether she'd been living or dead, blazed to the forefront of my mind. I knew I'd been neglectful, and on a couple of occasions Brian had brought it up, too. Post-partum and other explanations were given, but the result was the same. I'd been a poor mother then, and I was doing the very same thing even after her death. My life, no matter what shape it was in, always seemed more important than hers.

"Are you going to tell me you haven't been neglecting her?" I countered.

"What?"

"You lock yourself in that office and hardly ever come out. You've buried yourself so deep in your work that the only reason you've made love to me recently is because I threw Annabelle into the mix. How can you stand there and accuse me when you are more guilty than I am?" Blaming him had been the only ammunition I'd had left.

"Sally, I spend time with her. I'm not always alone in my office," Brian revealed, causing a large and unnaturally cold pit to sink into my gut.

Once again I found myself resenting Sonya, resenting the baggage of my own daughter. Sonya was no longer the living, breathing testament to a life gone awry. She was the undead imagery on a tombstone, an epitaph that read 'Neglect.'

"None of this is right," I said to Brian, grabbed up the grocery bags, and went to make myself busy in the kitchen with mundane chores that were the domain of the living.

Sunday brunch the next morning had been a quiet affair in which everyone attempted to act normal, and all of us agreed without a word about it to let the pretense stand. The Christmas holiday that followed on its heels was a hard one for Brian and me. The shadow of Sonya hung between us as though her spirit were always in the room, even though I sensed that she'd withdrawn into a part of the house where I'd never find her. I'd only see her again if she wanted me to.

My mother and father had bought and brought more presents for the two cats than for anyone else, spoiling them like the grandchildren we'd never be able to provide. A litter of tinkling balls, catnip mice, feather doorknob hangers, and fancy string wound up getting scattered everywhere. Larger items such a scratching posts, new litter pans, and hideaways were piled into a corner of the den until they could be given permanent spots.

The food was decent for two days, thanks to mutual efforts. And, we all took time to appreciate the snows by peering through windows and the holiday décor by looking and touching that had which had been strewn throughout the house since Thanksgiving.

"I'll help you get all of this down when we come over for New Year's Eve," my father told Brian and pointed to the long, braided holly wrap that made its way perfectly along the banister from first floor to second.

Brian nodded. "Thanks. I appreciate it."

All in all, the time spent was favorable. My mother and I seemed to be working past our largest issue, even if we no longer spoke of it. In fact, the secret we continued to hold between us might have been making us stronger. Every so often, I would see her glance in my direction, and then as our eyes locked with one another, two icy blue crystalline sets of orbs, we'd share a small smile. I sensed that I knew her better than I ever had before. And with what I'd gone through with Reggie, I may have also started to understand her. I could see why she'd fallen in love with him. I had, too.

With the basement having gone quiet once more and my parents packing up to return to the city bright and early Tuesday morning, I found myself with only one thing on my mind. The enhancement was especially heightened since Reggie had been removed from the equation of my life.

Annabelle.

I hadn't found enough time by myself to do a proper investigation. The vows and the stipulations I'd made to come to her rescue within twenty-four hours had lapsed, and she became yet another person added to the list of those I tended to neglect. Christmas morning had found the lights on in her home and some movement was spotted through the windows, but I hadn't been able to make out anything clearly. I hadn't seen her, and I was still concerned. She hadn't been over in a touch more than two days, and even though we'd gone longer, it was as if time had slowed and that stretch felt greater than any one prior. I'd neglected her and may have even betrayed our bond.

With those thoughts rattling around inside of me, I knew that as soon as I could I would make my way over there. I had to see her. Tuesday would find my parents gone, and if the weather held out, Brian would go to the office. I'd then make my way to Annabelle's. And, if I got no response from banging on the door, I swore I'd break in, even if it meant huge embarrassment later.

I had a sinking feeling just thinking of her in that house, alone with her father. I had an even worse feeling contemplating the possibility that he may have removed her from the house, taken her somewhere where I'd never find her. There was an aura about him, an essence that was most sinister. And, I went to sleep Monday night in a tense bedchamber with that as my last conscious thought.

I woke up very late on Tuesday to discover that my parents and Brian had already left.

People are always doing that to me, leaving without so much as a proper goodbye.

It was practically lunchtime when I'd gotten dressed and ready to trudge out into the snow. As I stepped out on the front porch and into the blinding sunlight, I caught the mailman coming up my steps. I saw more of an outline moving towards me and didn't quite make out who he was until he started speaking.

"I'll just hand this to you," said the well-bundled little man as he offered me a stack of letters and advertisements. "Happy Holidays!" And with that, he was off to the next house.

I went back inside to place the items on the dining room table, and then spied among them a packet from Ella.

The house paperwork.

That stopped me from my pilgrimage to Annabelle's. It wasn't so much the paperwork that awaited my perusal as the inkling that I should call Ella. I knew most of what there was to glean about the cursory history of my house, but what about #20? The storyline there didn't add up. Annabelle's admission in the car that she had always lived there, other than during college, and then simply moved back afterwards didn't fit. Her father hadn't owned that house the whole time. It was vacant when Brian and I had first moved in.

I couldn't be sure how much Ella would be willing to tell me, but I felt encouraged by the fact that she had said most of the information I'd been seeking on my own house was available to the public.

I grabbed my cell phone and gave her a call, holiday season or no.

After three rings she'd picked up. "Hello, this is Ella."

"Hey, this is Sally Archer. Happy Holidays!" I opened casually and with falsified good cheer.

"Well, Happy Holidays to you, too! How considerate that you would call me. I assume you've received the paperwork I sent you?" Ella's voice went from the coolness of a professional hello to a warm welcome of lyrical lilting.

"I did. Thank you very much for putting all that together for me," I responded with a gratitude that was a little less false.

"You're welcome. And, how are you and Brian? I hear you have little ones in the house?" she said in an anticipatory manner.

"Little ones?"

"The kittens. I heard you have kittens," and at that she laughed most heartily, almost too much so.

I pulled the phone away from my ear for a bit until she was done. "Oh, yes, we have them. I got them from the Hastings in #24. Their calico had kittens, and we took two."

"Well, that's very neighborly of you. What are their names?"

"Helios is the boy, and Selene is the girl."

"That's excellent. You keep them close now, and they'll do you some good."

Interesting choice of words.

"And, how are you and Brian?" she inquired further, always one for immaculate manners and appearance.

"We're doing all right. Thanks," I summed up vaguely. "Listen, I hate to ask, but I need another favor."

"And, what would that be?" she said, cooling a touch.

"I know this is something I could find on the internet somewhere, but I figured you might know off the top of your head and would be willing to share with me," I prefaced my request.

I felt the thickness of her waiting, as though she were in the same room with me, sharing the same space. She could have been staring at me, and it wouldn't have felt any more intense.

"Who is the owner for the house next door, #20?"

Ella laughed again, only a little lighter this time. "Now that's a silly question. You met the Taylors."

"Yes, I know, but who is the legal owner of the house next door?" I clarified to a fine crystal point.

Silence squatted on the floor and peered up at me with a large, invisible smile. I'd felt it was a game changing-question, a solid question, one with long and extensive roots.

"Annabelle Taylor," Ella at long last gave me an answer, and it rocked my world. I was pretty certain what would come next.

"And, how long was it vacant before she took over the property?"

Hesitancy, it was a favorite instrument of Silence, a close second only to stillness.

"A smidge over four years," Ella replied, sounding a tad automated.

"And, one last question, and then I swear I'll let you get back to enjoying the holidays," I tried to lighten, but neither of us was feeling it. "Who owned the property before her?"

"Dr. and Mrs. Gregory Taylor."

I wonder what happened to Annabelle's mother. Did she pass away? Did she run away? I know I sure as shit would.

"Thank you, Ella. I really appreciate it," I said as I sucked in a breath, unsure of what I'd walk into when I went over to #20.

"Sally," Ella said my name strongly before I could discontinue our call.

"Yes?"

"I know what you're driving at, and I know what you're doing. And, I'd like to give you a piece of advice before you go any further, if it's all the same to you." Ella rode the fence between warm and cool again.

"Go ahead," I encouraged with a hint of caution.

"It would be wise for you to be extremely careful as well as knowledgeable if you decide to go any further. Be those things or let it all alone, honey. Everything you're dealing with is both marvelous and malevolent. Willow Tree Court is a very precarious place to be," she warned, and I heard in her tone a sense of dutifulness.

That dutifulness irked me. "You know, all of that might've served me better if you'd said something before I moved in."

"Brian had already bought the house," she defended herself half-heartedly. I felt sure she knew the feebleness of her position.

"You should've said something to him if you were concerned."

"I wasn't as concerned about him – "

"Thank you, Ella," I ended our conversation, and I'd sort of meant it.

Chapter 9

I'd thought about opening the paperwork before going over to Annabelle's, merely to skim over it and see if it held any surprises, but that seemed so unlikely. I doubted there would be more in that envelope than what Margaret had already told me. Besides, the last thing I needed was another distraction. The paperwork could wait.

Let's try this again.

I stepped out onto the porch and into the blinding sunlight. With all the snow we'd gotten, the day was overly bright, and it was hard to know where to look that didn't involve squinting. I felt my heart rate jump as I made my way down the steps and across Annabelle's yard. I stood in front of the stairs that led up to her porch with a pounding pulse. What if it wasn't Annabelle that answered the door?

That's silly. Then I'll just ask if she's home.

There was no plausible, definable, rational reason in the world to be so nervous, unless I counted the fact that I had proof of Dr. Gregory Taylor beating on his poor, young daughter. But, I was not a helpless, senseless female in his keep. He couldn't harm me the same way he'd inflicted harm on her. I only feared the inevitable confrontation that hung like a specter in the distance. And, I was already forming unpleasant and illogical suspicions about that formidable specter.

I did my best to shake it off as I loped up the steps and stood boldly before the door. Without pausing for more fearful conjurations, I knocked.

The door was flung wide open in an instant. I'd barely even had time to draw my hand back. Startled, I felt myself jump.

It was Annabelle. She stood there, wild-eyed in the doorway, and questioned my presence without a single utterance.

"Annabelle," I breathed, placing a hand to my chest to slow my heart rate. "You gave me a start, woman," I said and smiled at her, feeling a rush of relief that she was ok. At the very least, she appeared to be ok.

"What are you doing here?" Annabelle asked softly in response and folded her arms across her chest, creating a barrier from the cold and perhaps from my intentions.

"What am I doing here?... I'm here because you disappeared the night of, or morning after, the viewing, and I haven't seen or heard from you since. It's been almost a week," I informed her with a tinge of disbelief that she would even ask such a question.

I've been worried sick! And, haven't you missed me at all?

Annabelle took a couple of steps forward and drew the door with her so that it remained open only a sliver. "Sally, you need to go."

"Why? And, where have you been?"

"I've been at home."

"No, you haven't. The house was dark for days," I insisted.

What are you hiding and why? I already know your dirty little secret.

"Sally," Annabelle spoke a fraction about a whisper, "you need to go. Go home," she pleaded.

It was the look in her eyes that made me sympathetic to her wishes, the expression on her face that made me want to comply. I saw those familiar embers in her dark ebony eyes and was lit from within by a blaze of emotions. "I'll go ahead and go, but why don't you come with – " and as I placed a hand on her arm to be encouraging, Annabelle recoiled in agony at my affections. The withdrawal happened so fast it was as if I had burned her.

Her eyes left mine and stared at the porch railings. "Sally, just, please – "

"Oh my god!" I rasped in exclamation, trying to keep my voice down. "What the fuck's been going on in there? Let me see – "

"No!" Annabelle shouted a little too loudly and gave me a shove out of her personal space. "No, Sally," she said quite a bit lower, and did a quick scan around her to see if anyone had heard.

I didn't know how to respond. I wanted to grab her by the arms and drag her, kicking and screaming if need be, to my house where we could both find sanctuary. But, I knew I had to stop myself from attempting that. If I forced her compliance, if I tried to physically dominate her in that way, I'd be no different than her father when it came right down to it.

"Annabelle, let me help you," I finally said, breaking the tense pause that had settled between us as she waited for me to leave. "It doesn't have to be like this."

"It's none of your business," Annabelle said in a flat tone I'd never heard from her before. A few seconds later, with no sign of my retreat, she simply shut the door.

I spent the better part of a week moping. Annabelle had never shut me out like that, and I would've been almost proud of her determination and ability to have boundaries had it not stemmed from blatant terror. To make matters worse, Brian and I weren't at our best either. There were times when the natural affections between us would be there, when the love that we'd forged would show itself, but by and large, he concerned himself with his holiday backlog of work. I, on the other hand, wound up bouncing between reading books, standing in the backyard for as long as I could, and aimlessly crafting up in the third floor studio.

With both Annabelle and Brian becoming more peripheral and the kittens needing less attention by the day, I found myself drawn to that heavenly space and all it contained. I wasn't quite ready to indulge myself in attempting any Tai Chi or yoga, but I did decide to do a sketch. With the warmth of the sun's rays on my shoulders and the light pouring onto my easel, it seemed a great way to pull myself out of the moodiness that had swallowed me and gain some clarity.

I'd just started putting pencil to pad when I felt a shiver run through the room. It was a delicate and withered vibration that barely caused a disturbance and yet it shook me. I put my pencil down and performed a brief look around. Over by the foam rollers was Sonya, ever young and preserved in purple plaid, she stood there with her ringlets shimmering in the brilliant daylight.

However, instead of sighing in relief that she was allowing me to see her, I gave an unintended sigh of frustration that I was being interrupted. Amid the guilt that it caused I held on to my frustration, as I was being steered away from progress.

"Sonya?"

She stood there with an intense gaze. "Mommy."

Mommy.

The word reverberated around my chest cavity.

"Yeah, sweetie..." I coaxed.

"I want to go outside and play."

Then go.

A combination of maternal instinct and regret overwhelmed me. "It's really cold outside, Sonya. Mommy can't be out too long," I said sensibly.

What is it about motherhood that makes me so tired?

"But, I want to go outside and play with the other kids, in the backyard," she was insistent herself, and she wanted me to be a part of her own childish whims and designs.

Other kids?

I admit that I was curious about who she was referring to, and that impulse drew me away from the sprout of creativity that had just broken ground in the studio for a new project. We walked hand in hand down the stairs and, with only a slight detour to grab my coat, I took her to where she wanted to go, to the backyard.

As I stepped outside with Sonya, I noticed that the sun had started to make its descent, its journey towards the immersive horizon and sleep. The dark shroud of evening would be upon us soon, and I would lose the precious light that had been pouring into my studio, onto my easel. It wasn't so much that I couldn't create in the dark; it was more that I had wanted to draw in the light in that moment, for my new project. My inspiration and sprouting creativity had been warmed and nurtured by it. But, instead I stood out on the back steps with my daughter, looking at our snow-covered yard and the barren trees.

"See," Sonya said as she pointed a finger towards the back tree line, jarring me from my melancholy. "I want to play with the other kids."

I squinted a bit as I tried to bring that far back tree line into better focus. As I did so, I started to see flashes of lighter colors emerge, and two distinct shapes darted in and out amid the oak sentinels. I watched for a while longer, still clutching Sonya's hand in my own, and then a third shape took form. It didn't take me very long to recognize her — Trina.

Trina and her children were playing amongst the trees in my backyard, what used to be their yard.

Sonya tried to pull herself away from me as I gripped her cold hand tight. "I wanna!" It was a basic child's outcry. But, I wasn't too sure how to feel about that. After the story the Hastings' had told, I wanted to be comfortable but couldn't quite get there. I reminded myself that Trina wasn't a bad person, and that it was evident she loved her children and vice versa. But, there was something amiss.

Trina peered out at the two of us, locking eyes with me in a shared semblance of sadness. I knew her grief, and I understood her struggle. But, my lot hadn't been hers, and there was still a barrier between what I understood and what I'd be willing to accept. I then saw Trina gaze at Sonya with all the tenderness any woman could offer to a child, hers or otherwise, and instead of being at ease with that, I became threatened.

You have your own children. You can't have my child, too.

And, I sensed that was precisely what Trina wanted. So, despite her protests, I took Sonya back into the house.

New Year's Eve started out as my father and Brian had planned it, with them taking down the holiday decorations. I sat around with my mother while they worked, drinking wine, loving on the cats absent-mindedly, and hoping that the new year approaching would be better than the old.

I couldn't get Annabelle out of my mind as the rest of the week rolled by, days peeling off one by one in a hapless blur. I'd talked to Brian about what had happened when I'd gone to visit, about her refusal to be helped and the abuse that constantly went on. To which he replied, "It's Annabelle's life. Other than calling the cops if things get out of hand, there really isn't anything else we can do." I was severely disappointed in him, and I doubted highly there was anything the cops could do. Odds were good that Dr. Gregory Taylor was beyond the law.

I had spotted Annabelle a few times through the windows in passing and had even glimpsed her from a second story window out briefly in her own unkempt backyard, adjacent to our own. I waved, but she made no motion to indicate that she'd seen me, although I suspected she had. She'd simply gone back inside after catching a breath of fresh air from the last day of December. I worried deeply when I'd seen her then, for she appeared to be quite literally wasting away. Even with the bit of distance between us, I could see the sinewy leanness and lithe outline of her frame. She looked faint, as though a strong wind gust would push her over. Her usually soft and silky ebony locks looked brittle and frazzled, and there was a gaunt weariness to her facial features, made prominent even in profile.

I'd also managed to become very selective of the time I spent with Sonya and where I spent it, as the week wore on. The new arrangements were making Sonya and me more miserable by the day, which then began to spill over into Brian's world as another wave of household unrest. I wondered if the ebb and flow that had become so common in my life would ever truly stabilize.

I really didn't mind Trina and her children being in the backyard and enjoying themselves. They weren't disturbing me at all, and it was something of a pleasure to see such a functioning family unit, alive or not. What did disturb me was Sonya's preoccupation with it and insatiable thrust to be a part of it. I resented that. Not only was that a dynamic she'd never found with me, but it was also a gift I'd never been given either.

"So, how've things been?" my mother broke into the discordant reverie of my thoughts.

"You mean since I saw you on Monday?" I snickered and polished off the rest of the red wine in my glass.

"Feels longer," came her casual observation. "I've never cared for the cold or the long nights. This time of year is just depressing."

Thanks for the pick-me-up.

"The days do seem to go by slower, or maybe it's just that there seems to be more space in between each day." More space seemed to be the likeliest explanation. The days flew by with so few hours of sunlight and the nights were so incredibly long that it felt an eternity to reach each new sunrise. It was as though I lay in a shallow grave all night with the sun, wanting to rise again and find the renewal I'd worked so hard for. Yet, I sensed more work; continued effort would be required of me.

"There's a lot to think about when you have nowhere to go," she went on.

"It hasn't been bliss for me either, being trapped in this house."

Not that I have anywhere else to go.

"You should come to the city soon, and we can spend the day together. Just you and me," she suddenly suggested with great gusto.

A mother-daughter day... I'm not sure how I feel about that.

"You think I should come to the city by myself?"

"Why not? There's no reason for you not to get out more. Is your license still current?"

I hadn't thought about things like driver's licenses in a long time. "Probably."

"Well, then, come on. You haven't been to the house in a while, and I'm going to begin basic planning of my spring garden beds soon."

Really? Just like that. You want me to help you plan the new arrangements for the garden beds, the same beds Reggie helped you turn over for the winter season?

It was all very hallmark, all very normal on the surface of it. "Gee, mom, I don't know..."

I poured another glass of wine, and while I was at it, I topped off her glass, too.

"Don't know what?" Brian asked as he strolled into the den.

"I'm trying to convince Sally that it would be a good idea for her to come into the city and spend a day with me, get out of this house more," my mother volunteered readily.

"She wants me to drive myself there," I clarified, thinking that somehow that particular specification gave more weight to my side of the tipping scale.

"So, why don't you? It sounds like a nice way to spend a day," Brian argued on behalf of my mother's suggestion.

"Well, for one thing, you have the car during the week," I brought up a pretty decent point for my case.

My mother immediately interjected. "It doesn't have to be during the week."

"Or, if it does, then I can simply work from home that day... so long as nothing requires me to be on site," Brian set down another mark against me. "Your license still current?" Pragmatic.

"I don't know, but I think so..." I said weakly.

"Then go," Brian pushed.

I didn't really know what else to say, other than to speak my main objection. "But, I haven't driven in years."

And, I don't want to drive now.

"Then it's time," my mother announced. "You're doing better, much better. It's time for you to start having a life again, a real life. You're young and you can get out there and contribute. And, there's a lot going on outside of this house and this court."

There's a shit ton going on here, too.

I looked at my mom and then Brian. "It's time to start living again, Sally," he spoke so kindly to me in that instant that a lot of the tension we'd held was suspended.

I want to start living, but it's just so hard when I'm also dealing with the dead. Not to mention, my terror at the thought of driving a car again.

I was out of discussable arguments.

"You ladies pick a day, and I'll see about having the car available," Brian authorized for my mother and me. And, then he turned to me. "Can I talk to you for a minute?"

"Sure," I said and sat back in the burgundy armchair with my matching glass of wine.

"Privately," he added.

I gave a dramatic and slightly playful moan to express my displeasure at having to drag myself from the cozy confines of my chair. I followed him out into the hall.

"Your mom brings up an interesting point," Brian began.

"She does?"

"Yes," he affirmed.

"And, what point would that be?"

"You should start to have more of a life again, a full and active life. You're doing so much better physically, and it might be time to leap on out there, stretch again. You used to do a lot of activities, and you spent a lot more time out of the home than you ever did in it," Brian recalled fondly.

Maybe that's because I hadn't been that happy in the house with you, in the beginning.

"I think it's a good idea for you to drive into the city for one day, and spend time with your mom."

"You've already gotten your way on this one," I reminded him.

"I also have another idea," Brian said as I braced myself. "Why don't you go ahead and make the most of that third floor studio space?"

"I use it," I said defensively.

I go up there, at any rate. I'm not sure I'm actually making enough use of it to claim any sort of progress or difference.

"I mean, use it for yourself. You should use it to push yourself forward and get back into all the things you lost. Don't try to make a point with it, or a business out of it. And, don't do it because you feel you have to prove anything. Just use the space because you want to and because you can. The space is primed and ready, no matter what caused that to happen. Why not make the most of it?"

he persuaded in his typical rational style, and I could see he'd had time to not only get comfortable with the idea and the manifestation, but also grow to like it.

I saw what he'd been trying to do, get me back into my pre-accident rhythm.

Find the rhythm and you find the key.

It was a concept I clung to in the earlier days of recovery, and something I'd heard in cognitive therapy before I'd abandoned it. It came around on the turning of a mighty wheel once again and lingered in my mind. The only problem was that I didn't exactly want to go back to my pre-accident life anymore.

"I'm trying to make the most of it," I finally responded to his prodding. "It's just that it can be hard to get much done up there. I mean, and this is going to make me sound like a neglectful parent all over again, but it's hard to get anything accomplished when..." I didn't want to say it. I thought it'd be easier if Brian could just intuit my meaning, sense where I was going.

He merely looked at me, and even though his expression revealed that he knew what I meant, he wasn't sure what to say either. Maybe he harbored similar feelings.

"I think it's kind of like you in your office. You're not alone in there, or, at least, not all the time," I went on.

Are you as frustrated as I am?

"We should both do the best we can," came his practical words of wisdom, words that would leave him guilt-free and also set the standard for as normal and perfect a life as one could hope to have in the confines of the court and situation.

The mild buzz from the wine was wearing off.

Something's got to give.

I spent the first couple days of the new year bundled up and out in the snow. I didn't want to be confined to the house, nor was I ready to try to make proper use of the studio again. I also didn't want to spend too much time thinking about the drive into the city I was inevitably going to have to make, especially since my mother was already texting me dates. With Brian back at work and the car gone from the driveway, I felt safe and contained and in control... for the most part.

I took a brisk walk around the court one morning, as time was a slippery slope once again. I settled for the slide so that I wouldn't have to be bothered with more troubling matters. I glanced at each house that was so much like my own and yet unique. They all may have resembled my house, but none of them were #18. All of them were built in the same grand old style that combined stone and wood and wrap-around porches. Original artwork windows glinted in the sunlight, and the stateliness of each home vibrated with a similar essence to all the ones around it. Yet, they all existed independently and of their own accord. Sure, some of the colorings, wood textures, and layouts varied slightly, but all of them held a closeness of character that was unmistakable.

As I arrived back in front of my own house and the willow that stood guard before its face, I contemplated all that had happened and wondered what was still to come. There was a trembling grief that shivered through me then, blending in with the muscle tremors caused by the cold. I'd let go of a love and lost a friend, no matter how damaged, in Reggie. Had I also lost Annabelle, too, my lover, and possibly the person I loved the most in this world? She'd shut me out completely, and after I'd grown so attached that it was hard to breathe properly without her. That hook in my ribs that tangled about the bones was still there, and the line in-between ached for her.

The sound of children laughing perked my ears and eventually stirred my brain from the fog of frustration and loneliness. It emanated from behind my house, and I immediately knew who would be there, whose children would be playing in the yard that was still very much their own. I made my way to the side gate and let myself in.

Some of the snow was starting to melt and the tops of grass tufts were peeking through. Trina had her children scattered about the yard making good, old-fashioned snow angels. I stayed near the gate and watched for a time until Trina turned to acknowledge me.

I smiled at her and wasn't sure why. She was a threat, plain and simple, but at the same time, she seemed so sweet and genuine. She felt like the closest thing I had to a friend in that moment, even with the bubbling discord.

Perhaps I'm lonelier than I thought.

It was only when she started to approach in that timid, mousy fashion that my hackles went up.

"Is it all right with you that we're spending time here?"

Does it matter how I feel?

"I guess it doesn't hurt anything," I responded hesitantly and with the edge of a chill.

"It makes Sam and Mary happy to be so close to home. I hope their noise isn't bothering you," Trina took a few steps forward, making the gap between us smaller.

"They're not that loud," I gave her. "Plus, I sort of like the sound of children playing."

Trina smiled and nodded. "It's refreshing. It makes me think of when I was their age."

"Yeah," I said wistfully.

"Would your little girl, Sonya, like to come out and play?" Trina inquired as though it were totally natural. And, what could be unnatural about dead children playing together?

It would be more unnatural if they played with live children, I suppose.

"Oh, I don't think – " and as I turned around to glance towards the house in thoughtfulness towards my response, I spied Sonya in an upstairs window looking down at us. "She's rather shy," I stated as I turned back to Trina.

"I see," she said simply. "Well, she's adorable. And, she's welcome to join us any time. I know I'd love to have her spend time with us," Trina admitted in a mother's radiantly welcoming voice. It was obvious Trina was already starting to fall in love with Sonya, such a sweet and lonely child suffering through parental neglect. No doubt she could identify it to the neglect her own children suffered through their father, and maybe even a little with her.

I felt so petty then, in the bold and stark light of it. Trina would love my daughter as no one before her had ever done, and my daughter was seeking out that affection. She hadn't been able to experience it in life, and so she was seeking it out after death. In as much, Trina was seeking reclamation, and not only through her own children, but as a mother in general. I absorbed the concept that the urge to nurture was resting at Trina's core.

I looked back up at the window that held Sonya's image and almost signaled for her to come to me, to join in the revelry, but when it came down to it, I held my icy position. It wasn't right in that moment. It wasn't right for me to make that kind of determination, at least not without first speaking with Brian.

"I think it would be nice for her to spend time with you, too. Let me talk with her and her father. Maybe something could be arranged," I offered with a bittersweet social expansion.

Trina lit up from within, her hoot owl eyes growing wide with hope. "I'd really appreciate that. And, it would make Sam and Mary happy, too."

I peered past her then to her two children, who had abandoned their snow angels in an attempt to build a snowman. "Good."

After a quiet dinner and a couple of glasses of wine from a bottle of pinot noir left over after New Year's, I made my opening move. "You were right," I said to Brian, pushing my empty plate away and snatching up another glass of wine. I sat back in my chair and waited.

He sipped at his wine a little bit more, and then met my words head on. "I can accept that," he said with a wink and a smile. "Right about what?"

"I have been neglecting her."

My response sat like a wedge between us, and I hoped he would judge me far more kindly this evening than he did the last couple of times we'd spoken about it.

Brian ran a contemplative finger along the rim of his glass, making circle after circle while he adeptly considered my admission. I could tell he was deciding the best course of action for a harmonious household, a goal he'd been striving towards for as long as I'd known him. It was sad really, as he had glimmers of it occurring along the timeline of our relationship, but it was a pinnacle goal of permanence that forever eluded him.

"I shouldn't have thrown it in your face like that," he held out an olive branch. "The situation is a hard one, and you shouldn't keep blaming yourself."

"No." He was letting me off the hook, and I wouldn't stand for it. "I was guilty of it when she was alive, and I'm doubly guilty now," I summarized with contempt for myself, mildly mitigated by the wine.

"I think you're drunk," was his first step towards being dismissive in a discussion that was likely to not go the way he wanted.

"God, I hope so. It might be the only way I can have this conversation."

Brian let out a heavy sigh to indicate his reluctance to go further with whatever I had planned, but I knew for the both of us to ever reach his ideal goal, I had to press on.

"I need to talk to you about Sonya, and about what's best for her."

Brian leaned in towards the dining room table, suddenly a tad bit more open. "Go on."

"You remember me telling you about the lady and her children that toured our house one day, a little while back? Trina and her two children, Sam and Mary?..." I attempted to jog his memory. "You were away at the office."

"Vaguely," he said. "I don't really remember the names. We've had a lot going on."

"Well, I think it would be best to surrender Sonya into Trina's keep." I just went ahead and hit him with my idea, figuring questions and explanations would have to follow, not precede.

"What would make you think Sonya would be better off with a stranger?" Brian asked indignantly. And, he had something of a right to be insulted, as he hadn't neglected her nearly as much as I had; he hadn't betrayed the same instinctual trust with her — maternal love, the most important pair bond.

"Because even though we love her, we neglect her... me more than you, but still. And, though she's our child, we can't give her what she needs now. Brian..." I paused as a lump lodged in the throat. It was hard to make the realization all over again. "Brian, our child is dead."

The words were like river rocks that clashed together in a surf which raged past my heart and through my throat.

I took him to the basement then and told him what I knew of Trina. I told him her story as recanted to me by the Hastings and then added a few new details of my own. I revealed the canvases hidden beneath the dusty tarp and the tale they told all on their own. And, by the end of it, I didn't even have to bother with dragging out the paperwork Ella had sent me in the file on #18 Willow Tree Court. When it all came down to it, the canvases spoke for themselves.

I let the flashlight shine on Trina's delicate features as Brian stood with Silence and attempted to take it all in. I was curious if it was harder for him to accept than it had been for me. I'd had the benefit of outside influences reassuring me of the experiential validity. Brian only had me. He would certainly need to have his own deliberation process, as Trina's story wasn't an easy one to accept; it wasn't easy to condone her actions. Sympathy was easier, but it was impossible to tell what Brian was thinking sometimes, his stony mask held tightly in place over any potentially revealing facial expressions.

One thing I knew we agreed on in the dark of the basement, with only a low golden light hovering around us, was that we'd been failures as parents, even more so than Trina had.

❖

Vivid dreams. If I hadn't considered myself prone to them before my accident and prior to the move, I'd sure felt prone to them ever since. And, as days and weeks and months went by in that house, the dreams became more and more vivid.

That night, after we made our way up from the basement, not even bothering to lock the door anymore, we went about getting ready for bed. Things no longer felt tense between us, but they felt sullen instead. There were no moves from either of us to make love, and there was no mutual comforting. We were each isolated in our own private worlds, sorting out the shit that we'd been handed, the hand we'd had a part in being dealt. The only bond that night was in our mutual acceptance of our own shit.

I'd taken a quick shower, brushed my teeth dutifully, and fell asleep naked beneath the blankets. And, I dreamed...

I walked from the bedchamber automatically, across the hall, to the door of the guest bedroom, drawn there by a familiar and unrelenting force. I knew I had to go there. I had no choice but to open the door and allow it to swing back in a wide mouth that revealed my grandmother sitting primly on the bed in the periwinkle suite. On each windowsill in that room she had arranged fresh and pungent lavender plants, and the arrangement seemed well known by me and intimate. On the bedside table she had a plate of rosemary bread and cinnamon sweet rolls, a favorite for us both. She looked at me as I entered, and she kept an eager watch.

"Why are you here?" I remember asking as I knelt in front of her, my nose picking up the overwhelming scent of the sweet rolls.

"You aren't happy to see me?" she said spritely in the tone I recalled from her life, although it was overlaid with a warbled and watery voice that only my soul heard. My ears heard quiet and the occasional rush of a breeze outside.

I smiled despite myself, and in spite of the fact that I knew I was dreaming. I was aware of it this time and knew she wasn't really there. "Happy as I can be."

"You are changed, but you are not there yet. You seem less diminished, but you are still not free," she whispered to my soul without her lips moving.

"I'm trying," was all I had to meet her with.

Her hands gripped my own and held tight. "Are you ready?"

The question felt monumental and was made even more so since it was asked without vocalization. "Ready for what?" I quizzed.

"Are you ready to live like you're dying instead of living like you're already dead?" I watched as her lightly shaded eyes grew dark in tone, grew to a deep, dark forest green, so green they were almost black. And, as I continued to peer into her eyes, I saw in the surface reflections the outline of a willow tree. It swayed in the breeze, the same breeze that rustled its leaves right outside.

I hope so.

Without my having to speak, my grandmother heard me and reached forward an ancient hand to run her bony fingers through my hair. She combed and combed my unsightly tresses until she found something, and I sensed it was something specific she'd been searching for. She pulled back her hand and held it open to reveal to me a seed, the likes of which I'd never seen before. It was simultaneously non-descript and astonishingly beautiful in its simplicity. It could've belonged to a tree, a vine, a shrub, anything.

I took the seed from her hand.

"Bury it," she instructed.

I nodded my compliance with her wishes.

"Bury it and let come of that what may," she instructed further and then pulled me deep into her leafy embrace where I couldn't tell if it was arms that held me or branches.

The morning after that catalytic dream, my heart broke for Sonya all over again, and this time it broke for Brian, too. I stirred to the sounds of an early morning storm and went immediately to the bedroom window that overlooked our backyard. Heavy, dark storm clouds were moving in from the southwest, and light rains had already begun. Apparently, the temperature had risen just enough and instead of getting more snow, we were due for some rain. That was dangerous.

What if it refreezes?

I feared for Brian if he decided to work at the city office. The thought of anyone being on the roads if that should happen was enough to make me paranoid. The thought of it being my own husband was a perpetual jolt through my system.

I got dressed and made my way to the bedroom door, but as I went to turn the knob and step into the hall, I heard voices. Brian was talking to someone.

He was speaking with Sonya.

Brian's tone was so gentle, and it was a paternal side of him I hadn't seen in years. We'd gone all the way around to find him in the same spot, one of diligent and dutiful fatherly love. All in all, he'd been a good father the first and only year of her life, and he remained an oddly ideal protector even after her death. We both may have been guilty of some negligence, but he'd been far more nurturing than what I'd proven capable of.

I heard him talk to Sonya of how much he loved her and how she would always been in his heart, and that if she got lonely or scared he would always be in hers. I listened as her light and waning voice responded as only a young child's could. There was an innocence that hung between them and a beauty of unrest and fervent ties beyond the veil. How I longed for that sort of connection, and how little I understood what might go into it. What came naturally to Brian was alien to a person like me. It may have been due to an innate selfishness or maybe a hardening of the soul. Perhaps like one of his work computers, I was simply incapable because I lacked the proper port for that type of attachment.

It was when Brian told her how much "mommy loved her, too," that I shattered. I broke into crystalline pieces like the panes of glass from my accident, for I understood that he believed I loved her; he wasn't about to condemn me further, and especially not to our own daughter. No, there was definitely no hint of failure in his voice, no tone to betray hidden and contradictory feelings. There was only the palpable reality of our unfortunate outcomes.

I wept for my child and for my strained marriage. With as much as I'd tried to quicken both since I'd lived in #18, I had to admit to myself that I'd been unsuccessful thus far, and the likelihood of success was waning.

Maybe it's because I've been living like I'm already dead?

A paraphrase of my grandmother's words from last night's dream rattled around a bit.

But, what would it mean to live like I was dying instead?

I wept for my failures and shortcomings and prayed to a nameless entity that might be merciful for a forgiveness I probably didn't deserve.

And for the first time, I cried for what I'd taken from Brian. I saw his losses sharply where I hadn't been able to see them before. In our apartment, in my wheelchair, in my walker, and in my caged misery, I'd only been capable of retreating inward and seeing my own suffering. But, his words to me from months before in our old bedroom rang true...

"I lost my child, too, Sally. I lost the life we'd been building and the wife that had made me so happy... I lost my ability to even try to give you another child."

I couldn't help but ponder how one person could screw up so much, make such a mess of things. The move to Willow Tree Court had given me so much, and somehow I'd wound up diminished all on my very own.

"I want you to go with the nice lady, Sonya," Brian said, in his best and most reasonable voice. It caused my ears to perk. He was being firm with her so that she'd have faith in him. "She's a friend of mommy's. And, you will always be cared for and always have others to play with..."

"Like a brother and sister?" Sonya's voice was shaky but surprisingly upbeat.

"Yes, yes, just like that," Brian assured so tenderly. "You trust mommy, don't you?"

I didn't hear a reply and could only hope Sonya was nodding.

"And, I trust her, too," Brian affirmed. "So, you can trust Trina, mommy's friend," he reasoned further.

Why can't I get along better with a man full of so many amazing qualities? Another shortcoming of mine, I suppose.

"And, Sam and Mary are going to love you! You'll see." Brian was good at pragmatic motivation, even with the dead.

I cracked a smile at that and had the thought that perhaps if Sonya could find happiness in the impending arrangement, then maybe Brian and I would find bliss afterwards. We could still work towards it, and I still loved him... even if that love was stretched to wrap around Annabelle, too.

You're a good father, Brian. You were an excellent dad for the small amount of time you got to be one. You were a good provider and a good protector. Too bad you hadn't been able to protect her from everything — you couldn't protect her from me.

I stayed in the bedchamber even when the hallway outside my door had gone quiet and I was sure Brian had left for the day. He'd gone to the office, and although the back of my mind churned with the potential refreezing issue, the thunderstorm sounds hid my sobs so beautifully that I felt thankful for the rains. And, somewhere in the early morning dark and the encroaching maelstrom, I let go of the territorial hold I'd had on Sonya since she'd come into the house. I let go of my claim on her after death.

A little while later, as morning was in the process of becoming early afternoon, the rains stopped. I heard the flushing of water from the gutters continue, purging the surplus from the downpour, but the storm itself, or at least the first wave of it, had passed. I got up from where I'd sat on the floor, in front of the bedroom door, and went to the window. Light cloud cover was over us and another band of pendulous storm clouds was holding very far to the southwest. Most of the snow had been washed into the ground and everything looked cold, miserable, and sopping wet. It seemed as though Mother Nature and I had both cried ourselves out for the moment, and the scene outside depicted my depleted inner scenario.

I brushed off the few carpet fibers from the ornate area rug and traces of dirt from the hardwoods that clung to my defiantly orange peasant skirt. I straightened my gray turtleneck that matched the skies, and then went to the chamber bathroom to splash water on my face. I'd been hoping for a better start to the day when I'd first gotten myself together. Instead, a blotchy and puffed reflection stared back at me from the looking glass. I was a shambles and the day nearly half done.

The cold water felt exquisite on my puffy and severely reddened eyes. I even took to drinking some from my cupped hands to ward off any symptoms of dehydration. By the time I was done reassembling what was left of me in the bathroom, I appeared mildly more human. And as a living human, I needed food. It was time to step out of the sanctuary of the bedchamber and make my way to the kitchen, never knowing what I might encounter along the way.

It turned out to be nothing.

#18 was filled with an unearthly stillness. Silence ruled over my house that day with an iron fist and a promise of a taste of his whip if I stepped out of line. I didn't dare break his impending order. In fact, by the time I'd filled my belly with leftovers from the refrigerator and drank a hot and hardy tea, I was falling into step with the quiet and the melancholy that reminded me of how very much I still felt, how very much I had the potential to give. All that emotion and all that energy could be put to better use than it had been in recent years. The ability to start again wafted across my finer and not so finite senses.

It was after tea that I saw the sun peeking out from behind a thinning barrier of pale clouds. The scene outside continued to look cold and foreboding, but with the sun came my desire to lean in towards a window and soak up whatever rays made it through the glass. I grabbed a beer and went to stand in the puddle of sunlight that streamed past the sink and onto the floor.

I closed my eyes and sighed at the life-affirming rays that glazed the skin on my face. I felt every exposed pore open up like a sunflower to the light and drink in what ultraviolet they could. Such a sense of renewal and rebirth was present in the sunlight, such a promise of another day and more provisions. I thought of myself then as a great and giant cat stretching out into the warmth of solar bliss, letting the heat provided by nature stimulate every fiber of fur and muscle. I shifted and stretched in my contentment. I heard a faint moan of pleasure escape my lips.

It wasn't until I heard contemplative mewing that I broke from my fantasy and opened my eyes. Standing directly behind me were Helios and Selene. As I turned all the way around to face them directly, they mewed again, one right after the other. I smiled despite myself.

Silence certainly has no hold over you two.

They stood on a tiny patch of sunlight as well and squinted upward to cry out in pathetic want once more.

"Oh... what?" I cooed in return.

A couple more feeble cries escaped them both as they sauntered over to their empty food bowls and then looked back at me.

"Well, that's pretty blatant," I said to the two fluff balls, whose eyes were already losing that baby blue and turning to a permanent adult color. I retrieved a bag of dry food from the pantry and poured a generous amount into each bowl, staring down at the kittens as I did so and really taking in their development.

Selene was the same shade of black she had been when I'd gotten her, but I started to notice a fleck or two of additional white that wasn't there before, and the fuzziness of her coat wasn't quite as pronounced. Of course, neither was her brother's. She had started to show green eyes, instead of a true baby blue. And, I thought to the large black male with the green saucer eyes at Margaret's house.

Maybe the calico getting pregnant was an inside job.

I turned my attention to Helios, whose orange stripes were gaining greater contrast by the day. He, on the other hand, was showing a golden glow to his complimentary orbs, the illustrious yellow eyes of his mother.

I squatted down and stroked both of them while they ate. They initially stopped and looked at me with matching expressions that conveyed the message, 'Do you mind?' But, I continued to stroke them anyway. They were so soft and supple and vibrant in being. In a second or two they went back to eating, ignoring my need to pet them, and we spent several minutes that way.

Eventually, Helios and Selene sauntered off, and I was left to my beer and my solitude in the kitchen. I immediately went back to the sunlight.

After polishing off my beer, I was heated and glowing from without and within, having sucked up the sun, food, hot tea, and a buzzing amount of midday alcohol. I placed the empty bottle in the sink and looked out the window to gauge the distance of the storm clouds, only to be disrupted by the flurry of rapid activity. I knew instantly it was the frenzied rush of children at play.

It was time to bury the seed.

I didn't even sigh as I made my way out the side door and into the backyard, forgetting to bother with a coat to ward off the chill. There was nothing more to sigh or cry about. On the contrary, I felt my pulse grow rapid and my breathing was shallow at best, and at my worst moments it was simply nonexistent. It might have been in my best interest to forgo the comfort of a coat, as the deep winter cold kept me sober and sharp.

I stood immediately past the last step and shivered in the grass as I waited. With each muscle trembling I felt sure I held awareness. I consoled myself with the fact that I'd be clear headed. I waited and watched Sam and Mary scurry about the yard, remaining unnaturally dry amid the wet grass and tree branches. Many oak and maple that lined my backyard had braches that were torn asunder from the onslaught of the rains mixed with the barrenness of the season. Sam and Mary played with those as well and stayed perfectly dry and eerily warm in their cheery seasonal ensembles. From just looking at them, it was impossible to tell that they weren't what they seemed, that they didn't live and breathe and grow. I sensed it though, both from prior knowledge and from first-hand experience with breathless lungs.

They are so carefree and beautifully preserved.

Time could not touch them, and Silence held no sway over them. They were exempt from Nature's mockery, as their energy patterns played on. I held a fervent prayer that it would be like that for Sonya as well. I shut my eyes tight and envisioned her playing with them in the wet and golden grasses, flitting amongst the barren black trees. I imagined her in that peculiar purple plaid I'd selected and thought of her as four years old forever. But, would she be?... Sam and Mary might not have aged in decades, but Sonya's spirit had aged, as the living would've done in the span of three years. My eyelids flew open.

What if she ages and flickers out? What if she leaves me to eventually be no more?

It was a thought no parent wanted to consider, no matter how real and probable. It was a thought most parents set to the side because the odds weren't great that they'd outlive their children. Would I have the unfortunate fate of outliving mine twice? Or, out-existing at any rate?... It weighed on me until I had to sit down from the pressure. I'd had no idea what I was getting into.

I back peddled to the steps, and even though they were made of concrete, and very wet and cold, I sat down anyway, burying my head in my hands. Maybe my compassionate plan wasn't the ideal solution I had envisioned. What if Trina and the other children accepting her and loving her wasn't enough? What if she had to be with me because she was tied to me? If I let her go, if I let loose what held us in place, she might be lost completely.

Something inside me rocked back and forth, and I heard in my soul the warbled voice of my grandmother. She matched the wet state of nature all around me.

"Bury it and let come of that what may."

Did I even have a choice? The current conditions weren't livable for me or sustainable for Sonya. And, sitting there on the concrete, that's when I finally sighed.

My thoughts roamed to Trina and I prayed she would come soon, that her spirit would visit me so the seed I'd held and let wither could be buried, for whatever it was still worth. I sat shivering and rocking, refusing to go back inside for even a minute to fetch a coat, fearing a window of opportunity would close on me, and I wouldn't find another one to open.

Time passed painfully slow, like maple sap dripping inexorably down frigid bark. And, it wasn't until I started losing feeling in my fingers and toes that I heard the crunch of footsteps on wet and slightly frozen grass. The steps sounded brittle and I glanced up, fully knowing whom it would be.

Trina.

My broken heart whispered her name, as she held one of the many keys that would be necessary to help me escape my personal purgatory and have a shot at reclamation.

"I'll wait while you grab a coat," she started for the both of us. "You look so cold."

"I'm fine," I lied.

"Are you?"

Silence placed a hand at the back of my neck and gave my flesh firm strokes so that I spoke not a word out of turn.

"People who are fine don't sit outside in the dead of winter without the proper clothes on," Trina said reasonably. "I said I'd wait. Please, go get a coat." It was as though she'd read my mind and saw to the center of my fear.

I nodded and obliged, quickly dashing through the house, donning a coat, and arriving right back at the exact same spot. It went by in a blur, and Trina was still solidly there.

"You could freeze to death out here," Trina smiled as though her words were humorous, but I'd failed to see it.

"Trina, I know about you," I said through chattering teeth, throwing off the hand of Silence.

"You do," she stated more than asked and eyed me cautiously.

"I heard about what happened to you, all those years ago. I heard about what happened to you and your children," I completed my thought.

Trina's hoot owl eyes fluttered to gaze at the ground. "I-I don't know what I was thinking..." her voice faded away, and it was then I realized that the incident hurt her just as much now as it must have all those years ago and ever since. She may have been able to pick up some of the pieces and carry the weight of them forward in an afterlife of her own design, but she hurt doing it nonetheless.

It was agonizing. I knew.

"You weren't. You weren't thinking," I said sympathetically, and I had tremendous sympathy for her. "You were overwhelmed by grief, deeply upset, and unstable. You didn't know what you were doing," I offered her understanding for her displayed remorse. "You may have hurt your children, but you love them. You loved them then, and it's obvious to me that you love them now. And, I know that like you, I've hurt my own child. I may love her but I still hurt her, and I do it over and over again. I don't know why, and I'm not sure things can be different with such a chasm set in place before Sonya and me. But, with the love that you have, there is hope. I have hope for myself because of your love." My words spilled forth like blood seeping from an open wound to trickle at the feet of a brown-haired angel with large owl eyes.

How many times in one life will I be sentenced to stitch myself back together?

"I can never take it back, Sally. And, neither can you. But, you have to live with it," she told me, point blank. And, it was undeniably true. In death she'd gained a renewed and constant connection with her offspring, something I may never have with the barrier that could not be lifted.

I nodded slowly and solemnly and for a long time. "I know. I have to live with it. But, in order to live with myself, I have to let Sonya go."

Trina nodded in rhythm with me, and we kept watch in that space on each other and for each other, as the partially hidden sun made its modest arc across the thunderous January sky. The storm clouds that had been on the horizon early in the afternoon were making their presence notably felt, and neither of us spoke again until the first slicing raindrops began to fall.

"Will you love her as though she were your own?" I asked with a tremble I could not control, a mixture of bodily cold and emotional turmoil.

Trina gave a faltering half-smile. "I will love her even though she is not my own, Sally. I will love her and respect that one day you will come for her, and I'll have to let her go."

It was then I saw that what I was asking of Trina, what I was visiting upon her was not a gift at all, but a curse. Perhaps for it to be a step towards reclamation it also had to be a punishment. She'd have to love and nurture a child that she would also one day have to relinquish without any say so. One day the barrier between Sonya and myself would fade away into nothingness, and I might be able to come for her again, to make things as right as they would ever be. If there was a heaven and a hell, interconnected as the words had once been displayed on the willow's bark, then this promising precipice was both of them.

I reached out and grasped Trina's tiny shoulders, surprised that they felt so solid. That aspect seemed to surprise me every time I touched one who had passed, as though death and all those contained within it should be hazy and hollow and of no mass. Death had weight and permanence. It had a strength and invincibility about its permutations, no matter how long they took. Trina was solid in the reality that held her and in the slow permutation of her pattern. "I will come for her." It was the only promise I could make, and the one promise I owed all three of us.

Trina leaned forward and pressed her forehead to my own. We were bound by what had happened in our lives, by our similarities, and our journeys. And, we were bound by the house, the court, and that moment in time with the agreement we'd made. As she pulled away from me gently, it was time for me to fetch Sonya.

A strong wind whipped up, and it wouldn't be long until a serious icy rain poured down on all of us, to only affect me. I was so cold already that it'd been hard to imagine it growing any colder. As I turned to go in the side door, I saw Sonya's face there, pressed against the glass. She held a seeking look; her blue eyes that mimicked mine were so full of countless questions.

I've failed you. I've failed you so many times and in so many ways. But, I will come for you on day, and we'll be together.

It was in that promise I knew I would not fail.

I opened the door and waved Sonya forth with universal motions of encouragement. She came right to me and glanced up as any expectant and trusting child would do. My heart skipped a beat in its torn condition, and I did my best not to sob. I knelt down and clutched her to my chest, her little arms attempting to wrap around me tightly. I held her back as tight as I dared and for as long as I could, until the rains and the ties were tearing us apart. It was easy to sense when I'd arrived at that moment, when it was time for her to go.

What really surprised me was not that I'd be able to let go of her, but that she'd be so ready and willing to let go of me. I let go not expecting her to follow suit, not expecting her to actually let me go. It was agony to feel that maternal tie shredded by such small hands that slipped from my body.

I wanted to tell her that I loved her, but she already knew it. I wanted to tell her to trust Trina, but I could see she already did. I wanted to tell her to be safe and to have a good time, but she would do both of those things with Trina looking on and my wishes beside her. The great tragedy was that there was nothing more to say and nothing that could make the outcome any better. I let out a hard and heavy breath, a great big visible puff of air.

I released Sonya from my embrace, and she flowed past me to take Trina's hand. Trina then bent forward and whispered something in her ear that made her giggle, and then they both started for the tree line. It was then that I saw all of the trees appear to shift without moving, their barks swirling in a spiral pattern that flowed the same direction without momentum at all. It looked like a grand optical illusion, something that wasn't real but merely played a trick on the viewer. I watched Trina and Sonya until the silhouettes of the trees and the steady downpour made it almost impossible to see them. But, in that last instant before I retreated into the house, I waved my unspoken goodbye.

Trina and Sonya waved back.

I'd felt hollow with Reggie and Sonya gone from my life and from the house. # 18 seemed to be yawning around me as it attempted to pull itself back together, to readjust. I could sense that changes were happening beyond what the naked eye could see, and I resolved to figure them all out in due time.

Right around early evening when Brian was due home, the rains changed from a chilled and cleansing water to a hard and threatening ice. I'd been so overwhelmed with joy when I'd seen his car pull into the driveway safe and sound that I put my own mourning on the back burner to throw open the front door and greet him.

But, as I waited for Brian to get his gear together and get out of the car, I saw another flicker of movement in front of my house and near the cul-de-sac. I tucked my arms together in front of my chest, braced myself for the low temperatures, and stepped out onto the porch to see who or what was out there.

It was Cynthia. She walked about undisturbed by the nasty weather. And, why should she be disturbed? Given who and what she was, the rain and ice wouldn't even faze her. And, her presence so near to her sister gave me a glimmer of comfort. It was poor but acceptable succor to think that even though Sonya was removed from my life in a way I'd never thought possible, she might not ever be that far away.

I waved to Cynthia, an acknowledgement of her closeness and perhaps Sonya's as well.

And, this time, Cynthia also waved back.

Chapter 10

Days and nights swirled by indiscriminately after Sonya left me. It was a lot like being caught in a vortex and not knowing how far down you were at any given moment. It was impossible to keep track of the hours, let alone the days, a chore at which I'd never been truly adept. It didn't help either that Brian decided to take some time off work, so the usual marker for days of the week was removed. He'd said it would be good to have some time off between the last big software release and the next one. I suspected it was more that he'd needed the time off for personal reasons, and simply didn't want to say it like that.

It was difficult to make those attempts at adjustment for the both of us, and our days together reminded me a lot of the first time we'd lost Sonya, the first time I'd returned to the apartment and found the nursery empty and my life in a shambles. There was the release of a perceived burden, yes, but there was also that dreadful hole at the base of my being that could not be filled. I sensed Brian felt the same. We were both in some sort of unspoken parental withdrawal, detoxing from a presence we'd gotten our hearts and minds used to. I spoke very little to him of Annabelle during that time period, as it was easy to tell he didn't want to be bothered with anything of that sort. He wanted to be in his home with his wife, to have a false sense of security. And, that created a hurdle for me to leap over, as Annabelle consumed a large portion of my daily thoughts.

I did find myself reaching out on several occasions to touch him, to be assured by Brian's company and physical form. We'd sit in the den and hold hands, or stretch out on the sofa and watch television, and at some point curl around each other for a nap. A few nights we'd found ourselves in bed together and wide awake. But, instead of gentle touching turning into foreplay, it stayed gentle touching, a promise that something and someone was still there.

Another false sense of security.

I think a full week must've passed that way. And, not only were we detoxing, but I sensed the house was doing the same as well. #18 had been through just as much as we had; it had endured two major psychic surgeries in the extraction of Reggie and then Sonya. There were gaping holes in its auspices, wounds that could get infected if they didn't heal over properly, and I hoped they would mend well in time.

I padded through the house quite a bit, touching it in what may also have been promise. I could be found placing my hands on the walls as I strode past or holding a doorknob and relishing the coolness. On the main level nothing much seemed to change, at least not outwardly. And, the basement had gone so very still that I avoided it as much as I tended to do with the garage, not even touching its cool doorknob. The emanations coming off it felt lifeless to me, and I thought perhaps something of the dead might remain down there, just not something that pertained directly to me, so I left it alone. After all, I'd felt I had about all I could take. The paintings, that insidious greeting card Brian had given Amelia, the wheelchair, and whatever else lurked in the dark recesses would just have to avoid the light of day, at least for a while.

The biggest change I noticed at some point in the span of a week or so was in Brian's office. I'd been walking by on my semi-usual circular route when out of the corner of my eye I picked up a strong flash of white. It was merely an innocuous flash, but the information provided was enough to convince my brain that something was amiss, out of the ordinary. I turned around, instead of heading downstairs, and peeked into Brian's office, where the door stood slightly ajar. But, what I beheld made my eyes grow wide, and I threw the door back all the way to take it in. The yellow and brown stripes that I'd painted so carefully and thoroughly were gone. Every single wall was white once again. At first I wondered if Brian had somehow done this without my knowing about it, but that intellectual inclination passed just as quickly as it came.

I should certainly know better by now.

I did know better. The room had changed on its own, as the house kept changing. Sonya was gone and the room reverted to form. I let loose a heavy sigh and allowed the door to stand open. Brian would see it soon, no doubt, and he'd have to come to terms with it.

Instead of heading back downstairs, as I'd originally planned to do, I decided to go upstairs to the studio, curious if anything had changed there, too. I took the steps slowly and methodically, bracing myself for whatever manifestation was to come. As I reached the top of the stairs, I was relieved to see that it wasn't so much that the studio had rearranged itself, only that it had come back to its roots. Everything looked exactly as it did the very first time I'd laid eyes on it, with only one key exception. The artwork I'd barely started on the easel was still there and begged to be finished. I was drawn over to it and quickly set to work. There was an easiness to be found in working.

Sometime later the sun started to set and a low light filled the room. I stepped away from my easel, stretched, and turned to peer out at the court from the massive window. I was able to see more than I had been the first few times, as in the winter with bare branches, I could spy more through the willow tree than when it was in full vigor. Still in all, my eyes were drawn to the tree and not through it. I wondered if those angry hands were still there. Were they as prominent in the bark? And, what of the raven? I thought about going down to check it out, but was feeling such a state of contentment in the studio that I thought better of it, and went to have dinner with Brian instead.

Why spoil a good thing?

It may have been two or almost three weeks by the time my mother called, suggesting a return to our Friday teas since the holidays were well past. She also brought up the subject of me driving out to the city to meet her for a day on the town, and I knew once we had tea there'd be no getting out of it. I'd have to give in and go to the city.

"So, I'll come out this Friday, and we'll catch up and set a date," she prodded in her flagrantly fluid way.

"Yeah, sure, that'll be fine," I said flatly, letting her know in no uncertain terms that I was not happy with being pushed into this.

"It will be more than fine, so stop moping around as if you've lost your best friend," she instructed me on more appropriate behavior. And, I would've been irritated further had I not also sensed she was trying to cheer me up with her tone and word choice.

The only problem is I have lost someone... and more. I have lost a friend, a love, and a child.

I decided to make a side step in the subject. "By the way, Brian may or may not be here for tea that day. He's taken some time off work before his next big project, and I'm not sure when he's going back to the office."

"Oh?"

"Yeah, so if you bring snacks, make sure you bring enough for three," I said.

My mother laughed lightly, and it sounded not unlike the delightful rustle of a summer breeze, a direct contrast to the weather outside, which was mildly improving. "Has that ever been a problem? I always bring too much anyway."

I smiled into my mobile phone. "True."

Friday afternoon brought my mother, ginger snap cookies, beer, and tea. The beer was Brian's addition to our little gathering, and as we sat in the kitchen it seemed that the three of us were as close to well-adjusted as we had ever been. We were sitting with hard realities that were challenging to integrate, but in the pauses between the dialogues it was easy enough to tell that we were all working on it.

"Sally tells me you've been taking some time off work," my mother turned to Brian for renewed conversation.

"I thought a few days off after the holidays were called for. We've been busy as a company, and I've been busy as hell dealing with it. One major software release was recently completed and we have another one coming up," Brian reported.

"A little time to catch your breath, that's nice," she replied courteously. "So, what have you two been doing with your time?"

Other than dealing with forces from beyond the grave, not much.

"Nothing much," Brian and I spoke in unison and then shared a small smile with each other.

"That was odd," I laughed at him.

Are we becoming the Hastings?

Brian shrugged and gave me a boyish grin that let me know he was happy in the moment, happy with the beer and the sudden onset of a small amount of normalcy. Would he ever have that as a mainstay in his life, in our lives? The mundane was such a rarity where we were concerned, and more so where I was concerned.

"Sally and I have been kinda taking it easy," Brian said, a casual return to the flow of the discussion.

I placed my hand over his. "Getting back into step," I added.

"Well, that's good," was all my mother had to offer in response.

"I, uh, I've also got a small art project going," I threw it out there, and did so cautiously, since the last time the two of them were together they'd felt very strongly that I needed to get a life again. Was this a valid enough start?

"You do?" Brian questioned with a hint of skepticism, for which I didn't blame him. It wasn't like he'd been privy to my plans or the start of my work, and I also hadn't gotten very far.

"What are you working on?" my mother asked more directly.

"It's a sketch, really. I've been thinking about turning it into a painted piece, though," I downplayed my work.

"What's the subject?"

I grinned at the awkwardness of it all. Talking about doing something productive for a change, talking about progress was not an everyday thing in my life. "It's a study of Helios... or more accurately, what I envision Helios will look like when he's done growing."

"Why Helios and not Selene?" Brian inquired.

Ah, little Selene. Are you becoming a daddy's girl?

"I don't know. I think maybe it's because he has his mother's eyes, and I thought it would be interesting to speculate." It was the best at an explanation that I could do, given the fact that I hadn't even considered my motivations for the muse at all. I turned to my mother. "How's dad?" I moved us along.

"He's well. Now that the holidays are over it's been full throttle at the warehouse with all the reorganizing, cleaning, and preparing for new inventory and shipments. After the holidays may be worse than the actual holiday rush this season. And, that has made it very quiet at our house. So, I've kept up with Pilates, done some minor redecorating, and am looking forward to planning out this year's garden beds," she summarized, bringing the topic back around to her.

Those damn garden beds.

I was going to have to get over it someday. Reggie was gone, but would he ever truly be forgotten? More than likely not by the two women sitting at the table in my kitchen.

"I can't wait for you to see the improvements I've made to the house. It's been so long since you've been there," she continued and made a nice and easy detour towards her agenda.

Here we go...

"So, when would you like to come out?" she persisted.

"Oh, I don't know," I began with the standard hesitation that was expected of me. "The weather is still so unpredictable, and I'm not comfortable with planning a date and time when I don't know what the weather will be like."

"The weather's fine," my mother halted my argument. "It's warming up. It's almost February, and spring is right around the corner."

I sipped my jasmine tea. "It can still snow and ice in February." I couldn't just let her have the argument.

"Well, if you wake up to snow or ice, you can call and cancel," she said, playing what was obviously the trump card of our current conversation.

"That does seem fair," Brian joined in with her prodding, but did so gently.

"Ok, let me get my phone, and we'll set something up," I relented and went to retrieve my cell phone from the cloakroom off the hall.

As I dug through my purse, trying to find my cell, I could hear my mother and Brian talking. The flow of their banter seemed smooth with an occasional chuckle, a lilt of laughter. I closed the cloakroom door behind me and held my position to listen for a minute. They talked so effortlessly with each other, and everything was so normal. When I had been in there mere moments prior, Brian had looked happy, happier than I'd seen him in a few weeks, maybe even months. He was truly in his element. And, it was in instances like that when he'd reached the summit of what he'd always wanted — a home, a wife, and some semblance of a functional family unit. It was then I realized that with Sonya now gone, most of my issues reasonably resolved, our house regaining order, and Annabelle distanced that Brian was finding the harmony he'd always wanted.

And, that realization strained me. I wanted him to have all of it. I wanted to pin down every last detail for him so that it wouldn't accidentally slip out of place and cause a whole new episode of chaos and discontent in our lives. And yet, I wanted Annabelle to be a part of it, too, or at least to be involved for the time being, and so much so that we could make her situation better. I knew Brian would rather forget all about that facet, hot sex aside. I knew Brian well enough to know that he'd readily forgo any future soirées with her if it meant he could have his picture perfect, well-contained, well-ordered world. It was an admirable trait in a husband, and I may have been the only woman alive that railed at it in destructive defiance, albeit subtly.

I tossed my curls about as if that would clear my head and then took a breath. Phone in hand and calendar displayed on the screen, I returned to the kitchen.

"Ok, mom, so when were you thinking?" I opened.

"How about next Friday? Instead of tea, you can do the day trip," she beamed.

"I hate to be a problem now, but next week is the start of a new release and that might be an issue. I'm planning to be at the office a lot." Brian looked from me to my mother and then back to me. "In fact, I may be away all weekend, from that Friday to the following Monday," he confessed.

"What?" My interest was piqued through anxiety. It had been months since Brian had done anything like that, and the very thought of it drew my mind magnetically to his mysterious and former phantom lover, Amelia.

Amelia.

I had to stop thinking about her and about the potential for unresolved issues. She didn't even work at his company anymore, and from what I could tell Brian had no contact with her since before we moved. But, jealousy and paranoia reared their ugly heads, and they were made even more potent due to the stress and unrest that Brian and I had found ourselves under.

I tried to console myself with the fact that Brian had shown so much loyalty and understanding to me as of late that I had no justifiable cause for thinking about her, or that he might be going off to be with someone else. I told myself that I had no real evidence to suggest that he might be making up the whole story for my benefit and, ultimately, his own. Odds were good that he was telling the truth, that the whole reason was a major software release and nothing more.

"Yeah, I'm sorry, but this is a big deal, and I plan to be at the office that entire weekend, if it's necessary. In fact, most of my team has already made the same plans." He gave more than a reasonable explanation, but it didn't sit well with me for all of my own personal reasons, consolation efforts aside.

"Why don't you drop him off on your way, Sally?" My mother offered a far too perfect solution to our dilemma.

"What?" I asked again, sounding like an echo of myself, or a person with a hearing impairment.

"That'll work," Brian said simply. "Then I can catch a cab wherever I need to go that weekend."

"And, Craig and I can take you back out here on Sunday." My mother wrapped our plans up nicely in a big, beautiful, proverbial bow.

"Are you sure that won't cut into your weekend too much?" Brian asked her, obliged to be courteous towards my mother, as he always was.

"Not at all," she brushed the suggestion aside and gazed at me. "So, it's settled. Next Friday."

"Next Friday," I agreed, feeling locked in.

"If you drop Brian off around nine, should I expect you at ten?" she continued to press.

"Ten it is." I acquiesced and placed the event with a few clicks securely in my phone's calendar.

It's as good a time as any for a car crash, I suppose.

I shuddered in a sudden and vehement burst that no one at the table seemed to notice.

I just know I'm going to wreck the car.

It wasn't until several days later that anything of real note happened. Brian continued to lounge about the house, fuss with a few small projects like tightening a loose knob and removing the latch and padlock from the basement door, as well as consistently making time to pop up to the studio where I would be engaged in my project. Life seemed blissfully and busily serene, and I was impressed with his attentiveness towards me and his willingness to remove the padlock. There were no locks or latches or screws that could hold at bay whatever might lurk in the basement. There was nothing that could be done outside of changing ourselves that could change our home or circumstances.

It was on the morning before he would return to work that I knew things were changing, that he was growing more open and aware than I'd imagined. I woke up on that amazingly bright and sunny morning to a stream of indirect light from our bedroom window smacking me in the face. I'd rolled over to crash into Brian, who was already awake and propped up on his elbow, and staring at me.

"What the hell?" It had been early, and I hadn't had coffee. So, that had been my best and most eloquent effort at expressing my dislike of being leered at while unconscious.

"Sorry. I was just watching you," he apologized half-heartedly.

I was sure he thought there was no need to apologize since he was my husband and had something of a right to stare, if only due to proximity.

"Yeah, I know. You freaked me out," I explained and sat up a bit, my heart skipping to a faulty rhythm. "I roll over and there you are staring at me. It's weird."

"It's not that weird. I was just thinking about you," he spoke so sweetly that I immediately softened my tone.

I rubbed my eyes. "What were you thinking about me? Or, do I need coffee first?"

"The coffee is on. It'll be done in a few minutes," he updated. "I went downstairs to make coffee and decided to take a trip to the basement." He made it sound so casual, like he was checking for leaky pipes or something of the sort.

"Why?"

Maybe I do need coffee first.

"To go get this," he said. And, it was then I noticed he'd been holding that damn greeting card. Would it ever dissolve or be destroyed? Its very existence was a testament to strings that would not detach, to feelings that Brian could not or would not overcome. It was a weapon that drove me further away from him and made me want to cling tightly to Annabelle, the woman who had shoved me aside.

And, just when things appeared to be going so well between us...

"It was still there."

"I can see that," came my snarky and witty rejoinder.

"I'm going to work on this. And, I think I've been holding on to it because everything else has felt so unstable since the move. I thought the move would bring us peace, but I know better now. We have to bring it, Sally."

That's a lot to ask from the historically unstable and dangerous one in the relationship.

I looked from the card to him, and then back to the card. The crimson used in the ink might as well have come from my bleeding psyche. "I've tried, Brian, but every time I fail."

"I'm not asking you to change who you are. I'm just asking you to help me build our lives to be what they once were, or what we once thought they could be."

It was a familiar refrain, but with enough of a twist that I was willing to hear him out.

"When we first moved here I thought it was going to be you and me. And, I'm sure neither of us thought it'd turn out the way it has. But, now that we're getting beyond a severe rough patch, let's try to make this work." It was an enticing offer, filled with sentiment, affection, and rationale. The only trouble with it was that it wasn't directly reflective of the reality I'd experienced since the move.

"Brian, I know it feels like one giant rough patch, and I'm not saying things haven't been rocky and even distorted, but it hasn't been all bad. I mean, just look at me," I declared. I was a walking testament to some of the miraculous that had occurred, some of the beautiful and benevolent. "Did you ever think I'd get better, be so whole again?"

"No," he answered honestly, "and I'm grateful every day that you're healed, more than you can imagine. But, that aside, things haven't been easy or even calm. And, I'd really like to try to get us back on course."

Somehow I always thought that if I healed, everything would just fall in line. How naïve.

"I accept you for who you are, and the house for whatever it is. And, I want every single thing that's caused us heartache to go away, so that it's only you and me." He sounded so much like a little boy with his simple and sincere request that it was hard to deny him. It was a lot like saying he was only asking for the world, and that's just one simple thing... but it was a big thing and perhaps beyond us, beyond most people. It was excruciating not to wrap my arms about him and agree to whatever it was he wanted.

But, there were other issues to consider.

"What about Annabelle?" I had to ask. The drive went beyond compulsion and into a realm of emotion even I didn't understand. My heart ached to ask, and I pined for my lost lover like nothing I'd ever known. I'd been fortunate and unfortunate enough to know many forms of love. Even speaking her name was painful, like an arrow piercing through my chest.

Brian ran a hand through his dark mane and lowered his gaze. "What about her?"

"I don't know," I resigned. "I thought I did, and I care for her very much."

"Well, if you don't know, then I can't possibly know either, Sally."

Fair enough.

"If you're asking me if I want her as a key part of my life, then I've got to be honest and say it appears to be more trouble than it's worth. And, I also don't care much for the fact that you'll be splitting your attention between her and me in a scenario like that. However, if you're asking me if you being with her is a deal-breaker, then no, it's not. But, what I really want is my wife back and another chance at the life we were building together." Straight to the point and unlike a man who had intentions of carrying on another illicit affair.

I reached out a hand to stroke the side of his face with all the caring I could muster, and all the caring that wasn't already squirrelled away in my heart for Annabelle. I felt him lean into my gliding strokes, lapping up the affection with as much gusto as I was doling it out. "I'll give it my best effort," I told him with great sincerity. "I love you, Brian, and every time we come back around to this point in our relationship, I love you more."

*It's hard to believe that at one point I didn't think I
loved you at all.*

"Sally," he breathed and kissed the palm of my hand.

"I wish I could give you a more definitive answer
about Annabelle, but I seriously don't know what to think,
with all that's been going on. And, I haven't talked to her in
weeks, I mean, not really talked. All I know is that I miss
her." It was as close to a full confession of my internal state
as I could come to in that moment.

Brian shut his eyes tight, and it appeared to be in an
effort to ward off tears. When he opened them again, his
eyes seemed mostly dry but slightly reddened by the effort.
"I can see that."

"I'm afraid for her," I admitted.

I yearn for her.

"I'm afraid for you," Brian said cryptically, while
clutching at the greeting card with an unsteady hand.

Many minutes passed with Silence perched on the
bed railing above us before Brian gave in to going
downstairs for coffee alone.

Later that day I found Brian asleep on the sofa in the
den with the television on low. I stood watch over him for a
few minutes and considered all he'd done for me and all I
felt for him. The relationship had never been entirely fair,
with him holding the short end of the stick. But, life wasn't
fair, and try as I may, there really wasn't much I could do
about it. The alternative was to lie to him and become
someone I wasn't, and that hadn't gone so well the first
time around. I'd only grown to resent him to a point
bordering on hatred, and I didn't want to go there again. I
had to do something about the situation with Annabelle; I
had to see her again and know where we stood with one
another. My love for her had developed to such an extent
that it outshone my affection for Brian, and all perspective
was lost.

I quickly and quietly put on my coat and made my
way outside, heading for the willow. If there were no clues

there in the bark, then at least I'd be able to serenely meditate outdoors and hopefully gain some insights.

As I stepped out onto the porch, a rush of warm air overtook me and made me second-guess my need for the coat. It had grown unseasonably warm, and had done so in only a matter of days. From snows to rains to temperate gusts of southerly wind — no wonder my mother had no fear of me driving in ice and snow. I opted to keep my coat on, though, afraid that if I exposed myself too soon to those unnatural winds, I'd get sick.

The sky looked as confused as I felt, a mixture of dappled rain clouds hanging from a bright blue backdrop with sunrays filtering in between. It could rain any minute or pass us by without a drop. I glanced to my left at #20 and saw nothing out of place, no indicators of any kind of activity, and so I made my way down the steps across the street and to the cul-de-sac.

I brushed past the still barren branches of the willow and made my way to the trunk. Placing my hands on it, I immediately sensed a thrum, a pulsation of life, spreading warmth. The tree was waking up from its winter dormancy and seemed as baffled by the high temperatures as I did. There were no buds on the branches yet, but I could tell that there soon would be if we didn't get another cold snap. As I circled the tree, I came to the conclusion that not much had changed on the surface. I wondered if winter slowed down the connections, the interpretations. If it did, it hadn't slowed down my propensity to dream or have visions while beneath the bows. I recalled the wailing of winds, the multitude of hands that had followed, the scurrying of animals, the attachment of other trees and plants, and the fire that had blazed all around me. The memory of that ethereal fire with a lion's gigantic roar stayed with me in a way few memories other than my car accident have ever done.

In fact, the only things that I saw that spoke of change in the tree were also adaptations of waning and lessening, even to the point of removal or nonexistence. The word 'doggie' that had scarred and faded was no more. I couldn't find a trace of it on the trunk as I came to stand before the exact spot it had occupied. The grooves of the bark looked seamless and blended harmoniously with the natural patterns of aged wood. I went to inspect the roots and spots higher up to find the same phenomena had happened with the emblem that had denoted Reggie's reappearance in my life: 'OMW' wasn't marring the roots any longer, nor the trunk. I sighed and leaned back against the tree. It had to be all over. It had to be. And, that thought gave me a sort of sick elation, while at the same time reminded me of a grim permanence to my actions that then echoed out to affect everything else around me.

I walked about to the far side of the willow so that I would be shielded from Brian, should he come outside looking for me. I needed to be alone, and I needed to think about Annabelle. I closed my eyes and pressed myself in as near to the tree as I could get, and in the perceived safe space I let my emotions run wild and free in a way I hadn't been able to do in a while, since the last time she and I had seen each other... and what a miserable encounter that had been.

With my eyes shut, I conjured up her image, how she looked before she'd displaced me from her life. Her dark eyes hiding smoldering embers and that intrinsic spark that had called to me alone, that hook which tangled about the bones. I contemplated the supple curves of her petite and nubile frame, and the hunger that resided within it. The start of a deep ache throbbed in me, rooted at the juncture of my legs and then spreading outward and upward. Gods! How I desired her still!

The winds grew unsteady and gusts became more frequent as my erotic envisioning went on, and sometime later I began to smell the heady scent of rain and earth and a hint of the sweet crispness of fresh apple.

Annabelle.

I was remembering her scent so vividly I could practically smell it.

"Sally," came the soft coo of a familiar and hauntingly erotic voice.

Annabelle.

My soul roared her name.

I raised my eyelids slowly, as though to move any one muscle too fast might frighten away the phantom I'd summoned. Once my eyes were fully open I saw her, only not as I'd envisioned.

"Annabelle?"

Are you real or is this a dream?

I laughed inwardly and to myself. Did it matter? For dreams were real enough.

It sort of felt like dream, but then so many real things did. A nagging voice returned to the back of my mind and shouted, 'You're awake!' And, I knew I was.

"Sally," she spoke my name again with a faltering intonation.

As I took her in, I could hardly believe that I was gazing upon the woman I'd made love to just a little over a month ago. Just as January was waning into February, winter starting to wane towards the burst of spring, so Annabelle appeared to be waning completely from life into the auspices of death. She looked so thin and frail; a mere shell of who she'd been in the prime of her existence. She'd gone quiet and sallow and almost sub-human. Her loosely woven rose-toned sweater top and long, petalled skirt hung from her as though it had been draped over a skeleton. There was no hint of a blossoming life form underneath those false flowers.

I reached out and drew her faint form to me, pressing her into myself and using the tree's strong body to support us both. She flowed into my arms like peonies bending forward towards the earth, perhaps because she'd wanted to and perhaps because she had nothing left to fight with if she hadn't. In either case, I had ahold of her and never wanted to let go.

"Oh my god," I whispered, as I started to stroke her hair and breathe in that unmistakable signature scent that swirled all around her. "I was starting to think I'd never see you again," I confessed, a victim of the lure in my own spellbinding.

I am so lost in her.

I felt Annabelle shudder violently as she tightened her grip on me as well, and then she started to cry. It was beyond heart wrenching to be in the presence of someone so fragile, gaunt, and yet somehow still elegant doing that, but I held her nonetheless until her tears subsided. My heart raced against the terrified beat of her own, and in that moment I knew I wasn't going to let the abuse she'd been enduring continue no matter what she had to say about it. The price to be paid could never be too high for me not to intervene.

I slowly pushed Annabelle back enough so that I could see her face, which she tried in vain to hide from me. "Annabelle, I'm begging you to get out of that house, to leave your father." I spoke with as much force and vigor as I had in my being. I was vehement. I had to convey the strong conviction I felt about this, and the passion carried for her. Those feelings and that unique passion had been earmarked in my being from the very beginning; they had been set-aside for her, long before we'd ever met. She had to hear it, I told myself. If she did, then surely it would jar her senses and set her free. What else was there?

Annabelle touched the blonde ringlets that hung wildly about my face and then pressed a finger to my lips. "You don't understand," she said with a sick determination as I studied the purple circles beneath her eyes.

"Oh, I think I do," I insisted and lifted her chin so that our eyes met, icy daytime blue to a brilliant night sky black. "I understand perfectly. Annabelle, please, please," I pleaded for all I was worth, "come back to me."

Annabelle shivered against the breeze, obviously unable to properly regulate her own body temperature, and she also couldn't manage to suppress the second wave of tears that rolled down her cheeks. "It's not that simple – "

"It is that simple!" I shouted, causing her to pull away from me a bit. "It is that simple," I spoke softer, and maybe even more convincingly, as I physically drew her in again. "It is, Annabelle," I assured, sounding more like I was talking to a child than my lover.

"You don't understand," she persisted with her severely flawed theoretical stance, and I could see I was getting nowhere fast.

"All right then," I stroked her shoulders and conceded, "then help me to understand."

It was then and there that Annabelle was stymied, at a total loss for words and therefore unable to form explanations, rational or otherwise.

I looked into the eyes of my broken friend, my torn and tattered lover, and I knew that I was the only hope she had of escaping this madness. She was clearly unable to free herself, and there seemed to be no one else in her life willing or able to do it for her. It was an honor to be the one holding a possible key to her release and scary, too. What if I failed?...

What if I fail at this the same way I've failed at so many other things, failed so many other people?

I'd already let her down once, even if she hadn't known about it. After the solstice night I swore to myself I'd come for her, retrieve her from the clutches of her father and bring her back to me, and maybe even back to Brian. But, I'd waited too long, and the spiral of her situation had already spun out of control by the time I'd gotten there. And, it was there, under that willow tree, that I grew to see we were at the same crossroads, with me bearing up under the yoke I'd have to wear for her. She was too frail and haunted to wear it for herself.

"Annabelle," I began cautiously, "I'm not sure what started all of this. I'm positive there are so many aspects of your situation that I don't know about. I don't know what caused it, what happened to your father to make him do these horrible things to you. I don't know what happened to your mother – "

Annabelle pulled away at the introduction of her mother into the conversation, and I could tell I'd hit a raw nerve that had never healed over, never gained a healthy layer of tissue to properly cover it. I let the sudden pause and painful pulsating hang between us until she relaxed enough that I could be sure she wouldn't dart away when I went on.

"And, I don't need to know all of that. What I do know," I re-engaged, "is that you don't deserve what's happening to you, not at all. For god's sake, no one does!"

"I don't know what to do, Sally," Annabelle burst into a crying jag that would not be stopped. She was hanging on to life and sanity by a single thread, and that thread was the cord that attached to the hook that went through my ribcage. With each new sob it tugged terribly.

I swept her up into another powerful embrace and let her weep. There really wasn't anything else that could be done to calm her. As someone with a wretched past, I knew that tears could bring about their own comfort; tears were sometimes the only way to get a message across. In so many old stories, even the gods were moved by tears. "I know he's hurting you. He's killing you, Annabelle," I said succinctly and let the terrible truth remain among our tenderness, travelling that solitary strand.

Annabelle wept into my shoulder, not daring to respond and probably not able.

"Why do you let him?" I questioned, knowing I wouldn't get an answer, at least not right away. "Why do you permit it? Do you want to die, too?"

The whole truth of what I knew slipped out in a single word, a single syllable – 'too.'

Annabelle suddenly stopped crying and was stone still. "What do you mean?" she asked back. But, I knew full well she'd known what I meant.

Freudian slip. Oops.

"I know your father's dead. The house records seem to indicate that it happened years ago," I told her, sounding a bit like a stalker.

Annabelle brushed past my prying into her life details. "House records... that's what gave it away?"

"That and you did just now." I smiled despite the sadness of our situation.

Annabelle leaned back and met my smile with one of her own that stemmed only from mutual recognition. There was no light in her anymore. But, her smile reminded me of the early days we'd spent together. She'd had more freedom and maybe even a deluded sense of control over her situation then. I'd had more cynicism and a naïve grasp on just how out of control a person could let their life become. And, together we'd both found out how off base and out of bounds we were.

"I don't know what to do," she admitted to me in a state of helpless abandon, holding her hands out palms up, as if I could place the solution in them.

I took her hands in mine and gripped them firmly, tightly. "Get your things together – "

Annabelle shook her head and started to object.

I squeezed her hands as tight as I dared. "Get your things together," I repeated, "quickly and quietly. I'll come for you," I swore, determined not to fail this time. "How long do you need?"

"Give me a day," Annabelle requested, catching a surge of energy from my plan and my resolve.

"A day... but no more," I warned. "You be here at this tree tomorrow afternoon," I instructed strictly. "And, don't make me come looking for you."

Annabelle gave one agreeable nod of her head to indicate that she understood, and then boldly lunged forward to kiss me with all she had left. It was voracious and starved and only a fraction of what it used to be. But, the kiss also held a promise of what it had the potential to become again. If someone were to nurture her, she'd no doubt make a speedy recovery. If she let me care for her, I would defy whoever and whatever it took to do so.

I kissed her back swiftly before she scooted on her way, carefully traipsing back to #20 and in through a side door.

Gone from me again.

I touched the willow for assurance that this still wasn't a dream, and that I wasn't about to awaken to the old reality. Everything stayed the same — the lingering scent of rain and earth and fresh apple, the gusts of warm wind, and the life strengthening within the tree.

I was all set to go back in the house and make arrangements for my new roommate, when I saw a flicker of movement off to my left. Margaret was flagging me down, motioning for me to come over and join her on the front lawn of her home. I hesitated only a moment to make sure no new upset took place through the windows of #20, and then slowly made my way up the street to her, the godmother of my cats.

"Hey, Margaret," I said on a more chipper note than I was actually feeling. "It's a freakishly warm day, don't you think?" It was my best attempt at casual, especially since I'd held the suspicion of her seeing what had just gone on between Annabelle and me.

When Margaret didn't say anything at first, I opted to keep the conversation light.

"I see you decided not to wear a coat," I said plain enough, reflecting the circumstances. "I was afraid of catching a cold if I didn't."

I studied Margaret further when she still didn't respond, and caught sight of the worry and frustration that were simmering right below the surface.

I worked at swallowing a growing lump in my throat.

"I suppose I'd normally ease my way into this, but I think we're well past that now," Margaret prefaced at long last, her choice in words as flawless as her outward appearance.

"Come again?" I said, choosing to play ignorant.
They say ignorance is bliss.

"I saw you with Annabelle, and believe me, I get it. I know what's going on and what's been going on with the two of you. And, I know all about her father, too, so there's no need for us to go all into that. So, let's have an open and honest discussion, right now. I think that would be best, don't you?" Margaret turned the tide from casual to deadly serious in a heartbeat, all the while remaining her typically charming self.

With all she'd done for me without expecting anything in return, I owed her honesty and a candid conversation, bare minimum. "Ok," I replied obediently.

"Thank you," she acknowledged my willingness. "Now, I need you to hear me, really hear what I'm about to say to you."

I nodded with a solemnity that I don't think I'd ever felt so strongly before. Margaret was a fount of knowledge and truth, an adept elder at the practice of understanding, and the severity she was portraying in that instant cut me to the quick. I was sobering up fast from my heady encounter with Annabelle.

What a buzz kill.

"Leave it alone."

"What?"

"Leave it alone, Sally. I know it may be very hard for you to do, but trust me, you want to leave this one alone," Margaret advised with equal parts sympathy and sternness.

I could hardly believe what I was hearing. Was she suggesting I turn a blind eye, and let Annabelle's father continue those torturous affairs with his own daughter? Was she actually expecting me to abandon the only person I'd ever loved more than myself? It called into question whether she grasped everything that had gone on with Annabelle and me in the first place. Her claims seemed invalid when backlit by the advice she was giving out.

"You can't be serious..." I diminished the importance of her words.

"I am. This is very serious. It won't end well for you, I can promise you that." She went beyond ominous with the blatantly personal.

I couldn't dismiss her again.

"And, how can you possibly know a thing like that?" I countered, and felt a little childish about doing so. It was downright petulant of me, but this had quickly become a hot button issue. A force inside me felt as though it had been called on to defend what I cherished most, and I couldn't turn it off or even tamp it down.

"I was there when Lionel Casey was dispatched, and that wasn't pretty for anyone involved, especially for my husband. I almost lost him," Margaret conveyed with a soul-churning sadness interlaced with a thread of fear.

I attempted to swallow that large lump again.

"I wouldn't wish that on anyone, not even my worst enemy, and I'm telling you that Gregory Taylor is far worse than Lionel ever was," she poured forth. "Leave it alone."

Margaret had spewed out threatening threads of ideas quicker than I could reel them in.

From all prior accounts, Lionel had been an awful person, a shameful husband and father, but it had to be a blessing to have him dispatched from our midst, and doubly so for Trina and her children. And, that had made a safe place for my child. How could Margaret even suggest that I let the situation between Annabelle and her father continue? And, I wondered what role Lyle had played in it all, although that was a secondary curiosity. He'd put himself in extreme danger over it, over Trina and the children, and that hadn't gone without repercussions, that much was certain from the few clues Margaret gave.

"Ok, first of all, there is no way in hell I'm leaving Annabelle trapped in this situation. No matter how it looks to you or what you may think about it, I love her," I practically shouted with a protective venom. "Secondly, if you were there when Lionel was dealt with, then just tell me what the fuck it is I need to do to get rid of Dr. Taylor." From venomous defender to righteous beggar all in one sentence, that was quite a grand sweep. Of course, I'd been known for them.

Margaret shook her head sadly. "This is Annabelle's mess. It's her hole to dig herself out of... or not."

"She can't!" I exploded in a raging roar, to which Margaret immediately signaled with her hands for me to calm down. "She can't," I said again with a bit more control and decorum. "And, if you can't see that she needs help, then apparently I'm talking to either a blind woman or someone who simply doesn't care. And, if you don't care then this conversation is over," I said and spun dramatically on my heels as I started to walk away.

"Sally!" Margaret called as I'd reached the adjoining lawn.

I stopped in my tracks but kept my back to her, making my position on the matter perfectly clear. I would not be swayed.

Choose very carefully the words you say next.

"It's not that I don't care," Margaret attempted to mend the threads that were quickly shredding between us.

I turned around. "Then what is it?"

"I care too much," she said, and those words were enough to send me right back to her. I knew what it meant to care too much, as I was caught up in the middle of it.

"Explain that," I demanded.

Margaret sighed and looked positively exasperated at having to go into even more detail. I could see that she'd wanted me to simply agree to leave well enough alone and go back to my house and my life. The only problem being that I could never call Annabelle's situation, or mine either, well enough.

I'm not well with a hook in my sternum.

"Sally, you seem to be doing pretty good, so much better. You're just starting to pull your life back together, and pieces of yourself in the process. You can have a bright future here, and build into it what you want. You can be happy, and so can Brian, I feel it. There can be so much more in store for you."

The winds seemed to whisper their agreement with her, a brush of encouraging warmth against my ears indicated that there indeed could be so much more.

"Things are now settling, as they should, each piece into its proper place. You've recently been doing the right things for yourself and your life, and it shows," she flattered with an edge of protective and meddling sincerity. "Do you really want to squander all you've gained on her?"

That really is the question isn't it?

Margaret had hit the nail of the head with that one. Did I want to?

I'd regained my physical health almost immediately after the move and my mental and emotional health seemed to bounce all around and then buoy a couple of months later. It only very recently felt as though I'd been working on gaining something even higher, something more ethereal. It might have even been a spiritual health or connection I was striving towards. My marriage was certainly on the fence for this whole wild ride, and who could say what else. Did I want to risk squandering it all for one person, for Annabelle? There was no guarantee on how anything would play out.

"Yes," I answered her, defiantly. "Yes, I'd give it all up tomorrow if it meant she'd have a shot at a better life."

Oh shit!

It was hard enough for me to believe those words could fly out of my mouth, and that I could mean them so much.

If Margaret had been made of sweet butter, she would've melted on the spot. As it was, her expression displayed a melting of emotion and an unquantifiable degree of admiration. No doubt she had been down this road before, with Lyle. I sensed she was experiencing something of a repeat of history in what flowed through our discourse.

"Yes," she reiterated. "I believe you would. You've gone that far."

Silence stepped in and gave us the gift of a prolonged moment to consider what was going to happen next, an exchange of powerful information that was riding an undercurrent of consent for all three of us. I felt that Silence had gone from tormentor to friend to noble conspirator in the span of time that I'd known him, or had taken note of him. And, I could use all the friends and conspirators I could get.

I watched with Silence as the sun was starting to set behind Margaret's house. The scene was picturesque, to say the least, and it looked almost perfect enough to be a snapshot on a postcard, cloud-matted sky emblazoned with hues of red, orange, and magenta.

Time then suddenly shifted from poised to perched as the winds were dying down. We were losing the light, too, and a blanket of heavier cloud cover had started rolling in. They were high clouds that held little moisture, so rain wasn't an immediate threat, but the darkness would soon encroach enough to lower the temperature and drive us indoors for refuge.

"Carve your intentions into the tree," Margaret revealed after carefully weighing her options, measuring the weight of each individual, available, and possible decision.

"What do you mean, exactly?"

"Carve some form of symbolism that is relevant to you and your intentions in this matter into the bark of the willow tree over there," she pointed to the old willow in the cul-de-sac, the one I'd come to associate on some level with my grandmother. "It will help. It'll set into motion a chain of events to bring you what you desire. "

I just stared at her, thinking thoughts I couldn't form into coherent ideas.

"It's how Lionel was dispatched years ago," she continued, "and how difficult actions and connections are initialized, and are inevitably made."

I successfully swallowed the lump and felt grounded.

"That tree…" Margaret trailed off and had to rally her courage to press on, "That tree is connected to all the other properties, the land, the other trees, and all the beings influenced by this court. You carve your intentions there, and it will be felt."

My head was swimming despite the groundedness of my body and spirit. "How do you know all of this?" That question may have been the riddle to Margaret's being for me.

"It's hard won knowledge I probably shouldn't be sharing," she said with a nervous wink.

"Thank you," spoke with tremendous gratitude. "Thank you for that."

"Think long and hard before you do it. Be careful and be certain, as there will be no going back. And, I can pretty much guarantee that you won't like how the intentions have to manifest."

Heavy words, a deep-seated and fearful warning. Are you remembering whatever it was that Lyle went through all those years ago? How much did you go through with him, Margaret?

"Ok." It was all I had to say to that. There were many questions in my mind, but I was hesitant to ask. I didn't want to push farther or harder than I had to, as I'd gotten the main nugget of information I'd been seeking. Everything else could wait.

Some riddles can sit on the shelf for a while without spoiling.

"It's a malignant business you're trying to manipulate, Sally. It will have harsh consequences and a steep price."

I nodded my understanding so fervently that my curls bounced in front of my eyes, the shimmer of a champagne mane. "Understood," I said and left her standing in the center of her front yard as I slowly worked my way back down the street towards my house, keeping a weathered eye on the tree.

Did you hear us?

I knew it did.

I paused in my walk about half way home, as a stark shift happened and the sky grew incredibly overcast all at once, blocking out most of what little light we'd had. A strong wind blew in and with it came lower, heavier clouds to provide us with a charcoal ceiling. I looked to my left and contemplated #20. A single light illuminated an upstairs window. I thought about what might be going on behind closed doors and deceptively gossamer curtains with the adjoining shades drawn low. And, I wondered if it was Annabelle's room that held the light, a low and flickering flame. I ruminated over where my lover was sleeping tonight, and whether or not she'd have nightmares before the new day dawned.

My house had most of the lights off, and the porch had gone unnaturally dark. It looked like a giant monster's mouth that certainly held tremendous teeth, only one wouldn't be able to see them until it was too late, not unlike #20. I had the undeniable sensation that something new and foreboding lurked there, something with an agenda, and the plans relied on me stepping willingly into that maw. And, that gave me pause.

I then turned my mind to more mundane matters to calm my nerves before I attempted to proceed. I contemplated whether Brian had already awakened from his nap. Most likely, as it had to be getting late with the sun almost all the way down. He probably had the table set and dinner waiting, which meant I should go in, I should attend to my own household and husband before dragging Annabelle unceremoniously into the mix tomorrow afternoon. I had to make sure all my ducks were as in a row as they could be, and not scattered about the pond.

I have to go home. I have to walk up those steps.

I screwed my courage to the sticking point and braved it. I dashed up the firm wooden steps, not giving myself another moment to reconsider. And, in the dark of my front porch, as I reached the very last step, the solid edge of the hardy wood expanse, I saw Ella.

Chapter 11

Ella sat on the ancient swing of my once welcoming warp-around porch. The swing rocked back and forth, all the while giving gentle creaks I hadn't heard until I'd been right up on it. I was alarmed to see Ella sitting there so expectantly, looking as she had the very first time I'd seen her, a blended icon of warm and cool, of grandeur and delicateness. Ella was perhaps the last person I wanted to see, aside from Dr. Gregory Taylor. She was also the person I understood the least, and that had me ill at ease.

"Ella," I said at last, "you surprised me." It was a definite understatement. "I wasn't expecting you."

"I know, dear. And, I didn't call," she said simply enough, and in that signature lyrical lilt that was so characteristic of her.

"Brian should be inside," I added. "Didn't you ring the bell or knock?"

"No, no, I didn't bother. There really was no need to do that, since I'm not here to see Brian." Ella sounded so logical and yet theatrical, implying that her visit had something to do with me without having to directly say so.

"Oh," lacking in words once again with her.

"I'm here to see you," she said unnecessarily, and she knew it. But, her declaration did give her position the emphasis she'd been going for. "Would you care to have a seat?" She asked, indicating that I should sit next to her on the swing, be close to her. And, part of me wanted to be, curiously enough. Part of me thought it would be nice to sit so close, and yet there was another part that concerned itself more with self-preservation and didn't feel confident not knowing what I was getting into.

"Thank you, but I prefer to stand," my voice wavered like my thoughts.

"You've been standing a long time. All afternoon, in fact," Ella replied, tipping her hand to purposely reveal that she'd been watching.

I shivered in an uncontrollable reaction to her voyeurism and the dropping temperature.

"Sally, I do understand that you're uncomfortable right now. You've been standing so long, and it's cold out here, too, even in that coat. Why not come on over and have a seat? Are you also that uncomfortable with me?" She asked with a slight head tilt, the cock of a polite question.

I looked her over. She was so slender and contained, long and tall and gangly in a sophisticated fashion that was only enhanced by her immaculate attire. What was there to be afraid of? The droop of her age? The sharpest thing about her was her steely gray hair. And, yet, she was such a haunted figure, nearly wispy in her contradicting physical firmness.

Ella smiled at me through heavy rouge and a hard line of coral lipstick, and I sat down beside her, ignoring my qualms.

"How long have you been waiting?" I casually asked, trying to lighten the mood around me, which had been grim all day due to others.

"I haven't been waiting, my dear," she corrected. "I've been watching."

Watching?

"Watching?" I verbalized my thought boldly.

Ella placed a hand lovingly on my knee, as though her touch might somehow be welcome. "Oh, yes, and I must say that I'm concerned about you, Sally."

I let her hand and her words remain in place for a minute or two before I reacted to both with graduated recoil. "Really? And, why would you be so concerned?"

"It frightens me to think of the steps you're planning to take in the near future, my dear," she said with an unashamed candor and near maternal warmth that reeled me back in. "The things that you are willing to do for Annabelle..." she let the concept wither while I pondered it.

How the hell could she know that? Margaret?

"What do you know about Annabelle?" I quizzed harshly of the uninvited woman who, in my mind, didn't even have the right to be occupying a seat on my porch swing.

"A lot, Sally. I know a lot about a great many things. Does that surprise you, too?" She asked of me in return.

Turnabout is fair play.

"Have you been talking to Margaret?" I poked more pointedly.

"Not lately, and not about this. No, I learned all of this from talking to you, from being with you... all this time." Ella's voice began to warble and distort as she'd finished her sentence, the tail end also a new beginning to a concept she'd wanted desperately to present. I understood that desperation about her if nothing else about her, to want someone or something to know you perfectly and not turn away. Her last utterances were said in a watery voice that I knew in the core of my soul, the stopping point of where it pierced. That voice had come to me in a dream, in many dreams, and it hadn't belonged to Ella. It belonged to my grandmother.

"No," I shook it off. "No, it's not possible," I insisted and tossed about my flustered ringlets.

"It is possible," came that voice again, only without the vocalization of syllables. "I've been with you all this time, in one form or another, in the most potent form I could take moment by moment. Why did you listen then but don't want to listen now?"

I stopped shaking my head at her and forced myself to take in her image once again. Ella looked as placid and serene as always, despite my proximity to a total freak out. "Who... What are you?" I finally got around to asking while pulling myself back together. "You are not my grandmother. I know you're not."

"Of course not," Ella spoke with melodious waters in her voice, the trickling of a delicate stream, and the clanking together of river rocks. "Although I am not ashamed to say that I quite like who she once was in life. She and I have a lot in common, according to your memories."

"Then who are you?" I asked again, ready to dive off the swing any second.

Ella stared at me for the longest time, considering. She could have been considering any number of factors in regards to an answer, and what all went into the determination, I'll never know. But, she opened her mouth to speak with that same warbled and watery voice once again. "I'm the willow, Sally."

I'm the willow, Sally.

It was a tidal whisper at the walls of my mind.

The truth beat against the barriers of my brain until it knocked the doors down and then raced along the corridors of my mind like a raging flood.

"I am the projection of this court, if you will," she once again returned to the more stable, albeit haunted form of Ella St. James, regulating her voice and committing to the image fully. "I'm its essence, the connection, darling girl. And, we've been communicating for quite some time, haven't we?" Her inquiry was rhetorical and an attempt to re-engage me in conversation, to help me come back down to earth, as if such a thing could ever be possible under such circumstances.

I nodded.

Ella chuckled heartily as if there were something funny about the whole thing. "There is no need to be afraid," she persisted. "You weren't afraid before, not really," she reminded me.

"What do you want?" I tried to cut to the chase.

"I want to tell you something you already know, but I want you to hear it from me. Perhaps it will carry more weight coming from me, perhaps not," Ella said.

Nothing so threatening there... is there?

"I'm listening," I opened for her, if only a crack.

"You are no longer so diminished, as you once were. You know that. You're well on your way, farther along your path than you have been in some time. And, that's no mere guesswork on my part, dear Sally. Just as I've connected with you and shown you all these things, so I have also connected with many here, including Annabelle, so that they might have a choice. It's a blessing, so they may experience something unique."

"What?"

"Their own sentience, in full."

"In full?"

"Their sentience in relation to the greater sentience, the greater awareness that exists in all things, if you will.

You see, my dear, just as you know the highlights and pitfalls of your own situation, so Annabelle and many others are quite aware of their own, too. It is not on you to rescue her, but to continue to restore yourself." Ella put it so eloquently that it was hard to argue.

"I can do both," I said, unwilling to let it go, despite the lucidity and validity in the case she was making.

"That may be, but you should know that Annabelle is responsible for herself. She moved back here and brought her father with her of her own choosing. It was all her own doing, conscious or not. Much like you were prone to doing, she takes from the living to give to the dead."

"It may be her own doing, but it is also her undoing. Her situation is far worse than mine ever was. She's in danger," I clarified for Ella, even though I knew then that she was perfectly capable of seeing it, of seeing everything.

"Sally," Ella cooed, "if you interfere, you will become a part of her entanglements. And, it is impossible to say how it will all turn out, what myriad of manifestations will come to pass."

"You don't know that already? You can't tell how it will all turn out if I go over there and carve my will and desires into the bark?" I spoke as though there were a threat there, as I pointed to the willow tree. And, maybe there was one.

"No," she admitted. "All I can tell you is that the manifestation will take the quickest and easiest route to get here. But, easy does not apply to you, only to the inevitability of the outcome. You may not like how it comes about, my dear. And, what you call will become your own fate, Sally. I can't help you with that."

Ella, the willow, the spiritual kin of my grandmother... whatever she was, she cared. She cared and Margaret cared. Odds were good my husband might care, too, if he actually knew what was going on, knew it from every conceivable angle. Maybe my parents might have cared as well, although they felt farther removed from my little bubble of a world.

The sharp sticking point remained well in place, though. I had a rich life full of people and beings who held a level of affection for me that deserved to be honored and cherished, and I was determined to throw it all away on a woman who had put me from her right when we needed each other the most. If I diminished, if I fell and could not get back up, it affected everyone and everything around me, and that included Annabelle. Was my interference more of a hindrance than help? Was that even possible given the state of affairs in Annabelle's web?

It doesn't matter. I have to do something about this.

That's what it kept coming back to for me. I loved her beyond myself. I loved her. There was no hope of anything more, of a further wandering down my own path if I could not also strive to set her free.

"You know a lot," I said to my mysterious companion. "You know many things, so then you should also know that I love her. I can't help it, and I'm ashamed to say that I wish I could. I wish I could overcome my feelings for her and my ties to her like I did with Reggie... with... with Sonya," I faltered as my heart skipped a primal beat.

Sonya. Are you happy? Are you safe?

I swallowed hard and set it aside. It was only distracting me, after all.

"I just can't do that with Annabelle. It's different. "

And, she's alive.

"You love her that much." It was more of an observation coming from Ella than a question.

"She may be the only untainted love I've ever known," I said in a moment of total bareness, an instant of blinding honesty. "Yes, I love her that much."

And, then it was Ella who had no words. The willow was quiet, and she nodded her acceptance.

"I can't turn my back on that. I can't turn away from her, not now that she's reached out to me. She's come back to me, Ella." I was begging her then, but I didn't know why. It had just felt the most natural in that space to plead.

"Has she?"

"Yes, you saw it today, under those branches," I reminded her.

"Yes," she agreed, cryptically. "I hope that you can accept whatever happens without bitterness forming in your heart, without it syphoning from you, diminishing who you are, who you've become."

I hope so, too.

"For better or for worse," Ella said to me, as though she were reciting a marriage vow.

"For better or worse," I repeated, feeling compelled.

And, somehow I knew then that we had both said all we'd needed to, that she'd said all she came to say, and there was no more persuasion to be doled out. I stood up from the swing and gazed down at her sitting silhouette.

"I knew you weren't quite who you seemed to be," leaving her with that non-melodious note, I went inside the house.

Brian was setting the table when I strolled in. "Hey," he greeted as I shoved my coat onto a hanger in the cloakroom.

"Hey," I regurgitated and joined him in the dining room, a little numb and raw all at the same time. It was weird to feel the pins and needles of elevated blood pressure, the distance of stress, while also experiencing the anguish and elevation of pure emotion.

"I saw you over at Margaret's a little while ago. Did you two have a nice talk?"

If only you knew the types of talks I had and the company I kept these days.

"Yeah, it was very in-depth," I said flatly.

"Well, dinner's ready. I was just about to bring it in," Brian said, checking me out, scanning me over in my aloof mood. "Brisket," he spoke as though that was some kind of spoiler alert, and I should be thrilled and thrown.

I smiled at him. "Very nice."

"Ok," he finally joined me in my lower vibration. "What's going on?"

I leveled with him. "Get ready for a house guest."

Brian wasn't overjoyed, and I hadn't expected him to be, especially since what I'd initiated was in direct conflict with the very desires he'd expressed to me, the future he'd envisioned for us.

It's not a deal-breaker.

I hung on to that reassuring tidbit, determined to proceed with moving Annabelle in, at least for the time being.

Brian had the fortunate distraction of having to return to the office the next day to keep him occupied, preparing for the software release that would dominate the coming weekend. That left him well situated in his sphere of intellectual and logistical endeavors while I made other arrangements at the house.

Helios had been hot on my heels all morning, even though both he and his sister were well fed and given copious amounts of attention. He made the amazing trek up a full flight of steps to follow me into the guest bedroom, as I attempted to make it more suitable to what I imagined Annabelle would like.

All morning as I worked I'd hoped she'd arrive early, sparing me hours of dangling expectance and an unsteady heartbeat. I was nervous. I was nervous about moving her into the house and being so close again. I couldn't even begin to predict what that would ultimately do to the relationship I had with Brian, or what my parents would say when they found out. It was also risky because her father couldn't be considered anywhere near stable, and it was anyone's guess what he'd do when he discovered her missing. I was a bundle of anxious energy, a potent mix of scared and excited.

And, I want to have sex.

Annabelle didn't come over.

By mid-afternoon, and approximately twenty-four hours later by my estimation, give or take, I stopped my fussing and fretting and decided to head out to the tree. She might have simply been waiting there as I'd instructed, but I should've known nothing about the situation would be so easy, few things in my life ever were.

I touched the window glass in my dining room for a quick temperature check, and as the day was a warm one based on that, I decided to forgo putting on my coat again. I figured I'd be warm enough in my sweater and smart gray woolen blended slacks.

Dress to impress.

And, I had thought at tantalizing length about seducing my new housemate once she was comfortable.

I stepped outside and made my way down the steps of the porch when I heard a very familiar voice off to my right. I looked over towards #20 and saw my mother standing on the front porch of the neighbor's house having what appeared to be a delightful conversation with Dr. Gregory Taylor.

What the fuck is she doing here?

I may have lost track of my days entirely, but I knew it wasn't Friday for Brian would've hounded me to drive him into the city and then meet my mother. And, she and I hadn't made any additional arrangements before then, which begged the question of what she was doing on the front porch of my heinous neighbor's house. How could she even tolerate talking to him and breathing in the sickly sweet stench that I couldn't erase from memory?

"Mom?!" I exclaimed, not even pretending to be delighted by this surprise, or even cordial.

Jeanna Dougherty, in flamboyant style, gave a swivel that would've turned heads had there been any around. With a flounce of hair that settled in whimsical waves about her shoulders, it was a swirl and a look that probably cost her an hour in the bathroom but suggested that she had only rolled out of bed. And, in an instant I saw the glow about her features, that same flush that accompanied undeniable attraction.

I think this display is making me ill.

"Oh, Sally, I was just coming to see you when Dr. Taylor here invited me over for a quick chat and some fresh-brewed coffee," she said holding up a steaming mug, oblivious to my distaste. "I wanted to drop by a day early and spend some time... and also make sure you are still planning to come visit tomorrow."

"Well, then let's spend some time," I said and motioned with a large arm wave for her to come over to where I was standing.

"Sally," Dr. Gregory leaned over his porch railing and considered me, looking like the doctor he must have once been going over a perplexing chart. "Sally, it's always a pleasure."

I took in the sound of his insincere words and the sight of his unhealthy pallor. Everything about the man made me want to vomit.

"I was just telling your charming mother that I must have the two of you over sometime," he went on, the edge of a torture master's blade in his tone.

I didn't know what to say, how to respond.

"Sally!" My mother expelled my name in huff of embarrassment. "Don't be rude. Accept the man's gracious invitation."

"Mom, if you need to talk to me, it's best if we make it soon. Brian might be home anytime," I lied, and did so out of a sudden onset of fear.

I don't want him thinking I'm alone in the house... cats or no...

"What are you talking about? It's the middle of the day. We have plenty of time. Why don't you come on over –"

"Mom!" I shouted and then attempted to regain my composure, attempted to keep the situation from spiraling any further. "Mom, please, I have a few private matters to discuss with you." I eyed Dr. Gregory intensely as my mother turned to apologize and then say goodbye to him.

I noticed he kept an eye on me, too, as he did his best imitation of listening to her, of reeling her in on a little leash.

"Thank you so much for understanding," my mother said as she departed.

"What's not to understand," he said to her from over the railing as she made her way into my yard. "Temperamental daughters." He and my mother shared a smile, and then he winked at me. "I'll see you later, Sally."

He knows!

That hideous grin on his morbidly curious face told me in no uncertain terms that he knew what Annabelle and I had been up to, and she had failed to leave the confines he had her in. He expected me to come for her, and soon.

And, I will.

As my mother followed me up the steps to my own porch and then flowed past me through the front door, I peered at the willow, squinting to see if I could make out Annabelle's shape or any sort of shadow that might seem vaguely human. There was no one there.

I sighed my resignation and knew I'd have to get rid of my mother fast, before Brian returned home at whatever point in the evening his work would let him go. I had to get her out of the way so that I'd be able to retrieve Annabelle, or at least put in the attempt.

"You should've called," I complained the moment the door closed behind me.

"I did call. Is it my fault you never answer your phone?"

Damn it!

My mother spun on her heels to face me, and I recognized that spin as my own dramatic flourish. "And, just what is so important that you felt the need to be rude to your neighbor?" She chastised me with her question.

"I told you some time ago that when it came to companionship or whatever the hell else you want to call it, to look elsewhere. Stay away from Dr. Taylor!" I demanded in a huff, not caring whether or not she rebuked my forward thrust.

"That's what all this is about? You think I'm attempting to have some sort of tryst with your neighbor?" She laughed in a series of exquisitely beautiful notes and then fixed her icy eyes on me. "That's not what's going on." Shaking her head in feign dismay.

"Then what is going on?" I challenged. "I see the way you look at him, and it seems pretty damn obvious to me."

"We get along," she said with a frozen fire in her voice, the remnants of socially acceptable speaking levels. "We have a lot in common. We're a lot alike, he and I. There's this sort of brokenness about him, and I've been broken for a long time, too, Sally." She played on what might be left of my sympathies for her martial plight.

It's just like what drew me to Reggie, our mutual bond of brokenness. It was the wounded predator that had pulled us so close to one another, had made us so wild for each other. It was what had made it so sick and so wrong... and so incredibly hard to let go of.

"Mom, please, believe me when I say you need to stay away from Dr. Taylor. He may be broken, but he's a wounded predator, and no good can come of any of it," I summed up with very little patience for further discourse.

Now I'm starting to sound like Margaret and Ella.

"Ok, Sally, if that's what you want," she hesitantly agreed, and caught me off guard by giving in so quickly. "I'm not sure what you're referring to, but I want you to know that it isn't what you think. And, I am trying to make things work with your father again."

Really? Is it beneficial to keeping up appearances in some way?

"You are?" I was skeptical, as my mother was not known for level-headedness or forgiveness, painful pragmatism and surface drama were more her style. Second chances were not common in her domain.

"Yes. We're even in couples counseling once a week now," she spoke with fleeting fondness.

"When did this happen?" I pressed, hungry for good news and hoping for sincerity, all with a cynic's tinge of doubt.

My mother seemed uncomfortable with the subject, but my interest spurred her on a little further. "It was a New Year's resolution that we'd made to each other, to try again. You and Brian are trying, and I think that's made us want to try."

My smile was so genuine in response to her exposition. There was a tremor of happiness running along as an undercurrent to her good news, and it circulated between us, humming promises of a new bond beginning to bud. I made the choice to let the doubt slip away.

"It has been such a blessing, such a gift to see you get well again, to see you start to live all over again. And, I want to make things better for all of us, Sally, one way or another."

Does she feel the same guilt I do?

Jeanna Dougherty may not have always been a nurturing caregiver, or even what some would've considered a good mom, but she was still a mother in the roots of her being. I sensed that she meant every last word in that abstract attentiveness that even a haphazard mother had to give. It was the nature of having bore offspring.

"Ok. Ok, mom. Thank you for that," I replied with what amount of gratitude I had at my disposal, as I also strived hard to have a moment free of distraction from what might have been going on next door.

"So, you will be at my house at 10am tomorrow, right?" she pushed her own agenda, which brought us back around to familiar behavior patterns.

"Yes, I'll be there," I bemoaned my fate.

"No excuses," she reminded me.

"Got it. No excuses," I echoed.

A quick tea for two and I ushered her out of the house as politely as possible, so as to not arouse suspicion or even too many prying questions. Time was of the essence.

I don't know what my motivation and pseudo-reasoning was in scooping up Helios before I ventured outside again. It may have been as a source of personal comfort while I attempted to figure out the best answer to the dilemma of Annabelle being trapped in that house. It may have been due to something Margaret had said in passing as she'd packed up cat supplies, something about cats being guardians, something about their understanding the balance between life and death. It stuck in my head and was revived right as I put on my coat to go skulk about my neighbor's property. Or, my choosing him specifically may also have been in relation to the fact that Selene had seen me coming and darted beneath the sofa in the den, wanting no part of my foolish endeavors.

A slave to logic and reason, just like her daddy.

The sun was dipping low in the sky, and I knew as I set foot on the grass that it was late in the day. The earth felt tired from bracing itself against the onslaught of bright sunlight that melted and the unstoppable cold that refroze. It was evening time and odds were good that Dr. Gregory

Taylor was lying in wait in that house for my next move. I had no hard proof from the small snippets of conversation that he'd known what I was up to, but I knew that he did. He knew I was coming for her. I could feel it in my bones, and there was nothing I could do about my disadvantage.

Helios, as if sensing the nature of our mission, as well as the chill on the breeze, burrowed deep into my coat where he could keep warm and out of sight.

More supportive than your sister, I'll give you that much.

I had no idea what my best move would be, as there seemed no blatant ideal. I stewed over it for some time as I peered up at #20 from my front lawn. A low light emanated from somewhere near the center of the house, but no shapes moved and no shadows altered. Everything and everyone had gone preternaturally still.

I guess I'll have to shake things up.

What else could I do, other than the most illogical tactic for an extraction? I walked right on to #20's front porch and rang the doorbell.

Silence snickered over my shoulder in a shuddering breeze. No one was coming to answer the door.

In defiance, I knocked and knocked loud. And, the percussion rang through a dead house to fall on dead ears. He was in there, and he was waiting for me. And, he had no need to answer, no impetus to set the wheels into motion. I would do that for him.

As a final attempt at brazen abandon and the element of surprise, I tried the doorknob and found it locked, as expected.

After several minutes on the porch, I walked back down the steps and meandered about the property, casting a glance through each window to try and obtain more information on what I'd be walking into. But, the windows were eyes tightly shut, and they refused to lift their shaded lids for even a peek. As I arrived at the tall red wood privacy fence for the backyard, I discovered that the gate had been left unlatched, and I cautiously trod inside to find a bleak world far different from the luscious sanctuary that was my backyard. It was a stark emptiness I hadn't been able to determine the extent of from the perch of my second story windows. Even after winter's toll had been taken, my yard looked like a paradise next to the dirt and debris that was Annabelle's. In her yard nothing grew, not even grass or shrubs. Even weeds had abandoned the earth here. It was a flat plot of land that sustained only dirt and whatever dead foliage managed to be blown in by the surrounding trees.

Is this whole place dead?

I didn't know what to think, but I had a suspicion that what I was looking at in that space was a terrible premonition of what I'd find in the house, some sort of horrible foreshadowing. If the property were this dead on the outside, what would it look like within the walls of #20 where a dead man reigned supreme? I couldn't even imagine, and it made me want to turn back, to get the hell out of there.

I could turn back now and be home in time for dinner, no questions asked. I wouldn't lose anything and my life can continue to get better.

But, part of me knew that wasn't the entire truth. There would indeed be a loss. I'd lose Annabelle for good.

I made my way through the remains of what was once a yard and around to the second gate that was nearest to my own house. I let myself out and found the side door immediately adjacent.

It's probably locked, too.

A tremor of fear ran through me and Helios as well, as he gave out a tiny cry when I turned the willing doorknob all the way and let myself into the makings of misery that was #20.

There are no words to describe it properly. I'd stepped into what had once been a kitchen; a few meager and rusted out appliances gave away its identity. The room was once a center of usefulness and familial gatherings, but no more. Unlike the hearth of Margaret's home or the practical utility space of my own abode, the kitchen of #20 was a husk, remains that could give indications but no more.

Within just a few strides I'd found that the walls had actually managed to shift without a making a sound, and I was suddenly and inexplicably in a room I didn't recognize. The lack of furniture and wall hangings hadn't helped me in trying to get my bearings, and looking around to then circle back only led me into yet another room I couldn't identify.

This place is a fucking maze! It'll be a miracle if I ever get out of here.

In no time at all I started to feel the origins of panic take root in my pelvic region. I wandered aimlessly, with no breadcrumbs for a trail. There was no way to be sure which direction I'd come, or which way I was headed. Doors would appear and then vanish while windows didn't seem to exist on the interior I occupied at all. I was trapped in a world with no definitive outlet and no recourse. And the roots of panic started to spread upwards.

"Great, Sally. That's just great!" I berated myself for blundering in to save the damsel in distress with no knighthood of my own or a well-hatched plan to fall back on.

I wanted to cry, but I had a vague feeling that tears would get me nowhere in this house. The gods weren't a part of this space. Heaven and hell and whatever may exist in between were blended together for a variation of an inconceivable purgatory.

It wants my tears. This house and all that's in it wants my tears.

The thought slammed into my brain from out of the blue and shattered into a million tiny, sharp pieces that dug into the gray matter with merciless ferocity. I could sense that what resided here wanted my confusion, frustration, and anguish. And, out of spite and a sense of self-preservation, I refused to weep.

Hours may have passed in that masterful maze until I finally figured that no further harm could come from me calling out. I was becoming exhausted, and Helios himself drifted in and out of sleep.

"Annabelle!" I shouted at the top of my lungs as I stepped across the threshold of a doorway only to arrive in another unfurnished and unkempt room. The level of filth had gotten dramatically worse since my entrance in the kitchen, and with each endeavoring stride towards the center of the house, the level of insanity and disgusting disrepair only increased. "Annabelle, where are you?!" It was practically a primal a scream.

Helios in sympathy, and perhaps with a fear and discontent of his own, started to cry. It was a piteous yowl I hadn't heard from him before, and it tore at the very soul of the residence, at the very fabric that gave it such an unstable and shifting nature.

I cried; he cried... but there were no tears, only primordial beckoning.

This went on until I was almost hoarse. And, then when nearly all energy had been expended, a stairway emerged, and radiating from the top down was a light, a low and flickering flame.

Perhaps it's coming from Annabelle's room?

I looked to my little companion. "Should we go up?"

He was speechless, yet seemingly drawn to the light and emerging a bit more from the folds of my coat towards its gleam.

"Annabelle?" I called out softer than before and with a great deal of uncertainty, fearing that I'd find her father at the top of the stairs, and that the light was really only hellfire that awaited me.

I began my ascent anyway. The stairs creaked miserably under my feet as though they would give out under an ounce more weight, and I walked up them with the appropriate level of caution and concern, near the same levels that I'd already given to the rest of the house.

As I reached the dusty landing, I saw a long corridor of rooms and a small oil lamp sitting on a hallway table just off to my right. That's where the light had been coming from, that dim and dingy lamp was the source.

Annabelle could be in any of these rooms or none at all. I can't wander around in here forever.

And, I was starting quake with a terrible tremor that grew from the thought that I'd never be able to find my way out no matter what happened, even if I did find her.

"Annabelle?" I called once more, still soft and hesitant.

The lamp on the table erupted into a geyser of flames. The heat it put off and the roar of the fire as an answer was enough to send me scurrying back a few feet to the unverified safety of the staircase. I watched as the flames slowly died down and returned to the parameters of their glass hollow. But, where they had launched up the walls, a message now glared at me with bold and dripping red letters, the gleam of a written wet surface against the flat matte of dirty walls — 'There is no rhythm and there is no key.'

It was a play on the axiom I'd clung to in the early days of my recovery after the auto accident.

Find the rhythm and you find the key.

It came around every so often, as though it existed on a particular spoke on the wheel that turned my life. Only now it was being used to mock me, to frighten me. And, I was afraid. The house was reading me, and I'd yet to be able to read it.

"Sally?" There was a timid voice whispering in my ear behind me, a rustling voice that sounded more ghost-like than human.

I spun around to stare directly into ember black eyes. "Annabelle?!"

She looked worse. Annabelle had become a gaunt and protruding figure from the shadows that I would've barely recognized. Her skin had degraded to a mottled state, a sign of neglect and a lack of nutrients. The bruises up and down her exposed arms were healing and welting all at once, and they were a shameful display of her abused and bedraggled state.

"I've been looking all over for you!" I breathed heavily, letting my rapid pulse subside to a pace closer to normal.

"I've been looking for you," she said in return. "I've been trying to get out of here all day. Sally, he won't let us leave!" And, with what strength she had left she fizzled into tears.

I gripped her shoulders as hard as I dared, feeling just as disoriented as I'm sure she was. "We have to get out of this house, now!" I commanded with what strength and energy I had left, and it wasn't much.

"What about my things?" she asked is a haze of minimized horror.

Are you fucking kidding me? We'll be lucky to get out of here at all. This place is all jacked up!

"Annabelle, we can't afford to go looking for your stuff. You'll just have to leave without it," I demanded and grabbed her by the wrist, pulling her flimsy frame down the stairs to the floor below, not even honoring her meager protests along the way. When we reached the bottom I hardly even recognized the house as the same space I'd walked through for hours to find her.

Everything still looked dirty and dusty, but there were furnishings and photos where there had been absolutely nothing on the first blur of a pass through. Paintings hung on colored walls covered with cobwebs and spoke of a time long gone by. Each room for as far as I could see around me appeared to have an identity, where there had only been a shape-shifting void prior. I knew I should've been comforted by the fact that a rhythm had appeared where I'd been assured of none, but part of me suspected it was just one more illusion in an infinite number of them, and I felt terrorized by the display.

"Annabelle, can you find your way out from here?" I asked, hoping that the manifestation of a pattern might be recognizable to her, and she'd remember the route.

"If it stays like this," she answered warily.

With a tug on her arm I brought her out in front of me and then gave her a gentle shove. "Let's go," I ordered from behind her and kept my head on a swivel as we proceeded.

We walked through what would've once been a grand main hall, not unlike the main hallway in my own home, only it had fallen into a state of dilapidation. The wood no longer shone with an unbelievable luster like mine did and instead lay dormant and rotting under a heavy coat of dust. The paint and wallpaper crumbled from the solid wall base, yellowing and pushing back and away like it was disgusted. There were paintings of friendly cottages and sailboats gone brown with age and numerous photos of family and friends with one woman acting as a recurrent figure in most of them. Whoever she was, she resembled Annabelle quite a bit; a raven-haired beauty with alabaster skin and an enchanting smile. It wasn't the same alluring smile as that possessed by my lover, but it was pretty darn close.

Is that your mother, Annabelle? Is that the woman who birthed such an amazing creature?

As the front door came into view, I breathed a premature sigh of relief, as I thought for sure at that point we'd make it out of the house without any further issues or hauntings. I was wrong.

Annabelle stopped at the door, and I noticed after a minute or two that we weren't going any further; we weren't well on our way to getting the hell out of there.

"What's wrong? Let's go!" I said, peering around the main hall and then looking to her for a response that justified our delay.

"It's locked," she said, her voice choked with fear.

"Well, unlock it!" I said pointlessly.

"I can't unlock the door without a key," she returned, sending the message that we were most likely completely screwed.

"What?!" I said and elbowed her aside so that I could check the door myself. There was indeed no way out without a key, whether outside the house or trapped within.

There is no rhythm and there is no key.

"There is no key!" I said out loud, cursing the double entendre. "Fuck!" I pulled and pushed at the door, banged and kicked, all to no avail. The door didn't budge one inch, and I was almost positive no one on the outside heard me.

If Annabelle had ever screamed and tried to escape, I'd never heard her.

"We're trapped in this house," Annabelle spoke with such perfect clarity to her voice that it shook me from my savage attack on the cage.

"Let's try the side door," I said with a glimmer of unwarranted hope.

"It'll be locked, too," she said with good merit.

"Maybe, but what do we have to lose?... And, besides, it was unlocked when I came in here," I told her.

But, how long ago was that? And, how much has changed since then?

It was impossible to say. If it were very late, Brian would come looking for me. He may even eventually come looking for me over here. But, would he find either of us?

"Ah, Sally," came a voice that stopped us both dead in our tracks.

I felt Helios dive down into the folds of my coat and out of sight.

It's him!

"It's always a pleasure," Dr. Gregory Taylor said, his usual greeting towards me.

I followed the sound of the voice through the low light to see him staring down from the upstairs railing at Annabelle and myself, although he was primarily considering me.

"Open the door," I said sternly, as though I had nothing to be afraid of. That wasn't how I'd felt, of course, and I could only pray my voice didn't betray my true emotions.

"Beautiful, willful, seductive Sally," he went on, descending a couple of steps in the process.

"Open the goddamn door!" I shouted and stood in front of Annabelle, as though that provided any sort of protection for her.

"I'm so glad you took me up on my offer. It's a delight to have you over. If only you had brought your mother, what a treat that would've been." He went on as though he had all the time in the world to toy with me, and it seemed as if he did. "But, you want to leave so soon... you know, your mother is right. You are being rude." He spoke with that cigar smoke rattled voice and gave in to a persistent cough that interrupted his toxic soliloquy.

"Please," I heard Annabelle break down from behind me, and I felt her curl up into a squatting ball.

I whipped around and grabbed her by the arms, hoisting her to her feet. "Get up. We're getting out of here," I said, not sure how or when.

"And, where do you think you're taking my daughter?" Dr. Gregory inquired, sharpening the edge of his voice like a scalpel that had never gone dull in the first place.

"Away from you," I hissed. "I know who you are — what you are... and what you do." It was a loaded sentence without a weapon to fire it.

I watched as Dr. Taylor made his way with a meticulous precision of steps down the length of the staircase. "I promise, this won't end well," and then he looked past me. "It won't end well for either of you."

Annabelle's finger's dug into my shoulders as a brace for her, and I didn't know what else to do. We were trapped.

The sickly sweet scent that accompanied Dr. Gregory at all times was growing overly ripe and pungent as he came nearer. I was starting to gag on the odor when he stopped short and the scent lessened considerably. A small mewing sound was making itself heard from inside my coat lapels. And, with each increasingly loud kitten's cry, Dr. Gregory stepped back further, the smell vanquished.

Margaret was right! I fucking love that meddling woman and her cats!

"Open the door," I said again, offering him a solution to removing the presence he found offensive.

"It won't change a thing," he uttered.

I unbuttoned my coat and whisked Helios out in front of me so that he was on full display, his visage there for all to see. Helios hissed and bared his claws in a heightened defensive manner at the sight of Dr. Taylor, yowling and carrying on as if he'd seen a ghost, and he had.

And, then came an enlivening sound, the click of a lock.

"Annabelle, behind you," I said, but she didn't move a muscle, keeping her fingers dug into my upper arms. "Annabelle," I said again, more firmly, "try the door. Do it!"

I felt that sturdy grip of hers release me, and then came the triumphant noise of a door opening, creaky hinges for dramatic effect.

"You bitch!" Dr. Gregory Taylor swore at me in a rage as he rushed the door we immediately backed out of. "It won't change a thing, not one fucking thing! You bitches!" he ranted as we stepped all the way to the far edge of the porch.

And, then there was a pause, a moment in which Annabelle froze and I froze with her, as she locked eyes with her dead father standing in the doorway of her home. He glared out at her with a cold hatred that I felt pass right through me to nest in her belly.

"Murderer," he proclaimed, and in a blink he was gone.

I tucked Helios safely back into my coat and ushered us all off the porch and across the lawn to the safety of my property. The sun was hanging low in the sky, at the exact same point it had occupied when I went into the evil embrace of #20. Time had held still while whole hours passed inside those walls. Nothing had changed in the outer world, but in the inner realms of that house a person could lose whole days or even a whole lifetime while no one else lost a single, solitary second.

I thought about Dr. Gregory's last word to Annabelle before we departed, and how it had passed through me to hit its target.

Murderer.

It was such a familiar decree, one I'd bore as a brand and burden on my own soul. It was a declaration Fido had heaped upon me with unspeaking lips and unblinking button eyes. And, in some form, he'd been correct in his label. And, that begged the question... Who was this woman that I sheltered in my home?

I'd placed Annabelle in the guest bedroom with tea and a mild sedative from my expiring medical stash. And, once she'd drifted off to sleep, I fed the cats and waited anxiously for Brian to come home. I couldn't even imagine what I'd tell him, or more so how, for I knew I'd tell him the truth. I had to; he needed to know, for he was as much a part of it all now as I was. Annabelle was in his home, too, and she posed a threat and a new angle in our relationship. And, I knew that in time with decent sleep and a good meal or two, she'd have a lot of issues that would need to be sorted out, both emotionally and mentally.

There was an uneasy Silence prowling the house after Annabelle fell asleep. #18 had reawakened in a new way with her nestled in it, and it felt alive, electric, and unsettled. It was as if the whole house had gone on alert as an alien dynamic was taking hold of it. I felt as though a net had been cast over my home, one in which Annabelle was meant to be trapped, and I was caught, too, by proximity.

Or maybe it's more like a cage...

That same caged feeling I'd experienced in Annabelle's home had now transferred to mine, and I only hoped that the walls wouldn't start to move and the very wood that I admired begin to decay around me. I thought about taking a sedative myself to ease into the life transition, but I wanted to stay on guard, for I had no idea what Dr. Gregory Taylor was capable of beyond the walls of what had been his dwelling in life.

It was well past sunset when Brian finally came home. I saw the headlights as he'd pulled the car into the driveway and quickly set about putting a sumptuous dinner on the table. It was a preemptive effort to appease what I figured would be a man turning into a beast. The hour was late, and he looked more tired than I could ever remember seeing him. The workday and the drive had sapped what copious amounts of energy he usually held in reserve, and so I tucked him in at the dining room table with a quiet meal and a few glasses of wine before attempting to bombard him with more life stress.

I watched patiently as he consumed his food with a mild vigor and then followed it up with an appreciation for the wine I'd selected. For me, it all tasted the same. The food had turned to ash in my mouth, and the wine might as well have been water, although it was even more tasteless than that.

It was only after the table had been cleared and Brian had plenty of time to detox, that I told him Annabelle was upstairs sleeping. I recanted the more mundane details of my story first; the abuse and neglect that had become so rampant that it required direct intervention. As he listened with keen interest and a supposed lack of judgment, I went on into the more fantastic aspects of my tale; moving walls, bloody messages, disappearing and re-appearing furniture, and the like. I saved the fact that Annabelle's father was already deceased for the last reveal, thinking it might put him over the edge after Reggie, and especially after Sonya.

But, Brian never reacted. He never jumped up from the table and stormed out or cut me off or yelled in outrage. He listened. Perhaps he was too tired from a long and arduous workday to do any of it.

"So..." I at long last led in, "What are your thoughts?"

I needed him to say something.

"Initially, I can't help but wonder if there isn't a slow gas leak in here," he said dryly. "I think it would all make a lot more sense if we were going mad."

"Brian," I breathed his name, exasperated. I breathed it so emphatically, wishing he wouldn't leave me.

"I know, I know," he replied, giving in to the horror we'd been plunged into, a nightmare wrapped in a dream that could still end like a nightmare.

I know I've done this to you, Brian, and I'm sorry. But, what else was there for me to do?

I awaited his judgment, his weighty decisions on the matter. And, just as he'd opened his lips with a wary look in his eyes to chastise me for my imprudent actions, Annabelle sauntered into the dining room and leaned back against the entryway frame of the pocket doors for physical support.

She was a shell, even in the soft light of our dining area and so late at night; she was a withered person, a damaged bird-like figure with tattered wings and torn feathers. The strands of her hair were tangled in knots all around her face, and her skin had taken on a faint bluish hue from all of the exposed veins underneath.

Brian didn't say a single syllable to her. He merely gaped in response to her presence. I'd had some time to see the decay, but this was the first real experience Brian had with it in his sight.

After several long moments, Brian got up from his chair. "Please, have a seat," he said, escorting her over to his spot, the chair already pulled back and available with open arms.

Annabelle allowed herself to be led to the chair and the dinner table. "Is there food?" she inquired, glancing at me and then at the vacant place setting where a plate should be before her.

"Yes, there's still plenty left from dinner. I'll get you some," Brian interceded and rushed off to the kitchen to make himself useful in the only way he knew how for the situation at hand.

He wants to fix it. Maybe not as much as I do, but he still wants to help fix it.

"How are you feeling?" I asked my estranged visitor.

"How am I supposed to feel?" she answered back with a question of her own. A response like that, which would've usually been taken as snarky, now seemed like a genuine seeking out of normalcy. How was a normal person supposed to feel under such dire circumstances?

I shook my head out of disappointment in myself and reached into her lap for her hand. "I don't know. I guess however you're feeling is how you're supposed to feel. It's all right now," I said, with no evidence to back up my claims.

Annabelle snorted in disbelief but clutched tightly at my hand in contrast.

Brian brought into the dining room an enormous plate of food that I knew Annabelle would never be able to finish, and set it in front of her. He also went about the task of pouring her a glass of wine as he took up a new seat, a gesture of normalcy and also what I suspected was an attempt at relaxing her, maybe even numbing her. He wanted a buffer to a possible breakdown.

"After you finish eating, I'll make you some more tea, and we'll get a bath started," I informed my beloved guest. "I also have some clothes for you and toiletries – "

"I can't stay here," Annabelle cut me off and dropped her fork.

"No, you can," Brian intervened before I could. "You can stay here as long as you need to."

As long as you want to...

I smiled at Brian, even though he did not see it, feeling more kindly towards him than I ever had. There was nothing else he could have said or done any better than what he did in that moment, in response to that dejection of hers. It was like finding him and falling in love all over again.

I think I've fallen in and out of love with this man too many times for one lifespan.

"He knows I'm here, and he'll come for me," Annabelle said, and she didn't need to elaborate further.

"Finish dinner and then we'll talk," I interjected into the conversation and then motioned for Brian to get up from the table with me. "We'll be in the den when you're done."

And, that's where we were when she found us, stumbling into the den with a half full glass of wine and a somber tone. I set her down in my favorite burgundy armchair and joined my husband on the small sofa.

We didn't have to wait long, for Annabelle wanted to talk.

"I've lived there most of my life, and I can remember when that house used to be a beautiful place, the most beautiful house in the entire neighborhood," she reminisced in a most pathetic fashion, for we always paint the past rosier than it was and the present darker than it is.

Maybe that's why the tantalizing idea of the future always seems so bright.

"Annabelle, those pictures that were throughout the house right before we left, the dark-haired woman, was that – "

"My mother?" she overrode me in such a delicate way it was hard to believe I'd been interrupted. "Yes. Yes, that was my mother."

"What happened to her?" I pressed, sensing the importance of this key piece of information.

There is no key.

I doubted that highly. There's almost always a rhythm and always a key.

Annabelle sipped at her wine and then looked at me with dark and forlorn eyes, the embers had gone out. "She died, a long time ago. She died while giving birth to me."

Annabelle's words felt cold, colder than they should have. But, I reminded myself that there would be very little love lost, as Annabelle had never really known her if her mother had died as she was being born. She may have missed her on some primitive level, felt a piece of her identity was lost, perhaps. But, Annabelle hadn't known her, so how could she have ever really loved her? Still, the chill bugged me.

"My father never forgave me for that," she paused for another sip of wine. "And, I don't think he ever will."

Especially since you look so much like her.

Annabelle's appearance must've been a constant reminder to him, and as she grew up and grew older I could see how he might have gone over the edge, turned mean. I'd grown so bitter after the loss of my daughter that it wasn't much of a stretch to imagine what could become of someone after such a tragedy.

"What happened with your father?" Brian joined in on the empathetic interrogation.

"He raised me by himself, and I can remember being happy as a child. I can remember what it was like when he was kind to me," Annabelle whimpered and set her empty glass down on the floor by her feet. "But, he turned mean, and I didn't help. I didn't want to help him at all." Annabelle shook her head terribly fast, as if to erase memories with the movement, and then brought her hands to her face to hide in. "I moved away. I ran away," she finally spoke again, in muffled derision of herself. "I went off to college, and he died while I was gone."

"Oh, honey," I felt sympathetic tears trace paths down my cheeks as I flowed off the sofa and over to her side. I slid an arm around her narrow, bony shoulders and let her feel my acceptance of her unfortunate and blood-splotched history.

And, I thought my parental situation had been a bad one...

"Do you know the last thing I said to him?" she suddenly spat, raising her face up so that it was in mine. "I said, 'I hate you!' I said, 'I wish you had died instead of mom!'"

And, there it was.

Murderer.

Dr. Gregory Taylor had spoken his own bizarre and twisted version of the truth. No doubt to his undead mind she was a murderer, having taken the life of her own mother and then being derelict for the rest of his. Her last words to him must've been a breathy wish played out like a rolling curse gaining momentum over the years that followed.

"Why did you come back here, after all that's happened?" Brian asked empirically. "Wouldn't it have been better to move away and start over completely?"

"Yes, it would have... but I inherited the house, and I wanted to come back. He wanted me to come back and set things right," she explained, and Brian and I both knew that she was well aware of the flaws in her thinking.

"He wants to kill you, Annabelle," I whispered the harsh truth softly to her. "He wants to take your life, as he believes you took your mother's and dishonored his. And, it doesn't matter whether that's true or not. You can never set things right with him. But, if you get away from this, beyond this, maybe you can make things right with yourself. Stay here," I suggested lovingly. "Stay here, and let me help you."

"How?" she asked, having very little faith that I could help her in any way.

"Just trust me. I'll sort this out," I swore, thinking to the willow tree, thinking on what would come to pass for it and for me.

The sooner I get out to that tree, the better. But, that could be dangerous all by myself... and it has to be me alone.

Chapter 12

I drew a bath for Annabelle and helped get her situated, while Brian worked on getting hot tea ready for her afterwards. Much like he had been nurturing with Sonya, I'd found him capable of being kind towards Annabelle in her shriveling state. It didn't shock me really, as I could also recall his attentive applications after my accident and all through therapy.

I'd gotten the water in the claw-footed tub going and arranged a mass of soaps and shampoos for her to choose from, raiding my own bathroom in the process. Brian and I never used the bathroom off the hallway, preferring the one adjoining the master bedroom instead. Once Annabelle had looked over what all was available and climbed out of her clothes, she readily settled herself into the tub's embrace, and the piping hot water.

I tried hard not to stare at her as she'd gotten herself ready for the bath, but every bone and every bruise beckoned me to bear witness. I took that knowledge, and those images that would never be erased, with me into the hall as I left her to her ablutions. I got together a good amount of clothing, about half my wardrobe, and drug it to the periwinkle guest bedroom that reminded me so much of my grandmother, who now made me think of Ella, the willow.

She'll be safe here. If there is any room in the house that would be safe, it'd be this one.

And, I'd been swayed more in my assumption when I opened that bedroom door to find both Helios and Selene occupying her bed. Selene who had been no help whatsoever with my earlier exploits now sat proudly atop the soft linens and purred contentedly, staking out her claim and taking up her fair share in our mission. Helios just eyed me as though I were of more concern to him than the room or its occupant.

I hung the clothes in the closet for Annabelle to have easy access to. I thought she'd admire the selection I'd given her, some of my finer and more delicate things. I wanted her to be enraptured by everything that surrounded her — the periwinkle blue guest bedroom that smelled vaguely of lavender, the bountiful albeit mildly disturbing willow right outside her window, the decadent apparel, and mostly the cats and the company right across the hall.

After I'd completed most of my task of stocking the guest bedroom, Brian appeared, as if on cue, in the doorway with a platter of hot tea and assorted cookies.

That's so sweet!

"You did the right thing," he said as he set the tea down on the nightstand beside the bed.

"I hope so," I replied, contritely.

"You did," he affirmed. "And, it's important that we keep doing the right things." It was a lead-in to a much larger topic, I could tell.

"What does that mean?" I asked, tired from my day that had more hours in it than it should. I could see he was tired, too.

"I want to go over a few items with you once you get her squared away for the night. I'll be in our room," and with that being all the further he would go without a longer bout of privacy, Brian left me to care for Annabelle.

As I made my way back into the hallway bathroom, Annabelle was wrapping herself in one of the soft, white terry cloth robes I'd left hanging.

I've always adored her in white.

She looked a bit better than she had only hours ago. All cleaned up with her hair and teeth brushed and some decent food and rest, there was a glint of life stirring in the bowels of her being. A purge had started somewhere inside her, and I initially sensed the stirrings of that cleanse. Her body was already repairing itself. In a few days' time, she'd be well on the mend. It was her mind and spirit that concerned me more.

"I'm so tired," she moaned, and I led her to her room and the tea that waited there.

"I put a bunch of clothing in the closet, along with fresh linens and additional items to make you feel more at home," I informed her like a well-rehearsed and gracious hostess. I felt like neither. I felt like a stressed and strained partner who merely wanted to crawl in bed beside her lover, curl up protectively, and go to sleep. But, I couldn't do any of those things that night. As it was, there was still much to be accomplished before my head hit the pillow, for real.

"And, two cats," she said eyeing Selene and Helios who didn't even bother to move when she sat down beside them on the bed.

"That, too. I think it'll be good for you to keep them in here overnight. But, if you need anything else, Brian and I are right across the hall," I said and started to make my way out of the room.

"Sally," Annabelle called as I was all set to close the door.

I opened the door half way and glanced in at her.

"Is it enough to say thank you?"

"From most people, probably not. But, from you, most definitely," I told her.

She smiled at me then with a hint of who she once was and who she would one day strive to become again. And, I smiled back with a sense of foreboding and abandon, but also a job well done. It was as though there were a seesaw in my heart that rested towards the middle instead of to one favored side.

"Get some rest," I instructed sweetly and shut the door as Helios attempted to follow me out.

Sorry. Not tonight, little man. You stay in there.

Brian had dozed off by the time I cleaned myself up and crawled between the sheets. I'd planned to shut off the bedside lamp and curl up briefly without disturbing him, so that he would easily drift off into a deeper sleep. But, no such luck.

"I need to talk to you for a minute before you click out that light," he said and rolled over to face me.

I did my best to hide the frustration, as I just wanted to shut the lights off and wait for him to drift into a sound sleep so that I could slip out again and do what needed to be done. There was no reason to take any of my emotions out on the man that had given in on so many issues, though, so I played nice.

"Ok," I said and opened myself up to his discourse.

"It's just a reminder, really. I wanted to make sure you knew you had to be up when I get up tomorrow, so you can drive me to work," he said blankly, but I knew he was expecting quite the reaction from me.

Tomorrow's Friday! Shit!

"Oh, I really don't think that's a good idea," I started in against his plans and my mother's.

"Sally, you need to go see your mom tomorrow, like you promised, and you need to start driving again. And, most importantly, you need to get out of this house for a while," he said sounding both bold and rational. His words brought forth memories of his utterances at the apartment, when he was trying to sway me to be amenable about moving into #18. "That last point is one I can't stress enough."

"Actually," I set up my counter-attack, "That's probably a really bad idea, given all that's gone on today. Annabelle shouldn't be left alone – "

"Annabelle is perfectly safe in this house, and you've been in this house long enough. You've been involved in all these things long enough. If Annabelle is going to stay here for a while, then she can't disrupt our lives or interfere in our plans," Brian summed up. He may have given in on a few key issues, but I could tell he wanted to continue to instill boundaries that promoted progress, much like the move from the apartment to the house was one of progress. And, who could blame him? "We still have to live our lives while she tries to recover hers." It was an offensive maneuver that was hard to rally against.

But, what if something happens while I'm away?

I felt myself nodding agreement I didn't entirely feel, and mostly because I understood his position and the rightness of it. I couldn't blow off my mother now that she and I were building what may amount to a relationship one day, and also since she was trying again with my father. I couldn't disregard Brian's wishes either, as he had fulfilled all of mine to the best of his ability. And, I couldn't take

Annabelle with me tomorrow. How would I explain it? And, there was no way in her current condition Annabelle could or would go anyway.

I briefly entertained the concept of inviting Margaret and Lyle over to sit with Annabelle while I was away, but I dismissed that flight of fancy immediately. I'd asked enough of Margaret, and she'd made it perfectly clear she wasn't in alignment with what I was doing. She'd been through something similar with Lyle at one point in the past, and she didn't want to revisit that. Odds were Lyle wouldn't want to either.

At least there are the cats. Small comfort.

But, given Dr. Taylor's strong aversion to them, the cats provided the best line of defense that I could see.

I watched Brian set the alarm and then turn back to me. I nudged closer to him on the bed for the sweet assurances his body provided, and I let him kiss me goodnight with all the energy he had left. I responded in kind before the lights clicked out and let in the darkness.

The bedchamber grew quiet, but I sensed a stirring in the walls. The house was awake, and all that roamed around outside kept it tottering on the edge of its foundation. I listened for any noise that would be out of place but heard none. I opened my eyes wide to let in more of the dark and adjust my vision so that I might peer around the room and spot a shape out of place. There was none. Nothing was amiss and yet everything was wrong.

❖

After a long while, as the night grew closer to the dawn, Brian's breathing became so rhythmic and throaty that I knew he was fast asleep. I could move about the room and never wake him, so long as I was careful and crafty.

'Be careful,' Silence warned from somewhere in the chamber's dusky gray abyss.

I slipped out of bed and quickly donned a pair of heavy stretch pants and a large sweater built more for insulation than fashion. It was easy to move around in the dark and find what I wanted after giving my eyes hours to adjust. The house grew quiet and undisturbed on all levels, as though it too had been lulled into a sound sleep, and along with that sleep came a false sense of security.

I inched the door open and stepped out into the hall, taking great pains to click it shut behind me with nary a peep. The floorboards didn't squeak as I made my way down to the first floor. From the bottom of the steps, it was easy enough to see by streams of moonlight, and to dash from there into the kitchen. I retrieved the sharpest kitchen knife I could find, as well as a flashlight, and made my way to the cloakroom.

With my coat buttoned securely around me, I stepped out into the night turning early morning.

Coming off my porch and onto the ground, I looked up at the brilliance of the moon as it shown its essence onto the dew of the earth and the moist suppleness of a land ready to live again. The great nightly majestic was waning in the sky, the lunar body going from brightest beacon to shrouded gatekeeper filled with potentials and promises. There was enough light to see very clearly by, and so I had no trouble making my passage effortlessly to the tree, with Silence filling in my fragile and slightly frightened footsteps.

I tucked the blade of the kitchen knife into the folds of my coat pocket and with outstretched hands, I touched the willow's ragged and aged surface.

Grandmother.

I thought of her first, but then realized my mistake in the illusion. It was hurtful to set aside what I'd wanted to see for what had been a more accurate and necessary portrayal.

Ella.

The winds picked up slightly, enough to make me think I'd been heard, even if that wasn't that case and I was only talking and thinking to myself. Every branch and twig on the tree trembled, and I wondered if it was at the thought of what I was about to do to the trunk. I circled around to the far side of the tree, the side that was hidden from view by #18 and its neighboring property, #20. Kneeling before the bark with the reverence of an adoring worshipper, I searched for the artistic scratches that had rendered the work of the broken raven with tattered wings, the raven trapped within that gilded cage. In short order I found it, and the angry hands, too. They were just slightly removed from touching the cage but held themselves in a loftier position than I'd remembered, as though they were hovering above the cage and the raven itself, ready to smash them both to bits.

This was it.

I was going into the city to be with my mother tomorrow. Brian would be at work. And, both of us... in fact, all three of us, needed an end to the madness. My life and Brian's needed to move forward since the brokenness of our existence had been brought into sharp contrast by the events that surrounded our move, by Reggie and Sonya... and Amelia. We'd been forced into a pressure cooker for months by those two souls and a solitary phantom, and now the additional seasoning of Annabelle and her father threatened to make the pot boil over. Annabelle had to want an end to it all, too, even if she was incapable of feeling it at the time. I wanted her to be free, and I wanted her to want it, too.

I want to set us all free.

I took the blade from my pocket and vigorously worked at defacing the hands that hung high above the cage, and attempted to hide themselves in the grooves. I stripped them completely from the trunk, pieces of bark peeling away with the slip of my blade, and then dug like a woman deranged to bury the bits of splintered wood that were the remains of that terrible image. I covered them over with dirt and prayed they'd never return, that they'd stay in the earth where they belonged, where all dead things must go.

As they say, ashes to ashes, dust to dust.

I then set my sights on the raven in the cage. At first I thought to deface that, too, to take it away completely, but then a sensation in the back of my arms that crept up to perch on my shoulders stopped me. It was as if gentle and guiding hands were signaling to me to wait, to think about it a little more. I eyed the artwork critically, and then saw what it was I wanted to do. I didn't want to deface it, strip away what was there already. I wanted to restore it.

I made a couple of deep slashes at the structure of the cage until it appeared broken, as though the fevered flurry of raven's wings had shattered what held the bird in place. The cage had surrendered to the captured. I sat back on my haunches for a moment and considered my handiwork. What I'd intended was for the raven to appear as though it had the strength to rip and rend the bars to shreds. However, the more I examined it, the more I saw that it looked as though some beast outside the bars had torn the cage asunder to release the bird. The slashes I'd made with my knife had come to more closely resemble claw marks than bird scratches.

Did I do that?

I didn't think so.

It didn't matter. The intent was there, and the spirit of it was freedom.

I focused on the bird — broken bones and tattered feathers. They needed the careful precision of fine detailing, something to be done with the tip of my blade. I took a deep breath and gazed upward into the branches of the tree. From my squatting position, looking high up into the sky through bare branches, the form of the tree as it stretched up and then cast its branches back down resembled that of a web, a large, interconnecting, intersecting web. How had I not seen that before? The branches and twigs were silhouetted against the smiling moon and the shimmering stars, and they cast a web up and out to the cosmos, and I was just as sure that the roots cast a similar weaving down into the earth and all there was.

Where am I? Betwixt and between?... In fairy tales, in ancient stories, hardly anything good and almost everything monumental happened there.

At the base of the tree I felt out of time and nowhere, and yet in the same instant I felt myself everywhere.

Inevitably, my mind came back around from tired and tedious wanderings to hone in once more on the task at hand. I began to augment the details of the raven that were already present on the tree, creating the illusion of fuller, healthier feathers, perfect for flight. I straightened the edges of the wings so that the bones were strong and would allow for lofty soaring. The expression on the raven was one of strength and renewal, of the moment before takeoff. Every single detail had to be ideal, and I labored over it until I heard the calls of a few birds waking in the trees, surrounding me on all sides. The sky was turning to an enlivening hue of purplish-red, and I felt the radiance of solar rays on my back.

My work had finished as night was turning to day, as the sun joined the moon for a brief interlude at dawn.

I stood and stretched. It was time to go back into the house and clean up. I'd have to take Brian into work very soon, and I'd need to get Annabelle all set up for the day before I left for my city adventure. I feared the day with my mother less and the car ride more, especially now that I'd missed a full night's sleep and would no doubt be exhausted on the road.

A little coffee might fix that right up.

I'd gotten good at convincing myself of things I wanted to believe. No coffee would save me.

I tucked the blade once more into the folds of my coat pocket, brushed myself off, and started for the house. It was then I noticed a fragment of light, a sliver of yellow movement out of the corner of my eye. I glanced to my left and saw the shadow of a man standing along the side window of #20 and peering out. I knew it was Dr. Taylor, although I had no idea how long he'd been watching or how much he'd seen. How much could he possibly be able to see in the early dawn?

No matter. What's done is done.

I strode past his house, Annabelle's house, and into my own with more confidence than I'd felt. There was fear in my steps and a minor sympathy in my heart as I locked the door behind me and shut out the world, if only for a little bit longer. After my episode with Reggie and a full viewing of my own sins, I was apt to be more understanding. I could comprehend how his soul may be suffering, how things could get twisted and distorted in life and even more so from beyond a heavy veil. But, in the end, it didn't change a thing. My mission, my will, and my desires were still the same. And, it was time to face the day and what was to come.

I crept to the periwinkle guest bedroom and found Annabelle asleep.

Perchance to dream?...

I watched her rest peacefully, or what looked peacefully, beneath a thick layer of blankets and two cats. Selene lay right on top of her back and gazed out at me through half closed green eyes that suggested I knew better than to disturb them. Meanwhile, Helios mewed and stood to stretch at the foot of the bed. I could tell that he wanted my attention, even after I'd shut him up in the room all night, dismissing his objections.

I walked over and began to pet him, careful not to make too much noise or motion. I didn't want to disturb Annabelle. If anyone needed more rest, it was her. In the tender light of a dawning day, she seemed practically rose-toned and nubile once again. Her face looked fleshier, and the skin was starting to take on the glow of the sunrise. Of course, I was sure many of the inflicted flaws would still be there in a harsher light of day, but it was endearing to see her as she was in that moment, wrapped in a rose gold sheen.

Helios at one pointed started to make such a fuss out of being petted, that I saw Annabelle roll over. I picked him up, as if that would help, but he only talked more, probably demanding to be let out of the room and fed.

Annabelle's eyes fluttered open and she smiled at me straight away.

"Hi," I said as politely as I could, being the cause of the disruption.

"Hi," she mirrored.

"I didn't mean to wake you, but this one had to get rowdy," I went on, indicating that Helios was the culprit.

"It's ok. I was more awake than you thought. I was just laying here, listening." She spoke with a sexy sideways smile and sat up. Annabelle patted the bed next to her as a sign that I should sit there.

I did just that.

"How are you feeling?" I asked, as might be expected.

"Some better."

"Did you sleep well?"

"I had dreams all night," she responded, and her tone of voice gave the hint that something about it wasn't typical. "I hardly ever dream," she filled me in.

"What did you dream about?" I pressed, fearful that the willow had reached out to her too much, had tipped my hand and my will. There were things I thought would be best for Annabelle not to know, at least not right away.

"I don't remember much now that I'm awake," she started, "but I remember they were good dreams."

What a relief!

"And, you were in them," she tacked on.

"That's nice," I said as normally as I could, given the wave of relaxation that washed over me when I'd heard her response, not to mention the sweet stab of heat.

Annabelle inched in closer to me, and I set Helios on the floor. A vibration of anticipation sizzled all around us, but I noticed that it was weak and off-kilter. "Sally, it felt like months," she breathed, leaning in towards my ear and then resting her head on my shoulder. "I thought I'd been in there for months at a time, especially between the last two or three times I'd seen you. He'd gotten so angry, especially after you and Brian..." her thoughts sort of halted there, and she didn't bother to give them a nudge onward.

I also thought it was best that those thoughts lie down and die. No point in reviving a memory or an issue that would only cause both of us further pain. I knew that her father had heightened his intense and insane grip on her because of what was growing between the two of us. And, with Brian entering the picture, with a sense of happiness and harmony almost complete, it had brought the theoretical roof down with Annabelle trapped in the rubble.

"I missed you," she finally surmised. "I missed you so much, and I thought I'd never see you again. When I sent you away that day – "

"Stop it," I said in a raspy whisper, the air and my heart thick with emotions. "Don't think about it. You're here now, with me, and that's all that matters."

Annabelle stopped speaking and instead nuzzled my shoulder and neck in response.

"I missed you, too. I always miss you when you're away, and it makes no difference how long it is," I told her with what words would come out and with what eloquence I could muster.

Thin and tiny hands lifted my sweater off and initialized a sequence that had me shed the rest of my pragmatic attire. Annabelle had already lain naked beneath the blankets, and she beckoned me in to curl up beside her. I had no idea what time it was, but I was sure that Brian would find me when I had to get up and begin the new day he and my mother had orchestrated. In the meantime, I curled around my beloved and placed my head to rest on a pillow that smelled of lavender, fresh apples, and new earth.

Brian had known exactly where to find me when I wasn't in bed with him. I heard rapping on the bedroom door, in response to which Annabelle and I both bolted upright.

"Sally," Brian called through the barrier of shiny wood, "are you in there?"

"Yeah, yeah, I'm here, and I know. Just give me a minute, and I'll be right out."

I heard Brian's feet pad across the hall and down the stairs.

I threw the covers back, stretched and wrapped myself in the robe Annabelle had worn after her bath the night before. "I have to take Brian into work today," I told her, as I began gathering up my few items of clothing. The small amount of shuteye I'd shared with her had made me feel worse than if I'd just stayed up the entire night. I felt sleepier now than I had when I'd crawled into the bed. "And, then I'm spending the afternoon with my mom. We're running around the city or something and planning garden beds," I summarized with a snort.

"So, you'll be gone all day?" Annabelle asked shrilly, clutching the blankets to her chest.

"Unfortunately, yes. And, Brian will be in the city, at his office, all weekend working on a software release. So, he won't be back until Sunday late," I said, filling her in on the pertinent details.

"Then what am I supposed to do?" she narrowly focused in on the horror of being alone in a house not hers, next to a house possessed by a spirit that wanted her.

Ok, so it's not an ideal arrangement.

"You stay in the house until I get home this evening," I instructed her in a manner stricter than I'd intended.

Strangely enough, Annabelle seemed immediately comforted by that strictness. "Ok, I can do that, but what if –
"

"I don't think anything can harm you here, not now. I don't think he can get in or that he'll even try, what with the cats and all," I said and walked over to where she sat up against the headboard. I gazed at her adoringly, sure that my eyes were dilated as wide as could be, given the amount of affection that I felt. "This house isn't his property, and he hasn't left the confines of your house since we left it yesterday. If he wanted to drag you out of here, he probably would've tried it by now... don't you think?"

Who the hell knows? It's not like any of this is rational or functional... or predictable.

"I guess so," she spoke with a measure of reluctance, greater than a tinge of uncertainty.

"And, it may or may not mean anything, but the cats are here," I offered again, further.

"I'm not sure that means anything," she said with a nervous laugh.

"Me either," I admitted, "but they do make me feel better, and it got us out of your house."

I headed for the door and opened it a crack before stopping to speak again. "There are plenty of clothes in your closet, and if you don't see anything you like, feel free to raid the closet in my bedroom. You'll have the run of the house, so make yourself at home. There's plenty of food and drinks in the fridge," and I left her with that, shutting the door in a soft yet definitive click.

I dressed in a hurry, put on a minimal layer of makeup for the day, and proceeded downstairs to Brian, following the aroma of freshly brewed coffee.

"I put yours in a to-go mug," he said as I rounded the corner into the kitchen. "It's getting late."

No small talk with you this morning, huh?

I accepted a mug of the bracing hot substance, as well as the car keys Brian shoved in my hand.

"Let's grab our coats," he declared the next step of the day's itinerary.

I followed willingly, wanting to get the drive and the day over with so I could return home to Annabelle and rest assured that all would be well when I got back. I threw my coat on over the eggshell white cashmere sweater I chose to be a suitable companion to my basic black slacks. I looked presentable enough for almost any activity my mother might have planned, and the outfit was warm and easy to move in. Brian looked ready for the managerial salt mines in his polo top and pleated khakis.

With a quick nab of my purse and the flick of a deadbolt, the house was secured and I was ready to face a day of independence and exploration about town.

Do I have to?

I knew the answer to that already, and climbed behind the steering wheel for the first time in over three years. A full cycle of life had concluded itself; I sensed the turning of another wheel, a wheel within a wheel, and was privy to a notch up on the spiral.

I can start over... or crash and burn as I try.

I put that possibility from my mind and turned over the engine with a twist of the key. It roared to life and then hummed in tune with the thrum of existence that sat alongside Brian and me.

"Here we go," Brian said with a measure of excitement at the prospect of me driving, at me making noteworthy progress. It was just he and I in the car, and once #18 and Annabelle were in the rearview mirror, he took on a glow of contentment. He had me and his work to look forward to.

The drive into the city was a long, arduous white-knuckle ride for me, and what on the surface seemed to be a pleasure cruise for Brian. He talked on and off about the project he had going over the weekend, and I half listened, paying more attention to the roads and the long stretch ahead. The morning was a terrific one for driving — clear skies, dry pavement, and a small amount of traffic. I couldn't have asked for better, and yet I resented it.

When I dropped Brian off in front of his office building, he leaned in and gave me a quick, customary kiss on the lips.

"Text me when you get to your mom's. I want to make sure you get there safely," he said as he stood outside the car, hovering.

"I will," I obliged.

"Got your phone?"

I rummaged around in my purse until I laid a hand on it and then brought it forth for him to see. "Yep, and it's got a full charge."

"Call if you get lost on the way there, ok?" Brian continued with his fussing.

Gee, who's the nervous Nelly now?

"I will, but I know the way, Brian," I said, shaking my head at him in dismissal.

"I love you, Sally," he said and leaned in for another brief kiss.

I kissed him back, and in doing so indulged in the exchange of compassion, interplay of energy that went on between two people that had seen and been through a lot together. There was a lot to honor in that.

"I love you, too," I said.

Our eyes locked for a moment, and then Brian shut the passenger side door. I pulled away from the curb and resumed the journey of my day trip, and the next stop was the immaculate cottage-style home that belonged to my parents.

My mother was on one of the white wrought-iron chairs situated at an angle on her concrete porch, waiting when I drove up. Although her house was positioned in the middle of an urban subdivision, with all the tall trees and sumptuous space between the houses, one could almost imagine it was a secluded glen.

She waved in a flawless flow at me as I completed my arrival text to Brian. I stepped out of the car and started up the stone path that led directly to her. It was disturbing how very much she looked like me, and I don't think I'd ever been so very aware of it as I was right then and there. Her long hair was a flash and flush of wanton blonde, and her creamy skin was a beautiful biscuit beige. As I got closer, the blue in her eyes captured me and reminded me of my own azure irises. She was long and lean and carried herself with the same determination that I did. I could see why Reggie had been drawn to her when he couldn't come to me.

"You made good time," she complimented, as she got out of her chair. "Come on inside. Have you had breakfast?"

"No, just coffee," I told her as she made her way in and held the door for me to do likewise.

"Good, I have a lot of food in the kitchen," she said and ushered in her long sought after guest with all the elegance of a happy homemaker. But, was this a happy home? It had never been overtly so during my childhood. Average may have been the best term to describe the vibe of my memories there.

I stepped into the great room, which was a combination of a living room and dining room space, perfect for entertaining. And, my parents had held a lot of parties there when I was growing up — birthdays, Easter, 4th of July, and of course, Thanksgiving and Christmas. They'd also held the occasional New Year's Eve party, and out of all of them those had been my favorite, for I got to stay up way past bedtime when I was only a few years of age. It had seemed like a forbidden world to witness and then cross over into the witching hour.

But, the great room from my memories was not the room I stood in now.

"What do you think?" my mother asked, taking my purse and then helping me off with my coat.

Where carpets had once been, there were now darkly stained hardwood floors that boasted an ornately patterned area rug, uniting the two definitive spaces of the room with palm leaf pleasantries. The walls had gone from off-white to a creamy sourdough, and where there were no palm leaf accents there was bamboo instead. It was not the room I recalled from my youth.

It's better. Not only is the style more modern, but also the fresh paint and lack of carpets takes out any sadness with it. This is a room in which a person can start over again.

And, that's why she'd done it. Whether she had started this project of redecorating the house while she was carrying on with Reggie, or she'd gone mad with mayhem afterward for the majority of it didn't matter. It was information sitting boldly on the surface that my mother was in the process of reinventing her life and maybe even herself.

"It's amazing," I admitted to her, wandering around the room as though I were lost in the intricacies of the artwork she'd selected, and I was. "I can hardly believe you've done all this."

"Well, I have," she boasted with a beaming grin. "And, every room has updates. Come, I'll show you."

I followed her into the hall. She was right in that every room had changed. Not only were there updates, but they were highly noticeable ones. The paint patterns were what caught my eye the most, for I could remember every room from when I'd lived there being either a shade of white, off-white, cream, or beige. And, I could remember thinking, 'what's the difference?' My mother had always defended her color palette, and more strongly when I'd grown into a teenager and wanted to paint my own room some vibrant hue of a grotesque color I knew she'd never permit. "It's a heavenly color scheme," she'd defended her position to a teenager she didn't have to explain things to and a husband that merely chuckled and rolled his eyes. "These colors are comfortable for everyone and offend no one. And, if we ever have to sell the house again, it'll make it easier."

Only, they never did sell the house and have never had any intentions to in the first place. She had been concerned with appearances, and at a young and tender age even I had been able to pick up on that. My father, more than likely, simply didn't cared and let her have her say.

But now, my mother had busted loose, and her house had exploded in an array of fine colors. They were gentle colors and a tad on the conservative side, but colors nonetheless. The bathroom was a muted aqua blue, walls and even ceiling. And, two bedrooms were a fine salmon color with opposite reddened earth accent walls. A third bedroom, turned work studio, was a mossy green with emerald accents and all wood furniture. And, finally our arrival into the kitchen erupted into a sphere of harvest yellows and golds, with a grounding black and white tile floor pattern.

I was speechless, except to compliment her. I was stunned to say the very least, and had to digest all the change along with the large breakfast assortment my mother had laid out before me. We ate in thrumming contentment, near Silence.

"So, what's on the agenda for our day?" I inquired as she cleared the plates and shoved them into the dishwasher. Leftovers found their way immediately to the refrigerator.

"I've planned something I know we both like... a trip to the Butterfly House," she said with indulgent appeal.

I smiled at her. "I do like the Butterfly House," I got on board. "But, you drive," I added a caveat. "I've had my fair share already this morning and will have to do that whole trip again tonight."

My mother sighed with a mixture of happiness and minor annoyance, and grabbed her car keys from off the hook near the back door.

A flurry of fluttering wings awaited us.

❖

My mother had always liked the Butterfly House. I suspected it was for several coalescing reasons — the flower-like insects, the wide assortment of plants, and perhaps most of all, the extravagant indoor landscaping. She'd always loved her work when she'd been in her prime, when her solo career had been at its peak. And, even though she'd aged a bit, had a small settling in of arthritis, and eventually retired, small gardens and growing indoor elegances continued to call to her. Space was sacred in her eyes, and I had inherited some of that worldview.

I liked the Butterfly House for all of the beauty and majesty in movement on display. Each insect, moth or butterfly, had its own particular floaty flight pattern that was unique to the species. And, all of the movement patterns were brilliant, a marvelous use of space. I, like my mother, also enjoyed the wonders of the growing, natural world, although I often found myself more interested in the symbolic and scientific information made readily available about each species in the House's collection.

We stepped into the unnaturally humid air and were greeted by a release of wondrous wings taking off in response to our sudden emergence. There were very few people in the House with us that late morning, so most activity was in response to us and typical butterfly and moth daily needs.

I recalled quite a bit from my earlier tours of the place, even though it had been years since my last walk through. I spotted right away some of my favorite insects. There were the blue tigers from Southeast Asia, greenbird wings from Australia, and of course the easily recognizable monarchs that were native to my own region as well as lands that stretched all the way down into Mexico. However, the few species from Central and South America were the ones that captured my imagination the most — cattlehearts, red rims, and the owl butterflies were out and about and apparently as happy to see me as I was them.

Do you know you are some of my favorites?

I couldn't help contemplating that as I walked around the indoor, climate controlled, tropical paradise.

As I neared the end of my first cursory circle through the place, I spotted the one butterfly that captured my heart and spirit the most, as it was the very first butterfly I'd ever learned to identify — the Achilles Morpho. I saw the bright blue bands on predominantly black-wings from several feet away. One was perched on the walkway near the bench that sat at the far end of the path. I approached it cautiously, not wanting to frighten it away and have it take flight before I could get a good, long look. However, as I got within only a couple inches, I realized that something was wrong. The lovely morpho hadn't taken flight from the path. It sat there on the stones, giving me only the infrequent and slow rise and fall of frail wings.

I got in so close that my breath rustled the scales of the poor creature's colorful display, and after a few minutes I stood to full height and looked around for one of the volunteer attendants that was often seen walking through, keeping a weathered eye on visitors.

I saw an older woman in an official green volunteer's shirt and went over to her. "Excuse me, I think there might be something wrong with one of your butterflies," I informed, and she followed me straight away.

I brought her to my beloved blue morpho, which hadn't moved an inch since I'd left its side. The old woman squatted down and took a quick peek, and then got herself back up. "It's dying," she frankly stated, and gazed at me as if I should just move on with my personal tour.

"Isn't there anything that can be done," I pressed, and when I'd heard my own words come tumbling out of my mouth, I realized how ridiculous it sounded. But, I held my ground and let the words sit between me, her, and the butterfly.

"No," she said in the same tone. "From egg to mature adult, they only live for about four months, approximately 115 days." And, with that being all the further she wanted to take it, she walked away to check on the other visitors and the healthier insects.

I peered down at the morpho, which gave another excruciatingly slow flap of its wings. The symbol for Venus and Aphrodite, the message of love and hope and happiness, according to the signage, lay dying at my feet. The metamorphosis it had gone through in life from egg to larva to pupa to adult was over. There was only one stage left, one more metamorphosis to be completed to end its individual story. I sat down on the nearest bench and watched. I watched the stillness and the random flutter. I saw the infrequent on-looker trudge by and the volunteer glance at me every so often in a rude questioning. And, I stayed in the spot, holding a vigil that seemed ludicrous even to me, but I couldn't help it.

Sometime later, my mother appeared and sat next to me on the bench.

"What are you looking at?" she asked, obviously not seeing what my eyes beheld, an increasingly still life form.

I pointed out to the speck of blue and black on the path a few feet away. "That morpho there."

"Pretty," she said in instant outward appraisal.

"It's dying," I informed her with a grimace.

"We're all dying."

"*Are you ready to live like you're dying instead of living like you're already dead?*"

My grandmother's words... no... Ella's words.

I turned to my mother, who had changed so much in such a short period of time. "You seem different to me lately," I finally summoned up the courage to say.

She patted the back of my hands that sat folded in my lap, as if they embraced a prayer. "I broke, Sally," she explained. "I broke into so many pieces, and I'm not even sure when all the shattering happened. I don't think it was all at once," she said, seeking an answer in herself that had never surfaced. "I think I've been broken for a while and only recently realized it."

"Reggie," I spoke the name of the dead and recently departed over the dying butterfly.

And, in the Silence that followed I knew it was because of him, for her. But, what was it for me?

❖

The entire day with my mother had been a surreal one, and overall a very good one. We'd returned to her house after the butterflies to sketch out basic plans for the coming spring's garden beds, the beds that Reggie had turned over for her in the early autumn. And, then, before I knew it, it was time for me to head home. The sky was growing fiery with the first hues of sunset, and I didn't want to drive in the dark.

"It's a shame you can't stay until your father gets home," my mother said as she walked me to the car.

I opened the door and sat down in the driver's seat. "I really don't want to drive in the dark, mom. I'm nervous enough as it is just driving back by myself."

"At least you're driving."

What does that mean, exactly?

But, I sensed that like Brian, she was happy to see me out and about. And, I didn't stay to question it. A parting hug and I was off on the long journey home, home to #18, which had been my own personal chrysalis. Back to Annabelle, who I hoped and prayed would be within the walls of my cocoon, safe and sound.

And, I hope I make it back there safely as well.

That terrible, palpable feeling of crashing the car hung with me on the drive. It may have been post-traumatic stress disorder. It may have been related to muscle memory. The imprinted sounds of crunching metal and shattering glass rung in my ears the whole way, while the inside of the car was quiet. It felt more and more like a reality the closer I got to home. As tall buildings and large clusters of houses melted into sprawling suburbia and then the rolling fields of the countryside, I grew more and more alarmed by the sensation inside me. In my mind's eye, I automatically mulled over the imagery of ravens and crows taking flight, fleeing the sound of a gut-wrenching crash. An unstoppable anxiety was coming into play. It sat beside me in the car while Silence occupied the backseat.

But, nothing horrible happened.

I turned onto Willow Tree Court smoothly, and then into my own driveway without a hitch. I breathed a loud and laudable sigh of relief as I threw the car into park and turned off the purring engine.

Home, safe and sound.

I texted Brian the news of my return.

I saw numerous lights on inside my house, upstairs and down, and found relief in that, too. Annabelle was inside and had probably turned on all the lights for comfort. Darkness is the enemy of those that can conjure up awful and plausible scenarios within it.

I got out of the car and dashed up the porch steps, letting myself into the house with the unlocking of the deadbolt. She was safe behind that door, a door that had been kept locked.

"Annabelle, I'm back!" I called out as I shoved my things haphazardly into the cloakroom. Coming into the hall, I was greeted by two madly mewing kittens, bent on wrapping themselves around my legs so that I couldn't move, couldn't leave them. "Oh, you silly things," I cooed and swept them both up into my arms. "You might have to get used to me being gone more," I told them and bestowed a tight hug before setting them down again.

I headed into the den. "Annabelle," I called lovingly, with a hint of play in my voice, "aren't you happy to have me home?"

Silence followed me around as I worked my way from the den to the kitchen to the dining room. I finally found myself back out in the hall, and Annabelle hadn't answered me.

And that was when I sensed it, the cold. It was a peculiar cold, a cold that was no mere matter of degrees Fahrenheit. It was more of a draining of warmth from the vitality of the living, and I recalled it from the stores of my mind as a feeling I'd had while in the basement some time ago. But, now it was right in the middle of my very own home, and it spread tentacles upstairs as I shot up the steps calling out for her.

"Annabelle!" I screamed, not caring if it was an over-reaction, which I highly doubted.

No response.

I did a thorough search to find her nowhere on the second floor. I bolted up to my studio, willing her to be there, studying my artwork or playing aimlessly with my old movement equipment. But, she wasn't.

I came back downstairs to the main hall and called out again.

Nothing. No one. It was me and the cats.

The basement. Maybe she went down there.

There was no reason for her to do so, but maybe she had anyway. The basement had an intrinsic pull to it sometimes that beckoned with an incredible force. I fled to find a flashlight in the kitchen and then opened the door to that void-inducing blackness. I flipped the stairway light switch and illuminated the steep steps down.

"Annabelle?" I said, softer now, hardly believing she'd go down there and leave all the lights off.

I clicked on the flashlight and headed down.

"Annabelle," I spoke a little more forcibly as I reached the concrete bottom.

Nothing... again.

I shone my flashlight beam around the main space of the basement to see nothing other than storage, and I decided not to go further, knowing already what resided in the other areas.

My wheelchair. Trina's paintings. Maybe even Brian's card to Amelia...and who knows what else now that Annabelle's been in the house.

I went back upstairs to the main hall where reality greeted me, striking like a thunderbolt. Annabelle wasn't anywhere in the house.

He's taken her!

I don't remember running out of the house or leaving the door wide open either, so that the two cats scattered into the coming night. But, I will never forget the expression on Annabelle's face, that look of horror and hypnotic suggestion in her eyes, as she banged against an unbreakable window in the house next door. She slammed herself against the glass and opened her mouth in a shout, a scream, and one I couldn't hear. No ears outside the walls of #20 heard her. She'd more than resembled that raven, wings spread aloft, slamming itself along the barrier, beating feathered limbs against the bars of its cage.

Our eyes locked in the longest moment I have ever lived through, before or since, and then a large shadow loomed and stole her away from the window, away from me. And, there was a frenetic vacancy held the spot where she had been, asking what I would do next, asking if there was anything that could be done.

I ran up the steps of #20 and pounded on the front door, screaming for all I was worth. I banged on the windows that would not break and yelled until I was near collapse, circling the house like some ravenous animal that could not be sated. I felt rabid and frothed inwardly.

"Sally!" came a booming, feminine voice in my ear as I made for the front door of #20 again. "Sally, stop! Stop it! Stop it!"

It was Margaret. She stood on Annabelle's lawn draped in a flamingo pink bathrobe and fuzzy pink house slippers. She was a serene essence of common societal sanity pitted against the parched madness of a sentient world that would not be quenched.

"Call the police!" I roared at her in abandon as I flung my body against the door, pounding and kicking.

Margaret's arms were around me in an instant, dragging me away from the scene of my attack. "Sally, don't –"

I shoved her off and started to pound on the windows again. "Call the cops, damn it!" I screeched. "He's killing her! He's killing her!"

Margaret ran back to her house and out of sight.

But, I knew there was no time left and nothing the police would be able to do. I ran around in circles looking for an answer, looking for a key. As my eyes scanned the ground, they settled on a large rock, about the size of a fist. I scooped it in hand and bolted up the steps of the porch again to hurl it at one of the windows.

The boulder bounced off and landed on the wooden wrap-around with a giant thud of failure.

I'm failing her!

I wailed out to the rapidly setting sun my terror, my torment, and my loss. It blazed back at me in fiery rays and continued its path, went on with its predestined decent.

I dashed down off the porch again and scurried about the grounds, seeking a solution and means to salvation for Annabelle and me. And, then a spark of clarity ignited in my brain, as I caught the glint of sunrays on the hood of my gray economy vehicle parked perfectly in the driveway.

Damn it! I just knew I was going to crash.

Grabbing the keys, turning on the engine, and backing out of the driveway elude me, too. The flash of activity from those seconds is gone from my brain, expunged, but I know it must've happened, as I lined the headlights of the car up with the front door of Annabelle's house.

A flicker of movement, a hovering shadow situated itself between the beams and then stood there for me to get a good look, to have a minute to think. It was Ella. She placed herself in front of the car in a wispy guise that I recognized as not stable, not solid, and totally impermanent.

Move!

My mind shouted at her.

Get out of the way!

It persisted.

Ella did not move, and it didn't matter.

It was the last moment of decision, that last chance I had to make a different choice, and create a better ending. It was upon me like a cloak of dying rays putting up one last scrap prior to the night consuming them. The manifestation of what I'd carved in that tree was upon me, and there were no other options readily available.

I threw the car into drive, hit the gas with everything I had, and ran the small gray vehicle up the front steps and in through the door... where we reached a smashing stop. It was a screeching and crunching halt, one I'd been through before, and my life shattered like the panes of glass in a hedonistic drizzle all around me.

I thought on the willow in that instant, as I hung suspended in the crushing maw of a metal monster. I thought of the visions I'd had while beneath the boughs. I recalled the wailing of winds, the multitude of hands that had followed, the scurrying of animals, the attachment of other trees and plants, and the fire that had blazed around me. The memory of that ethereal fire with a lion's gigantic roar soared before my eyes as the car engine caught fire. The flames spread along the front end up towards the windshield and then out along the wooden framework of the house, making short work of the wood and scorching the stone with unforgiving heat. I didn't feel any pain, but I heard screaming.

Is that me screaming? Is it Annabelle?

I tried to get out, but couldn't move. The flames, like the fiery sunset, grew more dazzling and kept coming closer.

Looking out at what was left of #20 being torn down from my lofty perch on an early spring morning was almost as hard as letting Annabelle go. But, I had to let her go. It was her last day sharing the house with Brian and myself, before to moving to the city and beginning a brand new career venture, and a very promising one at that. I had shut myself up in the third floor studio for the morning to contemplate it. I was also avoiding the pain associated with the transition. From lover to lodger to distant acquaintance was more than I was able to handle in such a short period of time.

Annabelle had been packing as I'd hobbled across the second floor hallway with my walker, and then made my way slowly up the steps. She'd heard me moving past and asked if I needed help. But, I couldn't let her touch me now, not now that she was leaving. I understood that it was for good, no matter what either of us said to the contrary. I understood that it was for good, even if she didn't. It didn't matter how much we'd planned to stay in touch, swore we'd keep in contact, our lines of connection were destined to dwindle over the months that would add up to years. Annabelle had to start again with nothing tied to her from her life before. She had to leave the cage of the court and fly away, and I had to be selfless enough to let her.

That has never been my strong suit, even with all the opportunities for practice.

Most of #20 had burned all the way to the ground the night I ran my car in through the front door. It had been mostly stone settings that had withstood the flames, like ancient sentinels telling an old story to any who dared to look on, to listen and learn.

New scars replaced the old ones I came in to #18 with, making my daily excursions to the mirror awkward and even agonizing. Something inside, some internal knowing, told me not to expect them to heal up in the same miraculous way. The scars and injuries I'd incurred that fateful February night were with me to stay, and I was working on making peace with it. It wasn't going well.

I gazed out the large studio art window at the willow in the cul-de-sac, the willow that had seen me go from walker to freely walking to wheelchair back to walker. The bark on it had changed in the two months or more that passed. There was no longer a raven beating fervently for release or a cat's claws positioned defensively. Instead, there were new emblems and elements that I wasn't adept at deciphering yet, and I went outside a lot less frequently as it required a lot more effort.

As I looked to my right at the lot that had once held Annabelle's home, I saw a figured weaving back and forth amid the broken earth. I squinted and leaned in closer to the gleaming glass pane. It was Margaret, tossing something onto the disturbed ground.

Curious behavior.

I popped open one of the window panels and shouted down to her, "Margaret!"

She glanced up but didn't register my presence.

"Margaret!" I yelled again.

She caught sight of me and waved.

I waved back. "What are you doing?"

"Salting," she responded and then resumed her task.

"If you do that, not much will be able to grow there," I warned her, thinking of perhaps a community garden being put in by me and my mother, as I worked towards regaining my strength and better use of my limbs. It was a project that suited both her and me, and we needed to continue bridging the gap.

Margaret stopped again and looked up at me. "That's the idea." And once more, she returned to spreading the salt.

Perhaps it's better. Summer is right around the corner, and it's getting a little late for planting anyway.

The land needed rest. It needed a season or maybe several to heal.

My mother's new beds, on the other hand, had already gone in as planned.

I shook my head, thinking about Margaret's task, positive that she had her reasons and would explain them to me one day.

As I kept the window open and breathed in the fresh air, thinking on the long road ahead of me for recovery, I heard the light lilt of a child's laughter coming from somewhere outside. It coalesced into the sound of children playing, although I didn't see any. And as I listened, I started to realize the sound was coming from somewhere in the back of the house, and it was echoing around the sides and up through my window. Another laugh and my heart skipped a beat.

Sonya.

I couldn't be sure mentally, but my heart overrode any need for intellectual knowing. It was her, and she was not alone.

Trina's children, has to be.

I relished that small tidbit of happiness that existed outside of me but also because of me, at least to a very small degree. I would come for her one day, and I would not fail. I hadn't failed Annabelle, and I wasn't about to fail my child. Failure was a thing of the past, and it belonged there.

I heard the soft padding of feet, a sound that made me surface from the depths of my thoughts and emotions. I'd looked down just in time to see Helios pounce on me and clamber up into my lap. As winter had melted into spring, he and his sister had started to grow quite large. They were older, stronger, and I sensed they were also that much wiser. Something had changed in them the night they escaped and then in the following days when they'd decided to come back.

Aren't we all wiser now? And, isn't it a hurtful proposition to gain such knowledge?

I looked to Helios and then to the easel that held the painting that was almost finished. It was the study I'd started of him, that had centered on his mother's eyes, the eyes of that mischievous calico that had gifted me with two of her offspring through Margaret. They were the eyes Helios had inherited from her that his sister did not. The artwork did resemble who and what he was growing into, but there was a power about Helios that simply couldn't or wouldn't be captured, try as I may, I just hadn't been able to get that aspect of it to come out right.

I'd felt haunted by it all then, just as I feel now. I understand it better though, and it's easier to see why that feeling stays with me. With the willow doing its dance of change, stretching forth towards the zenith of the summer months that are yet to come, and with #18 changing too, transitioning slowly but surely around me once more, I realize that places are haunted more by the living than they are by the dead.

Made in the USA
Lexington, KY
14 August 2013